THE
THIRD TERM

THE
THIRD TERM

★ ★ ★

DARRYL NYZNYK

Cross Dove Publishing Company, Inc.
Manhattan Beach, CA 90266

Cross Dove Publishing Company, Inc.
P.O. Box 220
Manhattan Beach, CA 90267-0220
(888) 871-8880

Editing, design, typesetting, and printing services provided by About Books, Inc., 425 Cedar Street, PO Box 1500, Buena Vista, CO 81211, (800) 548-1876.

First printing 1997

ISBN 0-9656513-4-7

LCCN 97-66088

ACKNOWLEDGMENTS

For My Ladies:

Loretta for the guts to encourage me to embark upon this venture and the strength and love to stick with me through it;

Laura, Sarah, Julia and Hannah for being the reasons for being; and

Mary, without whose inspiration and appearances in Medjugorje this would not have happened.

PROLOGUE

Los Angeles...March 22

He stood amidst the swelling throng, a man torn by the conflicting torrents of rage and compassion that had brought him to the brink of his own destruction.

Albert Smith didn't actually know he was going to die this night. If he had been able to give it any rational thought, he probably would have been able to guess, but rational thought was beyond his capacity now. He acted mechanically, as if possessed, knowing deep down he was wrong, yet unable to resist the strange force that moved him . . . a force grown strong from the seeds of his own anger and pain.

Smith shivered despite his heavy jacket and the intense heat of a Southern California evening buffeted by the dry desert wind known as the Santa Ana. Had he been totally aware of himself, he might have wondered why he shivered. He was not cold. In fact, his body's perspiration soaked the shirt beneath his jacket and his hair hung pasted to a wet forehead and neck. He might have wondered under different circumstances, but he didn't have the capability of wondering today. Albert was consumed by one thought, the thought that had brought him to this ill fated appointment.

The corner of Fifth and Grand in downtown Los Angeles is the site of the Biltmore Hotel, an ancient edifice whose recent facelifts had once again made it one of the city's premiere stops of the rich, famous, and politically correct. On the evening of March 22, the storied structure's Presidential Ballroom was serving as the election night headquarters of thirty-nine-year-old California Congressman Aidan Sullivan.

Outside the gothic structure, the westering sun blazed orange and washed the approaching motorcade in its eerie glow. The candidate's limousine, preceded by security men and police, rolled to a stop and the milling crowd suddenly fell silent in anticipation of its hero's appearance.

Policemen forced a path through the tightly packed crowd to the hotel's entrance. The candidate emerged from the limo and the crowd erupted in a wild cheer, an enormous headless creature suddenly jolted to life. Bodies beneath the beaming faces of his adorers pressed against the locked arms and backs of the security men and Aidan Sullivan smiled. He strode confidently among them. Arms reached for him and he offered solace for the hungers in their lives with a glancing touch and a gleaming smile. His followers' tear-streaked faces were flush with excitement and the burning desire to be a part of the aura that was Aidan Sullivan.

Political analysts had long ago rejected the possibility that Sullivan had even a remote chance of winning his party's nomination for the office of president of the United States. Most believed he was still too young. He needed more seasoning, particularly on the Hill. His political career had been limited to local and state office and this was only his first attempt at the big time. Besides, his party had two strong candidates, the winner of which would likely choose the loser as his November running mate and together form an alliance that would finally break the stranglehold the opposing party had on the highest office in the land. None of the political rhetoric mattered to Sullivan's followers, however.

To his supporters, Aidan Sullivan was the young, unbearably handsome last great hope for the survival of their country. Young people looked at him as the second coming of another president who had brought the hope and vigor of youth to the Oval Office in 1960, at a time when it was most needed to shake a country into a new birth. Although none of his young supporters was alive during John Kennedy's years in office, they longed for a prosperous time when they could dream of futures in which they, as Americans, could once again make the rules in the world and experience the rewards of such power, the way Kennedy had promised a generation so many years before. Aidan Sullivan was their man.

To the older people in the crowd, Sullivan represented a return to their own youths when idealism and a cause were the only nourishment they needed.

The candidate's ice blue eyes, set large and even in a sun-bronzed face beneath neck-length windswept light brown hair, danced at the unrestrained adulation being poured over him. He knew what the pundits said—they'd been saying it his entire public career. Always underestimating him. Even those handling his own campaign had little hope he would gain his party's nomination this time around. They felt he could make a significant noise, one perhaps that would carry him to victory in his next attempt. No one believed it could happen now. No one except Aidan Sullivan's starry-eyed followers who simply would hear none of the negatives. He was their man and he knew his time was now.

Albert Smith knew the truth. He had known it for some time and he knew if he didn't act immediately, it would be too late. He stood far back in the crowd. He was afraid he would not be able to get close enough. There were just too many bodies packed impenetrably together and the distance from Sullivan's limo to the front door of the hotel was far too short.

Sweat ran rivers beneath his jacket as he tried desperately to wedge his way through the crowd. He was scratched and shoved continuously. Faces turned angrily at him, spewing epithets, while arms propelled him into other bodies and more epithets. Yet he pressed on, oblivious to the pain inflicted upon him and the anger his charge engendered, knowing only he had to succeed. Struggling forward, Albert caught a glimpse of the candidate's light-haired head bobbing through the crowd toward the hotel entrance. Albert fought the pit of panic that surged up through his bowels and into his stomach and throat. He had to maintain some control and press on.

Suddenly, surprisingly, Albert found himself standing three people back of the nearest policeman whose back loomed straight and powerful in front of him, and he realized Sullivan had stopped. His quarry had not yet reached his vantage and he had stopped. What great fortune had befallen Albert. If Sullivan only knew what awaited him, he would never have stopped. He would have sprinted to the hotel's entry. But, of course, he couldn't have known and, as a result, he had stopped to shake a hand or offer an encouraging word, thus giving Albert one more hope they would meet this evening.

Albert's head began to throb. The crowd's noise became muffled and he again pressed forward, meeting stiffer resistance the closer he came. He moved in slow motion. The harder he struggled, the slower he seemed to go. He saw the smiles and tears of those about him as if in a dream. The fog in his mind clouded his path and he tried desperately to focus on his purpose, one from which he could not permit himself to be diverted.

Beads of sweat rolled down Albert's forehead into his eyes, stinging them and blurring his vision. He dragged one sleeve across his brow and elbowed past the last line of supporters until only the policeman stood before him. His other hand slipped beneath his jacket to grasp the smooth handle of the .357 Magnum automatic tucked into his belt.

Albert stared over the policeman's shoulder and shuddered involuntarily.

"Control yourself, Albert. It's almost time," he whispered to himself.

His eyes barely moved for fear of revealing his purpose, but when his quarry did not step into his view, the panic again surged upward. He craned forward, again pushing, leaning and drawing the ire of those around him. But he couldn't see him. There were too many people. They were everywhere and Aidan Sullivan was nowhere.

He'd missed him. Somehow, Sullivan had escaped him. It couldn't be.

Albert grew desperate and finally reached for the muscular blue-garbed shoulder when suddenly the entourage appeared. At first, he saw only security men. Dark blue suits. Concerned looks. No smiles. Then they separated, as if by magic. Aidan Sullivan was standing directly in front of him, smiling. His blue eyes sparkled at Albert and his arms came apart to envelop the entire crowd.

Come to me and be safe, Sullivan seemed to beckon the crowd. Then, staring directly at Albert with a wry smile, his eyes said, "I know what you intend. Do with me as you will."

"How could he know?" Albert wondered for the instant before his hand came out of his jacket clutching the handle of the massive weapon. He thought about how slowly he moved. Too slow. He raised the barrel and pointed it directly at Sullivan's forehead.

"A gun!" someone shouted.

Albert squeezed the trigger. The explosion was deafening. His eyes burned. His ears ached and suddenly he was on the ground. The gun was gone. Albert was covering his face . . . his body. Hands reached for him. Feet kicked him. He felt the weight of someone on top of him. It was a man . . . a very large man. Albert tried to push the man off but the man was too strong. He was too heavy. Albert struggled against the powerful hand that was squeezing his throat. He couldn't breathe. Then he heard a second explosion. It was very close. The pain in his chest told him he'd been shot.

"Martha," he whispered as the third explosion tore through his brain and left him dead at the feet of those who hated him.

CHAPTER 1

Laura Miller woke early Monday morning. She rolled out from under her sheets and stumbled to the bathroom. It was still dark in the room, but she didn't switch on the light just yet. She knew she looked awful after her weekend of revelry and couldn't stand the thought of seeing herself until she'd showered. She didn't want to lose the euphoria over the success of her story that had broken in the *Washington Herald* on Saturday morning. One look in the mirror before she was ready would destroy it all.

She fumbled in the medicine cabinet for the plastic bottle that felt like it might be the Tylenol. She held it close to her face and squinted through the darkness to make sure she wasn't holding some other drug container. Stepping back into the bedroom where the dawn's light was just beginning to filter into the room, she squinted again at the container and finally decided it was, indeed, Tylenol.

"Why don't you just turn the light on?" Tom Stafford rolled over and stared at Laura's naked silhouette in the bathroom doorway.

"Tom . . . I'm sorry. I didn't mean to wake you."

"I work too, remember?" He pushed himself up on an elbow. "Switch the light on. I could use an eyeful to get me going today."

1

Laura finally popped the lid off the Tylenol container and smiled, through her pain, toward the bed.

"I'm afraid I'd scare you off this morning," she joked as she stepped back into the bathroom and closed the door.

Laura dumped several caplets into her hand, separated two from the group and tried to replace the others. Some made it back into the container but a couple missed and ended up on the floor.

"I'll get 'em later," she told herself as she finally located a glass, filled it with water, and downed the pills.

She stood in the darkness for several seconds, leaning on her hands which held onto the counter. As soon as the Tylenol took effect, she'd feel great. Feeling great was important because this was going to be a big day for her.

Her story would tear the cover off the president's Teflon image. The American leader had been able to fend off all journalistic attempts to find a chink in his armor for the past six-plus years. No one had been able to get anything on him. It was as if he was perfect. It all suddenly changed, however, about three months ago.

Laura turned the control knob, adjusting the water temperature to the steamy hot she loved in the morning. Her thoughts wandered to that day, three months ago, when she was sitting in Murphy's Mill on Pennsylvania Avenue just north of the White House.

The bar was a favorite hangout of the younger aides and gofers of the capital's politicos. It was a place where journalists had been able to learn the backroom secrets of Washington from alcohol-induced loose tongues. During the current president's tenure, although those tongues had continued to wag consistently with regards to senators, representatives, and other lesser leaders, all tasty news about the president, his cabinet, and immediate advisers had dried up completely. It was as if the president had actually been able to surround himself with people who simply didn't talk.

The hot water soothed Laura as she slowly massaged the shampoo through her thick shoulder-length brown hair. She had plenty of time before she had to relinquish the bathroom and shower to Tom. He usually didn't get to the law office until nine-thirty and was probably comfortably into his *Wall Street Journal* by now.

★ CHAPTER 1 ★

It wasn't that Laura had anything against the president. On the contrary—she probably would have said he was a good president if the question were ever posed to her. It was simply that she needed a good story.

Laura had risen quickly in the ranks of investigative reporters since her days in the early 1980s with the *Los Angeles Times*. The eighties were filled with wonderful scandals in the business and political worlds of the United States. It was to these types of stories she gravitated after her studies in journalism at UCLA were completed. Although the *Times* and its readers were receptive to her tremendous writing talents and her tightly accurate investigations, she longed for a regular position in the nation's capital, on the staff of the *Herald*, the most widely read newspaper in the country.

She got her chance in 1992 when she wrote an expose on the democratic-led Congress and the amorous dalliances that had knocked them out of three consecutive presidential races. Her story, entitled "Why Are the Democrats So Dumb?," raised a furor of gargantuan proportions as she named names with impeccable accuracy. The article turned the party around and got her the notoriety she needed to be offered her dream position with the august *Herald*.

Laura felt herself falling into the lethargy of prolonged exposure to a steam bath. It was time for her wake-up call. She stood under the showerhead, hot water beating against the top of her head as she steeled herself for the sudden cold that would come as soon as she turned the control knob to C. It only took seconds for her lethargy to disappear. The icy cold rolled off her head, down her spine and made her skin jump. She turned her face up to the streaming cold for a few quick seconds, took a mouthful and quickly turned the water off. The rush was incredible. She was suddenly alive as she reached for her towel and began rubbing away the streams of water still coursing down her body.

Although her early years at the *Herald* were nonstop in their investigative intensity, the exciting stories had, in the past few years, become hard to come by. Business and lower echelon political corruption had become commonplace. Few people even bothered to read about it anymore. People in her specialty were finding it difficult to justify their larger salaries and, in many cases, their continued employment. Laura had been feeling the pinch, too. Her boss had even discussed the possibility of her becoming a beat reporter for awhile.

"I don't want to lose you, Laura. You're too damn good a writer," he'd said. "But the market's dead for your type of stories now. We've got to cut back somewhere."

Laura started questioning her purpose. Because her work had slowed down so dramatically, she found herself with a lot of time for introspection, a luxury she hadn't afforded herself for as long as she could remember.

She had begun talking to Tom about marriage, a family, something other than the, dare she think it, pointless articles she had been writing. Her mind even turned to religion. The thing she had banished almost two decades earlier. These thoughts only created conflict and nearly a breakup because Tom was just not ready for the "M" word and the commitment and responsibility it entailed.

Mercifully, all those thoughts came to an abrupt end that fateful day, when she first spoke to her "little mole" at Murphy's Mill. Laura again found meaning and purpose to her life. She suddenly had the story of her life. For Tom Stafford, Laura's return to sanity had come in the nick of time. He had become nervous and agitated with the pressure she was putting on him. His relief was obvious when the subject of commitment was dropped and they could get back together again under the circumstances that existed before Laura went off the deep end. Things were good again, although, unbeknownst to Laura, Tom continued to harbor fears she would raise the subject again.

Laura switched on the light and stood in front of the mirror brushing through her tangled hair. The overhead exhaust fan had sucked out enough steam to clear large portions of the mirror. As she pulled the brush through the last tangle, her already loosened towel fell from around her body. She glanced into the mirror as she bent to retrieve the towel and then stood again to steal a good long look.

"Not bad," she thought, content with herself for the first time in years. She scanned her body, still firm at the stomach, arms, and thighs. Her breasts were full and perfectly round with the inviting weight of a maturing woman. Her nipples were large and hard in the now cool drafts of air in the bathroom. "For a thirty-eight-year-old woman, you look pretty damn good," she said to herself, her light blue eyes shining as she smiled, embarrassed as if someone was watching her. She shook her head, wrapped the towel around herself again and walked back into the bedroom.

Tom was sitting on the balcony, wearing his motley terry-cloth robe and reading the *Journal* just as Laura had suspected.

"Your turn," she called.

The sun was shining brightly now. Although the spring air was still a little cool, it was fresh and wonderfully exhilarating.

As Laura got up from her morning cereal and a *Herald* article on new Russian demands for more financial aid, Tom walked into the kitchen.

"Still feeling sick, babe?" he asked.

"Just about this," she said as she flipped the paper and article to his side of the table. "It's amazing to me they're still so backward. From a major world power for so many years to a third world country now."

Tom glanced down at the article while Laura rinsed her bowl.

"Other than that, I feel great," she continued. "What a little Tylenol and a hot shower won't do for a hangover."

Tom pushed aside the front page in favor of the sports page and frowned when he read the Lakers had beaten his hometown Knicks again the night before. He didn't notice Laura was staring at him as if she wanted to say something, but wasn't sure of how it would be taken.

"Tom . . . I really meant what I said last night. I love you, babe." There, she said it while she was sober. That was her first time since she was a Southern California high school senior. Because of the excitement from her stories she had lots of room for a little vulnerability.

Tom wasn't sure whether to ignore her or make light of the whole thing. He had strategically avoided the subject during their passion the previous evening. He didn't want to get started on it now.

"I was that good last night, huh?" he joked with a painted smile.

Laura stared at him with a frown, not quite sure if she should continue. She really didn't want to ruin the feeling she had. Tom backpedaled.

"I'm sorry, Laura. You know I feel the same." He paused for a moment trying to keep control of the direction of the conversation. "Look, you go to the office and bask in your glory. I'll be home early tonight and we'll go out for dinner somewhere where we can talk. Okay?"

He smiled reassuringly. She finally returned the smile and nodded.

"You're a coward, you know that?" she said jokingly as she walked up to him and kissed him goodbye. "I'll see you later."

Tom grabbed her and pulled her onto his lap. He gave her a full-mouthed passionate kiss. "I can hardly wait," he panted as his hand moved across her breasts and made her nipples jump.

"You're nuts," she said, pushing herself up and pulling away from her groping lover. "I gotta go."

The walk to the downtown office of the *Herald* took her twenty minutes. Laura's mind returned to thoughts of glory and Pulitzer Prizes.

The Saturday evening news had been awash with the controversy generated by her story. Many simply couldn't believe the Teflon president had gotten himself personally involved in the drug and arms trading scandal that had been bouncing around Washington for over a year. Cynics and the few groups that opposed the president relished the news, however. Reporters even tried to contact Laura for additional information, but she was smugly tight-lipped. She still had two more parts to the story, and they would be the front-page stories of the Tuesday and Wednesday *Herald*.

★ CHAPTER 1 ★

National Public Radio had broken the initial story about ten months earlier. It seemed some powerful American businessmen had helped set up a drug pipeline from Columbia and several South American countries to the independent republics of the former Commonwealth of Independent States. Since the collapse of the Soviet Union in 1991, the independent republics had struggled to gain some sort of economic and political stability. They even made attempts to form a new federation or commonwealth. But it just hadn't worked. The worldwide turmoil of the 1990s had created a global recession not seen since the 1930s. As a result, aid to these former Soviet Republics was sparse and slow. The various leaders soon realized their primary trade commodity was their tremendous arsenal of advanced weaponry.

The republics found ready customers in the drug-producing countries of Central and South America. To stem the tide of government-sanctioned arms shipments, the governments of the United States, Japan, and several Western European countries stepped in to increase financial aid in exchange for weapons, which, they, in turn, destroyed. But the black market flourished.

In exchange for the weapons, the black marketeers received much-needed hard currency as well as drugs to control their own societies.

According to NPR's investigation, none of the trade was possible without the aid and active involvement of a very powerful "middle man." Central and South American shipping was harassed constantly by the American drug enforcement agencies. The black marketeers simply didn't have the ships to carry on their trade. Thus, according to NPR, the middle man saw his opportunity. The only problem was that no one could put a finger on the middle man. It had to be a powerful American who had powerful political support. Until Saturday, most people had believed aid was from lower levels of the U.S. government and the president was beyond reproach. On Saturday, that belief was destroyed. Laura's meeting at Murphy's Mill had given her the story of her life. According to her informant, the president himself was right in the middle of the whole mess.

Laura spent three months corroborating facts, following leads, and confirming the story. On Saturday, it all came out in the *Herald's* lead story and it was followed with another lead on Sunday. Both carried Laura's byline and sold more copies of the Washington *Herald* than any story in more than a decade.

The White House was in an uproar. Laura was ecstatic.

★ ★ ★

CHAPTER 2

The sixteen-story building that housed the *Herald*'s offices, built in 1926, was now a landmark in midtown D.C. Nelson Kursh, the great-great-grandson of the founder of the paper had moved the company to the building upon its completion. Its glass double-doored entry opened onto a newly refurbished marble floored lobby, which led to a first floor museum of history as seen through the lenses and recorded by the pens of the *Herald*'s long list of renowned photographers and writers for more than two centuries.

The lobby was crowded with early morning business traffic. Laura smiled confidently as she walked past a news/snackstand toward a bank of elevators.

"Hi, Miss Miller. Those were good stories you wrote," shouted the proprietor over the din. He was a short black man with a big toothy grin and grey curly hair.

Laura stopped and smiled, "Thanks, Charlie. Glad you liked them."

"Do you think it's really true, Miss Miller?" Charlie asked as his grin was replaced with a concerned frown.

"I wouldn't write it if it weren't, Charlie."

"Yeah, I guess so," he wasn't so sure. "Still, Miss Miller, I woulda never thought it of the president." He turned to take a customer's money for coffee and a copy of the morning's *Herald*.

Laura's smile disappeared as it struck her that maybe some people didn't really want to see their president's image tarnished.

"I'll see you later, Charlie."

Laura stepped into one of the crowded elevators.

"Ten, please," she said to a fat man standing in front of the control panel. The man didn't smile. He pushed the button bearing the number "10."

As the doors were closing in front of her she felt a chill prickle her spine. She shivered despite the warmth of the close quarters. The old car jerked upward and moved at a comfortable pace at first. Then she felt the eyes. They seemed to be boring into the back of her head. She dared not look around for fear of something she couldn't describe. She tried to visualize the faces she'd seen when she stepped into the elevator. She remembered no one was smiling but that was nothing unusual on a Monday morning. She recalled the fat man in front of the control panel, but his weren't the eyes she felt because he was staring somberly at the overhead numbers.

The car stopped at the seventh floor where two people exited and another joined the crowd. The doors closed again and the eyes bored deeper. Laura grew anxious. She'd never had problems with claustrophobia before, so she didn't know if this was what she was experiencing. All she knew was someone was staring intensely at her trying to open her mind.

"This is crazy," she thought. Yet she couldn't rid herself of those eyes. The deep, dark feeling persisted—a malevolent feeling of incomprehensible evil.

The eighth floor registered on the floor counter and the car did not stop. Beads of sweat formed on her brow. Panic surged up into her chest. It was overwhelming her. She had to get off . . . now!

The elevator stopped at the ninth floor. Laura pushed through the doors before they were fully opened. Stumbling across the hall to the far wall, she caught her breath and turned back to see the doors closing with half the occupants still aboard.

"Are you all right, Laura?" Jan Carlson had seen Laura stumble out of the elevator and followed her to offer assistance.

Laura stared, dazed and confused, at Jan for several seconds. She then glanced back at the elevator before she finally felt her head slowly begin to clear.

"Jan . . . yes . . . thanks," she stammered. "I'm fine."

"You sure?"

"Yeah, thanks. I just got a little dizzy, I guess."

"Can I get you some water?" asked her friend.

"No . . . thanks . . . really, Jan, I'm fine now," Laura tried to smile.

Jan returned the smile and patted Laura on the shoulder. She turned to walk away and then stopped abruptly.

"Oh, Laura . . . great articles this weekend. It's amazing isn't it?"

"What's that?" Laura was still a little dazed.

"I thought the guy was invincible, didn't you?" She shook her head. "It's really a shame he's involved."

Laura nodded at her as Jan walked down the hall.

"Good job anyway. They were well written," she called back to Laura.

"Thanks."

Laura stepped to the drinking fountain, took a long drink, and slowly regained her composure. Rather than try to understand the intensely uncomfortable sensation on the elevator, she simply tried to put it behind her, to chalk it up to anxiety and excitement. All she needed was a deep breath and a drink of ice water. When she stood up from the fountain, she felt better.

Instead of braving the elevator again, Laura took the stairs around the corner, up to the tenth floor. The receptionist there was a young black woman named Cherie. She worked an emery board around her long fingernails, oblivious to visitors. Occasionally, she punched buttons and spoke into the mouthpiece of the headphones she wore.

"*Herald*, please hold." She smiled at Laura. "Hi, Laura. Boss man wants to see you."

Laura smiled back, "Good morning, Cherie. Do you have anything else for me?"

"A ton 'o calls." She leaned forward to convey some deep secret. "White House people have been calling since I came in. The weekend receptionist said it was just as bad Saturday and Sunday." Cherie smiled slyly. "Guess you kind of pissed them off."

"Guess I did," said Laura, again feeling quite proud of herself. "Did you read the articles?"

Cherie looked surprised. "I work here honey. . . doesn't mean I gotta read the paper, too." She went back to her filing. Laura nodded and started to walk away. "Kinda wish I had though," Cherie spoke again. "I'd like to know what all the fuss is about."

"Is he in his office?"

"Yeah, he's waitin' for you."

"Thanks, Cherie."

Laura walked past desks crammed with computers, typewriters, phones, and other paraphernalia of the trade. The investigative reporting room was large and noisy and in constant chaos. The morning crew was just settling in on the phones, scheduling appointments, drinking coffee, and working leads on stories some had been following for weeks. Occasionally, someone at a desk would look up, smile at Laura, and wave between words on the phone.

John Bailey had just stepped out of Editor Bill McDonough's office and was walking toward Laura. "He's pissed. Be careful when you walk in there," Bailey cautioned.

"He's always pissed," smiled Laura.

Bailey stopped and turned, "No, Laura, he's really angry today. He's getting a lot of heat over your stories."

"That's good." She hesitated and stared at Bailey. "Controversy sells papers, right?"

Bailey shook his head, "Yeah, I guess. Hope so anyway. Be careful."

As John Bailey turned and continued down the hall, Laura knocked on McDonough's glass door. The editor stood at his desk, telephone receiver grasped tightly in his left hand. He glanced up and motioned Laura to enter.

". . . check it," McDonough finished a sentence and listened.

Bill McDonough was a big man in his mid-fifties with thick white hair and a ruddy complexion, which seemed even more so as he listened to the caller. He'd been in every phase of the newspaper business for thirty-five years. As editor of the *Herald* for the past eight years, he'd taken the paper out of the 1990s slump and again made it a national economic powerhouse. Although people knew him to be a driven and forceful taskmaster who demanded and got the highest level of production and reporting from his staff, Laura

"I'm sorry, Bill." Tears began to roll down her cheeks as she felt her world crumbling. "I don't know . . . ."

McDonough looked with a mixture of sadness, pain, and a touch of anger at Laura who again dropped her head hopelessly.

"Look, Laura, why don't you just go home?" He hesitated for a moment before continuing. "Go see your family in California for a couple of weeks. I'll deal with this. We're going to have to do some major apologizing here."

Laura nodded as Bill walked over to her and took her arm to help her to her feet.

"Go home, kid. Let it rest for a couple of days. Then we'll figure out what happened."

Laura placed the photographs back on the desk. She leaned against McDonough, dazed, almost in a swoon.

C'mon, Laura, walk outta here, she thought. You're stronger than this.

She walked to the door, which McDonough opened.

"Can I get someone to take you home?" asked Bill.

"I'll be all right. Thanks," she responded, still half dazed.

As Laura walked back toward her own desk, McDonough stared after her. Something wasn't right. Laura was, without a doubt, the best journalist on his staff. She was a superb investigator and a marvelous writer. It simply didn't fit that she could make a mistake of such enormous proportions.

McDonough remembered arriving at the office around five-thirty this morning. The photographs were already on his desk with a cryptic, anonymous note that read "This Is Your Informant." Who could possibly have known and how had the White House known? In every call he received, the caller threatened presidential retribution for writing a blatantly false story on the uncorroborated information of an escaped lunatic.

It just didn't track.

Laura stopped at her own desk to pick up messages and her weekend mail. She stared absently at the materials not reading them. Somehow the news had leaked into the newsroom and her associates avoided contact, none of them really knowing what to say. Laura didn't hear the whispers or notice the glances as she stuffed her mail into her purse and walked past Cherie to the elevator.

She didn't even notice the thin, well-dressed man who entered the elevator with her. She didn't notice, until the car was halfway down that someone was again staring at her. This time, however, the feeling was different. Someone was mocking her. It wasn't the painful boring of someone wishing her harm. It was more the smirking jubilation of someone who knew he had already done her harm.

As the elevator reached the first floor and the doors opened, she turned sharply to view the faces of those in the car. The exiting crowd pushed her backwards.

"What?" she yelled as she surveyed the faces. "What do you want?"

Several people stared at her in surprise, while others simply walked away as quickly as possible. The well-dressed man turned away from her and walked through the lobby to the front doors. Laura followed him with her eyes. As he disappeared out the doors, she looked around at the business people walking in every direction. No one paid any attention to her.

Laura Miller stepped into the bright warmth of the beautiful spring morning and felt a chill.

Michael Stoner sat bruised and battered in the corner of his cell. The walls were heavily padded and the room was brightly lit. He was wrapped tightly in a straightjacket, but he was beyond caring about such things. He'd fought those sons of bitches hard and all he'd gotten was this cell. They hadn't even cleaned up the blood and spit that marked his face, and he could do nothing to wipe it off.

Michael brooded in his corner. He knew he'd get another chance. He just had to be patient. He would have to wait until his time came again. He'd been railroaded into this hole in the first place. He wasn't crazy, but who would listen to him over the president? Another chance would come. He couldn't blow it next time.

Tawana Childess had been on the streets for ten years, since she was twelve. She knew her trade well. She knew the johns and how to make them come back again . . . to her. Tawana was a pro. Most of Tawana's customers were repeaters. She rarely had to walk the streets of the ever-shifting redlight district in D.C.'s back street slum anymore. Her tricks knew her number. They knew she was a classy hooker, not one of the usual filth normally found on the streets.

Tawana had her own place. It was cheap and rundown like the rest of the hovels in town but that was for good reason. She was saving most of the money she earned. With another two years of hooking, she figured she could pack it up and get out of this cess-pool of a city.

Tawana Childess was tall, black, and beautiful. She'd been able to protect that beauty on the streets by being tough and uncompromising. She could usually see the violent tricks a mile away and she'd never give them a chance. Only twice in her ten years on the streets had she been beaten up. Those times were enough to teach her what to avoid. She'd learned well and become known on the streets as Classy Bitch, a title she wore on her sleeve. It got her the best, most expensive tricks.

This spring evening, Tawana felt like being outside. It was unseasonably warm and the sweet smell of wild jasmine filled her with recklessness. Despite the lazy euphoria, however, she wasn't going to get caught with some sleazeball. In fact, if it wasn't just right, she'd just take the night off and enjoy the lazy uptown air.

As Tawana walked past shops, barred and closed for the night, others plied their trade to automobile operators who drove by to find their evening's pleasure.

"Yo' Tawana."

She turned calmly, recognizing the voice of her friend Arletta, known on the streets as Big Mama.

"So what's the Classy Bitch doin' on the streets again?" Arletta spoke at the top of her lungs. Her voice was deep and might have been sexy if it weren't so loud. She was a huge woman, fully six-feet tall, weighing well over 250 pounds.

"Hi, Arletta. How's it going?" asked Tawana as she and the big woman embraced.

"Great, baby. How 'bout you? Shit, we haven't seen you walkin' the streets for a long time."

"Yeah, I know," Tawana smiled at her beaming friend. "It's such a beautiful night. I just wanted to take a walk."

"Ha ha, baby," bellowed Arletta, arm around Tawana as she started to walk with her. "Business so good you can take a night off?"

Tawana smiled again, "It's been good." She turned and looked up into the clear night sky. Stars twinkled brightly despite the lights of the city just a few blocks away. "I feel like just enjoying the night."

"Yeah, I know what you sayin', baby," Arletta's voice dropped several levels as she too sensed the intoxicating warmth and aroma of spring.

They walked for several seconds in silence until Arletta spoke again.

"The Kiss-Man wants you back, honey."

The Kiss-Man was the street name for Malcolm Jackson, Arletta's pimp and the man who handled most of the hookers in this part of town. Jackson was a vicious little man who got his name because of the trademark kiss he gave his girls after he punished them and any of their tricks who hurt his girls or cheated them in any way. The Kiss-Man protected his assets ruthlessly. Over the years, several johns had been found beaten and some dead because they'd gotten on the wrong side of the Kiss-Man. Although he'd been questioned numerous times by the police, no one was ever able to pin anything more than pimping on him.

"The Kiss-Man say his little Tawana needs pertection," Arletta continued, barely containing her urge to laugh.

Tawana smiled, "Protection from what, Big Mama? I got you to help me if I need it. Besides, we're family here, none of us need that skunk." She stopped and turned to Arletta. "Why do you stay with him? You don't need his protection."

"You right there, honey. It ain't his pertection I need."

"Well why, Arletta?"

"Ah c'mon honey, look at me," Arletta spread her huge arms as if it made her more visible than she already was. "The little man gets me my tricks. Hell, I'd have to work all night just to get some guy to get over the fear of my size." She laughed. "The Kiss-Man takes care of that for me. When those boys come to me, they beggin' for Big Mama."

Arletta shook her torso so her ponderous breasts swayed under her tent-like dress. The two girls laughed.

"I love you, Arletta. You come with me when we leave this pit, okay?"

"I tol' you befo' honey. When you gone, I go with you. You gonna need pertection out there," pointing to the city, "and Big Mama be the only one who can help you."

They embraced again, the slender Tawana being buried in Arletta's ample flesh.

"I got to get back to it. I ain't workin for myself, like you. You be careful now, honey," the big woman warned Tawana as she turned to walk back to her corner.

"Bye, Arletta, I'll talk to you later," Tawana waved.

Tawana understood the warnings well. For five years, the Kiss-Man had been trying to get her back. He always warned her of the dangers of the streets and implied some of that danger might come from the Kiss-Man himself. But he never really bothered her much. Tawana figured Arletta had something to do with that. Although the Kiss-Man was Arletta's pimp, Tawana truly believed he feared Big Mama. Since Arletta looked at Tawana as a baby sister, the Kiss-Man knew better than to touch her.

As the night wore on, Tawana absently made her way closer to the middle of the city. The evening's warmth filled her with dreams of better times to come, when she could walk proudly among the rich folks. She and Arletta would find a place together, get respectable jobs, meet successful men, and have families. That was how it was going to be. Just two more years and she'd be free.

Tawana was still lost in her own thoughts when a black limo pulled up to the curb next to her on Twelfth Street. The street was dark except for the limo's headlights and a couple of street lamps whose bulbs had not yet been broken by the sharp shooters of the neighborhood. At first, she didn't notice the vehicle, but when she saw the high beams switched on and off, she turned.

The back seat passenger door opened and Tawana, still standing on the cracked and broken sidewalk, peered into the car.

She couldn't see the occupant clearly. All she saw were two slender white hands counting out ten one-hundred-dollar bills and laying them on the seat. Something in the back of her mind told her not to step any closer. She'd had plenty of rich folks before. Of course, none had ever offered her a thousand dollars. For that kind of money he'd probably want something kinky. Some of these rich white guys were weird and some were just plain sick.

The white hands shuffled out another ten bills and laid them next to the first stack. The intoxicating evening had turned Tawana's mind to mush. She wasn't as sharp as she usually was. That's why she failed to heed the tingling in her spine. The tiny voice inside her head screamed "no" but she didn't hear it.

Tawana Childess stepped into the limo. The door closed and the car moved away. It was too late for her to rethink her decision.

After Laura left the office, she wandered the streets of D.C.'s business district struggling to find the answers to questions she couldn't even formulate but finding only haze and confusion. By two-thirty, she found herself standing in front of her apartment building, staring uncomprehendingly at the rough-hewn stone facade of the decades old structure, when she suddenly realized what she needed most.

Grasping for the only thing that seemed at all clear through the fog of her brain, she thought of Tom Stafford and raced up the steps, past a slow-moving security guard and to the elevator which took her, all too slowly, to the fourth floor.

As she fumbled in her handbag for her key, she knew she had to call Tom. He was the level-headed lawyer, trained to sift through the slop and make sense out of seeming chaos. Surely, he'd heard by now, anyway. He was probably inside already, waiting to console her, concerned he hadn't been able to locate her for the past several hours. But when the door finally flew open, Tom was not at home .

. . and somehow she knew something else was wrong. That's when she found the note by the telephone.

"Dear Laura;" it started as the pit in her stomach suddenly took shape again. "I really don't know how to say this, babe, because I really do love you. You know that, Laura. We're right for each other, but I'm just not ready for marriage." Tears formed again as she understood immediately what was coming. "It's not you, Laura. It's me. I guess I just haven't grown up yet. You're on top of the world now and I'm still moving up. I need some time to think and figure out where we're going.

"I've moved some of my things to Peter's place until I get settled. I'll call, okay?"

And then he'd signed it, "Love, Tom."

"No!" Laura shouted as she crumpled the note and turned sharply in search of something upon which to vent her anger.

"You coward!" she shouted and hurled the phone at the framed photograph of Tom above the stereo and then crumbled to the floor in tears of anger at first, and then self-pity, after the cord stopped the phone's flight far short of its mark.

She spent the rest of the day wallowing in her sorrow, not really knowing what to do. She couldn't even think straight enough to analyze the day's events. She was a wreck and the wine she drank did little to soothe her. It only exacerbated her despair. Maybe if she drank enough, though, she'd pass out and her nightmare would just end. But it didn't work.

Even when she turned on the television in the hopes of finding something that would take her mind off the day's events, she was unable to escape. Every program was interrupted with special news bulletins about the hoax and the apology coming from the *Herald* as recriminations flew from the president's subordinates.

Despite her attempts to simply hide from it all, her mind raced with a jumble of tattered images, first of Michael Stoner and then overlaid with Tom Stafford and finally the president himself.

By seven-thirty Laura was well into her second bottle of Beringer's Chardonnay when she received a phone call from her mother who'd been watching the news across the country and had heard about the terrible scandal.

When Laura stopped crying long enough for her mother to speak, she said, "Come home, Laura. Dad and I will be home for Easter week. You can relax a bit."

That was the same suggestion Bill McDonough had made and Laura suddenly felt it was a good one. But she was in no condition to make the arrangements. Her mother told her she'd have a ticket waiting for her at Dulles.

The next morning, Laura didn't read the papers. She asked the taxi driver to turn off the radio. She grew hostile with the young Puerto Rican when he tried to bring up the *Herald's* blunder, and he quickly backed down. He'd seen enough hard cases in his short lifetime and he simply wasn't interested in conflict on this beautiful morning.

At one in the afternoon, Laura Miller found herself aboard a Delta Airlines 747 taxiing on the runway for takeoff. Earlier, she again had to use the relief afforded by the Tylenol to stop the throbbing of her second hangover in two days. By the time the jet lifted off the apron, the throbbing was gone although she was still a little slow.

As the plane reached cruising altitude, Laura drifted off to sleep while the passenger next to her read the *Washington Post* story of another murder in D.C.'s redlight district. Apparently a young black woman, a hooker, had been brutally murdered the night before. The article, relegated to the tenth page of section A, related the gruesome details. The woman's body had been found in an alley off "M" Street, gutted from throat to groin by a very sharp object, police surmised. The precision cut looked like the work of a surgeon. It was the third such killing in the last six weeks.

A large black woman named Arletta, whose tear-stained face appeared in the story's photograph, was quoted as saying, "You got to find this sonuva-----. We're people too!"

The dead woman's name was Tawana Childess.

CHAPTER 3

He'd cried often as a young boy, believing in his newly forming mind he cried out of sadness for the loss of his mother. She'd died suddenly, leaving him to a father who never cared and who ultimately turned him over to foster homes. There had been many of them . . . cold, sterile places where he sought the warmth of love and listened to the voices.

He'd heard the voices early on, even while his mother lived. They'd been conflicting voices in the beginning, some given strength by the overbearing influence of his mother, while the others, more subtle at first, grew in strength as he silently resisted her. When she died, the voices stopped for awhile and enabled him to truly grieve in peace. When they came again, the formerly stronger voices began losing ground steadily over the ensuing years as he associated those voices with his overbearing mother, the woman he gradually grew to hate.

It was in one of the last of the homes where he met the man who gave him the love he'd never felt before. It was not the love of a parent for its only child or even the love of one lover for the other. The man's love was the clinging love that grew from what the boy at first believed was evil physical contact into an adoration of the subject for his master. The man taught the boy much of the beauty of darkness and pain until he realized the boy's own strength and the power that came through the voices he taught the boy to heed.

It was at this time the adoration began and the boy, approaching his early teens, suddenly realized the man had served his purpose. It was time for the boy to follow the voices on his own and create his own voice. And so it was the boy left the man behind to die alone in the firestorm that took with it the altar to his adored boy. And so it also was that the boy began to truly understand the power he could possess.

CHAPTER 4

The president of the United States leaned back in his chair in the Oval Office. He nodded, raised his eyebrows, and gestured for Bret Cummings, his chief of staff, to continue. His press secretary, Simon Frieberg, looked on glumly.

"You're going to have to address the nation, Aidan," said Cummings.

Despite six and a half years in the most strenuous job in the world, Aidan Sullivan was still ruggedly handsome. He was, of course, older now, with greying streaks at his temples. The scar on his cheek, where the bullet had grazed him, was barely visible and added to his mystique. By far the most eligible and sought after bachelor in the country, he was public enough with his dating to dispel any rumors of homosexuality yet discreet enough not to antagonize the more prudish of his supporters. He now stared intently at his two aides.

Bret Cummings had been with Sullivan since the early days in California and, except for three of Sullivan's personal body guards, there was no one closer to the president. Although, at first the chief of staff had been jealous of the bodyguards and their positions of confidence with the president, he learned to accept the inevitable and clung to his own select position as, what he believed to be, "the right hand man to the greatest president in the history of the United States."

"I don't agree, Mister President," said Simon Frieberg. "We've diffused the impact of the articles. Everyone believes they're false. The *Herald* is backpedaling and stumbling over itself with apologies."

"And what are we doing, Mister Frieberg?" asked the president.

"Keeping the pressure on, of course," Frieberg spoke as if the answer were obvious. "We're going to get a complete front page retraction and apology. We're demanding the heads of those responsible for it."

The president nodded and leaned forward, "I agree with my friend, Mister Cummings, here." Bret Cummings loved it when the president gave him such deference. "It would be appropriate for me to address the people of this country, perhaps show the *Herald* some mercy. After all, we don't want such a powerful enemy do we? An eagle with clipped wings is still a dangerous foe." He stared hard at Frieberg, his blue eyes suddenly cold, calculating. "I'll hold a press conference this evening."

Cummings smiled as Frieberg nodded slowly.

"Set it up will you, Mister Frieberg?" Sullivan stood up signifying that the meeting had come to an end.

"Of course, sir." The press secretary gathered his papers and stood to leave.

After the door closed behind Frieberg, Bret Cummings turned back to the president, who stood staring pensively out the window overlooking the west lawn.

"Are you sure you don't want your doctor to look at that cut, Aidan?" He referred to a long cut on the lower cheek and jaw of the president's face.

"It's okay, Bret. I've just got to stop using those damned straight razors. I love the close shaves but this job causes too much anxiety for me to be using something so dangerous. I'll be all right."

Sullivan smiled reassuringly and walked back to his desk.

"How's the third term issue doing?" he asked.

"It's going well, Aidan. Your popularity is at its highest point. No president has ever been this high so far into a second term." He was jubilant, as if he was the mastermind of the marketing of a phenomenon.

"Danwood will be presenting a resolution to the Senate by the end of the week. A good speech tonight should convince them all that the country needs you for another term."

Sullivan looked into the idealistic eyes of his chief of staff. He was a good man for enhancing the president's image. "It'll be good tonight. Thanks. You can get back to work."

Although Cummings loved his work, he always suffered a let down when his meetings with the president were over. He tried to smile as he stood to leave.

"Oh, Bret, was my son out again last night?" asked the president.

The president referred to his twenty-two-year-old son, born during his marriage to June Wilson, his college sweetheart. They'd been married for three years before June died in a terrible auto accident when their son Jason was two years old. June had been pregnant with a second child who had also died in the accident. Aidan tried to raise Jason by himself, but when he turned his eyes further away from his criminal law practice to politics, he lost interest in the boy.

Jason had been born with Down's syndrome and during the years of his father's political climb, he had been shuffled in and out of sanitariums. Although there were times when it served the president's political purposes to have his "handicapped" son in the public view and Jason would spend periods of time at home in the White House, the staff and president were ever watchful because the boy had occasionally exhibited violent rages uncommon to Down's sufferers. Any new signs of such rage or anger would result in Jason's return to a hospital.

"Yes Aidan, he was." Cummings bowed his head. "Seems he got into a fight. Jack Thompson was with him. The boy was bleeding pretty badly."

The president frowned and turned away from his aide.

"Check with the Sunford Home. I want him taken there for awhile," said the president.

The chief of staff nodded and noticed the president's neck begin to turn red with the anger Cummings had grown to recognize. Bret marched quickly out of the office to do his idol's bidding while the president stood staring out his window, his hands clasped tightly behind his back.

Spring in Manhattan Beach, California, is a wonder. After the usual storms, rains, and heavy surf of winter, spring suddenly surges into the consciousness of the city's residents with a vitality of uncontrolled splendor. Tuesday morning was no exception.

Mark Tucker woke at five forty-five. The sun was already shining in a bright blue cloudless sky. When he stepped outside to find his morning *Times,* he was accosted by the salt spray ocean air. Closing his eyes, he turned his face skyward and breathed deeply of the refreshing tonic.

"What a day," he mused aloud.

Sparrows greeted him with their morning song and thoughts of his youth and baseball sprang to mind as the sweet smell of his neighbor's newly mowed strip of lawn mixed with the ocean aroma and reminded him of opening day in Little League. Mark Tucker's mind was free for those few seconds on this beautiful morning when no one else was awake and he could enjoy the wondrous beauty of his untainted world without interference.

Tucker's house was a small "beach cottage" on Ninth Street, one of Manhattan Beach's renowned walk streets, so called because there was no vehicular front end access to the homes. The walk streets were actually sidewalks the width of a narrow street, which ran entire blocks from west to east. On either side of these sidewalks were tiny beach lots with residences ranging from small, two bedroom, sixty-year-old bungalows like Mark's which were now worth over a half million dollars to enormous, four-thousand-square-foot, million-dollar edifices with not even a hint of yard. This housing diversity was one of the unique attractions of Manhattan Beach and certainly one of the things that brought Mark and his family there in 1991. In an age of planned unit development where it was less costly to construct tracts of housing clones, the variability of Manhattan Beach was refreshing.

★ CHAPTER 4 ★

The paper was under an overgrown hedge against the front of the house. The errant throws of the *Times'* delivery woman sometimes upset Mark, especially when the paper ended up in mud or a puddle of water after a rain. This morning though, Mark smiled, thinking only that it was always an adventure when he went paper hunting.

Once back inside, even the closed-in smell of a night's sleep in the old house didn't bother him. He simply opened the blinds and double-hung windows in the living room and kitchen to let the day in.

Tuesday was the first of three days of finals for Mark at the University of Southern California where he taught criminal law and procedure to first-year law students. He also taught several upper division courses in specialty areas of criminal investigations and psychology to second and third year students.

In his nonteaching time, Mark had become somewhat of a national celebrity as the result of his work relating to serial murders. His undergraduate psychology training naturally led him to the highly specialized area. It was the mind of the killer he sought to know as it was only through knowledge of that mind the world could ever hope to end the increasing violence of society. Law agencies from across the country had requested Mark's celebrated learning in that area to help in their investigations of serial killings. His specialty was in painting a psychological picture of the potential killer based on the nature of the killings and the clues left behind. On several occasions, these psychological paintings had led investigators to the murderer.

Mark glanced over the *Times* first page and saw a name he recognized. The byline for the column one article was Jake LaFord's. Jake was a constitutional law professor and a colleague of Mark's at USC. Mark could never understand Jake's fascination for the subject of his expertise. Even though con law, as it was known in the halls of academia, formed the basis of the American judicial system, Mark simply couldn't be bothered with constantly trying to determine what some guys who'd been dead for over two hundred years really meant when they said things like "equal protection" and "due process." He felt it was important, of course. It was just better left to others. Jake LaFord was one of those others.

Jake recently opened a small foundation in Los Angeles for the purpose of alerting the electorate to the horrors of unlimited presidential terms. The *Times* article was to be the first in a sometimes series on the issue that was beginning to attract significant interest throughout the country. In the article, LaFord, although vehemently opposed to unlimited presidential terms, wrote about the issue from an historical perspective from the time of the First Constitutional Convention in 1787 through the present day.

Apparently, as Mark read Jake's words, between that first discussion of the issue and the adoption of the 22nd Amendment to the Constitution of the United States, in excess of 225 resolutions to limit the presidential term had been introduced in Congress. It wasn't until the late 1940s, however, that the resolution that became the 22nd Amendment was actually adopted. It took the election of Franklin Delano Roosevelt to four terms in the White House to force Congress to write down the rule that, for over 150 years, had been followed through tradition only.

As Mark read the historical arguments presented with equal conviction on both sides of the issue, he smiled because they were exactly the same arguments being bandied about today. At various times, according to the article, each view had been the popular position depending on the popularity of the incumbent president. Today, the winds would blow in favor of repeal of the 22nd Amendment abolishing presidential term limits because president Aidan Sullivan was so popular according to all the polls.

Mark laid the paper aside and looked pensively out the window above the kitchen table. He intended to give some thought to his own position on the subject but was distracted by the warm breeze that carried the ocean to him and by the blond jogger in lime green spandex who ran past his window. He smiled and shook his head at his lack of intensity.

"Forget concentrating today. It's spring," he thought as he again closed his eyes and breathed deeply of the fresh air.

"Hi, Daddy," came the voice of Nickie Tucker, Mark's twelve-year-old daughter.

Mark was jolted out of his reverie. He turned to the love of his life.

"Good morning, kiddo. How'd you sleep?"

"Fine," she answered as she walked to a cupboard and reached for a box of cereal. "Nice morning isn't it?"

"Yeah," Mark responded slowly, lazily. "Can you smell the air?"

Nickie smiled and nodded as she sat down across from Mark and poured milk into her bowl.

"How come you're ready so early, Nickie?" She was already wearing the black and navy plaid skirt and white blouse that was the uniform at American Martyrs Catholic School.

"It's seven-fifteen, Dad."

Mark jumped at the time and glanced quickly at his watch.

"Damn!" he said softly "Guess I got lost again. Daydreaming." Nickie smiled knowingly. "I'll get showered and be ready in about twenty minutes," Mark continued. "Can you get your lunch ready?"

"Sure," Nickie replied. She loved her father more than anything in the whole world. He was a daydreamer at times, but that's what made him so much fun. She didn't mind fixing her own lunch.

★ ★ ★

Mark pulled his Saturn up to the curb in front of American Martyrs School. After gathering her backpack and lunch bag together, Nickie leaned over and kissed him goodbye.

"Have a good day, honey," said Mark.

"You too, Dad," she replied. Then stepping out of the car, she said, "I love you."

"I love you too, Nickie. Do well."

Nickie closed the door, waved, and joined a couple of her seventh-grade friends, just arriving at school. His daughter was growing up quickly. Her light brown hair was cut to her shoulders in a style that reminded him of Mary, the wife and mother he and Nickie had lost six years ago to the ravages of leukemia.

Mark and Mary liked the idea of Catholic School for Nickie. They had both gone to Catholic high schools and had enjoyed them. Neither cared much for the discipline at their schools, but they loved the sense of community and purpose they later realized came from the teaching of the common faith. It was important for both of them that God be in their daughter's consciousness on a daily basis. It didn't hurt either that American Martyrs didn't take a back seat to the excellent Manhattan Beach public schools academically. It was always ranked among the top schools in the state.

As Mark turned left onto Manhattan Beach Boulevard for his trip to the downtown campus of USC, he glanced quickly at this watch. It read 7:55, plenty of time to make it to his first class for the nine o'clock exam if he didn't hit any unusual traffic tie-ups.

Although Mary's death had devastated both Mark and Nickie, each became the strength the other needed to get through the loss. Mark's initial reaction was anger at God for taking such a wonderful woman away from him. Once he was able to look beyond his own self-pity to the pain his daughter was suffering, he realized she needed him to be whole. He explained to Nickie that God had called mommy to heaven and she would see them again, when they all got there. Until then Nickie's mother would be watching over and protecting them.

It wasn't until several years later that Mark really began believing the things he told Nickie. He knew somehow Mary was happy and he could go on with his life with his daughter. It wasn't easy, but the realization he was all Nickie had brought him back completely. He was determined to give Nickie the best life a child could have. What he received in return was the peace and joy of unconditional love. Mark's purpose was clear. Everything else was just filler. Even his work.

CHAPTER 5

The approach to Los Angeles International Airport from the east provided an awe-inspiring spectacle. As the giant 747 passed over the Mojave Desert and approached the backside of the San Bernardino Mountains, visitors got the first glimpse of the insanity that would soon envelope them. Houses and other human development drifted by in ever-increasing densities until suddenly the Los Angeles basin appeared as a concrete and glass carpet stretching as far as the eye could see in every direction except west. To the west lay the sparkling waters of the Pacific Ocean, the one natural wonder man couldn't seem to conquer and the one thing that granted respite from the swarming civilization on land.

Laura's plane touched down on time at three-thirty in the afternoon. The five-hour flight had given Laura considerable time to ponder her situation. She couldn't understand how it had all fallen apart. Every fact had been carefully corroborated. She had official memoranda on presidential letterhead. Memoranda from the president's own desk to his underlings. Swiss bank accounts had been confirmed. Michael Stoner had been one of the people on the inside. He knew it all, but he was a nut . . . how could she be so damn stupid?

She couldn't think about it anymore. Her head was in such a fog. Thoughts weren't coming clearly. She needed to rest and clear her mind so she could piece it together slowly, later in the week.

Laura spotted her mother when she stepped out of the pedestrian tunnel. Catherine smiled broadly, despite the drawn look on Laura's face. It would have been clear to even casual observers where Laura had gotten her beauty once they had seen her mother, sixty-three-year-old Catherine Miller. The former junior Miss California carried her years well. Her only concession to the wealth her husband had amassed as a partner in one of California's largest law firms was the slight coloring of her hair to cover the grey streaks. Cat and Jack Miller had been high school sweethearts who married right after graduation. They continued their lifelong romance through forty-five years of marriage and the raising of five children in the fast-paced lifestyle of Southern California.

"Laura," she greeted her daughter and took her into her arms.

"Hi, Mom," Laura clung tightly and began to cry.

Cat had always been available for all her kids. She loved them all so intensely she felt their pain almost as much as they did. Her three sons and other daughter were all married and raising families of their own. They all seemed to have found a life perspective and spirituality that gave each his or her desired level of peace and happiness.

Laura, her middle child, had always been so driven. Like her father, more than the others, Laura had always worked hard. Even by Jack's standards, however, Laura worked too hard. She never learned to balance her life the way Jack had done. Her father had been able to become one of the top business lawyers in California while devoting inordinate amounts of his time to his first loves, his wife and children. Laura picked up the drive but not the balance. That's why, whenever she had difficulties in life, her falls were so deep. Cat knew her daughter well. This fall was a bad one.

"C'mon honey, let's get your bags and get home. We'll talk once you're settled."

Laura held onto her mother's arm and let her lead the way to the baggage claim area.

Cat drove her new Ford Explorer out of the airport onto Sepulveda Boulevard. After passing through the Sepulveda tunnel, she turned right on Imperial Highway, then traveled the mile and a half to Vista Del Mar, the highway along the coast in El Segundo. A

left turn brought them parallel to the ocean along El Segundo's
Dockweiler Beach, a favorite camping spot for motor home and
camper enthusiasts. For locals the drive from LAX could be a beautiful one, particularly on a sunny day like this one.

The northernmost part of Manhattan Beach, along Highland
Avenue, extending south along Vista Del Mar, is a jumble of closely
packed condos, apartments, duplexes, small store-front businesses,
and single-family homes. Although there appears to be no method
to the madness of the city's main street development, it is that very
jumble and seeming chaos that lends the city it's life and character.
When the sun shines in Manhattan Beach, the streets are teeming
with bikers, skaters, halter-topped women, and short panted men,
at all hours of every day.

Cat maneuvered her Explorer over the narrow streets to the
Hill Section in South Manhattan nearest the border with Hermosa
Beach. The Hill Section was the most expensive housing area in the
beach city other than the homes along the Strand. The lots in the
Hill Section were large enough to contain any size home and still
have a yard, a novelty by the beach.

When Laura saw the large Cape Cod–style structure her parents
had built thirty years earlier, she sighed involuntarily as if she had
reached a safe place. A place where all the bad things would stop
for awhile, permit her to get off, and make some sense of it all.
Thank God she was home.

★   ★   ★

The president was enraged. Angrier than anyone had seen him
in years. Bret Cummings smiled though, because the president's ire
was directed at Bret's competition, the three trusted body guards.
They had again failed to keep Jason out of trouble and now Aidan
Sullivan was going to have it out with them.

"What in the hell happened?" asked the president of Frank Thompson, a burly white man with scars making tracks across his face.
The president didn't yell as he tried to control his anger, but his
tone was cutting and his eyes seemed to pierce to the very soul of
his subordinate.

"I lost 'im, Aidan. The sonuvabitch ran the minute the car was stopped long enough for him to bolt."

"Where?"

Thompson bowed his head as if he were a child preparing for punishment. The scene was almost comical as the six-foot seven-inch, 265-pound hulk cowered in front of the president, who stood seven inches shorter and weighed a full eighty-five pounds less.

"It was on 'L' Street." He looked up slowly and when he saw Sullivan's anger rising, he began to talk quickly. "He wanted a woman, Aidan. The kid begged me to get 'im a hooker. I left them in the car alone for awhile along the waterfront. When I got back, they were both gone."

"Well, what happened to him?"

Thompson shook his head slowly, "I dunno. I drove around for two hours looking for 'im. I finally found him kinda stumbling down 'L' Street. When I finally got him, he was covered in blood. He wouldn't tell me what happened, but I figured he'd got into a fight. You know how he gets."

"Did he say anything about what happened?"

"No, Aidan. He didn't say anything except about the monster again. He just kept mumbling about the monster."

Sullivan turned away from Thompson. As the president walked to his desk, the big man glanced furtively at Bill Jackson, a black man comparable in size to Thompson, and at Charles Gilbert, a thin, wiry white man who was easily the most presentable and least fearsome looking of the trio.

"I'm not going to put up with you any more, Frank." The president walked pointedly up to the bigger man and jabbed a finger into his huge chest. "You know what I'm trying to do here? I've kept you with me for years because you wanted to help. You're not, Frank. You're fucking it up."

Sullivan turned and walked away slowly. The big man was scared. The president leaned against his desk and stared hard at Thompson. He then raised a finger and spoke in a low, venomous voice.

"One more time. You've got one more chance with me. I will not accept another failure. Do you hear me?"

36

Thompson was ecstatic. He was like a puppy, excitedly, assuring his master he'd do better next time. He nodded vigorously.

"I want him out of sight, now. You'll take him back to the hospital. Tonight! I don't want any publicity." Sullivan turned to Charles Gilbert. "Charlie, you go with Frank. Make the arrangements and do what you have to do to keep it quiet."

Charlie nodded.

Aidan's eyes rested for a moment on Gilbert. It would be done right if Charlie went along. The smaller man was a perfectionist who never made mistakes, simply because he was always so well prepared. There was something more about him Aidan Sullivan liked, however. He was ruthless in his dealings with foes of the president. He never permitted emotion or feelings to disturb his thought processes. He was like a computer of efficiency.

Bill Jackson dwarfed Charlie Gilbert. He stood with his arms crossed over his massive chest, a man as powerful as Frank Thompson. Where Frank Thompson's strengths did not include intelligence, Bill Jackson was a genius. He too was unemotional, though not ruthless like Charlie Gilbert. Jackson simply didn't let emotion crowd his analytical thinking.

All three were loyal to a fault. Each would willingly lay down his life at a command from Aidan Sullivan. And none would have any qualms about killing another human being if the president requested it.

Aidan Sullivan needed men like these for the difficult times to come. He didn't want to lose any of them, yet. They would be too hard to replace. His eyes returned to Frank Thompson who fidgeted, a stupid grin covering his face.

"Don't let me down, Frank."

"Oh . . . I won't, Aidan, I'll do it right. I promise," assured the big man.

"That's all gentlemen. Bill, stick close this evening. I may need you."

"Yes, sir," responded the former marine.

Sullivan stood and extended a hand to the three men. Each, in his turn, took the hand and bowed until it touched his forehead.

Frank Thompson was the last of the three. As he bowed awkwardly, Aidan placed his other hand firmly atop Thompson's head.

"Don't forget this day, Frank."

Thompson felt the cold from Sullivan's hand seep through his brain to his spine. The chill spread to his limbs and he rocked forward on the balls of his feet almost falling into the president.

Thompson's smile disappeared as Sullivan lifted his hand and the big man caught himself and stepped back. Fear was again etched on his face.

"Go now and do as I've instructed you," Sullivan nodded reassuringly.

As the three men filed out of the office, Bret Cummings poked his head in.

"They're setting up, Aidan. You go on in one hour."

Sullivan stared toward Cummings but didn't seem to see him. A crooked smile was painted onto his face.

"Aidan?" frowned Cummings. He stepped further into the office. "Aidan, are you okay?"

Suddenly the president snapped back, "Oh, Bret, I'm sorry. I must have been daydreaming." The anger and strange power of the president was suddenly replaced by the calm veneer that had publicly marked him.

"You go on in one hour, Aidan. Are you okay?"

"Sure. Don't worry. I'll be ready." He smiled to reassure Cummings.

Cummings nodded warily.

"I'm fine, Bret. Just give me fifteen minutes."

Bret Cummings nodded again, closed the door behind himself and wondered what had happened.

The sun was slowly drifting down toward the western horizon when Cat called Laura for dinner.

Earlier, Laura had taken a swim in the pool in which she'd spent so many happy summers. After the swim, she drank orange-spiced iced tea and sat back in a chaise lounge enjoying the sun's warmth.

Toward dusk, Laura moved to the upstairs deck off her room and sat quietly trying to forget her troubles. She wanted to remember a more carefree time.

When her mother called, the bottom edge of the sun was touching the ocean. The sky was alight, a bright orange, like flame that danced on the water.

Jack Miller had come home early and was busy barbecuing steaks by the pool.

"C'mon down, Laura," yelled Cat from the deck below. "The steaks are almost ready, honey."

Laura threw on her bathing suit coverup and walked downstairs. The television in the living room was broadcasting President Aidan Sullivan's address to the nation. In spite of herself, Laura stopped to watch.

"Good evening, friends. I'd like to speak to you, briefly, about a subject that is abhorrent to me, but must, in my mind, be dealt with.

"As most of you know by now, a pair of stories in this past weekend's *Washington Herald* cast considerable doubt on my integrity and that of my administration. It is my sincere hope you all know by now these reports were false . . . a cruel hoax by enemies of our very way of life."

Laura cringed. Was it possible she had been so terribly off base?

The president stared somberly at the camera and despite his youthful appearance he looked like a father teaching his children.

"My advisers suggested I not speak to you about this horrible thing this evening," he continued. "They argued you, the American people, knew it was false and it would serve no purpose for me to address you. Obviously," he smiled, "I disagree.

"I will not try to convince you the reports were false. That is up to each of you to determine on your own. I believe you all know me by now. I believe knowledge will lead you all to the right conclusion. It is only with the proper conclusion we will be able to continue the work we've started.

"Together we've again made the United States of America the most powerful and prosperous nation in the universe. We no longer cowtow to Arab oil sheiks, because we control the oil. We no longer take a backseat to Japanese manufacturing being dumped at below cost on our soil, because we have solved that problem. There is no country in the world that dares mock us or endanger any of our citizens abroad, because they know the wrath that will befall them. My friends, we've done this together with trust in each other. I submit to you, trust cannot be broken by falsehoods from those who oppose us."

Sullivan's words had built to a crescendo as he pounded his desk with a vehemence that had become the speech characteristic that moved his live audiences to wild cheers. Laura quaked as she realized the hammer was about to fall. The president suddenly became calm, however. He was again speaking to his children.

"As I said, I'm not going to defend myself this evening. I come before you, rather, to show some mercy, which is, after all, our American way.

"The *Washington Herald* is a marvelous newspaper. Over the years, it's true its management has opposed many of our administrative moves and policies," he hesitated. "But that is our system. That is the beauty of our system, the right of all people to say what they truly believe without fear of retribution. Until now the *Herald* has been a paragon of that right. Last weekend, however, the *Herald* stumbled."

Catherine walked in at that moment to see the president's handsome face glaring out of the television screen. She looked at Laura who was transfixed. Cat shook her head before she picked up the remote control to turn it off.

"Leave it, Mom," said Laura.

"You shouldn't be watching this now, honey. It'll only make things worse."

"Mom . . . leave it, please. I want to see what he says."

Cat stared sadly at Laura whose attention went back to the screen.

". . . must pay. Because some zealots have caused great pain and turmoil, it doesn't give anyone the right to punish all those associated with the zealots.

"The management at the *Herald* is publishing a complete and unequivocal retraction in tomorrow's edition. The people most responsible for the lies will be terminated. But . . ."

His pauses were magical. Aidan Sullivan knew how to hold his audience.

"I forgive the *Herald*. I will not destroy a two-hundred-year tradition because of the mistakes of a few wayward souls.

"We will continue to be attacked. Every day of our lives, those who envy us will come after us to take away what we have earned. You will read of attacks from the religious right which believes we don't pay enough homage to each of their gods. We will be attacked by all kinds of minority factions in this country who want to bring us back down to the drifting loss of identity in which we found ourselves in the nineties. We still have enemies in other countries who wish to see us fall. It is a fact of our superior life, my friends. Everyone in the world wants to be what each of you is, a member of the greatest society the world has ever known. There are those who see their own power bases disappearing, who, for their own reasons, will not join us, and who will try to bring us down. But they will fail!" Again he pounded his desk.

"Now, however, we must remember to forgive. Don't punish the *Herald*. Most of the people there are part of us. It is for them we must forgive. In forgiveness, they will join us in a stronger bond that will help us conquer new obstacles as the greatest people in the world.

"Thank you all . . . and let us remember always who we are."

The president smiled a forgiving, fatherly smile as the picture cut to two WBC commentators. Both sat speechless for several seconds, mesmerized until one realized they were on screen.

"Ladies and gentlemen, you have just heard the president of the United States give one of the most eloquent and moving speeches of his career," said Sam Franks as he shook his head dumbfounded. "What did you think of the speech, Tom?"

Tom Bracken simply smiled, "He's something . . ."

Catherine switched the television off.

"Let's go eat, Laura," she said softly.

Laura continued staring at the television screen for several seconds. She struggled to capture the thought that was playing on the fringes of her mind. Something was terribly wrong with the man. She knew it. Something he had said, or maybe it was in his delivery, gave her the alarming sensation there was considerably more to the man than any of his public could sense. She knew her stories were accurate. But there was something more.

"Laura, are you all right, honey?" Catherine could only see pain in her daughter. She didn't recognize the flickering recognition and the determination that was suddenly beginning to take root.

"I'm okay, Mom. You go. I'll be there in a minute," Laura smiled and patted her mother's arm. "I just need to finish a thought."

Catherine nodded slowly and stared into her daughter's eyes, which suddenly began to show some life.

"Don't be long."

Laura nodded and tried again to recapture her thoughts, but she couldn't get back to the clarity she'd had for just a fleeting second before the interruption. Her career at the *Herald* was over. Suddenly, however, that didn't matter so much. There was something bigger she would have to deal with. Something that was now beyond her capacity to grasp but something that was there somewhere. She just needed time to think clearly again.

After dinner Laura sat with Cat and Jack on the pool deck, sipping Bailey's Irish Cream on the rocks. The balmy evening air made it easier to discuss difficult issues. It didn't seem like the end of the world.

"It's hard to believe it's over," Laura said quietly, lapsing again into self pity. "You know, it's still kinda like a dream."

Jack, although a warm and supportive father, was never one to pull punches. Usually, Laura appreciated that from him, but on this occasion she thought she would have liked a little patronizing.

"I think you're right, kid," said Jack. "Do you know what happened?"

"Not yet, Dad," Laura replied. "I'm working on it, though. I'm still a little foggy on the whole thing."

"It's a tough business, Laura. Like law, I guess. Cutthroat. I know how hard it is to keep a perspective."

"I guess I should have listened to you and mom before. Maybe it really is just a sleaze job."

Jack smiled. "No . . . I think maybe I was wrong." He paused and stared across the pool to the lemon and orange trees at the back of the yard.

"It's what you make of it. If you're out trying only to win, with no regard for doing the right thing, it's wrong. I still believe that."

"Thanks, Dad, for making me feel good," Laura tried to joke.

"I'm sorry, kid, I don't mean to hurt you. I just think you've got to find your balance. You're a talented writer. That's obvious. But you've got to use that talent for giving, good and truth."

"I did it right, like I always do," said Laura defensively. "I followed up every lead, every fact. It was solid."

"I believe you." Her father leaned forward and looked her straight in the eye. "I also believe it's the truth."

Laura was surprised. She valued her father's opinion above all others. He wouldn't lie about his beliefs. That knowledge was a powerful constant that had given her own character the strength of her convictions over the years.

"But right now the truth of what you wrote doesn't matter. You could spend the rest of your life trying to clear your name, Laura. And if you did that, you'd be lost. You've got to remember what this whole thing is about. This . . . this life of ours."

Jack hesitated as he took his daughter's hand. He knew her feelings on the Catholic faith in which she'd been raised. She'd made it clear on several occasions the church's structure was too controlling and she simply wasn't interested. Jack and Cat had found a peace in their faith in Jesus Christ. They often tried to convey that peace to Laura and their four other children without preaching, knowing full well each would have to make his or her own spiritual journey. Still, they tried to offer guidance.

"Jesus told us it's love of others that matters. It's a simple message." Laura fidgeted inadvertently and Jack took it as discomfort at what he was saying. "Please, Laura, hear me out on this and I'll keep quiet.

"If you try to beat this guy for you, you'll lose. If you act from the heart, out of love for the people of this world, if you use your talents to help those who have no voice, we'll all win because you'll get help from places you never dreamed possible."

Laura stared hard at her father. Surprisingly she was not at all offended by his mention of Christ. Although she had given up any practice of religion, she still had some level of respect for a God . . . on those rare occasions when she thought of it. On this occasion, it surprised her the mention of Christ felt good. It conjured thoughts of another world, a safe place, away from the evils of small beings. Laura felt the truth of her father's statements. She didn't understand it all but she knew he spoke the truth. She smiled and gripped his hand.

"Thanks, Dad. I think I know what you're saying. I just need some time to sort things out."

Laura knelt in front of Jack and hugged him. She felt like a little girl again in her daddy's arms. Tears came to her eyes. "I'm fine, Dad. I'm gonna go up to my room and get to sleep early."

Laura hugged and kissed her mother good night. Before she got to the door she turned and spoke again. "Thanks for bringing me home. I love you both."

"We love you too, Laura," said Cat.

Laura slept fitfully that night. When she went to bed, she felt a strange peace, as if her father's words had touched her soul and awakened it. In sleep, however, she was troubled.

She dreamed of evil things. Black shaped demons devouring worlds, grotesque faces of death and fear swirling around the leering misshapen head of President Aidan Sullivan. When the face suddenly turned red and the eyes yellow, she could feel the dream creature coming for her. She screamed, a fearful "No!" and suddenly woke, wet with perspiration amid disheveled bedding.

A shadowed figure sat over her, frantically stroking her brow and whispering.

"You're okay, honey. It's just a dream."

Laura stared, frightened and disoriented until she recognized her mother in the moonlit darkness of her room. She was shaking with an unknown fear as Cat soothed and whispered, "It's over, Laura."

Slowly, she stopped shaking and grew calm as she snuggled close to her mother.

"Jesus, protect my child," she heard Cat whisper and memories of her childhood prayer of protection came to her.

As Laura's eyes closed again, she heard her mother again, "Jesus, protect her," and she drifted off to sleep again.

Michael Stoner sat quietly in a plastic chair in the lock-up ward of the Sunford Home. The lock-up ward was for those who'd made at least one break and for the other hard cases. The ward was completely barred and impregnable. He'd been there once before when they first brought him in, six months earlier. That's when he first threatened the White House with exposure. They wanted to fire him, because those wimps below the president were afraid of him. When he threatened to go to the papers, they had him committed. There wasn't any basis for it, of course, but they could get anyone committed. Shortly after his first arrival, the lock-up had become too crowded as a result of an influx of hard case lunatics. Michael was released to a lesser security ward. That's how he was able to escape. This time, though, he'd be in lock-up for a long time.

He brooded after watching the president's speech because he could see the president mocking him from the screen. The man he once loved blindly was a bad man. He knew that now. In fact, he'd known for some time, although he would not permit himself to acknowledge it in the beginning. Soon, however, it became impossible to deny, and it was then he made the threats, hoping he could stop the evil and get back to the love he truly wished to express. But he had failed. When he realized what could have happened to him had they really wanted to get rid of him, he knew he had to act decisively. It was because he was still alive he felt compelled to do something. He was given a chance and he would have to take advantage of it. He was the only one who could do anything because he was the only one who knew the truth.

When the wardroom gate was unlocked a few seconds later, Michael glanced up to see a very large man wearing a too-small suit accompanied by a thin, wiry man. He knew these two men but they did not even look his way. They had a purpose. They escorted Jason Sullivan into the ward.

Michael knew Jason, too. They'd talked a lot in the past. He smiled despite his anger, as he realized an ally had just joined him.

CHAPTER 6

The warm weather broke suddenly in D.C. Charcoal gray clouds, dark and forbidding to match his mood, greeted Bill McDonough in the morning. The weather forecaster promised a terrible spring storm but no one really believed the balmy weather of the past few days would end, especially the people of the capital city who had waited so expectantly through the long, cold winter for the sun's warmth. But it looked like the weather forecaster was right.

McDonough had gotten official word the previous evening just before the president's speech. He wasn't surprised at his firing because the screwup was just too big. If you were going to go after the president of the United States, especially one as popular as Aidan Sullivan, you had damn well better know you were reasonably within the ballpark with your facts. The *Herald* and the editor who had been the envy of every newspaper in the East's major metropolitan areas had become the butt of every joke writer's material. To hear people talk, Laura Miller's story was so far off base even the greenest of reporters would have seen through it. That's what got to Bill McDonough, the now-former editor of the *Washington Herald*.

Bill was cleaning out his office, packing boxes with memories of some of the greatest journalism the Untied States had ever seen. He'd given his life to the *Herald*, starting at the bottom as a runner and gofer right out of high school more than thirty-five years before. Through college he continued to work at the *Herald* and by the time he graduated with his master's in journalism from George Washington University, his incisive pieces on the anti–Vietnam War movement had earned him numerous awards and a reputation as an uncompromising chronicler of the American psyche.

During the 1970s and 1980s, McDonough had been offered many positions with radio and television companies, including NPR and CNN. Bill's love, however, had always been with the written word. He loved the paper presentation, and although he grew up in the age of visuals and sound, he couldn't bring himself to leave the *Herald*. He was rewarded for his loyalty when he was made the *Herald's* editor-in-chief. During his tenure, the newspaper exploded in circulation and became the nation's number one daily.

McDonough was sorry to leave. Yet it wasn't that sorrow that so clouded his mood on this particular morning. He couldn't believe he and Laura had made such a huge mistake. They were both experienced journalists, meticulous in their detail and careful to the point of being absurd. "Corroboration" was their watch word.

Something didn't fit. Every time he thought about the photographs, he felt a chill, deep down inside, as if something evil were touching him.

He wondered how it was possible those photos had appeared on his desk Monday morning at five-thirty. It had to be someone from the paper . . . but who?

Even as he searched for a traitor with his mind's eye, his thoughts drifted. How did someone, the photographer or the deliverer, even know this crazy man was Laura's informant? Unless it was a setup from the beginning. Laura had rubbed many influential people the wrong way. But it simply wasn't possible she could have pushed anyone so far the person would go to so much trouble to bring her down. She was nothing in the whole scheme of things. Just a good kid and a great writer.

His thoughts moved to Laura. She was the best journalist he'd ever worked with. He figured he owed it to her to call and let her know she'd been fired too, before she read it somewhere or received her notice. He flipped through his Rolodex and found the number for Laura's parents in Manhattan Beach, California. It was already eleven o'clock in D.C., eight o'clock in California. He hoped she'd be awake while he was still using the *Herald's* quarter.

★ ★ ★

When the phone rang, Laura was sitting on the balcony in a white terrycloth robe. She was calmer now despite her dream. The sweet smell of gardenia's conspired with the clear blue sky to bring a smile to her face.

"It's for you Laura," yelled Cat from the patio below. "It's Bill McDonough."

Laura lifted the receiver of the phone in her room. She hadn't wanted to talk to anyone from the office. Bill was different, though. He had raised Laura in the business.

"Good morning, Bill," she even sounded happy.

"Hey, kid. You sound good. Everything okay?" McDonough asked.

"I'm fine. Nothing like home and Mom to make you forget your troubles."

"Yeah . . . Laura, listen," he hesitated, not quite sure of how to raise the issue. Finally, he did as he always did, he got to the point. "We've both been let go. I . . . I wanted to tell you before you heard it on a street corner."

"Oh, Bill . . . God, I'm sorry," Laura was surprised. She hadn't expected Bill would be fired. "Why you?"

"It goes with the job. The buck stops here. I knew it when I took the job."

"I'm so sorry," Laura said as tears came to her eyes. "What'll you do?"

"Listen, Laura, don't worry about me right now. Hell, I'm almost relieved. Nell's been bugging me for years to take some time off. I'll be okay. What about you?"

Laura wiped her eyes and caught her breath as she spoke, "I expected it, I guess. I'm just going to stay here for awhile and decide what to do."

"That's a good idea. It's kind of hot here right now. You don't need all the reporters. It'll cool down in a while."

Laura nodded slowly, not knowing what to say.

"Oh, listen, I'm having your things boxed and brought over to my house. You can get them when you come back," Bill continued.

"Thanks."

"Yeah . . . well you take care, will you?"

"Sure." Laura's eyes were dry, but she still felt so badly for Bill. The *Herald* had been his whole life.

"You know, Laura, it just doesn't make much sense to me," Bill spoke as if he had suddenly become pensive. "There's something wrong here."

When Laura didn't respond, he continued, "We'll talk about it when you get back, okay?"

"Yeah, Bill. Thanks," she said softly.

They said their good-byes and hung up. Laura thought about Bill's last words. "Something is *definitely* wrong here," she muttered.

That same morning democratic senate majority leader John Danwood of Pennsylvania proposed Senate Resolution Number 20131 calling for the repeal of the 22nd Amendment of the Constitution of the United States.

As was expected, the initial arguments for and against the resolution fell along partisan lines.

The republican minority's position was eloquently posited by the senior senator from Washington state, sixty-nine-year-old Zac Morgan. Gentleman Zac, as he was known to his colleagues, was well respected by all members of both houses of Congress because of his genial, self-effacing manner, country wit, and intuitive genius. He rarely engaged in the day-to-day banter and argument of the other congressmen because, as he was oft quoted, "These other fellas are a whole lot smarter than me. If I open my mouth too often you people'll know just how dumb I really am." Instead Gentleman Zac sat, always listening attentively and speaking only when he was moved by what he called "this august body's minor misunderstanding." He usually left his listeners entranced and begging for more.

Senator Morgan had strong feelings about the road upon which the Senate was embarking under Senator Danwood's proposed resolution. He was a young man when the 22nd Amendment was adopted, and although he had known the basic issues back then, he didn't truly understand them until now. Zac carried a pensive look to the lectern as he took his turn to speak. He began without the patronizing preamble with which all the others started.

"It seems to me human nature is the real issue here. All you folks are talking about our president, Aidan Sullivan. Some say he's the best president we've ever had in our history, that our country has never been so prosperous nor has it been so respected by our overseas neighbors. Others, my republican comrades, mostly," he smiled his folksy, well-what-did-you-expect smile and drew laughter from the other senators, "see things a little differently. They see prosperity but only for those who make a difference in the polls. They don't see respect from overseas so much as fear because our president is so willing to use our mighty military to push the American ideal.

"Lord knows I've disagreed with Mister Sullivan a lot of times, but . . ." he glanced sheepishly around the room, "I guess that's why I'm still here after thirty-five years and he's up there being the boss."

Again his words drew laughter from his audience. Morgan looked around the chamber, his blue eyes shining beneath his thick, white, collar-length hair. Slowly his toothy grin faded and he grew serious.

"Seriously folks, we're not here to argue about Aidan Sullivan. Those arguments will all fall along partisan lines and we'll never resolve anything. I believe we're here to discuss human nature. It is the nature of all of us to seek the highest possible goal and many times, in seeking the highest goal, it is our nature to forget our true purpose on this planet.

"The office of the president of the United States is the single most powerful position any human being can hold. The position controls the mightiest military machine the world has ever known. From that position, a person has the power to control the thoughts, customs, spiritual beliefs, and understandings of an entire country, which in turn dictates those thoughts, customs, and beliefs to an entire world.

"We are the most influential human force the world has ever known and the office of the president is the pinnacle of that force. What greater goal could one seek than the presidency of the United States?"

Zac hesitated as he searched the faces of his audience. He lifted his left hand, index finger extended to make his point.

"It is a goal to which each one of us would aspire. Every single man and woman in this room. Given the time, we would each strengthen our hold to take the next step. The only logical step for a motivated human being . . . the step of world domination.

"Human nature thrives on power and prestige. We all love it. Oh, we like to think we get into politics to do some real good, and when we're younger, we probably do some good. But the longer we sit in a position of power, the more mundane the requirements of that position become and the more we seek a higher position, a greater challenge . . . more power.

"Until Franklin Roosevelt sat in the White House, no president had ever been elected to more than two terms. Even Mister Roosevelt's four-term run was in a time of great national peril, when the country arguably needed the stability of a continuous management team. Prior to Roosevelt, we believed the rigors of the job and our former presidents' own restraint kept them from seeking that greater power of which I spoke earlier. The position of our former leaders is commendable. Yet to think all our future leaders will show the same restraint or be as worn after eight years, is naive.

"This world continues to harbor many Adolf Hitlers, Joseph Stalins, and Saddam Husseins, who seek the ultimate goal on this earth. Why, the very reason we're here today is because our current president wishes to seek a third term. Already, the traditional restraint of our forefathers has been lost.

"If we repeal the Twenty-Second Amendment of the Constitution, my friends, what restraints will we have against the madman who has the charisma to gain the highest office in the land the first and second time? I say to you we will have none. With all due respect to Senator Danwood's resolution, I urge you with all my heart to vote no and stop the process here on the Senate floor."

★ CHAPTER 6 ★

Zac Morgan stared at his audience and knew he'd missed. The nods and head shakes were still firmly moving along partisan lines in favor of abolishing the restriction and reelecting the popular democratic president. Morgan knew if the resolution passed the Senate, it would fly through the heavily democratic House. The big fight would then begin as each state considered the proposal and conducted its own constitutional convention. Two thirds of the states would have to vote in favor of repeal. President Sullivan was so popular among the wealthier voting class his chances were good.

Zac sat down, disquieted. As other speakers praised his eloquence and pleaded their own cases, he feared for the road his country was traveling.

Although he had sensed the power before and had even used it on the most basic of levels, he never really understood it until the fire.

The boy sat stoically as the man fawned over him . . . adored him. This same ritual had occurred over and over again for the past three years. Although the attention had been welcome in the beginning, the boy was now becoming bored. He no longer felt the warmth of a caring touch because he had made contact with a far more powerful force. A force he had only experimented with until this very night.

He stared hard at the man who suddenly fell away from him, his hands tearing at the growing pain in his head. The man's eyes were wide as an intense fear gripped him. The man had known for a long time it might eventually come to this. He had recognized the boy's power long ago and he had nurtured it as a loving parent nurtures the strengths of his own child. And, like a parent, he hoped the boy's need for nurturing would never end. But it did. And when the time came, the man was not ready for it.

The pain cut deeply for several seconds until the boy released him. The man felt relief that the boy was not in complete control, knowing he would still be needed, at least for a short time, so he could complete the boy's education. But the relief was short-lived.

When the man looked into the boy's piercingly beautiful blue eyes, he saw the truth . . . the boy was truly in control now. He had met the master and the man was expendable. The world lay before him alone. The man was no longer necessary.

Without remorse, the man accepted his fate. He stared at the boy lovingly despite the renewed pain, as his body moved mechanically, controlled by the boy's will. His hand reached for the kerosene canister, in the middle of which burned the flame of his devotion to the boy. It sat atop the wood shrine he had built and he pushed it over.

The pungent liquid spread the flame quickly as the boy stood and moved slowly away from the growing conflagration, continuing to concentrate on the control of the man's mind. The man sat amidst the flame, his eyes fixed on the receding figure of his worldly devotion until once again his mind was released, and he felt the searing pain to which he'd been numbed when the boy had controlled his mind. It was too late. The man could not move; he only screamed.

Outside the man's living quarters, black smoke billowed above yellow-orange flames that tore through the paper-thin walls and stretched high into the night sky to spread its eerie glow beneath the canopy of heavy cloud cover. The boy slipped behind the overgrown shrub of bougainvillea across the yard and watched the frantic attempts to douse the flame, until the screaming stopped.

For the first time in his life, the boy was at peace. He knew he would never be alone for he had finally understood and fully accepted the only lord he would ever need.

CHAPTER 7

Jake LaFord followed the Senate debate closely. He knew the arguments well. Particularly the one posited by Massachusetts Senator Jane Cruzack who chastised Zac Morgan and others opposed to the repeal for their lack of faith in the American people. She argued the electorate could make proper decisions. The voters wouldn't permit a power-hungry leader to stay in office. They would still have elections every four years and if anyone overstepped her bounds, she simply wouldn't be reelected.

"Sure," argued LaFord to himself as he ran off the last copies of his newsletter for distribution the next morning, "just like our intelligent voters permitted free speech and rights to women and blacks before legislation was adopted to protect those rights."

LaFord had great confidence in the American people. That's why he knew they could be lulled, like any other people, into complacency. They'd fight if they were pushed hard enough, but that need to fight was slow to come. As long as things weren't "too bad," the American public would let it rock along until it was absolutely necessary to stand up and fight. By then it would be too late if Cruzack and her group had their way with the repeal of the 22nd Amendment.

Jake was afraid of Aidan Sullivan. His concern wasn't the generalized concern about human nature, expressed so diplomatically by

Senator Morgan. Jake was genuinely afraid Aidan Sullivan would actually win reelection to a third term.

As Jake scanned his final product for the millionth time, he thought again about his heavy burden. With the recent loss of the Washington *Herald's* contrarian voice, he was the only one left to continue the fight.

President Sullivan was on the very course feared by Senator Morgan. In his first year in office, the president had stepped in quickly to prevent the lurching effect of yet another OPEC oil embargo. After years of bickering amongst themselves, the Arabs had finally agreed upon a program of strict controls. The price of oil tripled overnight and the American economy came to a standstill. While Congress debated, the president threatened immediate military action.

The world watched in horror as American smart bombers hit Ryahd, Baghdad, and Tehran. After only a few days, all three cities were in chaos, mosques and government buildings lying in rubble. Then came the troops and within days it was over. A grim-faced President Sullivan stood in front of his desk in the oval office and issued a warning: "Never again will the American people be subjected to the greedy whims of the rich sheiks of the Mid-East. We will control the oil and we will show the world American fairness."

American troops protected the oil fields of the Arab world and American business interests controlled world distribution from those fields, thus ensuring an endless supply of cheap oil to the United States. Although prices to other countries were significantly higher, that was justified by the fact it was American lives keeping the wells flowing freely, and the higher cost was to compensate the United States for that sacrifice.

In the fourth year of his presidency, Aidan Sullivan again used the American military on an international scale. That time however, he looked west . . . to Japan.

Throughout his entire first term, the president had cajoled Japan's Prime Minister Fukujama in an attempt to end the trade imbalance in Japan's favor. He demanded larger payments for the stationing of American troops on Japanese soil until eventually he was demanding that the payments each year equal, in cash, the amount of the U.S. deficit with Japan.

Naturally, the proud Japanese demanded immediate removal of the American military. They would henceforth take care of themselves. Peace factions in Japan and not-so-veiled threats from President Sullivan won the day, however. Now the tide had changed. The deficit in favor of Japan had turned completely. Japan's markets were wide open to American goods to the tune of two hundred billion dollars per year. Virtually all of Japan's imports were now from the United States. President Sullivan's intense efforts had paid off.

Jake LaFord understood all too well where it was leading. Germany was the only country in the world with enough strength to oppose the United States. All of the other European allies pretty much followed the U.S. lead because they knew they would also profit from America's success.

Things seemed to be going well in the United States under Aidan Sullivan. Jake LaFord knew better, however. And he, by God, would fight that sonuvabitch until the rest of the country understood.

He placed the last stack of newsletters by the delivery door at the back of the room. He stretched, looked at his watch which read nine o'clock, and realized why his stomach had been growling for the past hour. He'd stop and get a sandwich and bottle of wine at Giuliano's on his way home. He loved to relax on the balcony of his fourteenth-floor apartment overlooking the chaos of Los Angeles. It was a warm night, the kind of night he could use to relax, if only for a little while.

Jake switched off the light, locked the door behind him, and stepped out onto the sidewalk.

A black BMW 525i, the kind driven by the East Side's drug kingpins, pulled away from the curb up the street from Jake's printshop.

As Jake turned to walk East, he heard the roar of sudden acceleration. The faint outline of the black vehicle was barely discernable on the darkened street where none of the overhead lights were working and the car's headlights weren't on.

Jake peered through the moonlit darkness at the oncoming car and realized too late he should run. Suddenly he was staring down the barrel of a machine gun clutched tightly in the hands of a black man. A man he'd seen before . . . somewhere. The first burst cut across his stomach, tearing him open as he clutched in surprise at the blood that was spilling through his fingers. The second burst caught him in the chest and threw him backwards through the plate glass of his store front.

Jake LaFord was dead before he hit the ground.

The next day, the newspapers carried the story as another deplorable driveby shooting. But Jake LaFord would have told them differently had he been able to speak.

CHAPTER 8

"Good morning, Aidan," Bret Cummings ran up to the president as he strolled the south lawn of the White House, his secret service bodyguards at strategic locations throughout the grounds. For the first time in many years Bret could see shaded half circles beneath the president's eyes.

"Are you okay, Aidan?"

Sullivan nodded pensively. "I'm fine. What do you have?"

The president didn't tell his chief of staff about the dream that had kept him awake most of the night. It had been continuous. Every time he'd closed his eyes, the pain returned. He'd seen himself atop the world, arms outstretched basking in the adulation of his people . . . until suddenly that woman appeared. He couldn't quite make out her features although with each recurrence the face became a little clearer. It was as if some great battle was being waged with one side trying to reveal the woman's identity and the other side trying to conceal it.

He strained and peered ever more intensely to try to discern her features, but she always turned away before he could see her clearly. And then she acted. She exhibited tremendous strength, pulling him from his pedestal. She tore his world down around him and people jeered. They pushed him aside and that woman stood to the side mocking him, urging his former supporters to turn on him. He struggled desperately to pull her down and destroy her but he could never reach her. He always woke, remembering only her smile.

As he lay in bed shaking with rage, he thought again of the women who had so often stood in his way. First there was his mother, a fanatical southern Baptist for whom life on earth was to be a constant struggle until the ultimate reward was attained. She hadn't been with him for a long time, but when she was she'd bludgeoned him relentlessly with the "word of God" as only she knew it. Over time he'd grown to hate her. She had died, never knowing he was destined for greatness, a greatness beyond anything she could ever imagine.

It had been the same with all the girls in high school and college. They couldn't understand his purpose. They all stood before him to prevent his ascent, their magnificent flesh tempting him, teasing him. That is, all except June Wilson. He met her in his junior year at Georgetown University. She gave herself freely to him and she seemed to know for what he was destined. She was not a hindrance . . . until they were married and she suddenly became, as she called it, "responsible." Then June abandoned him for the responsibility of motherhood and she lost the vision.

Now they were both gone and so was that bitch from the *Herald*. The one who'd tried to ruin him. She, too, was finished. Her career was gone and she was nothing.

Yet there was this other woman. He'd seen the smile before, in prior dreams, but he couldn't place it. This dream, like all his others, was a message. It was from his lord and all he had to do was be patient. It would be made clear to him. Yet it was driving him crazy. He wanted to know, now! Things were moving quickly and he had to rid himself of his obstacles . . . NOW!

"It looks real good, Aidan," continued Bret Cummings after finally dismissing the president's appearance as an anomaly brought on by concern over the recent events. "The Senate is moving straight along party lines, except it looks like we'll also get a couple Republicans."

They walked together toward the president's office. The chill that had come with yesterday's rain still hung in the air. The sky was cloaked in a grey that promised more precipitation.

"We're continuing to receive rave reviews on your speech and the *Herald* is falling over itself to make it up to us. I don't think we've got a thing to worry about, Aidan," Bret finished jubilantly.

"We still have powerful enemies, Mister Cummings," responded the president morosely.

Cummings was surprised at the formality. Undoubtedly the president was more concerned than he'd thought.

"What about Zac Morgan?" asked the president.

"He spoke well, Aidan," Cummings shrugged, unable to understand the concern. "But he didn't move anyone. Our supporters are firm. Morgan was their best shot and he missed."

The two stopped on the steps leading to the Oval Office. The president turned and stared into his subordinate's eyes. Bret Cummings felt a chill under the penetrating gaze.

"Morgan isn't finished, Mister Cummings. There's a lot of fight in the old sonuvabitch. You keep an eye on him."

Bret nodded, stunned at the president's tone. He stood transfixed as the president turned to walk up the last steps. At the top, Aidan Sullivan turned again.

"Ah, Bret," he hesitated, "listen, I'm sorry about my mood. I'm not feeling right, today."

The weight on the chief of staff's shoulders suddenly disappeared. He smiled and bounded up the steps to the president's side, relieved. Sullivan was still pensive as he spoke again.

"I'd like to just sit and think for awhile. We'll talk more, later," he said as he turned and walked to the entry. "Send Charlie Gilbert in to see me, will you?"

"Sure," Bret frowned as he watched his leader disappear behind the doors of the White House.

Charlie Gilbert preferred to stand when he was being addressed by his commander-in-chief; it was his marine training. President Sullivan understood that, but it still irritated him to have to look up at the meticulously groomed, well-dressed soldier. Although he no longer wore his uniform, this former lieutenant-colonel looked every bit the soldier with his ramrod straight back, close-cropped hair, and unfaltering obedience.

The president stood up, walked around to the front of his desk, and leaned back against it. "Charlie, do we have any idea what this . . . this woman from the *Herald* is up to? Do we know where she is?"

"Yes, sir, we do," the soldier responded crisply. "Bill McDonough spoke to her yesterday from his office at the *Herald*. He called her at her parent's home in California."

"What's she doing there?"

"On the tape it sounded as if she was hiding, sir. It seemed like she simply didn't want anything more to do with the matter. She's apparently accepted her firing."

"Anything else?"

"Yes, sir. She seemed more concerned over Mister McDonough's firing." He hesitated as if to properly formulate his thoughts. "I believe Mister McDonough will not let the matter lie."

The president nodded as if he suspected as much. "What makes you think so?"

"His final words to Ms. Miller were that nothing made sense to him. He suggested she call him when she returned."

"Is she coming back?"

"We don't know. She said nothing in that regard."

President Sullivan pushed himself up and walked back behind his desk. He leaned on his hands and spoke again.

"I want you to keep an eye on her."

"Yes, sir."

Sullivan was pensive for several seconds before he spoke again.

"We'll see about Mister McDonough."

Jake LaFord's murder shocked Mark Tucker. Although they were never the best of friends, they had talked at some of USC's faculty-student mixers. They'd even had lunch together on campus and discussed their respective expertises. It had always amazed Mark that LaFord was so obsessed with such an esoteric subject as the intricacies of constitutional law.

★ CHAPTER 8 ★

Mark didn't believe the newspaper reports of another random driveby killing. It was certainly done to look like one, but it simply couldn't have been. First of all it was in the wrong part of town. You just didn't get drivebys on the west side. Occasionally, one would occur, but not in a business area and certainly not unless rival gang members were in the vicinity.

Although Mark was not expert in gang activity, he knew enough about it to know gang shootings usually dealt with turf control or retaliation. Neither of these fit.

LaFord seemed harmless—except, of course, when he was challenged on a subject on which he was master. Clearly, the issue of unlimited presidential terms was one such issue. It had become an obsession for LaFord. Mark wondered what terrible thing Jake had done to someone. He wondered what kind of man had really lurked behind his intellectual facade.

CHAPTER 9

Laura spent the rest of the week helping Cat prepare for Easter dinner on the upcoming Sunday. They were expecting the entire family this year. Everyone had arranged with their respective spouses to have springtime in Manhattan Beach. They'd all be staying the weekend, so it would be crowded at the house with the spouses and ten grandchildren. The siblings were surprised to hear Laura was home to join them. It would be a real reunion.

Father John O'Connell promised he'd come this year. Although Laura was looking forward to seeing her siblings, she was positively ecstatic at the prospect of seeing Father John, one of Cat's brothers and a favorite uncle. The priest was in his mid-seventies, and as Laura remembered from her last visit with him two years earlier, as spry, agile, and sharp witted as he had been in his earlier days. Father John still ran a Northern California parish in Auburn, a picturesque town in the foothills below Truckee and Lake Tahoe off Highway 80. Because of the dramatic reduction in the numbers of young men joining the Catholic priesthood, the church had found it increasingly necessary to keep the older priests working long past their normal retirement years. Although many priests complained of the continued responsibilities, Father John O'Connell thrived on it. "After all," he would say, "I have given my life to Our Lord's work. As long as I have life in this old frame, I'll try to do his bidding."

Laura hoped she'd get the opportunity to chat with Father John alone for awhile.

In addition to the family, Cat invited Mark Tucker, his daughter Nickie, and another Manhattan Beach resident who didn't have any local family. Laura knew nothing about Mark Tucker, except he'd worked with her father's firm on a few occasions and had become very close to Jack. Tucker and his daughter had even used the Millers' home in Palm Desert.

The other Manhattan Beach resident was old Mr. Radson, an eighty-six-year-old widower who lived up the street from the Millers. He was bringing a girlfriend with him.

Easter morning in Manhattan Beach dawned with the same soothing warmth and aroma of the past several days. To many residents of the seaside community, the year-round wonder of the climate had become commonplace, almost mundane. The weather drew comment from the residents only when it turned grey. To the Miller brood, however, it was a reminder of days past in the secure comfort and joy of their childhood home.

Initially, Cat tried to get everyone up and ready for nine-thirty Mass. It soon became apparent, however, that it couldn't be done. With ten grandchildren ranging in age from a constantly underfoot one-year-old boy to a sullen sixteen-year-old girl and mothers and dads trying to find clothes not completely unpacked, she realized they'd be lucky to make it to eleven-thirty Mass on time.

Cat was determined, however. She assigned one family to each of the home's five bedrooms, with Laura graciously agreeing to sleep downstairs on the family room's sleeper sofa. In each room, a husband and wife slept with at least one of their children. Cat and Jack had four of the older cousins in sleeping bags in their room, and ten-year-old Casey slept with Laura downstairs. Although the accommodations were extremely tight, they all loved it. The children viewed the whole experience as some great adventure with their cousins.

★ CHAPTER 9 ★

When the three full baths weren't enough for people to work out a sharing arrangement Cat quickly assigned family times to each bathroom. Each group had a specific bathroom and time limit within which to work. Naturally, it brought fights and groaning from those who didn't want to shower or dress with their brothers or sisters. Finally, however, by ten forty-five, Cat was able to smile at her spotless brood of nineteen grandchildren, children, and children-in-law. She didn't bother with the war zone upstairs. That would wait 'till after Mass.

Three minivans were required to carry the entire clan to Mass and it took two full church pews to hold them all. As the family knelt to pray before services started, other parishioners gawked at the huge turnout of Millers.

Jack smiled as friends patted him on the back.

"Had a few more recently, huh, Jack?" whispered Sam Granoulis as he walked by.

"God bless you," said the widow, Mrs. Flores.

"God bless us is right," whispered Jack to Cat as they sat back waiting for the service to start. "I feel like I'm on a powder keg that's ready to blow."

Cat smiled. "What are you talking about?"

"There's no way they'll all make it through Mass." He turned and smiled nervously at the finely groomed pack of children surrounding him. Already, Justin's cowlick had defeated the water pasting it had taken, and it was making his drying hair stand up like a haphazard display of needles. The six-year-old's eyes were darting back and forth excitedly. It was only a matter of time. Jack had been through it before. With five kids of his own, Sunday mass was always an ordeal. So much so, that in their early years, neither Jack nor Cat ever had any idea what the priest spoke about in his homily.

Cat patted his leg and smiled happily, "Quit worrying, Jack. Just relax and enjoy it. Remember," she said with a twinkle in her eye, "you're not the parent now."

Jack nodded and smiled again, "Thank God."

Jack sat back and let his children worry about the grandkids. He was able to hear every word of Father Tom Thibideaux's homily about the daily significance of Christ's resurrection.

After mass, Laura and her older sister, Hilary, accompanied Jack to the airport to pick up Father John. His plane was arriving from Sacramento at one-thirty.

"This is nice, Dad," said Hilary as she leaned back in the front passenger seat and smiled contentedly. "It's so hectic with the kids, it's nice to be away from them for a few minutes."

"You only have three, Hil. Imagine what it was like for your mother and me with the five of you."

Laura and Hilary had their difficulties when they were younger. Hilary was three years older than Laura and Hilary had always tried to mother her. As Laura got older and more stubborn and independent, she pulled away from the intensely clinging materialistic need of her sister and Hilary resented it. Through the teen years, Laura's independence continued to grate on Hilary. It really wasn't until she had her first child that the tension between them began to ease. Now after three children, Hilary and Laura had actually become friends. Hilary had her hands full with her own kids, the oldest of whom was sixteen-year-old Robin.

"You look good, Hil," said Laura from the middle bench seat. "You've lost weight?"

"Yeah, a little" she smiled and turned in her seat. "Are you okay? We really didn't get much time to talk yesterday."

"I'm okay. Dad and Mom are taking good care of me."

"We'll talk later, okay?"

"Sure," said Laura. She suspected they probably wouldn't have too much opportunity to talk. Hilary usually had so much planned for the family when they visited Southern California from their home in Seattle. But something seemed different about Hilary. She was calmer, more at peace somehow. And it wasn't just the drive to the airport without the kids. Laura had seen it the previous day. She smiled a lot more and seemed to be more at ease, even in the face of her children's demands.

At the airport Laura spotted Father John first as he disembarked. She ran up and hugged him.

"Laura," he beamed, "and Hilary. You're both more beautiful than you've ever been."

Both girls grinned at the always-charming man, who despite his years and the Roman collar was very attractive.

"Hello, John," Jack smiled and grabbed his brother-in-law's hand. "Glad you could come, old man."

"When Cat said both girls would be here, how could I refuse?" Jack lifted Father John's bag. "Is this it?"

"That's all I need for one night." He threw one arm around each girl and followed Jack to the car while they discussed his flight, the weather, and all the preliminaries.

Aidan Sullivan was not a religious man. His only faith was in himself and the strange power and charisma he possessed. When he was nine years old, he first began to realize he had a special gift. By thirteen, he truly understood the significance of his gift, even when very few others did. His was a gift that made him a powerful leader, a man to whom others looked for their strength. In his way of thinking, a belief in God was nothing more than a crutch for the weak. He needed no crutch.

Easter at the White House was no different for the president than any other Sunday, or for that matter, any other day of the week. He, of course, had to honor the tradition of the day off for his other staff, as he did every Sunday. He even mockingly paid lip service to the Easter bunny for the children of his country. But, for Aidan Sullivan himself, it was a day of work to attain the ultimate goal. Charlie Gilbert, Bill Jackson and Frank Thompson sat with him in the Oval office as he brooded over the recurring dream.

"I want you to send your best man to California, Charlie. Watch her. I want to know what she's doing all the time," said the president.

Charlie Gilbert nodded. Aidan Sullivan leaned back in his chair and swivelled to the side, eyes fixed pensively on the west wall.

"I can't see it clearly yet, but it's her, Charlie. I feel it." He rubbed his eyes slowly. "What about McDonough? What's he up to?"

"He's snoopin' around, Aidan," responded the bass voice of Bill Jackson. "He's not buying the hoax. He believes the bitch's story."

Sullivan nodded slowly. "Has he tried to contact our friend Stoner?"

Jackson shrugged and the president drifted into his own thoughts again.

"Stay close to him. We'll let him stumble around for awhile as long as he's just trying to rehabilitate his reputation. He can't find anything that can hurt us." His eyes scanned the faces of the three men in search of doubts. He then leaned back in his chair, grew pensive again and spoke barely above a whisper. "We'll have to see about Stoner."

Easter dinner was served at four o'clock at the Miller house. Jack expanded the dining table to its greatest length and brought in the ping-pong table to attach to one end so everyone could sit together. Even with the two tables, however, the middle five kids and Nicole Tucker sat at card tables set up just to the side of the main tables. Dinner was loud and happy as everyone seemed taken with the fact that the entire family was together for the first time in seven years. Even Mark and Nickie Tucker and old Mr. Radson and his girlfriend could feel the sincere familial warmth around the dinner tables.

After dinner and the obligatory one hour wait to avoid cramps, the kids went back to the swimming pool and the warmth of the coming evening. The adults maintained safe distances from the water and sat in groups sipping their after dinner Bailey's, Amaretto and Brandy.

While Mr. Radson regaled brothers Adam and Bill and his own girlfriend Ms. Sophie Jansen with stories of World War II and the Nazi scourge, the others sat and talked to Father John.

"So what's going to happen, Father?" asked Mark Tucker.

Laura hadn't talked much to Mark after their introduction when he and Nickie had arrived. He was attractive enough for her tastes and seemed intelligent, but there were too many people around to have any kind of meaningful discussion.

As for Mark, he thought Laura was beautiful. He'd seen pictures of her mixed in with those of the rest of the family on previous visits to Jack and Cat's house. No photograph he'd seen had done her justice. He saw a sadness in her, however. A sadness he wanted to explore.

"That's a tough question, Mark," said Father John. "You saw the church today. As I understand it, it was barely three-quarters full . . . and this is Easter Sunday. It was the same in my parish in Auburn and it is that way throughout this country. There is apathy toward our Lord."

"It seems like people aren't hurting enough now," said Jack, Jr. "Maybe they don't need God as much as when times were tough."

"Unfortunately, I think you're right, Jack," said Father John. "And I must say, I believe it comes from the top. Our own president has made it clear, on numerous occasions, God has no place in the modern world. God is nothing more than a safety device for the weak."

"He's sure getting a lot of people to believe him, John," interjected Cat. "Seems like everyone is starting to believe what he says about being the greatest people in the world. I don't know about the rest of you, but he scares me."

No one spoke for several seconds until Cat continued.

"Maybe we shouldn't get into politics right now. It's such a nice night. Can I get anyone another drink, coffee or dessert, yet."

Several hands went up to coffee but everyone begged off on dessert until later in the evening. When Cat and Jack's wife, Carla, returned with the coffee, Bill's wife, Sarah, was asking Hilary about her recent trip.

"I've heard a lot about Medjugorje, Hilary. How was it?"

She referred to the small village in the foothills of Yugoslavia where it had been reported the Virgin Mary, the mother of Jesus Christ, had been appearing to six young people since June of 1981. Almost from the start, millions of religious pilgrims had trekked to the remote village from all over the world to bear witness to the events. Stories abounded of cures and other miraculous events. In the early and mid-1990s the pilgrimages had diminished dramatically because of the bloody Civil War that had torn the country apart. With the Civil War's end, however, the coming of the new century and the dramatic resurgence of American might, wealth and prestige, the pilgrimages began again. For those who found America's new path unfulfilling, the pilgrimage gave them a life purpose. Such was the case with Hilary and her husband Bob.

"It was a great trip," she hesitated and smiled. "Actually, the trip itself was very hard. Long and arduous but well worth the time."

"Why?" asked Jack, Jr.

"Because it's really happening, Jack. Mary is really appearing there," Hilary responded.

"You didn't see her did you?" asked Laura, ever doubting.

"No. Very few people actually see her," she looked up into the dark sky searching for words. "But I know it, Laura. We both do." She gestured to Bob who nodded in support.

Hilary looked around the circle at the expectant faces. They wanted more.

"We were struck first by the intense devotion of the people in the village. I mean, here they are, dirt poor and just coming off a deadly Civil War and they're all smiling, praying and giving all they have and are, to rich westerners who come demanding everything."

"It really stunned us at first." She looked at Bob and he joined her in a shrug that expressed their unease upon first arriving in the village.

"We come from the West and movies and restaurants and money and we're immediately overwhelmed by people who don't begrudge us that," interjected Bob. "All they want to do is pray and show us how to pray. You kinda get suspicious."

"By the second morning, though, the suspicion is gone," Hilary interjected. "I mean, we prayed occasionally before we went, but there we prayed all day. And it brought us such overwhelming peace and contentment we simply didn't want to leave."

"Yeah, you didn't want to get back to the kids," said Carla with a laugh. Hilary and Bob smiled with Carla before Hilary continued.

"I thought for awhile that was it, Carla, but I realized, finally, it wasn't. We were really zapped over there."

They all laughed except Father John who sat quietly listening and Laura who was wrestling with her demons, wanting to hear her sister, but not really able to believe the reports from Medjugorje.

"Very quickly, before we move on to something else, I'd like to tell you one miracle we actually witnessed with our own eyes," Hilary continued.

Everyone, of course, was immediately attentive at the mention of miracle.

"Prior to going to Medjugorje, Bob and I had heard about something called the miracle of the sun," she glanced around the group as no one showed recognition. "When Mary appeared at Fatima, in Portugal in 1917, it was reported over a hundred thousand people witnessed something they called the miracle of the sun. Apparently, the sun did some kind of dance in the sky at the time of Mary's appearance. Bob and I had no idea what the sun was supposed to have done so, in our typical American way, we fully expected to see something if Mary really was appearing there."

"At six o'clock every evening, at Saint James Church in the village, the Croatian priest would begin praying a rosary inside the Church. The Church was always packed, so Bob and I, along with several hundred other people, would kneel or sit on the steps outside the Church and say the rosary with the Priest. The Church had speakers outside to carry his voice to us.

"At six-forty, when we were almost done with the rosary, the visionaries would suddenly kneel down in unison, in the Church's choir loft, and go into ecstasy."

Hilary used the term that referred to the trancelike condition into which the visionaries fell when Mary appeared to them. During this state they were oblivious to the entire world around them. Under the most intense testing by doctors and scientists, bent on establishing the whole issue of the apparitions was a hoax, the visionaries, when in ecstasy, felt no pain and were unable to have their attention diverted from what they reported, afterwards, was the appearance of the Virgin Mother of Jesus Christ. Even those most cynical scientific minds were moved by the six young people whose brain waves and eye movements were identical and showed they were seeing something in common when they were in that state.

"An observer in the choir loft motioned the priest to stop the rosary when they went into this ecstasy. There followed complete silence and prayer for several minutes until the visionaries, whose mouths moved without sound during the apparitions, suddenly found their voices while praying the 'Our Father' in unison. The observer would then motion the priest the apparition was over and he could continue the rosary.

"For the first five days of our trip, after each apparition, I would look up at the sun to see if it was doing anything unusual," Hilary smiled as she recollected this. "You all know when you look at the sun with a naked eye, even for fifteen seconds, your eyes burn and you must turn away so you don't destroy your eyes. That happened to me for five days."

"On our last full day in the village, as I prayed the rosary, I prayed to our Lord and said I didn't need to witness anything more. I'd seen rosary chains change from silver to gold and I'd seen an intense devotion which convinced me Mary was really appearing and trying to help us all.

"As the rosary ended that evening at six forty-five, I walked away from the church steps and saw a group of thirty or forty people standing in a clearing, staring up at the sky. One of the people was a man from our group, so I approached him and asked him what was going on.

"Without turning to me, he simply pointed up into the sky.

"When I looked up, I saw the sun blazing hot as usual, except something strange immediately started to happen."

Hilary dropped her head and swallowed hard trying to compose herself as tears came to her eyes. Finally, she lifted her hands with her left thumb and fore finger forming a circle and her right hand, fingers outstretched placed over the top of it. She held her hands above her head and stared up at them.

"The flame of the sun seemed to gather across the face of the sun," she slowly closed her right hand and moved it in a fist to the left, leaving only the left hand with the thumb/forefinger circle still above her head. "It moved off to the left and disappeared. What remained of the sun was a perfectly round white circle, like the Holy Eucharist at Mass," she referred to the round white host of bread, which Catholics believed is converted to the body of Christ during the mass.

★ CHAPTER 9 ★

"It started to spin," she moved her arm in a circular clockwise motion. "With each spin, a wake followed it around. You know, when you put something in a bowl of water and spin it, a wake follows it. The same thing was happening to the sun. And with each turn, a circle of pastel color would move out away from the sun. Very subtle oranges, pinks and yellows," she held the forefingers and thumbs of both hands together forming one big circle and then slowly, and in stages pulled them apart to depict the manner in which the pastel circles moved out away from the spinning orb.

"When the spinning finally stopped, the sun began to beat or pulse like a heart. And with each beat or pulse, a cone of intense flame-orange color shot out from the bottom of the sun to the earth."

Hilary hesitated now and looked at the faces around her, "I stared directly at the sun for fifteen solid minutes with a large number of people seeing exactly what I was seeing. When I finally turned away, it had no impact on my eyes. No dark spots, no pain, no blindness. I could see as clearly as I ever had."

Everyone sat in silence for several seconds until Jack finally spoke.

"Did Bob see any of this?" he asked.

"Yeah, Dad," answered Bob. "I was at another part of the church grounds praying when I glanced up and saw the same thing. I thought I was nuts because no one around me was seeing what I was seeing. I got up and went looking for Hilary. I found her in the clearing, staring at the sun, so I joined her and saw the whole thing."

"The sun was real low on the horizon right?" asked a skeptical Carla.

"It was in the summer, Carla," answered Hilary calmly. "The sun was still high in the sky and there wasn't a cloud in sight." Hilary smiled with a deep contentment. "The most powerful thing in our lives is the sun. It controls our entire livelihoods, yet it was being controlled in a way that no scientist has been able to explain since the apparitions began," she nodded slowly, "It's really happening."

"But why?" asked Adam's wife Sarah.

"Mary is asking all people to come back to God," said Bob. "To pray and fast and surrender ourselves to God. She warns of the coming of ten chastisements or punishments which will strike the earth when she stops appearing. Only the visionaries know what these chastisements are and when they will occur. But they are coming. When they do, it will be a time of great pain and suffering for those who have not come back to God. For those who have, the time of chastisement will be a time of great peace." Bob nodded slowly. "It's really happening," he echoed his wife's words. Everyone sat in silence for several seconds. Laura had tremendous difficulty with the whole concept. She knew Hilary as a storyteller from childhood but she'd always had the highest regard for Bob's veracity. How could this possibly be true? She'd read and heard about other reported apparitions around the world, but she paid very little attention because she felt there were all kinds of people out there looking for their own piece of notoriety. People who would do anything to be noticed. Many of these, so called, apparitions had proved to be false and Laura was convinced it was only a matter of time before they'd all be shown as hoaxes. After all, this was the real world she was living in, not some fantasy world of good and evil and princesses and demons.

Still, Laura was disquieted. Hilary had definitely changed. From the moment she arrived on Saturday morning, everyone saw the peace and contentment. And Bob, a man who always seemed to have his feet on the ground, was saying the same thing. It just didn't make sense.

"I've heard about Medjugorje for several years," Mark Tucker finally spoke, "but you're the first people I've ever met who have been there. If it's for real, this country of ours is in for some trouble when those chastisements start."

Everyone nodded in agreement.

"What do you think about all this John?" asked Cat of her brother.

Father John had listened intently to Hilary's story without uttering a word. Finally he spoke, very slowly and deliberately.

"I agree with Mark's assessment, here. If it really is happening, our country is in for tremendous suffering. I have met others who have been to Medjugorje and all seem to be as taken with the experience as Bob and Hilary are. The problem, however, is that the church will not take a stand. The Vatican has been sending investigators there for years but no official position has yet come down."

Laura smirked, thinking that was typical of such a huge bureaucracy, more interested in it's own survival than in something that might conceivably be good for the people.

"I have heard, however, in private, the Pope is a firm believer in the apparitions and in the message our Holy Mother is reported to be conveying."

"Well, what do you think, Father John?" asked Mark Tucker.

Father John smiled, acknowledging he was going to have to respond to a direct question.

"I believe it. I've never been there and officially I am forbidden to take a stand. But I believe wholeheartedly that our Holy Mother is appearing and begging us all to come back to her son before it's too late. It's up to people like Hilary and Bob, who have actually borne witness to spread the word to those who will listen."

For the rest of the evening, they spoke of many things. In the presence of the Tuckers, Mr. Radson and Ms. Jenson, conversations moved from religion to politics to world events. The majority seemed to be basically supportive of Aidan Sullivan's policies. They didn't care much for the military force he used so freely, nor did they care for the seeming decline in basic human kindness.

"It's all greed," bellowed Mr. Radson. "When I was younger, people helped each other. Now they're all out for themselves. I've been a Democrat all my life because it was the party that helped people. Now its just the same as the Republican Party. Money and power is all they want."

Everyone nodded and acknowledged what Mr. Radson said, but everyone was content to let it be. They were all doing well financially and it was a damn sight better this way than it was before Sullivan became president, when no one was doing well.

By eleven-thirty, the Tuckers, Mr. Radson, and Ms. Jenson had gone home. The kids were all in bed, some even sleeping, and the adults were starting to fade into their own rooms. Laura sat quietly outside staring up into the night sky and the millions of stars which, despite the lights of Manhattan Beach, were still faintly visible.

Father John strolled out of the house and pulled up a deck chair to sit next to his niece. She smiled at him and they both stared for several seconds in silence, out over the pool and backyard.

"Your mother told me about your job Laura," Father John finally said as he looked at her to see if he was treading on a subject too sore to discuss.

Laura's eyes dropped.

"Yeah, . . . it's been tough dealing with it," she said. "Coming home was a good idea. It's been quiet. I've been able to do a lot of thinking."

"Have you come to any conclusions?" asked Father John.

Laura shook her head sadly. Tears came to her eyes but she fought them back.

"It's been my whole life, Father John. I love to write," she hesitated. "It's gone."

"There are other newspapers, Laura," he offered.

"Not after the *Herald*. Everything else is minor league." She glanced away, still fighting the tears. "How do you go from the top of the world to any other position?"

"Maybe it really wasn't the top of the world."

"It has . . . or maybe had is the right word now . . . the widest circulation of any newspaper in the world. It was quoted and cited by more people than any other periodical. Its writers and photographers have won more awards than any other single publication."

"You brought in some of those awards didn't you?" asked Father John.

"Yes, I did," Laura answered wistfully.

"You can continue to write. You are a marvelous writer. No one can take that away from you."

Laura was exasperated but she tried to mask it. She was beginning to feel that her Uncle had perhaps lost some of his insight since she last saw him. He simply didn't understand the significance of what had happened. Because she loved her Uncle, she didn't want to make him feel badly, however.

"No one would consider hiring me now. My name will be dirt in the industry," she shook her head. "Maybe I'll become a nurse or something."

Father John smiled, knowing well Laura was trying to hide her frustration. "Not a bad profession Laura, if it was really something you liked."

Laura turned to him, surprised he'd fallen so far as to even suggest that. When her eyes reached his face, he wore a broad smile. She couldn't help but smile back, realizing he was kidding.

"That's better. Now that I know you can still smile, I'd like you to hear me out."

Laura glanced at him again and smiled, inviting him to continue.

"Laura, I read your articles as I've been doing with every article you've ever written. These articles were wonderfully written. They were tight, well structured and extremely readable. But if I may be so bold, they lacked something. They lacked your heart."

Laura turned now to face her uncle. He bowed his head as if trying to find the right words.

"They were written as if you really didn't care. You were going for the big story rather than something that really mattered to you. I believe you would have won awards for the stories had this terrible thing not happened. But we both know these were not from you."

"I know I did it right," she tried to defend herself. "Every fact was corroborated. Everything fit. I still can't believe it was all a hoax. The facts fit perfectly."

"What did you think about your sister's story about Medjugorje?" he asked.

"I don't know," Laura grew pensive. "I believe Hilary believes she saw these things, but they can't be real. I mean things like that don't happen."

"There was a time you believed they did."

"Yes, when I was a kid. I believed in fairy tales. Not now, though. This is a tough world. We take no prisoners. You can't go through life believing in fantasy."

"Is that what I have done all my life, by devoting myself to God's word? Is our Lord a fairy tale?"

Laura knew she had gone too far. She didn't mean to belittle the priest's profession. She backtracked.

"No . . . I mean God exits. I believe that. But ghostly appearances. It can't happen."

"Why not? If God is all powerful, why can't he send his mother to earth to help us find our way back to him?"

Laura couldn't respond. She never gave it any thought, so when the question was posed, she had no answer. Of course, she believed in God on some level. God had just never fit into her real world after high school. Now she couldn't figure out why God couldn't send his mother to earth, which was the position she wanted to support. She sat deep in thought until Father John spoke again.

"There is a terrible evil afoot in our world today, Laura. It is an evil that breeds greed and selfishness. It seeks power over all and it is winning.

"You have a wonderful gift, dear girl. Our Lord has blessed you with the gift of words. It is people like you who must fight this evil. Because you have an audience, you must use your gifts for good. Not just to follow the crowd and do what everyone else does. You are better than that."

"I've lost my audience. I'm through at the *Herald*."

"Then find a new vehicle. Stop feeling sorry for yourself. Take that gift of yours and fight a fight that can do some good. Help your readers see past their own selfish interests to the pain in this world." Father John leaned forward and took Laura's hand, "Take them by the hand, Laura, and lead them back to goodness. You have the ability to lead people away from this evil. I know you do. But you must look beyond your career and you must ask for His help." Father John glanced up to the heavens as he finished.

"Something is happening, my dear. Our Lord needs your help to fight it."

Laura was stunned. She had never seen such emotion from her Uncle. It was real, though. She knew it was real. He was not interested in consoling her, which is really what she had hoped for. He had seen something in her tragedy that had moved him to a position she'd never seen.

"What can I do?" she finally asked, not wanting to argue but not knowing what else to say.

★ CHAPTER 9 ★

"You must ask Our Lord to show you the way. I know you've had little interest in religion in recent years. And I'm not suggesting you come back to religion. What I am saying though . . . perhaps begging, is that you come back to God. Ask him to show you the way. The *Herald* is now in the past. You must go forward and use your gifts to show others the proper path. Not to clear your name but rather to open hearts to hear Our Lord's name."

Father John spoke with such clear conviction and emotion that Laura couldn't help but be moved. Her favorite Uncle seemed to see something about her that she simply couldn't see. He was desperately trying to reach her and she wanted to hear so she wouldn't disappoint him. Yet it wasn't clear. She bowed and shook her head.

"I don't understand all of this. How can I possibly know what to do?"

Father John could see he was just scratching the surface. She didn't understand and neither did he. He only knew what he said was true. He had no knowledge of why or how he knew.

"Pray Laura. You will find comfort in even the simplest prayer. Through prayer, you will find your answer."

As she dozed off to sleep that night, Laura was even more confused than she had been before. Her Uncle's words ran through her brain. She fought them and ran back to the comfort of defending her work at the *Herald* only to be carried back to the ominous words of evil. When she finally did get to sleep, her dreams were troubled. And when she again saw the demon eyes looming larger she woke with a start and screamed.

"Are you okay, Aunt Laura," asked ten-year-old Casey, who still shared the sofa bed with Laura.

"Casey, I'm sorry. Did I wake you?"

"You were having a nightmare," said the young girl.

"I'm okay now, honey. You go back to sleep, okay."

Casey nodded and lay back down on her pillow with a concerned look on her face. She then said, "My mom tells us to say 'Jesus, protect me,' whenever we have nightmares. It always works."

Laura smiled at Casey. "Thanks, honey. You go to sleep. I'll be fine."

Casey closed her eyes and Laura mumbled the words softly to herself, "Jesus, protect me."

In the next room, lying on a rented rollaway, Father John listened to Laura and Casey.

"Please show her the way," he prayed.

CHAPTER 10

Even after the fire, the boy didn't truly understand his gift. He knew he'd touched a powerful force and he knew without question he could manipulate that force to influence those with whom he was tightly connected. Beyond that, he knew nothing for the only two people in his entire life with whom he had had any connection were dead.

His connection with his mother had been the first, but he had not known his gift in those tender years. He only knew the physical contact with an overbearing mother who suckled him until her death when he was six years old. Even when her nipples bled as a result of his growing strength and teeth, she continued because deep down, she knew he needed it. The initial shock of her loss was intensified by the fact he no longer had that one comfort. Her death forced his weaning and drove him in search of other contacts he believed were to satisfy his need for love. But he could never find what he sought.

He lashed out in those early years after her death, physically hurting all people who dared come in contact with him, all the while dealing with the conflicting voices that battled in his mind. When the man was finally thrust into his life, he made his second contact and began to learn about his gift. Yet true understanding came slowly.

In high school, he rarely made friends of any kind because of the anger people could sense lying just below the brooding outer shell. That anger combined with the raging torrents of adolescent desire drove him even further from people until he made the next discovery of his power and took his next step.

Like most teens, the boy desired the chance peek at a young girl's naked flesh or the elbow's brush of a firm breast. And, like most, he dreamed of such contacts, one minute berating himself for such evil thoughts and the next minute longing for just one look or touch.

One day, he stood beneath the football bleachers, staring at the girl's tennis team as it completed its workout and headed for the locker room. He fixed his gaze on Elaine Gibson, the beautiful blond captain of the team and one of the most popular yet most unattainable girls in the school.

As the last of the girls entered the locker room, giggling and joking, Elaine held back, leaned against the wall and lifted her left foot to adjust something in her shoe.

The boy stared with unabashed longing at the girl's firmly muscled thighs protruding beneath the short tennis skirt and he focused all of his thoughts and energies on his desire.

When Elaine turned suddenly and stared with a smile directly at the boy, he turned away, embarrassed that he stared so lasciviously. Elaine frowned, shook her head slowly as if to clear it and began to turn away when the boy heard the voice clearly.

"She is yours! Don't let her go!"

He lifted his head and again concentrated on her retreating form until she suddenly stopped, turned to him again with a quizzical look and then smiled the inviting smile he demanded.

His mind beckoned her and to his surprise, she walked towards him, unbuttoning the silky white tennis blouse and pulling it slowly from the top of her skirt. When she reached him, she opened the blouse and he reached for her slowly, wordlessly.

His hand touched her firm right breast and her nipple leapt through the fabric of her athletic bra. His own loins ached as he lifted the bra and now felt supple flesh, firm and ever more inviting . . . like nothing he'd ever felt before. He pulled her to him and covered her nipple with his mouth as his mind willed her to reach down the front of his shorts.

84

★ CHAPTER 10 ★

"What the hell is going on here?" shouted the principal who ran from the gym directly at the two young people. "Elaine Gibson?" he said quizzically as the young girl covered herself and shrunk away from him. "Elaine Gibson . . . what are you doing with this young man?"

The principal stared hard at the boy who smiled, satisfied for the first time in years and finally understanding his gift was even greater than he'd thought.

As Elaine skittered away, sheepishly stealing glances back at the now seemingly handsome boy, the principal howled angrily at the boy, but the boy was unfazed. He knew he'd have Elaine Gibson again. He'd have her and many others whenever he wanted them.

CHAPTER 11

The Miller clan spent the morning after Easter packing. Adam and Jack, Jr. were taking their families to the Miller mountain home in the Lake Tahoe area for the children's Easter break while Billy, Sarah and their kids were heading to San Diego to spend a couple of days with Sarah's parents. Hilary and Bob planned to stay the week at their parents' home in Manhattan Beach, as a base of operations. They'd promised the kids trips to Disneyland and several other Southland attractions. This morning, they'd gotten up early and were off to Universal Studios with Nickie Tucker whom their second daughter Carole had befriended.

Father John's flight for Sacramento was to leave at two o'clock in the afternoon. Jack had taken the week off from work to spend as much time with his family as he could while they were in town. He was particularly looking forward to Disneyland on Wednesday.

Everyone was gone by ten after enjoying Jack's early-morning breakfast concoction of eggs scrambled with anything he could find in the fridge.

After seeing the last of the guests off, Father John, Jack, Cat, and Laura spent the rest of the morning out by the pool, reminiscing about the old days. They talked of how the whole family had been shocked when the oldest brother had decided to become a priest. He had been, without a doubt, the least likely of Cat's two brothers and two sisters to join a clerical order. The women loved him in his early years and he, being a gentleman of the highest degree, tried to accommodate them all. When he wasn't charming the women he was usually boxing the heads of some town tough who happened to look at him the wrong way. The family was shocked at John O'Connell's decision, particularly since all believed so strongly he was headed for a lifetime of jail or a bullet from some irate husband's gun.

Before he boarded his plane to leave, Father John remembered he had something for Laura. He fumbled through his pockets until he found what he wanted in the inside breast pocket of his coat. It was a silver chain from which hung a simple silver medal bearing the image of the Virgin Mary on one side and her Immaculate Heart on the other.

"I want you to keep this, Laura." He looked at Cat who recognized the medal. "My mother . . . your grandmother . . . gave this to me on the day I was ordained. She told me if I kept this symbol of our holy mother close to my heart it would be a constant reminder to me that all I need do if I am ever in need is to call on her to intercede for me with Our Lord."

"I can't take this. It's Grandma's gift to you," Laura protested.

"It's now yours, Laura. It has served me well. Now let it do the same for you."

He unclasped the chain, turned his niece around and hung it around her neck.

Laura hugged her uncle and waved as he boarded the plane. Father John turned one more time at the end of the tunnel before stepping aboard.

"Your uncle's worried about you, Laura," said Cat as they watched the plane lift off the tarmac.

"I know, Mom. I'll be alright."

When they returned home, Laura and Cat immediately went about straightening the house after the weekend's chaos. They didn't intend to do too much because Hilary and her family would be back to undo it all after their day's excursion. Cat and Laura were happy working together and joking about the weekend's stories.

Jack listened to the two messages that were recorded on the answering machine while they were out. Both were for Laura, the first from Bill McDonough just after they'd left and the second was from Mark Tucker, minutes before they'd returned.

"Laura must be home, Cat," Jack shouted sarcastically from the kitchen. "Only two calls and they're both for her. Think we should make her get her own line?"

"Sure Dad, I may just move back in with you. You'd love that wouldn't you?" Laura smiled as Jack feigned heart failure.

McDonough's message was from a pay phone somewhere in upstate New York, where he'd apparently taken his wife Nell to a cabin, out in the woods. He said he'd call back at noon the next day, because he'd found some things Laura would be very interested in. If he couldn't reach her, he'd be back in Washington by the end of the week and he'd like her to call.

As for Mark Tucker, he sounded a little nervous. He finally got around to asking if Laura would call him back so they could, maybe, go out to lunch.

"Mark's a very nice man, Laura. Call him," urged Cat.

"I'm not ready for anything right now, Mom. I mean it's only been a week since Tom and I split."

"You've got to strike while the iron's hot, honey. Mark's a great catch. And look how nervous he sounded. You can't turn him down," Cat pleaded.

"Dad, help me," begged Laura as Jack threw his hands up and left the room.

"How can it hurt to go to lunch? Call him, please."

"Alright, Mom. But it's just lunch, okay?" agreed Laura.

Laura caught Mark just as he was leaving to get some groceries. They arranged to meet the next day at eleven forty-five at a small beachside restaurant in Hermosa Beach, known as Good Stuff.

That night, despite Laura's assertions it was nothing, Hilary was ecstatic to hear her little sister was going on a date with Nickie Tucker's gorgeous father.

"She's a very nice girl, Laura. He's obviously a great father," Hilary pointed out.

Laura would be happy when it was all over. Anyway, she'd decided to leave for D.C. on Friday and, if nothing else, her departure would bring an end to any romantic intentions Mr. Mark Tucker might have.

Jason Sullivan was restless that night. He tossed and turned in his bed and couldn't sleep. Something terrible was going to happen, very soon. Jason knew it as well as he knew himself.

It was a horrible sensation the knowledge brought: The knowledge of a diabolical evil that prowled the night. Jason knew it well, but he couldn't explain it to anyone. For some reason the words just wouldn't come. His thick tongue couldn't form them clearly and his brain couldn't conjure the right ones.

He'd tried to warn them all, but no one would listen. They all thought of Jason as a child, to be controlled. They didn't want to hear what he had to say. Nobody, that is, except his friend Michael Stoner.

Michael had seemed like a nice guy to Jason when they'd first met at the White House, several years earlier. Somehow he was able to speak to Michael and the words came more clearly. At least it seemed that way because Michael always acted like he understood.

Jason was surprised when Michael showed up at the home for the first time six months earlier. He wondered why Michael was even in the home. He seemed so smart to Jason, who thought the home was for dumb guys like himself. He'd heard Michael was there because he had done real bad things while he was working for Jason's father. They said he was crazy. To Jason, Michael didn't seem as crazy as a lot of the other people who worked in and visited the home.

On this particular night, Jason was terribly concerned. The Monster was coming again, real soon, and he had to get out and warn them before it did. He didn't really know how he'd go about getting out, though. They'd all be mad at him if he did.

As he sat in the darkness pondering his situation as best he could, it struck him that maybe Michael could help him. His friend had tried to help him with a problem before. Maybe he could do it again. He lifted his huge frame from the bed and stood quietly, listening for any sound. Jason was a hulk of a man at six feet six inches tall and weighed 275 pounds. Yet despite his massive size, his hands were delicate and gentle like his mother's, whom he remembered only in dreams.

The big man tiptoed to the door of his private room. The guard would be outside the door as he always was. Jason's father was always trying to protect him, so he never let Jason be alone.

Slowly, he turned the knob and pulled the door open. The hall was half lit and quiet. In fact, the only sound Jason could hear was the staggered snoring of his guard, who leaned back in his chair against the wall outside the door.

Jason stepped into the hall, careful not to make any noise lest he wake the guard, a man Jason didn't like too much because he was always so mean and smelled of alcohol.

Michael Stoner's room was down the hall and to the left. He shared a room with two other men, one named Bobby and the other Clarence. Jason thought he liked Bobby and Clarence, except sometimes they made fun of him so he wasn't really sure. Michael, though, never made fun of him when the others did. Michael would get mad and tell them to shut up and leave his friend alone.

It didn't take long for Jason to find Michael's room because it was right at the end of the second hall. He stepped quietly into the dark room. The only light was the dim moonlight which filtered in through slightly cracked mini-blinds.

As he moved slowly to the middle bed, he smelled something terrible. Like rot, he thought. Maybe someone had gotten sick and puked in the room. It smelled kinda like puke, only worse. Michael would be real happy if Jason woke him up so he could get out of that smelly room.

He found Michael's bed and walked to the head of it. As he crouched down to whisper and wake his friend, the stench grew worse. Holding his nose with one hand, he reached for a shadow which he thought was Michael's shoulder, with the other.

"Michael," he whispered. "Wake up, Michael. It's me, Jason. I need help."

When Michael didn't move, Jason leaned closer and shook his friend by the shoulder. As he applied more pressure, his foot slipped on something and he fell across the bed and the body of his friend.

Jason tried to push himself up. He extended his hands and pushed but felt something wet and sticky.

"Michael, I'm sorry. I slipped."

Jason was beginning to panic. His friend was not moving and his hands were wet from something. The stench was unbearable.

"Michael, hurry and wake up. Something's happened, Michael."

He heard rustling on the other two beds in the room. His head bobbed frantically from bed to bed and back to Michael. He shook his friend again. A sickening thought struck him as he felt the cold sharp blade lying amidst the sticky wetness near Michael's body.

Suddenly, the hall light, outside the room, glared brightly. Jason glanced up, quickly, as he heard his guard running and calling his name. He looked down again and saw the blood for the first time. Gallons of it, he thought, and the grotesque, pained expression on Michael's face.

Jason screamed, a low, animal wail at first, that crescendoed into a howl of utter terror. He pushed himself away. The knife blade clutched in his hand cutting deep into the flesh of his palm. Again he screamed, stricken by terror. There was so much blood. And it was all over him.

The room lights were switched on and Jason fell backwards across Bobby's bed. Bobby, who was already awake, shoved the huge body away and started screaming a terrible, high pitched continuous scream of utter horror.

Clarence too was awake. But he was quiet. He simply stared at Michael's mutilated body and blood-soaked bed.

Hands grabbed at Jason. He struggled to break free.

"Michael," he screamed. "It's the Monster, Michael. The Monster came for you."

Two orderlies ran into the room summoned by an alarm that woke the entire ward. With the guard they were finally able to subdue Jason and wrestle the knife from his bleeding hand. A third orderly ran in with a needle. He jammed it hard into the big man's arm.

Jason didn't feel the needle but suddenly his head was swimming. He was losing consciousness.

"Michael," he mumbled. "The Monster. It's coming again."

"Shit," came the voice of one of the orderlies. "Look what this sonovabitch did."

Within seconds, Jason was unconscious. The guard was quickly on his feet staring at the horror in the room. Blood was spattered everywhere from the struggle with Jason and the stench was unbearable. One of the orderlies ran out of the room and threw up in the hall. The guard, whose name was Milt Franklin, was disgusted.

"Get them all outta here," he shouted. "Damn," he thought, "I don't need this now."

Milt knew he was in trouble for drinking on the job and for falling asleep. He had no choice. He had to call Mr. Gilbert, before word leaked out in the morning. He swallowed hard, knowing if he didn't call, his life wasn't worth shit. There was nowhere he could hide from Charlie Gilbert. He knew that well from his days in 1991 as a Corporal in Lieutenant Colonel Gilbert's troop in the first Arab War. If he reported it now, he'd at least have a chance of survival.

"Shit," he said again as he ran to the phone in the main office. "Why'd he have to do it on my shift? I thought he liked the little creep."

Charlie Gilbert was at the home within a half hour. The first hints of the coming dawn belied the gruesome sight that met him and Bill Jackson.

Charlie immediately spoke to the night doctor in charge who would have to make a report of the death for the official records.

"It looks like a suicide, Doctor Esfani," said Gilbert. "The wrists are cut to the bone and the chest wound occurred when he fell on the knife. It's all quite obvious."

Dr. Esfani knew better than to argue with the steely eyed ex-marine. "Yes, Mister Gilbert. That's how I see it as well," he said.

"I want the names of everyone on duty tonight, Doctor. I want to know who was in the room and who helped carry the president's son. I also want to know the names of the people who are cleaning him up. Can you get me that information?"

The doctor nodded slowly. He was afraid for every name that would appear on the list. He fought the urge to fear for his own safety. He was the doctor, a man who would be missed. Still, he quaked as Mr. Gilbert and the massive Mr. Jackson stood before him piercing his soul with their eyes and thoughts.

"Word of this tragedy will not go beyond these walls Dr. Esfani," commanded Charlie Gilbert. Then very deliberately he continued, "The president will hold you personally responsible for any leaks. Is that clear?"

"Yes, sir!" Dr. Esfani felt weak. He sat down in the nearest chair to catch his breath as Charlie Gilbert turned to Milt Franklin.

"You're through, Milt," started Gilbert.

"Oh, colonel, it's not my fault, I—" Milt pleaded.

"Don't insult me, Milt. You were drinking again. You fell asleep."

"Please, colonel, I'm sorry . . . . Don't —"

Franklin whimpered and cowered before his boss as Gilbert raised a hand to shut him up.

"Enough. We gave you a chance and you fucked up. The president trusted you. He honored you by inviting you to join him and this is how you repay him."

Milt started to speak again but Charlie Gilbert glared a deadly look that stopped him short.

"You're through, Milt." He said again. "If I see you in D.C. or anywhere near the president, I will personally cut your balls off and feed them to you. And, if you breathe one word of this to anyone, that will be your last breath." Charlie turned to Bill Jackson, "Get this scum out of my sight."

Jackson grabbed Franklin by the arm. Although Franklin was a big man in his own right, he was nothing compared to the mountain that was Bill Jackson. Jackson dragged him to the door of the office and threw him into the hall.

Franklin immediately sprang to his feet and ran toward the exit, breathing a sigh of relief knowing he was lucky he was still alive.

"Have the room cleaned immediately, Doctor. We will take the president's son home tonight, and you will log him out as of six-

thirty this past evening. We will expect a secure wing when we return him here two days hence. Do you understand that?"

Dr. Esfani nodded slowly and mumbled, "Yes, sir."

Within twenty minutes after their arrival Charlie Gilbert and
Bill Jackson were on the road again with the unconscious son of
their leader lying face down across the back seat of the limousine.

CHAPTER 12

Laura woke late the next morning, somewhat surprised she'd made it through an entire night without being awakened by her dream or other thoughts that had been haunting her for over a week.

She threw her covers off at nine o'clock, stretched as she sat for a moment on the edge of her bed, and looked through the mini-blinds to the bright day. Laura always slept with the mini-blinds or drapes partially open so she would be awakened by the morning's light. She hated waking up to darkness. She learned long ago that a dark morning was usually the portent of a tough day.

Laura opened her French doors and stepped onto the balcony. She shivered a little, not expecting the chill that met her. An unusual arctic storm had apparently done as yesterday's weathermen had predicted. It sent pockets of cold air south. None of the prognosticators predicted rain, but Laura could see bulbous white clouds floating lazily from the north. She crossed her arms in front of her and rubbed away the chill. A morning bird serenade and the aroma of freshly cut grass greeted her.

After a quick shower and a glass of orange juice, Laura dressed for a bike ride along the Strand to Hermosa and her lunch with Mark Tucker. She wore black spandex riding shorts and a loose fitting shirt over a lime spandex halter top. On her feet, she sported white socks and a pair of Nike jogging shoes, since she didn't own any special riding shoes. After pumping up the tires of her mother's thick-wheeled, eighteen-speed mountain bike and wiping off the rainy season's dust and grime, she was ready to go. It was only ten o'clock, almost two hours before her "date" with Mark. She decided to take a circuitous route and enjoy a longer bike ride before lunch.

"Take my helmet, honey. It's the law," Cat said as she tossed a red biking helmet out to her daughter.

"Since when?"

"For some time now, Laura. That Strand is dangerous, particularly when all the kids are out of school."

Laura fastened the helmet and waved as she wobbled out of the garage, down the driveway and out onto Dianthus Street. Cat cringed at her daughter's initial unsteadiness on the bike but, as Laura disappeared over one of the street's rises, she smiled with relief, realizing Laura had again quickly gotten the hang of it.

"This is harder than I remember," thought Laura. She fiddled with the multitude of gears until she finally found one which gave little resistance. "Whatever happened to one-speeds?"

Laura had no intention of making this a difficult ride. It was obvious, by her physical appearance, she was not adverse to strenuous physical activity. In fact, at home in D.C., she worked out regularly. It was just that she wanted a leisurely scenic ride today. Nothing too hard. Nice and easy.

She followed Dianthus to Eleventh Street, preferring not to go the extra block to Manhattan Beach Boulevard where there would be considerably more traffic this Easter break week. On Eleventh, she turned left and coasted downhill to Ardmore, using her brakes occasionally to slow her descent. A right on Ardmore brought her to a quick left on Manhattan Beach Boulevard from where she walked the bike past the downtown shops to the pier and bike path.

As she suspected, the town was already swarming with beach goers. The morning chill had given way to a subtle warmth, which promised more intense heat in a short time. The early beach goers from out of town would take up the few offstreet parking spaces in town within the next half hour. Later visitors would have to choose the beaches of Hermosa or Redondo, slightly further down the coast.

★ CHAPTER 12 ★

Laura mounted her bike again when she reached the bike path. In Manhattan Beach, the bike path meanders along the beach at sand level from five to fifteen feet below the sidewalk level of the Strand. The separation of pedestrian and bike traffic was an excellent idea for safety reasons and Manhattan was the only beach that provided the distinct separation in the South Bay.

The path wasn't too crowded yet, as it was still relatively early. Laura pushed out onto the Strand and began pedaling. She paid little attention to the few racers who shot past her. She concentrated on staying to the right of her lane and attaining her own comfortable pace.

She traveled North at first, intending to ride to Playa Del Rey before turning back and retracing her path to Hermosa Beach and her meeting with Mark Tucker.

Groups of bronzed bodies warmed up for the volleyball games at the nets that hung from hundreds of posts along the entire Manhattan sandscape. Laura marvelled at the reckless play of the women and young girls whose bathing suits were so skimpy, it was a wonder they weren't lost with each dive, bump, or slam. It reminded her of her own days on the beach when she did exactly the same thing. Had it really been fifteen years since she'd permitted herself the time to spend idling away an afternoon playing volleyball, lying in the sun and flirting with beach gods?

Although Laura had felt some initial uneasiness, as if she were being watched as she struggled to control her bike, she grew more at ease the further she rode.

At the northernmost end of Manhattan Beach, the path made a ninety-degree turn out towards the water and then another less severe turn north again. The path carried her past the sewer treatment and electrical power plants as well as the camper parking at Dockweiler Beach. The beach area along Dockweiler was considerably less crowded in the morning as the out of town beach goers were still on the highway, above, trying to find parking.

Those who were on the beach contrasted sharply with the beach goers in Manhattan. The vast majority of noncampers at Dockweiler were Hispanic, black, or Asian, whereas Manhattan's beaches were almost exclusively white. At first, it concerned Laura although she'd grown up in the area with full knowledge of that distinction. As she rode on, however, she realized ashamedly that her dealings in the inner cities and the desks of major metropolitan newspapers had infected her with the hypocrisy of prejudice. She reminded herself she had no more to worry about from the families who frequented Dockweiler Beach than she did from the self indulgent "me-firsters" in Manhattan and Hermosa.

By the time she reached Playa Del Rey, it was ten-forty. She had a little over an hour before she would meet Mark. Turning around, she headed back along the same path, riding harder on the return trip and reaching the Manhattan Beach pier in twenty minutes. She stopped there and grabbed a drink of water at a pier drinking fountain. She would ride at a more leisurely pace into Hermosa, a much shorter trip.

Laura was sweating profusely when she reboarded her bike. She had hoped she wouldn't be sweating and bedraggled when she met Mark. Then she laughed to herself and thought, "What the hell? It's only lunch."

As she pedaled south, she again felt the strange sensation she was being watched. She tried to shake the feeling. It persisted, however, and she glanced back several times but could never get a clear look at the bikers and inline skaters behind her. As the bike path approached the sidewalk near the south end of Manhattan, she stole yet another glance over her shoulder, but could discern nothing unusual. Laura swerved several times, barely avoiding collisions in her attempts to see behind her.

At the Hermosa Strand she stopped to walk her bike down the steps and suddenly the feeling disappeared. She stood for several seconds staring back up the path and glaring into the faces of people who passed her and tried to maneuver their way around her.

"You're blocking the path," yelled one blader as he zoomed past in a speed skating crouch.

Laura moved her bike flush to the curb and continued to stare up the path toward Manhattan. Nothing. She could neither see the person nor even sense the eyes she knew were watching her. Whoever it was was back there somewhere, waiting. But for what?

Finally, she lifted her bike and walked down the steps. The Strand was a slightly wider path at sand level with no other separation between the houses and the beach. Nor was there any separation between bikers, skaters, and pedestrians. All used the same path immediately adjacent to the three-foot-high retaining wall along the sand side.

Laura looked straight ahead and realized she was now on the obstacle course. No more leisure riding here. She was glad she'd been riding for over an hour already so she knew how to handle her bike. She began pedaling, slowly at first to gauge the pedestrian speed in front of her. Most of them stayed to the right of the path, but there were enough who didn't so she was compelled to proceed more slowly and stay constantly vigilant.

Suddenly, she felt it again. The prodding, staring violation. Those eyes were watching her. They were following her. She hazarded a quick glance back and regretted it as she saw nothing and almost collided with a mother pushing a stroller.

Thoughts of the elevator came to mind. It was the same feeling. A probing, as if someone were trying to read her mind. But that was ridiculous. That kind of shit didn't happen. Yet, there it was.

Laura found herself going faster, more recklessly. She had to shake this feeling. In broad daylight, she was beginning to panic. She knew someone was back there, coming for her. She weaved carelessly past reeling pedestrians until she caught herself and realized what was happening. She breathed deeply and tried to concentrate on a plan to discover her pursuer. Staring ahead, she discerned a definite pattern of movement. Clumps of people, followed by a bare space where there was virtually no crowd followed by a few people until again it became a large group and then nothing.

Again, she pedaled faster but more in control as she went around one large group. Ahead of her was another large group that was still far enough away to enable her to implement the plan that was beginning to take shape. Although the amoebalike groups changed continuously, there seemed to be a basic consistency. She continued to accelerate, maneuvering quickly around and through pedestrians, ever watchful of the amorphous larger group ahead of her. As she accelerated, her watcher's grip wavered. The eyes weren't penetrating as deeply as if the watcher was forced to concentrate elsewhere in an effort to stay with Laura.

Laura's speed grew dangerous. She pedaled faster and faster until, finally, she reached the large group she'd seen from a distance. They were teenage kids who were laughing and jousting unpredictably. The amoeba was changing quickly, too quickly. She swerved and dodged, brushing the arm of one young man who shouted angrily after her as she shot past. Luckily, her guess was correct. Beyond the group was a clearing.

She rode into it at breakneck speed to a point where there were people again. Squeezing her back hand brakes with all her strength, she caused the bike to skid and swerve dangerously. She dropped a leg and leaned away from her swerve in a maneuver she'd learned as a child.

Laura stopped with bike turned diagonally across the bike path to provide her a clear view of her pursuer. He was on skates, careening out of control around the amoebic group of young people. She knew it was him. He wore jeans and a tee shirt but he was too finely groomed. His clothes simply didn't look right with his moussed black hair and white eastern skin.

As he rounded the amoeba, he made eye contact with Laura and in trying to hide, he lost control completely. One leg came off the ground and his arms twirled like helicopter blades on either side of his body until he went down, skidding several feet. Laura gripped her bike handles to turn and accost him, but her luck had run out.

An inattentive biker, approaching from the opposite direction, suddenly glanced forward and in trying to avoid two slow-moving skaters, swerved and plowed broadside into Laura's bike. They both fell and the skaters, unsteady to begin with, fell over both of them.

Laura struggled out from under the pile, her elbows scraped and her legs bruised and aching where her bike had landed on her.

"I'm sorry," screeched the other biker, an overweight man in his mid-thirties. "Are you okay?"

Laura sat up and looked back up the bike path past the group of teens which was now upon them. She strained to see, but realized her pursuer was gone. He had simply disappeared.

"Are you okay?" the other biker was frantic. "I didn't see you."

"I'm fine," Laura finally answered. Then, to assuage his fear, she added. "Look, it was my fault. I shouldn't have been stopped."

"Damn straight, lady," said an angry young man of about sixteen from the group she had brushed. "You almost killed me back there. You and that sonuvabitch on the skates."

"I'm sorry," Laura winced from the pain in her right leg as she stood up.

The angry young man backed off when she stood rubbing her leg. He stared for a moment seeing for the first time how beautiful Laura was.

"Hey, are you okay?" he finally asked in a calmer voice.

"The man on the skates was chasing me. Did you see where he went?" Laura asked.

Suddenly, he was her protector. While his friends ministered to the two skaters and the other biker, he turned and pointed with grim self-importance.

"Yeah, he took off up that street." The boy then laughed. "He was really stumbling, man. He didn't have a clue on skates." He turned back to Laura. "Hey, but I don't think you got much to worry about from him. He went down hard. Bleeding real bad on the arms and legs. I think he hit his head too, on the wall, there."

Again he pointed up the path and Laura's eyes followed his finger.

"He ran off then?" she asked.

"More like stumbled and crawled," he laughed.

Laura nodded and turned to retrieve her bike.

"Hey . . . let me help you," the sixteen-year-old offered.

"Are you okay?" Laura asked the women skaters and the other biker. "I'm really sorry."

They all nodded and the two skaters pushed out on the path again. The other biker looked over his bike to make sure it wasn't damaged.

"Is it okay?" Laura asked.

"Yes, I suppose. But you should be more careful, you know. Biking is not a sport for amateurs," he finished as he straddled the bike and pushed off. The bike wobbled and almost went down again before he finally gained control.

"Whoa, that dude was out of it, man," the sixteen-year-old said, laughing.

"No," said Laura, "he had a reason to be mad. It was my fault."

"Hey, do you need any more help?"

"She's fine, Will. Let's go," said a pretty young blond who was part of the group.

"I'm fine, Will. Thanks for your help."

"If we see the other dude, we'll take care of him for ya, okay?"

"It's okay. I have a feeling he's more dangerous than you might expect. Thanks for your help."

Laura pedaled away and Will stared after her, saying to one of his buddies, "Wow man, she's hot."

The pretty blond slapped Will on the arm and they all laughed as they strode onto the sand to join another group at one of the volleyball nets.

At Fourteenth Street, Laura disembarked because bike riding and skating was not permitted through the Strand business area in Hermosa. It was nice to walk the bike the last two blocks to her meeting with Mark.

It didn't come to her until she'd left Will and his friends where she'd seen her pursuer before. It made sense. The sensation of boring, probing eyes could only come from the same person she'd encountered on the elevator at the offices of the *Washington Herald* over a week before. It was as if the man had a special power to see inside, or at least make one feel he was seeing inside. She recognized her watcher as the slim, well-dressed young man who had walked out of the lobby as she was frantically scanning the faces of the people exiting the elevator.

Laura made one more discovery as she dismounted the bike. Once she had come up with a plan to discover her pursuer, the probing stopped. He continued to follow, but he was no longer in control of the situation. It was as if she could see him following but she was no longer scared. Once she took control of her own mind, he was powerless.

As she made two important realizations Laura was faced with an even bigger question. Why was she being followed? She could understand it to some extent in D.C. where she'd written the devas-

★ CHAPTER 12 ★

tating articles. But why out here in California, where she was doing nothing at all?

When Laura chained her bike to the wrought-iron fence surrounding the eating area of Good Stuff, Mark was already sitting at one of the outdoor tables. He stood and waved as Laura followed the fence to the entry. She smiled, acknowledging to herself he looked good in blue swim trunks, white T-shirt with a designer emblem over the left breast, and blue thongs.

"Hi, Laura," Mark said as he pulled a chair away from the table for her. "Glad you could make it."

Sensing Mark's nervousness, Laura suddenly realized she felt a little tight, too. She tried to convince herself her feeling was attributed to her recent ordeal, but she knew better. It was exciting to be meeting a new man. She hadn't realized it before because Tom Stafford had been her only male companion for more than two years. She had quite forgotten the nauseating excitement of the first date. It was flooding her now. She couldn't think of a word to say.

"What happened?" Mark pointed to the scrapes and slow drying blood Laura had neglected to wipe away. "Did you fall?"

She glanced down at her scraped and bruised arms and legs and frowned. "I guess it looks pretty bad, huh?" she said.

Mark nodded, a look of genuine concern on his face.

"Are you okay?"

"I'm fine, Mark. Thanks. I just got going a little fast," Laura explained. "Some guy and I collided."

"It's pretty dangerous out there."

Laura finally smiled "Actually, it was all pretty funny once we found out everyone was all right. Two roller skaters fell over us. It took awhile to get untangled and back on our way."

They both laughed at the picture each envisioned and suddenly they were talking freely.

Lunch moved along surprisingly smoothly with neither one of them treading on any controversial subjects. Laura thought Mark could definitely be someone she could get interested in if she wasn't in such turmoil. As they were finishing their sandwiches and sipping their last glasses of iced tea, Mark asked how long she was staying in town.

"Just a couple more days. I'm leaving Friday morning for D.C." Expecting him to frown she finished with, "I've got a lot to do at home."

She was surprised at Mark's response.

"That's great. I'm heading out Sunday night for D.C.," he said.

"What for?"

"I've been asked to come and help with an investigation out there."

"Really?" she was suddenly interested. "I thought you were a law professor at USC."

"I am, but I have a secret life too," he lowered his voice for dramatic effect. He continued, "Actually, I do teach criminal law and procedure. But I'm kind of a serial killer buff. I've written a few books on some pretty awful people. I guess some people look at me as an expert. Anyway, the D.C. police are flying me out for a couple of weeks to see if I can help them."

His self-effacing manner was very attractive to Laura. Here was a man with some significant level of notoriety and no one would have ever know it. He acted like the carefree college professor, yet he dealt with crimes that would turn her stomach.

"Do you know anything about the crimes they're calling you to investigate?"

Mark nodded and motioned toward the beach, "Do you have time to sit on the beach for a while? I think they need our table."

The line waiting for a seat was long. Laura nodded and followed Mark.

"I know exactly what killings they're talking about. I've been following them for some time. You may have read about them."

Laura looked at him quizzically as they walked out onto the sand and wended their way through sunbathers towards the water's edge.

"Three prostitutes have been brutally murdered within the last six weeks. In fact, the most recent one was just last Monday evening."

★ CHAPTER 12 ★

Laura shook her head, "I didn't hear about that one, but I remember hearing something about the others."

They sat on the sand near the water.

"The murders were gruesome. Jack-the-Ripper types. The women were cut up pretty badly. It's got the D.C. police a little concerned."

"I would hope so."

"It's not such an obvious concern, Laura. They have terrible murders in the red-light district every day. The problem with these though is that they're not the only ones. Six years ago in the same general area, over a two-month period four other women were murdered. Then again, three years ago, another three women. All of them cut almost surgically with a sharp object from throat to groin."

Laura blanched at the thought of it.

"It doesn't end there, either. Eight and ten years ago, five prostitutes were murdered in the same way right here in California. Three in Los Angeles and two in Sacramento. I'm not sure if all of these are connected, but the method used to kill them is the same. It would be a hell of a coincidence."

Laura stared hard at Mark.

"How do you do this?" she finally asked.

"What's that?"

"This work. How do you deal with such horror?"

Mark looked out across the ocean and smiled.

"My wife wondered the same thing in the beginning. I even wondered myself. The only way I've been able to explain it is by saying I just don't get too close to the killers. A lot of people say you have to become like your quarry to understand and ultimately catch him. I don't think I ever believed that. I certainly don't now."

Mark picked a sea plant bulb out of the sand and threw it into a breaking wave.

"My wife and I were very religious. After she died, I pulled away from God. I was madder than hell at him for taking Mary away from Nickie and me. Actually at that time, I was a whole lot more concerned about myself than Nickie. Anyway, I dove into my work to the exclusion of all else, even Nickie, until I found myself getting

107

closer to the people I was studying. It scared me enough to make me pull away for a year and try to find myself."

He smiled and shook his head before continuing.

"One day I woke up and realized I still had a daughter who loved me and who needed my love in return. I convinced myself God hadn't done something to us. Maybe he had something better for our Mary. It was difficult for both of us for a long time. When I got back into my work, though, I realized it was only a job. Nickie was my life and all this other stuff was just work.

"You want to know how I really stay sane working on this stuff?" he asked.

She nodded.

"I pray a lot. Ask for perspective and I spend a lot of time with Nickie. It helps me keep my priorities straight and I deal with my subjects as just that."

Mark again stared out over the ocean and sucked in a deep draught of salt air. Laura sensed his peace and warmth.

"You've done a great job with Nickie, Mark. She's a wonderful girl."

"Thanks. She actually takes care of me most of the time. Sometimes I think she wonders who's the adult and who's the kid.

As they walked back to the restaurant and Laura's bike, Laura said, "Maybe you can look me up when you get to D.C." Who knows? It could turn out to be interesting.

When they reached the sidewalk again, Laura heard a familiar voice.

"Hey . . . we saw that guy again."

Laura turned to see Will and one of his friends walking toward her.

"He was in pretty bad shape. Pants and shirt torn. And blood! Man, he musta had a million cuts."

"Where was he?" asked Laura.

"He was walking along the Strand. Limping actually. He didn't have any skates on either. He was looking all over the place. He finally saw your bike over there," Will pointed. "That's when I went up to him and told him to leave it alone."

"Did he say anything to you?"

"Naw, he just gave this dirty look and took off. He didn't look too tough to me?"

"Thanks Will. I think you should stay away from him, though. He might have some dangerous friends."

"So do I," he laughed and pointed to his large, well-muscled body. "What's your name?"

"I'm Laura."

"Okay. Listen, Laura, if you need any help, look me up. I'm down here all the time."

"Thanks."

Will and his buddy walked away and Laura shook her head and smiled after them.

"What was that all about?" asked Mark.

Laura worked on the lock combination as she tried to decide how much to tell Mark. Finally she chose to tell him all, particularly after he'd bared his soul to her.

"Those boys helped me after the bike collision. The guy they were referring to . . . was following me."

"Did you know the guy?"

"No. I mean, I'd seen him before. In D.C. But I didn't know him."

"Do you know why he's following you?"

"Not really. Although, I think it's got something to do with what happened to me in Washington."

Mark didn't respond. He didn't want to push Laura to discuss a sore subject and Laura appreciated that.

"That's one of the reasons I'm going back so soon. I've got to find out what really happened. How it happened I suppose," she offered.

"Maybe I can help you when I'm in town. After all, I do have a passing acquaintance with the criminal mind," Mark smiled.

"I'd appreciate that," Laura smiled back at him. "Thanks for lunch, Mark. Call me when you get to D.C."

He waved as she started pedaling back to Manhattan Beach. His heart beat quickly in a way it hadn't for years.

★ ★ ★

Laura returned home to another message from Bill McDonough. She felt badly she'd forgotten he was going to call. She really wanted to hear what Bill had learned.

Cat explained Bill would be home by the weekend. They could talk then.

"How did he sound, Mom?"

"I don't know him well, Laura. He was speaking very quickly, though. Perhaps it was because of the pay phone."

Laura didn't believe that, but she kept her thoughts to herself, just as she did about her experience on the Strand. She didn't want to worry Cat any more than she already had. Until she'd figured things out, she'd keep it to herself.

CHAPTER 13

Aidan Sullivan had been angry a lot lately. Things had not been going well since those damn articles in the *Herald*. He'd known all along they were going to be written. He'd even known when.

The president didn't actually plan the whole thing. As it turned out, however, he couldn't have thought of a better way to get rid of the *Herald's* opposition while, at the same time, dispatching another woman that would have been a thorn in the side of his move for a third term . . . and beyond.

It had been a marvelous play. Two enemies completely debilitated in one shot. He should have been ecstatic. And he was, until he realized he'd misunderstood.

For more than a week his dreams had been troubled by the inscrutable face of a mysterious woman. Finally, yesterday, he demanded a clear vision. He needed to know, or it would drive him crazy. He knew the forces he was dealing with. He'd known them well for years. And he knew how to get what he wanted from them. For some reason, however, it was so difficult this time.

There had been considerable resistance, as if someone or something was trying to hide the face from him. Last night, just for a second, that contrary force failed.

Aidan Sullivan, on the fringes of deep sleep, made his demand. While he dozed he used his own considerable powers to focus on one thing. The image of the woman. It had taken the whole night. A night of battle between the combined power of his will and the force that assisted him against the other evil force. Finally, he'd won. Her face had come in a flash and then it was gone. But the flash was enough. He knew this woman.

During the previous week, the circles under the president's eyes had grown darker and Bret Cummings was worried. He had also been worried about the president's terrible mood, a mood he had seen before. It was anger, but more than anger. Cummings could sense a deep brooding hatred.

Bret canceled appointments and made excuses for the president, saying he was ill with the flu and was being attended by his physicians. After three days, however, people began to wonder. He hoped the president would snap out of it soon.

On Thursday morning the president smiled. Sullivan's dark circles were still apparent but his mood was lighter.

"I want a full report on the senate vote this afternoon, Bret. I'll see you at two-thirty," he said when he walked past his chief of staff.

In his office, Sullivan's smile disappeared. Now that he knew who she was, he could deal with it. No more need for total concentration. He had to get back to work and let someone else take care of that bitch.

★ ★ ★

Wednesday and Thursday passed quickly for Laura. She'd spoken to Mark a couple of times, once to turn down a date she really wanted to accept but for family commitments and the other to give her D.C. phone number to him.

The whole family was excited that the "lunch" had gone well and Mark was going to D.C. on "business." Cat, of course, was already thinking marriage although she would not dare actually broach the subject in Laura's current state.

Laura's flight to D.C. was scheduled for departure at 8:30 in the morning. It was going to be a crowded flight so she planned to follow the rule of thumb and be at the airport an hour before takeoff. She packed the night before and settled in for a good night's sleep.

Friday dawned cold, dreary and wet. The arctic storm had finally broken through the Southern California inversion resistance and the clouds had rolled in, black and ominous, during the night. As a result, the expected morning sunshine never appeared and Laura woke at 7:45. She was frantic. Cat assured her, however, it would only take fifteen minutes to get to the airport.

The rain had started quietly during the middle of the night. By 7:55 when Cat and Laura were sitting in the Explorer, it was falling in torrents. Both of them were drenched as they sat in the vehicle and Cat turned the ignition.

When nothing happened, Cat tried again. This time she pumped the gas several times. Again, no response.

"What's wrong, Mom?"

"I don't know. It just won't start," Cat responded.

She tried the ignition and pumped the gas several times. Again, nothing happened. It was 8:00. Suddenly remembering a previous similar problem, Cat pushed hard on the gearshift to make sure it was firmly in Park.

"Sometimes this helps."

Again she pumped the gas pedal and turned the ignition. The engine turned over, but it still wouldn't start. The smell of gas was overpowering in the vehicle.

"Flooded," said Laura. She was nervous. "Let's take Dad's car."

8:05

Cat pushed the button for the garage door opener. As it was opening, they both jumped out, grabbing bags and slogging through the rain to Jack's Bronco.

Mercifully, the car started on the first turn.

8:08

Cat backed out quickly, shifted into drive, and drove as fast as the pouring rain would permit.

8:10

They reached Manhattan Beach Boulevard and turned right to Sepulveda. Because of business traffic and long lights, they had to wait through two signals.

8:16

The rain caused major tieups along Sepulveda.

"Damn! We're not going to make it," said Laura anxiously.

"Be patient, dear. We'll be there as soon as we can."

They hit Imperial Highway at 8:23. Still enough time, if they hurried.

At 8:28 they pulled up in front of the Delta departure terminal.

"You go, Laura, I'll check your bags or send them on the next flight."

"Bye, Mom. Thanks."

Laura bolted out of the car and ran through the terminal like the TV ads. She dodged baggage and people. Thankfully there was no line at the metal detector.

8:30

She made it to gate five just as her plane was pulling away from the boarding tunnel and onto the runway. Looking desperately at her watch, she thought, "The first time it's ever been on time. And on a rainy day!"

Laura ran up to the flight counter.

"Excuse me, I'm . . ."

"One moment please," said the attendant.

"I can't wait, that's my plane!" Laura shouted.

The attendant was unnecessarily angry at the interruption. She very deliberately typed the last digit on the computer and turned to Laura.

"Now what's the problem ma'am?"

"I'm supposed to be on that plane. Can you stop it?"

"I'm sorry, ma'am. Flight three eighty-four is full."

"Listen, I've got a ticket right here," she put it on the counter and pointed, "so it can't be full. My seat is empty." She was yelling now as the plane was next in line to takeoff. "Call someone."

"I'm sorry, ma'am, we can't—"

"Look," Laura glared at the attendant and then suddenly realized it would do no good. She would have to wait for the next flight. A loud clap of thunder shook the terminal and brought an avalanche from the heavens as Laura tried to calm herself and finally smiled.

114

She spoke calmly, "I'm sorry about my insanity. I missed my plane. Can you get me on the next one?"

The attendant smirked victoriously and punched up ticket sales for the 9:30 flight.

"Yes, ma'am, we have several seats available. Would you like a window or aisle?"

"Window please."

The attendant prepared a boarding pass and handed it to her.

"Flight four seventy-two will be boarding at gate seven down the hall."

"Thanks," Laura said as she turned away. She went back down the entry to the terminal where her mother was arguing with a porter who kept saying the plane had already left.

Laura and Cat had a cup of coffee after checking the bags for the 9:30 flight, laughing together over the crazy drive to the airport.

Secretly, Laura was happy she'd missed the earlier flight. She had a terrible fear of flying in turbulent weather. By nine-thirty, the torrential rain had stopped completely. The black clouds turned to gray and blue sky could be seen clearly through the dispersing cloud cover.

★ ★ ★

Delta Flight 384 from Los Angeles to Washington D.C.'s Dulles Airport was one seat short of being full. It was carrying 480 men, women and children bound home, early, to beat the weekend rush after Easter break. The flight captain ordered seat belts be worn until the plane cleared the storm that was flooding Los Angeles. It was an unusual storm for this time of year because of its intensity. Captain Stan Zumwalt hadn't seen anything like it in his thirty years of flying the massive airliners. At least over Los Angeles International, he hadn't. Zumwalt was a pro, however, and he knew his plane well. He could handle her in any conditions, even the fluke Southern California spring storm.

As the plane sat in line waiting for its turn for takeoff, Captain Zumwalt wondered if the flight might be delayed or even canceled because of the weather. It'd happened before. Although he'd flown in snowstorms and other weather that was comparable, the Los Angeles traffic controllers weren't used to it. He could envision them pulling the planes back until the storm abated.

It didn't happen that way, however. After the United Airlines jumbo jet in front of him lifted off without mishap, it was Zumwalt's turn. As the first officer read the gauge settings aloud, Zumwalt listened carefully until he heard the traffic controller's voice.

"Delta Flight three eighty-four, you're cleared for takeoff."

"Roger, three eighty-four rolling," Zumwalt answered as he pushed the throttles full forward and the huge craft jumped.

The plane gathered speed quickly with the first officer calling out air speeds. As the craft reached optimum speed, Zumwalt rotated the nose of the plane by pulling back on the yoke and the front wheel lifted off the ground. The aircraft continued to thunder forward until finally it had enough speed to lift completely off the ground.

What surprised Stan Zumwalt as the plane came off the tarmac was that he didn't feel the buffeting, bouncing, and wind changes normally associated with a heavy storm. In fact, as the tires left the pad, it seemed as if the storm's intensity suddenly diminished. The ascent was easy, with a minimum of turbulence.

Out of the airport, Zumwalt directed the craft west over the Pacific Ocean. Passengers could barely discern the roiling gray waters through the cloud cover. Over Catalina Island, the plane reached the Dolphin Intersection at which point the Captain turned the craft east. He was still climbing as he reached Dolphin and made the turn.

"Strange," whispered Zumwalt when they finally reached the clear blue skies above the clouds at fourteen thousand feet.

"What's that, Stan?" asked copilot Ted Hilgenberg.

"That was the damndest storm I've ever seen. I thought for sure we'd have a rough go of it on takeoff. It was a piece of cake. Almost as if there was no storm at all."

"So what are you bitchin' about? It makes our jobs easier," Ted laughed.

"Yeah, I guess," smiled Stan. "I just thought it was unusual that's all."

At thirty-five thousand feet, Captain Zumwalt announced they had reached cruising altitude. Passengers were permitted to move freely about the cabin, although he did warn them to continue to wear the belts when they were seated.

It wasn't until they were flying over the great Salt Lake that Stan became worried.

The flight captain first noticed something was wrong when the plane's Loran System started to act up. The Long Range Navigation System, known as Loran, enabled the huge craft to fly on it's own. When it wasn't working, the plane could be controlled manually, by the pilot. In such a case, however, altitude and navigation were controlled by sight.

Captain Zumwalt asked his copilot to call the nearest tower in Salt Lake and ask for assistance as he surveyed the other gages on the panel before him. The tower would still be able to pick him up on their radar. When the radio didn't work, however, it was apparent that either the storm over Los Angeles had done some damage, after all, or someone had brought some electrical device aboard the aircraft. The plane's electrical equipment was so sensitive, even a small transistor radio could interfere with it's functions.

"Ted, have Janice get her crew to check the cabin, will you? We've got some kind of electrical interference."

Ten minutes later, Janice Peterson, the head flight attendant, reported that they had found nothing.

"I'll check below," Ted offered.

Captain Zumwalt had dealt with electrical interference before. It normally wasn't a major problem. They would usually hit a particular patch of turbulence and the electrically charged air would throw the system off for a few seconds. The challenge he now faced stemmed from the fact that the system had now been down for fifteen minutes and there were no clouds in sight. They were completely out of touch with the ground and the plane had dropped in altitude to fifteen thousand feet or so, to enable him to see landmarks by which to navigate into Salt Lake's international airport.

At the front cabin hatch, Ted Hilgenberg noticed that two of the four screws were missing and the remaining two were loose. He took them out completely, pulled off the hatch, and peered into the hole before descending. Because it was dark, he switched on his mini flashlight. He saw the device immediately.

The black metal tool box was lodged tightly between two pipes. Above the box, taped with black duct tape was a three-quarter-pound package of plastic explosives.

"It's a bomb!" he shouted.

Seconds later, the device exploded. The craft's outer skin, at the control cabin, peeled back instantly and opened a gaping hole to the passenger compartment. The plane disintegrated before anyone knew what was happening as a second explosion tore through it's luggage compartment.

As expected, the House acted quickly on the Danwood Senate resolution. The large majority of Democrats made it an easy call. What was most surprising was the number of Republicans who crossed party lines to vote in favor of repeal of the 22nd Amendment when the most likely beneficiaries of that repeal would be the Democrats and their incumbent president, Aidan Sullivan. Fully one-half of the House Republicans supported the repeal initiative.

The vote would be put to the states next. The U.S. congressmen would be taking the Danwood Resolution to their respective state houses and giving their opinions on how the vote should go. Even though none of the federal legislators had any direct say in the outcome of the state votes, they certainly had clout.

Once the states had the resolution, some of them would hold constitutional conventions with delegates elected from each of the state's districts while others would hold special elections to get the vote of the people.

The constitutional amendment process was one that could take years, as it had done with the Women's Rights Amendment, added to the U.S. Constitution in the late 1980s. Senator Danwood's proposal, however, had a momentum that would move it much more quickly. In fact, state legislators in the south and northeast had already been arguing the issue for almost two years. President Sullivan's army of supporters had begun fighting the fight just after his landslide reelection to a second term. By the time Senator Danwood made his proposal official on the Senate floor, half of the states were already scheduling their special elections and constitutional conventions.

The president's network, run by the efficient Bret Cummings, would keep constant pressure on the other states to move quickly. After all, the primaries started again in less than one year. It was Bret's intent that the decision be final by Christmas. With twenty-five states solidly in the president's corner on the issue, he only needed another nine. He felt certain he could accomplish that on time, even though twenty-two of the twenty-five remaining states had republican majorities in their state houses.

Aidan Sullivan was happier Friday morning. He had slept exceedingly well Thursday night. In fact, after his head hit his pillow at eight o'clock in the evening, he didn't budge until thirteen hours later when his housekeeper, Sylvia Bertrand, checked in on him to make sure he was okay.

Sylvia didn't intend to wake him. She had no desire to incur the wrath that had been exhibited so readily over the past week. She stepped in only to see if something was wrong with the president since he never slept past seven.

She opened the door slowly and peered into the darkness. The only light in the room was that which filtered in through the opening she'd just made and a few wayward sun beams that struggled through the space between the drapes. When she could see nothing, she opened the door further and tiptoed into the room. She could barely discern the dark figure of the president as her eyes began to adjust to the darkness. It looked as if he were sleeping sitting up, leaning back against his headboard. She stepped closer and bent to see if the president was breathing when suddenly she saw the pale whites of his eyes.

"Good morning, Sylvia."

She jumped back, startled. Her heart leapt to her throat and she reached reflexively for the crucifix at her chest.

"Oh . . . I'm sorry, sir. I didn't mean to wake you. We were worried . . ."

"It's okay, Sylvia," he interrupted calmly. "I appreciate the concern."

Sylvia shivered at the cold calmness in the president's voice.

"Please open the drapes for me."

She ran to the window and drew the cord, flooding the room with the morning sun. The president closed his eyes and turned his head away from the window. Slowly, the eyes opened again and he smiled at the forty-five-year-old Cuban matron.

"Thank you. Please tell Mister Cummings that I'll see him in my office at eleven o'clock," he instructed her.

"Yes, sir," said Sylvia, half-bowing and moving quickly out of the room.

She breathed a sigh of relief as she closed the door behind her. "I've got to get a new job," she whispered to herself. "That man scares me."

At the eleven o'clock meeting with Bret Cummings, the president received an update on the third term issue. He knew about yesterday's House vote, but Cummings' word that only nine more state commitments were needed was exhilarating.

"Now that's the way it should be moving," thought the president. Things were starting to look up for Aidan Sullivan. He'd taken care of that nagging dream of his and now nothing but positive news from his chief of staff. Not even his concerns over his son could dampen his spirits today. Besides, with Jason safely locked away in a secure wing of the Sunford Home, he wouldn't be able to cause any major embarrassment.

Aidan knew that Jason hadn't killed Michael Stoner. Anyone in their right mind, who had done any real investigation, would have seen that. It was the appearance, however, that he and Charlie Gilbert were concerned about. If his enemies ever got wind of what appeared to have happened, those spineless fence sitters, who went with the most popular cause would jump over to the opposition. All he needed was to keep Jason under wraps for another year and a half. After that, it wouldn't matter anymore.

All in all, this was going to be a great day for him. After the business, planned for the afternoon, he was escorting the beautiful Marianne Cornhauer to a White House dinner honoring her father John Cornhauer, chairman of one of the largest computer conglomerates in the world and one of the president's most ardent supporters both vocally and, of course, financially.

The president would speak eloquently of how the brilliant Mr. Cornhauer had devoted his life to the American dream and become one of the richest, most powerful men in the world. How upon reaching the pinnacle of success he had looked at the world's less fortunate and formed the Cornhauer Foundation to distribute food and teach the merits of capitalism to third-world countries. He smiled when he thought about the arrogant sot who strutted proudly in front of the peons but bowed down reverently before the president.

Sullivan could see through it all. Despite the fact that Marianne Cornhauer was twenty years younger than the president, her parents fairly leapt with glee when Aidan Sullivan cast his eyes her way. Like other influential families in the country, John and Madeline Cornhauer practically threw their daughter at the president. What a coup for the family whose scion found favor in the beautiful blue eyes of Aidan Sullivan.

Marianne Cornhauer had found that favor, at least temporarily. It had been in the back seat of the presidential limousine where the erstwhile debutante had given Sullivan the blow job of his life on the way home from yet another presidential fund-raising party. Since that enlightening event, Aidan Sullivan had spent several evenings with Marianne Cornhauer. The tabloids ate it up. This was finally it for the most eligible bachelor in the country, they speculated. He had finally found his Venus in the raven-haired beauty, Marianne Cornhauer.

For Aidan Sullivan, however, she was a nice diversion. One he needed badly this night. After the past two weeks of strain, he was ready to let go and the insatiable Marianne Cornhauer was the perfect tonic.

CHAPTER 14

As time passed, the boy's anger returned.

At first, he was delirious with his new-found capability. He was like a young child who has just been given free reign in his favorite candy store. However, as it was for that young child, the lack of control and resistance began to turn the candy store into just another mundane part of a life that required greater thrills. For the young man, it turned again to the lonely life and the voice of the force that was suddenly his only real companion.

The other young men wanted to be a part of him because of his obvious prowess with the ladies, while silently they wished him dead. He simply smiled and controlled any opposition, knowing full well that he could have whatever he wanted whenever he wanted. It was then that he began to expand the scope of the experiment.

He could already influence, manipulate and control, to various degrees, the minds of those who gave themselves to him and even those who didn't, but were too weak in mind and character to resist him. Through sheer boredom he tried to enter minds and soon learned that through some people he could sense what they sensed as if he were actually part of them. He even realized that he could make others do his will and satisfy his own carnal needs through this sensory sharing.

But there were restrictions. For the first time he realized there were others with wills, minds, and characters he could not so easily control. He worked hard on sharpening his skills and pulling closer to the force that moved him to greater heights of control and domination. One day he knew he would be strong enough to control them all.

Through it all, however, the young man brooded.

He was destined for greatness, he knew that. And so he made the right moves and followed the path laid so bright before him. Yet deep inside a cauldron boiled with a hatred bred by longing for the one true human relationship he could never attain again, the relationship that could replace the overbearing mother he'd grown to hate so much.

CHAPTER 15

Laura's plane touched down at Dulles at six o'clock eastern time. Although it was a quiet, peaceful flight with a minimum of air turbulence, it had taken a little longer than normal because the plane was required to detour south of Salt Lake City. The captain said they wanted to avoid the air space over Salt Lake because of an electrical storm.

Laura hailed a taxi and took the short ride to her apartment. She was exhausted.

When she opened her apartment door, she immediately noticed that something was wrong. It wasn't the musty smell of a place closed for two weeks but the mess of papers, drawers, and cabinets that she didn't recall.

Her immediate reaction was anger at Tom Stafford who, she assumed, had come to clean out the rest of his belongings and left a huge mess. Sure enough, on further investigation, she found all his things were gone as well as some of her own.

Nice welcome home, she thought as she resolved to call him Saturday morning at the office and find out what the hell his problem was. At the moment, however, Laura wasn't interested in dealing with the mess. She wanted to savor the last memory of her visit home before jumping back into the frenetic world of Washington, D.C.

After dropping her bags in the living room, Laura walked back out onto the street and turned toward Rosen's Deli, a favorite hangout a couple of blocks south of her building. Rosen's Reuben sandwich had been on her mind for over a week.

She walked slowly, assuming the pace she'd so quickly donned back in Manhattan Beach. Laura breathed deeply of the early evening air and saw everything for the first time in years. It was amazing how one could get caught up in the hectic pace of the city with the honking, smoke spewing cars and the running suits and briefcases. At the normal pace, one could easily miss the world around her. That was certainly the case with Laura. The thing that was suddenly most apparent was the poverty on the streets.

Laura had always avoided the panhandlers and street hoods, firmly believing they should all get jobs and quit feeling sorry for themselves. Even while she was in Manhattan Beach, where everything was beautiful, she avoided the homeless beggars.

Suddenly, however, she saw something different. She didn't really understand why she was seeing them for the first time, but she was. It wasn't only bearded vagabonds who smelled and looked pitiful. Entire families with young children cowering beneath trees and holding signs that read "WILL WORK FOR FOOD" were everywhere.

Her walk revealed other signs of destitution in the nation's capital. Many smaller business establishments were closed. These were ones she had never frequented, her own preferences running to the trendy, newer establishments around the capital. Now, however, she was seeing what was really happening.

When Laura reached Rosen's Deli, she'd lost the craving for her Reuben sandwich. Instead she bought a half dozen hot dogs, french fries, and five milks. On her way back to her apartment she crossed the street to the parkette where a young father held the "Food for Work" sign and his wife hugged their two children to her. Laura extracted one hot dog and a half pint of milk from her bag and handed the rest to the man. His eyes bugged open in shock. He stared at the bag and then at Laura as if it were a joke.

"I can do some work for you," he said awkwardly.

"I'm sorry, sir, I don't have any work. I was expecting guests tonight and they just called and said they couldn't come. I didn't want it to go to waste."

★ CHAPTER 15 ★

The man held the bag gingerly. He turned slowly and handed it to his wife who smiled as tears began to roll down her face. The two children, a boy who looked about ten and a younger girl, faces stained with mud and dirt and hair oily and slick reached for the bag and smelled the warm dogs and fries.

The father turned back and extended his hand slowly.

"God bless you!"

Laura took his hand and squeezed it tightly. When she turned away, the man was holding the twenty dollar bill she had put in his hand.

"God bless you," yelled the mother, tears streaming.

Laura scurried across the street and back to her apartment with tears of her own wetting her cheeks.

The next morning Laura called Tom Stafford's office. He was always in on Saturday. "Part of the obligations of the partners," he used to say. She'd pretty much straightened out the mess but was still upset at the effrontery of her ex in leaving her papers and things strewn about.

"Myers, Jonas and Bottomworth" answered the efficient-sounding receptionist at Tom's office.

"May I speak to Tom Stafford, please."

"I'm sorry . . . Mister Stafford has been on vacation all week. He won't be in until Monday. May I take a message for Mister Stafford?"

Laura was angry, at first, that he could go off on some vacation, probably with his little blond secretary, just days after he dumped her. She would have liked to leave an obscene message but decided against it with a smile.

"Please tell him Laura Miller called."

"Oh, Miss Miller. Yes, I'd be happy to leave that message."

"Thanks."

"You're very welcome."

Laura hung up and then immediately lifted the receiver again. She punched the buttons for Bill McDonough's house. After four rings, Bill's machine answered and Laura left a message that she was back in town and would like to get together with him. Apparently he and Nell had stayed an extra day and would be back later in the day or perhaps on Sunday.

"Two strikes," she thought. "I don't think I'll try for a third."

She spent the rest of the day determining how much money she still had and how long she could last before finding another job. After a couple of hours, she discovered that she had seventy-three hundred dollars in savings and, by her accounting, another twenty-five hundred in her checking account. It always amazed her friends when they learned she actually had a savings account. After consideration, however, most of the friends realized it was because she never spent money. It wasn't that she was a skinflint or anything, it's just that she had been so obsessive about her work, that she rarely found time to spend. On those occasions when she and Tom ventured out on the town, he and his 250,000-dollar-a-year salary usually picked up the tab.

Although her savings were fairly substantial, they wouldn't last long with no job and two thousand dollars a month for rent. She'd have to give her notice to vacate on May 1 and have the last month's rent payment she and Tom had put up at the beginning of the lease cover the final month. Laura would have to spend some time looking for a smaller place, that is, if she really was going to stay in D.C. That decision would be made as soon as she determined how welcome she was in town.

On Sunday, Laura read the newspaper for the first time in two weeks. She'd avoided it purposely, even in California, because she didn't want to know what was going on in the world. After reading the lead story, she wished she had waited another week or two.

The headline read "DELTA DEATH TOLL IS LARGEST IN U. S. HISTORY."

The article summarized the prior day's lead story about the crash of Delta Flight 384 from Los Angeles to Washington, D.C. Observers from the ground reported seeing a bright flash and then hearing a terrific explosion high above the ground. Apparently, the plane had lost considerable altitude before the explosion. Pieces of the shattered hulk hit the ground as far as five miles away and bodies lay scattered for hundreds of yards around the Utah field in which the main part of the plane fell.

Laura sat, mouth agape as she read and reread the flight number, the departure venue and the destination. All 480 passengers and 22 crew members were dead. The photograph depicted a gruesome scene of torn plane wreckage and mutilated bodies.

"Investigators are searching the wreckage to determine the cause. It is believed that it was mechanical failure," the article concluded.

She dropped the paper and leaned back in her chair. Laura stared out her window, shocked beyond belief that she had come so close to death. Just as suddenly as that thought crossed her mind, another thought, one even more perverse and unbelievable began to take root.

Maybe it was no accident. Her mind raced to the elevator at the *Herald* and the bike path in California, to the wicked little man so finely groomed who was bleeding and angry because she had seen him. Was it possible that the plane crash was meant for her? Was the murder of five hundred innocent people intended to cover up the death of insignificant Laura Miller?

It couldn't be. She couldn't accept the ridiculous notion that she was important enough to anyone to want her dead. Yet someone was definitely interested in her. It flooded her consciousness with a clarity she hadn't experienced in years. Yet it simply wasn't possible that anyone was interested enough in her to want her dead.

She struggled to make sense out of her confusion and her mind moved again to Michael Stoner. Everything he had told her was true. Every fact was clean. They'd all checked out. But somehow that didn't matter. There was something deeper. The hoax was on the world not on Laura. Someone had made Laura, Bill McDonough, and Michael Stoner look crazy. Someone was afraid of them.

Why else was she being followed? She was certain of that. Any doubt was banished when sixteen-year-old Will had seen the man near her bike. Someone was afraid of Laura. Afraid enough to try to kill her? But why? What did Laura have? And on whom? The president?

She shivered, unable to control the fear coursing through her body. She glanced again at the article, at the words in the third paragraph, which read, "A list of the dead is being compiled and will be released after the next of kin have been notified."

Maybe they believed she was dead. Maybe they wouldn't find out for a few days and she'd be able to hide or something. Maybe.

"This is ridiculous, Laura. Get ahold of yourself," she said out loud. "If it is the president, where can you hide? You've got to think. Figure out what's really happening. That's it. Relax and think. There's got to be an explanation. Some way to clear this up before anything else happens. I mean . . . you're nobody. They've got you wrong."

Laura spent the rest of the day alone in her apartment watching every news program she could find. She jumped when the phone rang and breathed again when it was the wrong number.

There was considerable speculation concerning the crash with most of the thought going to engine failure or other mechanical malfunction.

Laura tried Bill McDonough's number several times but couldn't get through to him. She really needed to talk to Bill. She wished he'd get home.

By that evening, Laura had calmed down considerably. She had ordered pizza and was eating a piece of sausage and mushroom when a special bulletin, announcing the first break in the terrible plane tragedy, came on the air.

Los Angeles' NBC affiliate, Channel 4, had received a call from a man identifying himself as "Moses," a leader of the rebel group known as the German Alliance For Peace. Moses claimed responsibility for the destruction of Flight 384 saying that "American imperialism will be stopped by our German fatherland, abroad, and by our brothers in peace in this country."

Reporters accosted President Sullivan at Camp David, the presidential retreat, where he'd gone early Saturday morning with his escort, Marianne Cornhauer, to enjoy some sun and quiet away from the rigors of the White House.

Even with a microphone stuck into his face, he looked fit and commanding.

"This outrage will not go unpunished. The German Alliance will not be permitted to run free in our society. I promise all of you that this 'Moses' will be brought to swift and uncompromising justice."

He bowed his head, pensive, as the cameras stayed on him.

"To the families and friends of those who lost their lives," he continued somberly "my heart goes out to you. Know that these brave people did not die in vain. They lost their lives while living the American dream. As you all are. You must all understand that we are at war with those forces who would pull us down. Those forces, led by animals like this 'Moses' and others. I failed you this time but I will never do so again. The German Alliance will fall and so too will all of those who oppose us."

The president stared hard into the cameras for several seconds. Even Laura was mesmerized by his words and eyes. No reporter asked questions as he turned and ran to his helicopter waiting to carry him back to the White House.

Laura went to sleep that night, wondering if she was crazy. She was disgusted with her paranoia. Someone had been following her alright. But c'mon, who would want to kill her? It just didn't make sense. Maybe if she saw Michael Stoner, she could start to decipher things.

CHAPTER 16

Mark Tucker's flight from Los Angeles arrived Sunday night at nine-thirty. He was met by Commander Raphael ("Ralph") Escobar, head of the task force investigating the Ripper killings, as they were being called because of their gruesome similarities to the murders committed in Whitechapel, London, over a century before. After introductions, Commander Escobar drove Mark to the Hyatt Hotel near the airport. He told him to be ready early in the morning, as Escobar was sending a car for him at seven-thirty.

"We've got to get to work since we're paying so much money to keep you here," smiled the commander.

Although several others under Escobar's command had bristled at the thought of an outsider coming to help with the investigation, the commander himself didn't mind. Escobar had been in charge since the second of the three current murders. When it became apparent that there was some kind of lunatic on the loose who liked to cut women up, rather than a one-time killer, the mayor decided it was time to put a task force together.

Escobar had been on the force for thirty years. He was well aware of the seven previous similar murders. However, because they were in the red-light district, people paid little attention to them. When money was finally set aside for the task force, Escobar quickly realized he'd need some help. He was unable to find any pattern to the killings, which now numbered ten in D.C., and, if the California ones were indeed linked in some way, fifteen all together. No one could determine what it was that brought the killer out every few years for a group of killings or what put him on ice afterwards. It wasn't even clear that all the killings were by the same person, although some signs, common to all the killings, that were never revealed to the press, pointed to a single killer. If the California corpses had similar marks, Escobar felt certain they were linked.

It was Escobar who asked for Tucker. The commander had been to a course several years ago at Georgetown University where visiting lecturer, Professor Mark Tucker, gave his audience some hints into the psychological make-up of the serial killer. Escobar even read one of Tucker's books. The man knew his business. Still, with money tight they'd have to work quickly.

Escobar had an officer knocking on Mark's hotel door at 7:30 sharp. Once at the station, Escobar showed Mark to an austere room whose only furnishing was a large aluminum table in the center. The table was stacked with files in various states of use and disrepair.

"Go ahead and take a look at those. When you're through, we'll talk."

"Thanks, commander. Looks like a nice way to start the morning."

Mark smiled and then turned back to the table.

"I'll send some coffee in," said Escobar.

Mark sat down and picked up the first file. They were arranged chronologically from the most recent case to the oldest. It read "Tawana Childess" on the title tab and it gave the date. Mark winced when he saw the first photograph of the mutilated body. There were a dozen similar photos as well as one posed shot of the girl. She had been pretty.

He shook his head sadly and started reading the reports.

★ CHAPTER 16 ★

Laura wondered if her car would start. It had been sometime since she'd driven the five-year-old Shadow. The red car sat quietly in its stall beneath her building. For just a second as she walked to the car, it flashed through her mind that she should check to see if any bombs were wired to the ignition. Since she wouldn't have any idea where to look or what to look for, however, she cast the thought aside. Besides, if someone wanted to kill her, they wouldn't have to stoop to some obvious movie trick.

Still, Laura winced as she turned the key. When the car started immediately she breathed again, relieved that someone wouldn't have to peel her body parts off the garage ceiling.

She let the engine warm up for several minutes before shifting into reverse. Laura backed up out of the stall, shifted into first, and drove to the exit. Manuel, the day security guard, sat munching on a burrito at the gate.

"Hey, Miss Miller, welcome back!" he shouted.

"Thanks, Manuel. That'll kill you this early in the morning, you know!"

"Naw, I been doing this for years, and look at me," he slapped his ample belly, "fit as a burro."

He laughed aloud as Laura smiled and waved. She felt grateful that he was so friendly. He didn't think she was such a fiend for writing such terrible things about the president.

"Hell, he probably doesn't read the paper anyway." she mumbled. That was probably the right idea anyway. Maybe it was better to go through life oblivious to the world's troubles.

Laura followed New York Avenue east out of the capital city to Highway 50, into Maryland. She intended to check in on her friend Michael Stoner at the Sunford Home near Annapolis.

With the convertible top down, she was able to take full advantage of the warm, sunny morning. What a change from the rains of the past few days. Laura loved to drive with the top down. It gave her a sense of freedom, particularly when she hit the highway and got to the country outside D.C.

Lush green hills dotted with spruce and oak rolled by and the sweet aroma of spring flowers was intoxicating. Laura smiled as her senses raced with the beauty of the open road.

The forty-five minute trip to the Sunford Home gave her time to work up a line of questions for Mr. Stoner. He'd have to talk to her and do some major explaining.

The home was nestled amidst bucolic surroundings that belied the tension of insanity within. The grounds were surrounded by an eight-foot-high cinderblock wall topped by three feet of barbed wire. A guard station at the front gate was manned by two armed security people.

The building itself was a large structure built in the 1800s as a hotel getaway for the well-to-do from the surrounding metropolitan areas. The original owner, Shamus Greenberg, had called the place the Greenhouse Inn. After his death in 1910, ownership passed to his grandson, John. During the depression of the 1930s, the place was shut down when John Greenberg, depressed over the loss of his entire family fortune, shot himself and his family. For years the inn sat vacant. Although several buyers made attempts during the 1950s, 1960s, and 1970s to get the inn up and running again, it never caught on. Some said it was because John Greenberg's ghost walked the halls.

Eventually, the property was taken over by the state of Maryland because of failure by its owner to pay taxes. The property sat empty until 1982, when some bright young politician suggested using it for a new mental home. No one would be too concerned about the ghost of John Greenberg. He'd fit right in with the lunatics who would be housed there.

In the spring of 1983, the Sunford Home, named after the politician who thought of the idea, accepted its first patient. In 1991, the place was renovated to become one of the most state of the art facilities in the East. The disturbed members of some of the East's most famous families found themselves spending time in the Sunford Home.

Laura drove through the guard gate after showing her Washington *Herald* press badge and saying she had an appointment to see the head administrator about a story she was writing for the *Herald*.

The guard didn't even check with the main office. He was mostly concerned with stopping people from getting out. The people inside would take care of unwanted visitors. Besides, she looked official. Laura was quite pleased that she could still flash a press credential and give the appearance of sufficient importance to, at least, gain access past a guard who really didn't care.

She walked into the lobby, which bore no resemblance at all to a hotel lobby. Office cubicles had been built to provide work space for the nurses, orderlies, and doctors who moved purposefully about the facility. She walked up to the reception window.

An overweight black girl in her late twenties sat quietly, looking bored and waiting for the phone to ring.

"Excuse me," said Laura.

The girl looked up without saying a word. Laura smiled in an attempt to get some reaction out of the girl. She was about to start waving her hands in front of the girl's face when the girl finally spoke.

"Yes?"

Laura nodded in appreciation. "I'd like to see a patient of yours, a Michael Stoner," she flashed her press credentials at the girl.

She barely looked at the credentials, instead glancing at a list on the wall in front of her.

"Wha'd you say his last name was?" She took the list of names and held it close.

"Stoner . . . S-T-O-N-E-R."

"Let's see here."

The girl moved her inch-long fingernail down the list and stopped.

"We don't have nobody by that name here."

"You must," Laura said in surprise. "I mean, he was here. Just last week he was here in the Sunford Home."

The girl stared at Laura as if she'd gone into another world. Laura was about to snap her fingers when the girl seemed to wake up on her own.

"Stoner? You say his name was Stoner?" Laura nodded. "Michael Stoner?"

"Yes, that's it."

"I don't think he's here no more. On accounta he's daid."

"What do you mean?"

"I think dat's da fella who died las' week." The girl was suddenly coming to life. "Lemme check somethin' for you."

She stood up and walked out of the cubicle into an office or filing room in back.

Laura was sure she was mistaken. She leaned over and picked up the roster card. Running her finger down the list, she confirmed that there was no one by the name of Stoner. Then just as Laura was going to replace the list she saw the name "Sullivan, Jason (violent)."

Unlike the rest of the names, it had no room number next to it. It looked like the guy had a whole wing of rooms to himself. She ran her finger down wings and rooms of other patients and none of them had the same wing reference as Jason Sullivan. She wondered if the secure wing was because the patient was someone important, maybe even related to the president in some way.

"Here he is," the girl said as she waddled out of the back room carrying a file.

Laura replaced the list of names.

"Michael Stoner," read the girl. "It say here, he deceased las' Wednesday. Yep, I remember now," she looked up. "He's daid."

Laura was stunned. When she didn't see his name on the list, she expected to hear that he'd been transferred to another facility. The girl said he was dead.

"Does it say how he died?" Laura was anxious.

"Le's see."

She looked at the report and then read out loud.

"Says here, suicide." She looked up. "Looks like he kilt hisself."

Laura felt like she'd been hit in the face with a shovel. She couldn't move or think clearly. What's going on? She stumbled back away from the window.

"Hey, you okay?" the receptionist asked.

Laura's left hand came to her mouth to cover the shock. She looked around, not knowing where to turn. What was happening here?

"Hey lady, you okay?"

Laura shook her head and looked at the receptionist.

"Yes . . . I mean . . . yes, I'm fine." She hesitated as if to say something else, then turned and ran out of the building. She stopped on the porch and looked out frantically over the yard, closing her mouth and breathing deeply through her nose. She tried to stifle the tears and calm herself.

Slowly regaining her composure, Laura stumbled down the steps to her car. A minute later she was on the road heading home.

"Michael Stoner is dead," she said softly. "Suicide?"

She stared ahead barely seeing the road or any of the signs that sped past her.

"No! Dammit, no!" she shouted. "This isn't right."

Laura glanced down at the speedometer. The needle was pressing ninety. Lifting her foot off the accelerator she slowly rolled to a stop on the right shoulder of the road.

"Okay, kid, it's paranoia time again. I've got to talk to Bill. We've got to figure out what's going on."

Nodding slowly, she again stepped on the gas, resolving to speak to Bill McDonough right away.

The first black limousine pulled into the parking garage at the White House. The American flags, waving on either side of the hood, alerted observers to the fact that this was a military vehicle before anyone saw the occupants. Although it was not unusual to see such a vehicle enter the White House parking garage early on a Monday morning, people had not seen four such vehicles so early in the week since the Japanese and Arab crisis early in the president's tenure.

Since resolution of the Japanese issue, President Sullivan had made regular visits to the tank at the Pentagon to maintain a vital link of communication with his power. A meeting of the joint chiefs at the White House was a portent of something big, however.

Five-Star General Homer Peters was head of the joint chiefs. He was lifetime army and had served the United States in Vietnam and every skirmish since. During the first Arab conflict, when the United States destroyed Iraq's vaunted military machine, General Peters was overlooked by President Bush and the then head of the joint chiefs, Colin Powell. They chose Norman Schwartzkopf to lead the American invasion. That escapade had made Schwartzkopf and

Powell American heroes. Peters, who had remained stateside and had very little direct involvement in any of the planning or implementation, was put out by what he believed was a slight by the president and General Powell.

Although Peters had to admit that Schwartzkopf's handling of the whole affair was masterfully done, he resented the general. He considered early retirement with the thought that he'd show those assholes in Washington what they were losing. He hung on, however, realizing that the military was his life and he simply wouldn't know how to deal with the "real world." He would just have to hope for another chance.

When that chance came with the shocking election of Aidan Sullivan, Homer Peters grabbed it. After the assassination attempt, things had moved so quickly for the young presidential hopeful. Peters could see it happening.

At first, there was the sympathy vote that got people looking Sullivan's way and won him his home state of California, as if he had no competition. Then it became a movement. A wave of support that grew and grew. People began listening to him speak and they came alive. He said all the right things. He said American's were the greatest people in the world. He spoke eloquently of an American spirit that turned a vast wilderness into the greatest country the world had ever known. He spoke of those foreigners who tried to bring America down. Those who dumped their goods and scoffed at the once powerful nation. And he spoke of lethargy. A palpable quiet that had taken hold of the people and destroyed their will to defeat the enemies of their destiny.

General Homer Peters had also been caught up in the young candidate's rhetoric. Suddenly, he realized that the republican old guard of the Reagan and Bush years was gone. This young man was his chance to attain the position he'd always aspired to, the one position for which he alone was best suited.

In the months after California, Peters worked tirelessly, espousing the virtues of Aidan Sullivan. Despite the scoffing of the powerful republican elite, he moved many in the military. When Sullivan was a surprise victor in November, the old guard was stunned. They fell over themselves trying to change their colors. To the new president's credit, however, he saw through it all, cleaned house, and left the door wide open for General Homer Peters. When the president invited him, Homer jumped in.

It was Homer Peters who directed the lightning strikes of the American military against the Arabs in the second conflict. It was Homer Peters who deployed the troops in the Pacific and brought Japan to heel. And it was Homer Peters who was in charge of the most powerful military machine the world had ever known. A military machine that had large contingents of its five million strong force in every major country in the world except Germany, China, and Ukraine.

At the large mahogany conference table in the White House's Situation Room, General Peters sat patiently with the heads of the four major military branches. Peters sat to the right of the seat left for the president. To his right was Admiral James Houston, head of the navy and Major General MacArthur ("Mac") Stevens of the army. Across the table from Stevens was Air Force General Dwight McCoy and next to McCoy was Marine General John ("Bull") Yocum. To the immediate left of the president's chair was a seat reserved for Bret Cummings, a nonmilitary man General Peters didn't care for, except that he seemed to be totally committed to the president.

At the other end of the table were three seats for the president's personal body guards. In the beginning, Peters wondered why the president invited these three to the meetings of the joint chiefs, especially when he rarely invited his own vice president. However, it had quickly become clear to Peters that all three were military men and Charlie Gilbert, at least, was a brilliant tactician.

When the president walked in with his retinue of Cummings and three personal men, the joint chiefs stood and saluted him.

"Thank you, gentlemen. Please be seated," said the president. "No doubt you all read or heard about the destruction of Delta Flight 384 on Friday. I am personally disgusted that a group of paramilitary foreign assassins could pull off such a coup within the borders of our own country.

"I have been assured by the German government that they had nothing to do with the affair and that the so called German Alliance for Peace is a nonsanctioned rebel organization. Well, I say to you gentlemen here today . . . bullshit!"

The president, still standing, slammed a fist to the table and glared at his military commanders. As his eyes moved from face to face, be began to calm.

"Before we get into any significant discussion on how to handle the matter, I'd like you to listen to Bret Cummings."

The president sat down as Bret dimmed the lights in the room and hit another switch that illuminated a map of the world through the now translucent surface of the conference table. The military commanders were surprised at the clarity of the map's images showing through the maroon surface that had seemed like solid mahogany when they entered the room. On previous visits to the situation room, a map of the world had been placed atop the old conference table when war strategy was at issue. Now the map was actually built into the table and illuminated by fluorescent bulbs, which outlined the continents and countries with such clarity that one would never guess it was below the surface of the table.

"Gentlemen," began Bret Cummings, "as you can see, the areas of greatest U.S. influence are colored in red. Those of lesser influence are lighter shades of red, pink, and white. Those areas of the world where the United States carries little or no military influence are blue in color."

The brightest red areas were in the United States; the Arab countries of Saudi Arabia, Iran, Iraq, and Kuwait; and in Japan. Canada, Mexico, and the Central and South American countries were pink in color as were England, South Africa, Australia, and several Pacific Island nations as well as several of the former Soviet Republics. Much of the rest of Europe, Asia, and Africa were almost white, signifying little military influence but some level of favorable economic and political influence.

The blue areas on the map depicted the independent nations of Germany, Ukraine, and China. They had withstood the controlling world influence of the United States and formed a second world power center to which those countries not totally committed to the United States could gravitate. By far, the most powerful of these three nations was the highly industrialized and militarily powerful Germany, under the leadership of Chancellor Heinrich Adler.

Although China's population made the country a formidable opponent, China's leaders were still struggling against the tide of capitalism that had swept communism from the world over a decade earlier. They simply could not figure out how to deal with their unbelievably enormous human resource.

As for Ukraine, the one former Soviet Republic that had been able to make a smooth transition to capitalist democracy, it was still a baby, working through its early growing pains. Because of their subjugation throughout history, the people worked unceasingly to develop their own national identity and, although they traded their wondrous resources with the world, they would not tolerate outside influence.

"As you can see, gentlemen, our influence throughout the world is significant. You all know that it is this influence and President Sullivan's vision of a unified world that has brought such enormous prosperity to America. At this point it is clear that only a few countries stand in the way of this marvelous vision."

They all stared at the obvious holdouts as Cummings, who had learned some tricks from his boss, waited to let them all fully understand the map.

"If the problem were just Germany, Ukraine, and China, we could deal with it diplomatically, over time, without difficulty. As you will see in a moment, however, the problem is much larger.

"We have just received word that German Chancellor Adler has called a meeting of the heads of the European Community. For the past three months Adler has been pushing the European alliance to break economic ties with the United States until we reduce the price of the oil we control and begin sharing our superior technological knowledge with them."

"In short, gentlemen," interrupted the president, "Mister Adler is trying to drive this country back to the days of weakness under our former presidents. The Germans want us to give them our oil. They want us to give them our technology. It's very clear, gentlemen, that they want a fucking fourth reich. They figure if we were weak enough to give it to them once, we'll do it again.

"The Japs tried to do it to us in the eighties and nineties. We showed them what America is made of. We're sure as hell not going to give to the Germans what we took back from the Japs."

Cummings stared at the president. No one spoke for several seconds, their eyes glued to the map before them.

"But we've got Europe tied up, sir," said Admiral Houston. "What can Germany do now anyway?"

"Look carefully, admiral," interjected Bret Cummings. "Although we have economic influence and some political pull in Europe, England is our only true ally. They are forever linked to us and they are the one voice in the EC that will stand by us. But the others are wavering.

"Our main hold on France, Italy, Spain, and the other European nations, including the Scandinavian countries, is the oil. Although the French are still colored as allies on the map, President Gisgain has been spouting off recently about what he believes is U.S. imperialism. The French are so damn proud, they can't see past their own personal interests to the potential strength and prosperity of a unified world. It wouldn't take much to turn the French blue," Cummings finished as he pointed to the map.

"And if the French go with Germany, so too will many of the weaker European nations," added the president.

"We can stop the Germans, Mister President," said General Peters. "We have the military might to do what we did with Japan."

"The Germans also have a formidable military, General Peters."

"Yes, sir, that's true. But you know we would all bet American drive against that German stubbornness any day. Besides, sir, we've got our big guns surrounding them. All we have to do is aim and fire. They don't have anything on our side of the Atlantic. They sure as hell haven't been aiming any long-range weaponry our way or we'd know it.

"I say we give 'em the same ultimatum we gave Japan, sir. Follow our lead or we nuke 'em."

The older military leaders nodded slowly, appreciating the bravado of General Peters.

"Gentlemen, if I may. Sir?" Charlie Gilbert asked the president's leave. Sullivan nodded and waved his hand for Gilbert to continue.

"Gentlemen, we face a very delicate situation here. Like you, I feel our military is superior to anything the Germans or, for that matter, any combination of European countries could muster. However, as we all found out in Vietnam, where we didn't have it, and in subsequent military actions, where we did, it's essential that we have popular support at home.

"The bombing of flight three eighty-four has certainly raised the hackles of most Americans. More will be needed, however, to get full support for a military campaign that would be considerably more difficult than anything we've seen in recent years.

"There's one other very important factor to consider. As you know, President Sullivan is nearing the end of his second term in office. Under current law, that's the end of it. All our plans will end abruptly in less than twenty months."

For the first time, it struck Homer Peters and the other military leaders their positions were not as solid as they had all come to believe.

"Now Mister Cummings has better information on this than I do, but I believe the Senate and House passed resolutions to repeal the term limits amendment. It's going to the states, for their vote, as we speak."

"I'll take it from there," interrupted the president. "Mister Gilbert was leading to a very important point. We are gearing all our efforts to repeal of this amendment. It is the only way we can all be assured that America will stay on its present course. Thus we cannot make any precipitous moves that will sway the vote against us. However, we also cannot let the matter lie, or when we are finally reelected, the die will have been cast and our enemy will be strong."

"What do you propose, Mister President?" asked General Stevens.

"Diplomacy, my dear general. Our secretary of state, Mister Henry Trotter, is, at this moment, flying to Germany to meet the chancellor. We will make some concessions, diffuse their ire. Meanwhile, gentlemen, your troops in Europe will remain on second-level alert at all times.

"And, as Mister Gilbert suggests, we will do our part here, at home, to ensure popular support if and when we need it. This unfortunate tragedy on flight three eighty-four has had a silver lining, as we can see. I want this 'Moses' caught and executed, and I want this rebel group exterminated. I will handle these matters through our intelligence network, gentlemen. Your job will be to keep your troops ready at all times. Are we clear?"

They all nodded and wore stern, committed faces. The military leaders were in their element now. They could again prepare for a coming storm. It was what they were all trained for and it was what they all loved.

CHAPTER 17

By noon, Mark Tucker had completed his review of the files on the D.C. murders. He had read every word and studied every photograph meticulously. When he finished, he was convinced the killer was the same person who had committed the California murders almost a decade before. The gruesome gutting of all the women would certainly lead the casual observer to that conclusion. It was the other body marks, however, that absolutely convinced Mark Tucker. No copycat killer could possibly know all the gory details.

After completing his review, Mark asked Commander Escobar to transmit a computer description of the crimes to police forces throughout the country, to see if anyone else had anything similar. Although Escobar indicated that the request had previously been made, Mark convinced him to make the request again as a top priority. Instead of just three recent murders, the various jurisdictions would be notified that they were dealing with a bona fide serial killer involving at least fifteen murders over the past decade. The details given were pretty basic: "Prostitutes, mostly black, no particular pattern in terms of size or appearance. All were cut with a sharp instrument from throat to groin. All bore other unusual body markings which will be discussed if basic case similarities exist."

Before commencing the next phase of Mark's investigation, his visit to the crime scenes, Escobar decided it was time to grab some lunch. For the third time that morning, Mark attempted to reach

Laura by telephone before they left the station. His attempt met with the same incessant ringing and no response.

"Got any ideas about our man . . . or should I say person, professor?" asked Escobar.

Despite Mark's request that he be called by his first name, Ralph Escobar liked to use the term "professor." It rolled nicely off his tongue and enabled him to keep Mark at a distance, something Escobar preferred in his line of work. The commander only called people by their first names when he got close to them. The professor was just hired help. To be sure, he was someone Escobar had requested, but it didn't mean they had to be friends.

"No, I think it's safe to say we're dealing with a man here. Unless we've got one hell of a powerful woman. On some of those bodies, it would have taken some major strength to make the kind of cuts I saw in the pictures." Mark didn't bother to mention his assumption was also based on the fact that the vast majority of serial killings were perpetrated by men. On that basis, he felt he was fairly safe. He also suspected that Commander Escobar already knew that fact.

"So what do we have?" asked Escobar again.

"I'm not sure, commander. The ruthless nature of the killings describes a man angry at the world. Certainly, he doesn't have much regard for women. Definitely not prostitutes, anyway."

He paused in thought, "We're not dealing with a killer who has a consistent pattern, though. Since the killings occurred in groups, with long intervals in between, it looks like something happens to set him off on a spree. Then when his appetite is sated, he doesn't kill again for years, until something sets him off."

"What do you think it is that sets him off?"

"I don't know. It could be almost anything. Something that happens to him personally or maybe a world event. We've got a lot of work to do. I think we'll start with the world events occurring at the time of the killings and then move down to local events. Hopefully, we'll be able to start painting a picture of our man."

"That's why you're here, professor."

★ ★ ★

Laura must have called Bill McDonough's number a half dozen times after she arrived home at noon. By six she was frantic with worry. Bill and Nell were supposed to have been home on Friday night. Laura had tried to reach them several times over the weekend but couldn't. She was sure they'd be back by Monday.

She tried again fifteen minutes later and a male voice answered. "Yes?"

"Bill?"

"No, I'm sorry, Bill's not available."

"Do you know when he'll be home?"

"Who is this?"

"I'm a friend of Bill's. My name is Laura Miller."

"Yes, Miz Miller. Bill's mentioned you," the voice cracked.

"Who is this?" asked Laura.

"My name is Ned. I'm . . . Bill's brother." The voice cracked again.

Laura grew anxious.

"What's the matter, Ned?"

"I'm afraid there's been a terrible accident, Miz Miller." Laura could hear the restrained sobs. "Bill's dead."

For the second time in the same day Laura was thrown backwards in shock. It couldn't be Bill. Not Bill.

"What . . . what happened?" she stammered.

"They were hiking. They fell. Both of them fell off a cliff. They were found yesterday."

Laura started to cry. Over and over, her mind told her it couldn't have happened to Bill and Nell. Such wonderful people. How could it be true?

"Miz Miller, are you still there?"

"Yes . . . I'm here. I'm so sorry." Laura had to get off the phone. Through sobs of her own, she spoke again.

"Ned . . . if I can help, please call me."

He thanked her and was polite enough to listen to her phone number before saying, "Bill really thought you were something special, Miz Miller. He spoke of you often."

"Bill was special to me too."

Laura replaced the receiver mechanically. She leaned back in her chair, unable to make sense of any of it.

What had started as the story of her life, the culmination of all her training and experience to this point, had turned into her greatest nightmare. Her dream of honors had resulted in the deaths of Michael Stoner and Bill and Nell McDonough, and, who knows, maybe even 500 people aboard flight 384. As hard as she tried to believe none of these deaths were related to her stories, that they were just accidents of some uncaring god, she couldn't help but think she was only kidding herself.

As she leaned forward and buried her face in her hands trying desperately to understand why Bill had to die, the medal of Mary, given to her by her uncle at the airport, fell out of her blouse. It dangled on its chain between her arms. She opened her eyes slowly and started to run her hands through her hair in frustration, when she caught sight of the medal.

Laura leaned back again as she grasped the medal with her left hand, closed her eyes and lifted her face toward the ceiling.

"What's going on?" she pleaded.

She sat that way for several moments, neither praying nor thinking, just sitting with her head back, eyes closed and her hand holding the medallion, when suddenly the phone rang. She stared, wondering if she should pick it up. After four rings she had still not moved. Maybe it was Ned and she should pick it up. But she knew he hadn't written down her number.

If it was her mother, Laura's frantic voice would only scare her and there was no need for that. Laura had to work things out for herself before she spoke to her mother.

It rang twelve times before it stopped. Finally, she lifted the receiver off the hook and laid it on the table next to the phone so she wouldn't hear it during the night.

Mark Tucker hung up the phone, exasperated. He wondered why she didn't have an answering machine. He'd just have to stop by and leave a note or something after he left the station. However, he didn't get the chance that night because Commander Escobar didn't drop him off at his hotel room until 11:30 P.M. He debated whether to call so late and decided against it. He could wait another day before he took drastic measures.

★ ★ ★

CHAPTER 18

Jason woke with a start very early in the morning. It was still dark outside. The barred window in his room gave way to only faint hints of the coming dawn. He tried desperately to stop shaking. He pulled his blanket up over his shoulders to stop shivering, but the shaking persisted. He wasn't cold. Jason was afraid. He'd seen the Monster again and he knew it was coming. Not for him, yet, but it was getting closer and someone else standing in its path would be butchered soon.

The big man wished he could think more clearly, like Michael had been able to do. His friend was always able to explain to him how things should be and what he should do. Even after those occasions when Jason blacked out, only to wake up later lashed to a bed within the constricting embrace of a straightjacket, Michael would soothe him. The blackouts always occurred just when the Monster was ready to move. Michael explained that because Jason was unable to do anything about the Monster, his brain got so frustrated, it just stopped working. He never understood what Michael meant when he used the word "frustrated," but he figured it was just that his brain got too mad and shut off.

"You only get real violent when you black out, Jason," Michael had explained. "You look like you're asleep, but you start screaming and carrying on like you really are crazy. That's when you start breakin' stuff." Michael smiled. "Boy, you should see how many of

153

'em it takes to hold you down. It's really kinda funny seeing six guys wrestling and fighting with you."

Jason never thought it was funny. He only remembered always feeling sorry he had been so bad. "Listen buddy, it's not you when these things happen. You just have some real weird things happening in your head and some other person just seems to come out of you," Michael assured him. "It's this Monster you keep talking about that is making you be bad."

That explanation had always made Jason feel better. Deep down, however, he knew he'd have to stop the Monster. He couldn't just let it keep coming out of him and making him bad. It had gone on for too long. Even before he could remember clearly, it had been happening.

Jason felt the approach of the Monster the night of Michael's death. That's why he'd snuck out of his room and gone to see Michael. Although he'd yelled to Michael's corpse that the Monster had come, he now knew it had not been the Monster at all. The Monster hadn't come yet. It had just been playing with him. It was only a matter of time.

Jason couldn't understand why Michael had killed himself. Maybe he had felt the Monster, too, and he just wanted to die, so he wouldn't have to feel the Monster anymore. Maybe that would work for Jason also. Maybe if he died, the Monster would go away and never come back. He wished he could talk to someone about it, but now there was no one left.

Dawn's earliest light was coloring the eastern sky and Jason could see the shadowy hulks in his room disappearing. They were being replaced by the dressers, chairs, and other furnishings. Gradually, he stopped shaking, knowing the Monster never came during the day. He smiled, relieved he could lay back down and rest again before it was time to get up. His rest was only for an instant, however, as he remembered words Michael had spoken to him once before.

"If you're ever going to stop the Monster, Jason, you've got to stop it before it comes."

Although the statement had never made clear sense to him, he didn't ask Michael to explain it because he didn't want to sound more stupid than everyone already thought he was. This morning the meaning of Michael's statement suddenly, miraculously, became clear. He knew where the Monster would be and he'd just have to get there before the Monster. He'd have to stop it before it came and did that terrible thing that it always did.

Jason threw off his blanket and dropped his enormous legs over the side of his bed. He lumbered to the closet, careful not to make any noise that might arouse the guard outside his door. His street clothes, a pair of denim bib overalls and a light flannel shirt, hung next to his "home clothes," the standard light blue loose-fitting materials worn by all patients in the hospital. He liked the home clothes, because they were so loose and comfortable on him. They had been specially made, his doctors said, because he was so big. He couldn't wear them outside the home, though, because people would know he belonged there, and they'd send him back before he could stop the Monster.

The big man struggled with the clasps for the shoulder straps and with the buttons on his shirt. He usually had help with these when he wore his street clothes. He couldn't have that help today, however. He was finally satisfied with fastening just the top two buttons on the shirt and the bib clasps. His shoes were much easier. For some reason, he had learned and remembered how to tie his shoes. Although buttons were tough, his shoelaces had always been easy for him.

Jason crouched in front of the mirror and dragged a brush across the top of his close cropped blond hair. The brush didn't do much to make the hair lie down, but Jason was satisfied with the result. He brushed his teeth quickly and stuck the toothbrush into his pocket, figuring he'd need it later after he ate.

As he walked toward the door, he realized he couldn't get out that way. The guard at his door was probably still sleeping, but the whole wing was barred and sealed and there were other guards all over the wing. Jason turned and stared at the window. The metal bars looked thick and strong, but he had no choice. He'd have to try to get through them because the sun was rising quickly and he wouldn't have much time.

He lifted the bottom half of the double-hung window and the warming morning air flooded into his room. Reaching for one of the bars outside the window, he shook the cage. It moved slightly. He shook again, harder this time, and he could feel the weakness in the metal contraption. He gripped a bar tightly in each hand and pulled, straining with all his mighty strength to pull the bars apart. They wouldn't move. Not even a little.

Jason tried again, pulling sideways. Then pushing out. Nothing.

He began to panic. If he couldn't get out, the Monster would come again. No one would be there to stop it. He struggled desperately, straining his considerable strength to no avail. Sweat poured from his brow and under his shirt. It wasn't coming.

Suddenly, he remembered some words he'd heard once, after one of his blackouts. They were spoken by a big strong guard. One of the men who had strapped him into that tight jacket and then onto a bed.

"That's one strong son of a bitch. Did you see him tear up that cage?" the guard had said.

Jason remembered. He'd broken bars before. During one of his blackouts. He had broken right through them, as if they were paper. These, in front of him, were thicker. They looked much stronger. But Jason understood what he would have to do. It scared him to think about it, but he knew it was the only way. He'd have to be quiet. Very quiet.

Jason began to shake as the fear again gripped him. He grew angry at himself for shaking, knowing that if he lost control, he'd wake the guards and they'd get him.

"Don't be stupid, Jason," he said to himself. "Be smart for once."

As the shaking subsided, he closed his eyes and called to the Monster. It was there, somewhere, hiding, not wanting him to stop it, but he kept calling and slowly the rage in him grew. The hatred of the Monster was alive. It was a part of him that acted, almost on it's own. He never had the strength to control it. Now, however, he desperately needed that strength. He felt his hands reaching for the bars and he continued to call for the Monster, demanding that it come, now.

And then it did.

The Monster streaked past his consciousness as if released by a spring—suddenly, too fast to see clearly. Not too quickly, however, for Jason to grab it. With his mind, he reached out, across the void and caught hold of it. It was evil. A terrible, hurting evil that Jason wanted to release, but couldn't, or he wouldn't get out. He struggled with it. His head ached. And suddenly it was before him. The grotesque bulbous head, red and deadly, with hate-filled yellow eyes and clawed hands that reached for him.

Jason's hands squeezed the bars. The muscles of his massive arms bulged. The fear, the hatred, and the loathing coursed through him as his mind clung to the Monster while struggling at the same time to cast it aside. One bar came loose.

His right hand turned and twisted and the bar snapped from its attachment joints. Then the second bar came loose in his left hand. And then the third and finally the fourth.

The Monster screamed a banshee scream. With flames raging around it, it opened its mouth wide and lunged at him with razor-sharp teeth. Red from the blood of the dead the Monster had devoured mercilessly. Then suddenly it was gone. Jason had released it. He fell back on the floor before the window, spent from the struggle. As he looked up, he realized that he had done it. He had made an opening just large enough to squeeze through. He glanced around to make sure he hadn't disturbed anyone. No one came through the door.

The sun was rising above a distant hill and birds were singing their good morning welcome when Jason slipped outside, onto the dew covered grass, across the lawn and over the eleven feet of wall and barbed wire. He barely even noticed the pain of the wire as it tore through his clothes and into his flesh. Jason had made it out. Now he had to get there before the Monster. He had to stop it.

"Damn!" yelled Aidan Sullivan. "How in hell can I run this country if you people can't handle the small things? What happened?"

Charlie Gilbert had stood quietly before the president during previous tantrums. Although Charlie would never take this abuse from any other man, the president was the greatest leader the world had ever known, and if he had to vent occasionally, Charlie could take it. Besides, the screw up posed a major problem.

"He tore the bars apart, sir. He snapped them right out of their frames."

Aidan Sullivan was not surprised. His son's awesome strength was well known to him. He had seen its results before and despite the president's own powers, the physical strength of his son was something that caused him fear. He glared at Charlie Gilbert, knowing that Charlie had not done anything wrong. He knew also that Charlie was the best man he had working for him. The supreme assassin as a soldier, Charlie had placed his talents and cunning at the disposal of the president and had shown unflagging loyalty and surprising composure through some very difficult times. Although Aidan Sullivan could destroy Charlie Gilbert, he needed to have this man at his side.

"I want him found, Charlie," said the president more calmly. "Now, before he does something."

Charlie nodded.

"Get someone to do it. I want you and Bill to stay close by. Keep Frank here too. I want you three to join me this afternoon. Take care of it."

Charlie nodded before saluting his commander-in-chief and turning to leave.

The president didn't need this now. He was scheduled to speak in front of the Washington Monument in three hours. He would rail against his enemies and those of the new American order. He didn't need the distraction of his son's escape. Something would have to be done about the idiot. Maybe it couldn't wait until after the next election.

The intercom buzzed and the president's secretary, Lisa Klaus, informed him that Mr. Cummings would like to see him. Cummings walked into the office looking glum.

"We're going to have some problems, Aidan. Zac Morgan is trying to put together a coalition to oppose the repeal of the Twenty-Second Amendment."

"That's nothing we didn't expect," the president responded caustically. "He's been opposed to us all along."

"That's true, but he seems to have more support than we expected."

When the president said nothing, Cummings continued.

"He's a sly old fox, Aidan. When he saw he'd get nowhere in Congress, he started his state campaign. His own state of Washington is clearly beyond our reach. He's working hard on all of the western states and, surprisingly, our people in California tell us he's having some success there."

"We only need nine more," said the president, somewhat absently. Cummings could see he was preoccupied and knew he had to get his attention.

"Please, Aidan, it's not that simple anymore. Of the twenty-five we thought we had wrapped, Alabama and Pennsylvania are showing signs of movement away. Because both states are still mostly Democrat, we should take them, but it'll require some major politicking. The thing that's more worrisome is the other nine. If Morgan gets California, it's going to have an influence on the other states. We all know what California can do."

The president shook away thoughts of his son and listened intently to Bret. He grew angrier with every word uttered by his chief of staff.

"Well, don't let it happen." He leaned forward and slammed a palm onto his desk, "What the hell is going on here? Can't anyone do his job? That old son of a bitch can't beat me."

Sullivan was working himself up to a rage. Bret Cummings could see it coming and he tried desperately to head it off.

"We'll stop him, Aidan. Our network in California is strong enough to bury him. We'll stop him."

The president glared at him. He slammed both palms on his desk, stood up suddenly and walked to his window. He was tense, on edge. The chief of staff stood and slowly walked up to the president. He stood behind him and closed his eyes, breathing deeply of the warm aroma of his idol, an aroma tinged with anger. He slowly reached out and placed his hands on either side of the president's neck, atop his shoulders. He began kneading and pinching the taut muscles and tendons, trying to relieve the tension.

"I'll take care of it, Aidan."

Slowly, he felt the president begin to relax.

"C'mon. We've got to get you ready for your speech."

The president was always ready to speak. Whenever he had an audience, words flowed as if by some magic force. He rarely had anyone prepare a speech for him and definitely never when he was to speak before the common people. He always knew just what words to use.

Yet when he was angry, the president could slip. He'd always been able to cover the slips in the past. At such a critical time, however, with a foe like Zac Morgan listening intently to every word he uttered, even a minor slip could prove costly. Bret had to keep him calm.

"Have you gotten the list?" asked the president without turning.

He referred to the list of dead from Delta flight 384.

"Yes, Aidan, this morning."

"Get it to Charlie Gilbert."

Cummings dropped his hands slowly to his side, put out again that the president chose Charlie Gilbert to do something for him over Cummings himself.

"I can do it, Aidan."

The president turned to Cummings, a wry smile appearing on his face at the sight of Cumming's bowed head. Sullivan relished the pain he caused his chief of staff. It was important, however, to keep the man happy at a time of such great significance.

"I've got other work for you, Bret. Don't look so damn unhappy. This is pissant stuff that Charlie can handle."

Cummings looked up and smiled. Charlie could handle the little stuff. Right now they had a speech to deliver.

Laura had a difficult night. Thoughts of death kept her rolling over in bed and unable to sleep until two in the morning. Once she had drifted off to sleep, her dream returned. The hideous creature had come after her, reaching, grabbing, wanting her just like it had wanted and gotten Michael Stoner and Bill and Nell and 500 people aboard flight 384. It was pursuing her and it was gaining.

She woke just two hours after she'd finally fallen asleep. She was angry. Why was she being bothered? She shouted, "Leave me alone!" and then sat quietly listening for her neighbors who might have been awakened by her shout.

She dozed off again at about four-thirty, her mind too tired to think any longer. At eight-thirty she awoke again in a sitting position. Her neck and back ached. Her eyes were heavy from tears and lack of sleep. Even her left hand ached. When she looked down and stretched her fingers, she saw the Mary medal she had apparently torn from around her neck during the night. No wonder her hand ached. She was probably squeezing the damn thing all night. She considered throwing the chain and medal aside, but decided against it when she remembered it was a gift from her uncle. She laid it next to her watch on her night stand and then rose.

Laura stood in the shower longer than usual. She quickly gave herself over to its warmth, letting the soothing heat beat against her head and body. She hoped the steam would remove the black circles and anxiety of sleepless nights from her face. She soaped herself slowly, wanting to stay in her steam cloud for the longest possible time. After a while, however, her mind drifted back to the predicament she had been trying so desperately to understand.

In her parents' home while watching the president's speech that had sealed her fate at the *Herald*, Laura had recognized something she had never seen. The president was a very strong man who simply wasn't satisfied with the most powerful position in the world. Even to most casual observers, his purpose was clear, as in his so-dubbed "forgiveness speech." He played his politics. He used the forum to again subtly attack his enemies on the right while forgiving the "innocents" who really had nothing to do with the misguided efforts of those at the *Herald* responsible for the stories. The president had known that, in one fell swoop, he would garner the support of everyone at the *Herald* except the two nobodies and in so doing he would turn a newspaper that had traditionally taken contrary views to his own, into an ally. It was a brilliant and masterful political move.

Laura also sensed an evil in the man. She, of course, believed her stories were true but, as she watched, that wasn't her concern. It had suddenly become clear that he would have to be stopped. From what she did not know. Just as suddenly she lost that flash of insight. Had it not been for the events occurring after that television address, she may never have felt it again.

First there was her father's strange statement about not pursuing the truth of her stories for herself. She had almost understood until Hilary related her story of the mother of God and how she was warning of coming disaster in a world filled with greed and evil. Then when Father John told her he believed she had a larger purpose, to help rid the world of an evil that was growing stronger, she lost all perspective. What could she possibly do? She was nothing.

Although Hilary's story had been interesting, Laura simply viewed it as a story with no significance in the real world, despite the dire predictions of catastrophe. The same held true for Father John. If God was trying to tell Father John that Laura had some high and mighty purpose, why didn't he just tell her? Hell, he could simply appear at night if he didn't want anyone else to see, and whisper in her ear, "Hey Laura, there's some bad shit going down in this world and you've got to do something to stop it."

She'd heard nothing. She'd received no message. No, she felt, there was nothing to this for her. She had simply lost her job at the *Herald*. She couldn't get her mind mixed up more than it already was. After her discussion with Father John, it was all too complicated. Everyone was trying to convey messages to her that just weren't getting through. She would just have to work on putting her life back together again. Perhaps she could find some quiet, out-of-the-way place, maybe even start a "Dear Laura" column in some small-town newspaper. Thoughts of anything more boggled her mind and she didn't need that. She couldn't take it.

Then there was the man following her on the Strand. He was the same person who had been behind her in the elevator. All of this skulking about could only have been related to her stories. The president or someone close to him had to be behind it. She had toyed with the idea that the follower had been a love-crazed psychopath but quickly discarded the notion.

Finally, the deaths. First, innocents aboard flight 384. Then Michael Stoner, now Bill and Nell McDonough.

Why was it all happening?

Laura toweled off and dressed quickly, as if she was compelled to take some action.

It had to be more than the stories. If, indeed, the president was behind all of this, there had to be a greater purpose. After all, she and Bill had already been thoroughly humiliated. Their careers were over. The president was cleared by the public even if the stories were true. The issue would never be raised again. They could do no more harm with the facts they'd gathered.

It was becoming clear to Laura that there was something else. Something beyond her claim that the president had been involved in the drugs/arms trade between Central and South America and the former Soviet Republics. That allegation didn't even seem to matter anymore. If all the events were connected and Laura was somehow involved, she had no idea how.

She stepped out into the warm spring morning. A slight breeze still carried some of the chill from the previous week's storms, but it looked very much like Washington was now into spring. Any rains from then on would be warmer and for the sole purpose of creating the humidity that made summers in the East suffocating.

At the corner bakery she bought an apple fritter and carton of milk. She hadn't eaten since the previous morning, but wasn't interested in sitting down to a healthy meal. She wanted to keep moving, so her thoughts would flow more freely. The sugar of the fritter would keep her moving and the milk was her concession to health. As she emerged from the bakery, stuffing her face with the apple fritter, the ten-year-old boy from the homeless family stepped away from the wall of the bakery and into her path. He held his little sister's hand and in his other hand he clutched the stems of some wild yellow daisies. Laura stopped short. The boy held out the flowers.

"Here, ma'am. These are for you on account of you look so sad. Momma said flowers brighten a day and always make people smile."

Laura juggled the donut sack and milk as she shifted them to one hand and reached out with her free hand for the straggly bunch of flowers.

"We wanted to thank you for what you done the other day. Momma cried, she was so happy." He looked down at his little sister. "That just made Hannah cry, too. But the hot dogs were real good."

"Thank you," Laura stammered, stunned at the selfless little boy and ashamed at her own selfish concerns.

"You're welcome. Well, we got to get back. It's going to be a nice day," the boy smiled and pulled his sister's arm. The little girl followed absently, as she stared, blue eyes wide and alive, at Laura. Laura turned to watch them.

"Wait," she called, as she caught them and reached into her pocket. "What is your name?"

"I'm Sam . . . and this here is Hannah, ma'am," the boy answered.

"I'm Laura," she said as she held out a ten-dollar bill. The boy stepped away shaking his head.

"No thank you, Miss Laura. We didn't bring those flowers for no money." Sam was crestfallen. "You just looked real sad and me and Hannah wanted to help you like you helped us the other day." He shook his head as he eyed the bill.

"Sam, please take it. It'll at least get you another meal."

"No thank you, ma'am," he responded. "You've done enough for us, and we appreciate it."

He smiled at her.

"Sam," Laura called once more as the children began walking away. She knelt down in front of the little girl. "Hannah, can I have a hug to thank you?"

Hannah dropped her brother's hand and threw her arms around Laura's neck. Laura lost her balance momentarily and then regained it before falling. She squeezed the little girl tightly and slipped the ten-dollar bill into the pocket of the ragged coat she wore. "You give this money to your Momma, but don't tell Sam about it, okay?" she whispered.

The little girl nodded and then released her. Laura looked up at Sam who made it clear he wasn't interested in a hug. He held out his hand. Laura took the hand and shook it. The two children then walked away, looking up and down the street before they crossed.

Laura held the flowers up to her nose and smiled. These people knew something most folks didn't.

Two hours later, Laura found herself wandering around the park surrounding the Washington Monument. Her body kept reminding her that her morning sugar fix wasn't enough to satisfy its need for nourishment. At eleven-thirty she purchased a hot dog at a corner stand, buried it in mustard, ketchup, and relish and sat on a bench with yet another carton of milk.

She was feeling somewhat better about things. Her meeting with Sam and Hannah had given her a different perspective. Maybe she was just overreacting and the world was not such a terrible place after all. Maybe her predicament wasn't all that bad. It really was unlikely that the president of the United States was pursuing Laura Miller, everyday average citizen. After all, if he really did want to hurt her, she was an easy target.

As she finished her hot dog, it struck her for the first time that the grounds around the monument were swarming with more people than one would usually find, even near the lunch hour. In fact, it looked very much like something big was happening as the crowd around the monument swelled and grew more dense.

From her vantage point, Laura could see the podium and microphone at the base of the massive structure. Workers busied themselves making sure everything worked perfectly.

"Test . . . test," a speaker in a tree near her crackled to life. That was the first time she'd even noticed the speaker.

"Test . . . one . . . two, three," the tester continued. "Sounds g . . ." he said as he switched off the mike.

The crowd continued to grow and spread back through the park closer to the bench upon which Laura was now standing. Stepping off the bench, she stopped a young man dressed in a dark navy suit.

"What's going on?" she asked.

"President Sullivan's giving a speech," he answered, as he hurried past, briefcase banging against his legs.

The crowd continued to grow. Everyone tried to get as close as possible to the podium. Laura joined the throng, then felt herself walking into the melee, being swept along by a great tide. People of all ages clamored for position. Older people used canes and wheelchairs to fend off intruders to their space. Mothers and fathers held young children high on their shoulders for just a glimpse of their president. Even older children had left school for this momentous event.

Television cameras and sound equipment were everywhere as technicians completed last-minute preparations.

Laura marveled at the turnout and at the adoration etched on the faces of almost everyone who got through the police cordon on the outer perimeter of the park.

Traffic along Constitution Avenue was very heavy. Thousands of people were already crowding the park, and thousands more were still coming.

As the tide continued to push Laura backward toward the monument, she noticed something unusual. The police were not letting everyone into the park. There were some people carrying placards and others without placards who weren't getting onto the park grounds. Apparently these few people were opposition voices. Clearly, the vast majority looked like followers, but the few who weren't quite taken with the president, were detained.

Laura found herself shoulder to shoulder in a sea of humanity when she heard a loud cheer that grew as more people began to realize he had arrived. Pushing herself up onto her toes and craning her neck, she was still unable to see anything until the president's entourage mounted the podium and he emerged from among his bodyguards to wild cheers and shouts of "Aidan! Aidan! Aidan!"

The faces in the crowd were all smiles except for the police and plainclothes security men. Several were very near Laura. They all watched carefully for the one lunatic who might suddenly raise the gun to snuff out the president's life, like that man tried to do so many years ago. Laura's mind wandered back, seven years, to the time in California when the attempt had been made. She had been with the *Herald* for a short time and was busy on a story about congressional game playing in an election year, when she heard about the attempt. After the November election they all discussed how that single act of violence had done more for the campaign of Aidan Sullivan than his stand on any issue affecting the country. She mused about why that nondescript man had taken such a step, when suddenly the president's voice filled the air.

"Americans!" he shouted to a roar from the crowd. "We are Americans!"

The crowd erupted in a resounding roar and cheer that continued as the president raised his arms high above his head in a stance reminiscent of former President Richard Nixon except this president did not cut the comic figure of the former president. Aidan Sullivan closed his eyes and bowed his head to the continuous roar. His hands were open, palms facing the surging crowd.

The president stood for several seconds exulting in the adulation of the live crowd and the millions more who watched on television. But his exultation was somehow tempered. It wasn't complete because he sensed something from the depths of the cheering throng. Some evil. Something that would pull him down.

He continued to stand, transfixed, as the cheering subsided in anticipation of his next words. He didn't speak. It was out there somewhere. His mind reached out to find the evil. To expose it, so he could rid himself of yet another enemy. He searched their minds. As if he was no longer standing there. He walked among them, knowing their thoughts, sifting through them to see what evil they planned for him. In the vast majority he saw pure, unadulterated passion and affection. In a few, who had slipped through the police cordon, he felt evil intentions. There were those who didn't want him. Those who would cheer his fall. None, however, was the one he sought. The one who could actually topple him and destroy the dream to which his life had been directed.

Then suddenly, he found it. Unprotected. Open for him to invade. There it was. This person was even now working to undo him but didn't know it. The seed was there, deep in the subconscious, moving inexorably forward until the person would know and then act.

He would stop this person now!

Aidan Sullivan focused intently on the mind he had pierced. He reached deeper for the seed, to crush it as only he, with a power that few suspected, could do. He peeled away the layers of brain and cast them aside until the seed was exposed. He smiled and reached for it when suddenly he flinched in excruciating pain. He almost fell back with the force of a strength he had yet to experience. He'd lost his grip. The contact was gone, and he couldn't find it again. President Sullivan shuddered as he regained his balance and slowly opened his eyes to glare at the multitude.

Laura felt the probe. It was subtle at first. Imperceptible, really, except that she'd experienced something like it before. On the elevator at the *Herald* and on the bike path in Manhattan Beach, but this one was stronger.

At first it simply flitted by and she thought she was mistaken. Then it returned and immediately took hold. She felt the pain. It was subtle, at first, much like a headache. She raised her finger to the bridge of her nose and squeezed to relieve whatever pressure was suddenly causing her discomfort, but the pain quickly intensified. It was like no mere headache she'd ever before experienced. This was a searing, blinding pain that seemed to be tearing her mind apart, laying it open for some unknown attack. She could not resist it. Grabbing her head, she squeezed it to contain the pain, which pulsed through the tissues, but it only grew worse, and with it came the sense of utter humiliation, as if her very soul was being violated and she was doing nothing about it.

When she tried to scream, no sound came. Laura was falling, becoming dizzy, unable to hold herself erect, until suddenly, from somewhere deep inside her, she heard a voice and then remembered. The violation she sensed was indeed an overt act of some being, as opposed to a physiological disorder. She could feel a presence in her brain. It was an evil presence she had to resist.

She'd fought off such a presence before. On the Strand the follower had lost his grip when she had taken control and refused to panic.

She strained through the excruciating pain, pushing and struggling to remove the force that invaded her mind. With all her will, she beat back the attack until it was gone. The barriers of her mind rose to fend off potential new attacks which came quickly but did not penetrate a second time. The pain slowly disappeared as Laura opened her eyes and focused on the people standing over her staring, spreading away from her.

"Give us some room," a man shouted. "She fainted. Give her some air."

The man knelt next to Laura, holding her head. He was concerned.

"Are you okay, miss?"

Laura's eyes moved around the circle of concerned faces as she slowly regained consciousness.

"Yes," she said, warily, conscious of her continued need for concentration.

She sat up slowly, shaking her head.

"I guess I just got too excited," she stammered an explanation.

The man helped her to her feet, still not certain she was okay.

"Maybe we should get you to the back, out of the crowd," he said as he held her arm to steady her.

"No . . . thank you. Really, I'm fine now," she shook her head again and smiled to reassure him.

"You sure?"

She nodded and touched his arm in gratitude, as she noticed for the first time her hand clutched the medal her uncle had given her.

Many of the others had already turned back to face the podium. After another quick look and a reassuring smile from Laura, the man too, turned to the president.

The cheering had stopped. Several seconds had passed since it stopped. The president dropped his hands and was standing at the lectern glaring out at the throng. He seemed to be searching as the crowd stood silently, staring, wondering what was wrong. Why had the president stumbled backwards?

"We have enemies amongst us." There was a perceptible relief in the crowd when he spoke.

"Even here in America, there are those who would try to destroy what we have built. What you, my friends, and your fathers and mothers before you and all the fathers and mothers before them have struggled for and died for, others wish to destroy."

Despite the earlier distraction, Aidan Sullivan had to proceed. His audience was too large to show any weakness. He would find this enemy and remove it before it had a chance to do anything. For now, however, he had to speak.

"You have all heard the enemies. Those who rail against us because we use force to protect American interests. The peace fanatics and so-called spiritualists who claim their god forbids us to use our might. And what about those who claim we no longer give our wealth away to foreigners. They claim we're not meeting our obligations to mankind. Where were these people, my friends, when you were all crying for help during the nineties, when you were all suffering through the worst economic times this country had seen in more than sixty years? I'll tell you where they were, they were taking money to third world countries. They were sending jobs to our competition. They were kissing the backsides of the leaders of every country of the world, while we Americans were dying at their feet."

As one, the crowd roared. The president had them. They were almost ready.

"Now we face another threat from another foreign power, which, though it denies involvement, sends terrorism to our soil. We have the foreign enemy amongst us, and he has already acted.

"Last Friday morning, we suffered one of the greatest tragedies in the history of the United States. The murderous destruction of Delta flight three-eighty-four in which five hundred Americans were mercilessly killed."

An intense hush fell over the crowd.

"This evil deed was perpetrated by a terrorist group, exported to our country by our so-called allies in Germany. I vow to you today, my friends," as he pounded the podium, "that your president will crush this German Alliance for Peace, as it dares to call itself. We will destroy them for their act."

Another loud cheer.

"I also vow that we will go beyond this puny group, to the head that supports it and we will cut off that head and we will hang it atop the highest pole for all the world to see and know that no one . . . NO ONE will ever again challenge the United States of America!"

The ovation was deafening. It thundered as people screamed and clapped and stomped their feet. The president raised his hands and spoke again.

"We are the greatest people the world has ever known. True Americans are the most literate. We're the richest. We are the cultural leaders, scientific leaders, and military leaders of the entire world. No one can stand in our way if we Americans don't choose to let them. We are destined to rule the world as the true superior nation."

Again a wild cheer and huge smiles of American self-righteousness.

"As we stand here before you, know that we are hunting down the animals who destroyed flight three-eighty-four, but we must do more. Over the next year, we will.

"We have commenced a program that we have been studying for years. With the downing of flight three-eighty-four, it is more imperative than ever before that we implement it now, for the protection of all true Americans."

The president slowly lifted his right hand and turned it so that the knuckle side faced the crowd.

"For those who can see it," camera's zoomed in on what appeared to be a one-inch square American flag tattooed at his wrist joint, "I have become the first to be marked with the seal of America. This seal, depicting our American flag will show the world who the real Americans are. Everyone who is part of us will have his or her own with their own number of registry that cannot be counterfeited."

People stared, not quite sure how to respond and the president had to take hold again.

"Only Americans will wear this symbol of our country's power. Only those who take an oath of eternal loyalty to our American life and ways will have the right to wear it. In this way, we will know the enemy. At all times. For those who don't wear our flag proudly on their wrists are not true Americans. They are not heirs to the world destiny that is America. For those who do, the world is theirs. I, as your president, promise you that. America, above all, for true Americans." He shouted the last statement and clenched the right fist.

The crowd again exploded. For several seconds it continued as Aidan Sullivan smiled triumphantly, full of himself on the masterful performance he had just given. As the roaring began to diminish, several in the crowd turned as another loudspeaker, from across the street crackled to life.

"And the Lord said to our brother John," yelled the voice and the crowd grew quieter still. "And the Lord said to our brother John," it repeated, "if anyone worships the beast or its image, or accepts its mark on its forehead or hand, he too will drink of God's wrath, poured full strength into the cup of his anger. He will be tormented in burning sulfur before the holy angels and before the lamb and the smoke of their torment shall rise forever and ever!"

People turned now and listened to the voice. Police and other security forces scrambled to the front door of an abandoned building across from the park. As if the speaker could see that his time was running short, he continued more quickly.

"There shall be no relief day or night for those who worship the beast or its image or accept the mark of its name. Revelations, Chapter 14, verses nine through eleven."

There was a brief pause. Aidan Sullivan glared at the building and sent his mind probe after the person whose voice carried such an ominous warning. When he found it, he felt the struggle.

"And the Lord said to our brother John," the voice repeated, this time with less force, as if it were struggling with someone, "if anyone worships the beast or its image or," and then very deliberately the voice said, "accepts its mark . . .." The speaker went dead, suddenly, and the voice was gone.

The crowd seemed lost. They had all been enthralled and now there was concern and fear because no one was quite sure how to react. Some opponents in the crowd suddenly began to raise placards which read "Stop Sullivan" and "We want peace, not Sullivan." From some parts of the crowd, shouts of "Devil Sullivan" could be heard. Slowly the questioning looks of those who, only seconds before, were cheering wildly, gave way to mumbling about God and what was happening.

Bret Cummings sensed his dreams for Aidan Sullivan crumbling. His eyes darted across the roiling crowd as police removed clubs and mace to fend off what they feared might be coming. All it would take was one leader to make a move. Cummings looked to the President who glared at the people. An almost maniacal smile crossed his lips before he began to speak. Bret held his breath.

"What is the problem?" Sullivan asked into the microphone, very quietly, almost imperceptibly. Some people turned and he spoke a little louder. "What is it, now? Do you have so little faith that you are swayed so easily by one you don't even know?

"Where was this man who reads from a book that has no meaning in our modern day? Where was he when we were all suffering without jobs? Where was he when all of you were crying out of fear of your futures? And where was his god?

"How many of you had your prayers for prosperity and wealth answered before our presidency? How many of you ever knew the comfort of world superiority and domination that America now has?"

He stared for several seconds at his audience, most of whom had turned to him and were now listening, almost begging for a way to go. The president's face showed a disappointed sullenness. He was making it clear that he was disheartened by the sudden turn. He spoke softly so people had to strain to hear him.

"We made the decision together, long ago, to show the world what an American is. We've done it. However, there's so much more to do because of our enemies." He hesitated and shrugged, palms open to the sky. "I don't know now what you want. If you can be so easily swayed, I'll simply step away and let this," he pointed at the building across the street "person take his place before you."

At that, the president turned and stepped away from the lectern. Complete silence followed him and Bret Cummings continued to hold his breath as he looked frantically over the crowd. Then, from deep in the audience, they heard a shout.

"No! We want Aidan!"

The president's back was still to the crowd, his head bowed in concentration until another voice and then another shouting "We want Aidan!" could be heard.

Soon several voices began a chant of "We want Aidan." As it gathered momentum and began to race through the crowd, the president turned his head slightly so his profile was clearly visible and more voices joined, until thousands shouted in unison, "We want Aidan."

Finally, Bret Cummings was smiling broadly as Aidan Sullivan turned to face the crowd. He hesitated, soaking every ounce of the drama of the spectacle. He finally stepped, again, to the lectern. The crowd erupted in a wild roar that continued unabated for several seconds as the president stood solemnly, staring at them. Slowly, the cheering subsided and Sullivan spoke again.

"If you want me, I will never leave you."

Another deafening roar and the president began to smile.

"We don't need these Bible thumpers!" he shouted to another roar. "We don't need their god," he shouted again. "We are bigger and more powerful than their god! We are Americans! We are the only god this world needs, and I'm here to lead you all to your destiny!"

Some were shocked at the blatant blasphemy, but the roar was so intense that those who were opposed did not resist. Bret Cummings stared in shock that the president had even said it. But his incredulity turned to excitement again when the monstrous crowd bought it all.

The president turned to Charlie Gilbert. "Charlie, bring my car out there," he said as he pointed beyond the crowd. "I want to walk through them."

"No, Aidan," interrupted Bret Cummings, "it's too dangerous out there."

Sullivan glared at Cummings. "They won't touch me. I'm their god."

He turned as Charlie ran back behind the monument to instruct the drivers. Cummings immediately started instructing security men to form a wall around the president who was already stepping into the crowd to a continuous roar.

★ ★ ★

★ CHAPTER 18 ★

Laura was suffocating as the crowd surged forward. As one entity the crowd pressed in on its hero, each of its parts trying desperately to beat the other, to see, and possibly touch, the president of the United States.

The prophetic words of Revelations which had, for several moments, interrupted the spell that Aidan Sullivan had initially cast over the throng, reverberated through her consciousness. She'd heard the words before during her religious studies in grade school and high school, but they had never stuck. Was it possible that this man was the anti-Christ that so many had prophesied for years? It had always been a fairy tale before, until he actually stood there and told them that all true Americans would bear the mark of their loyalty on their right hand. Yet no one cared.

Arms and bodies strained against Laura. Despite her attempts to escape the throng, she couldn't move except in the direction the crowd surged . . . forward . . . ever forward. Again she rose to her toes and craned to see. She saw only the backs of heads until finally between two of them she saw two enormous men. One black, the other white, they pushed through the crowd toward her. The crowd separated before them as if they formed a wedge behind which strode their king.

Laura struggled, trying desperately to break away. And then she felt it again. He was probing her mind. Again her initial reaction was panic; she struggled harder against the immovable bodies surrounding her.

"Hey lady!" shouted one man against whom she pushed with all her strength. "Back off!"

He shoved her hands aside and glared angrily at her. Her head hurt as she stared back at him, consciousness again taking hold and gradually turning to anger as she began to understand the game he was playing. She didn't know how, but she knew he was playing with her and she'd be damned if she'd let him win.

"What's your problem?" he shouted again, over the roaring crowd.

"Screw it," she shouted angrily and whirled away from the man toward the oncoming entourage. She stood concentrating, casting aside the probe, knowing if she could not hide from whatever was coming, she'd face it and deal with it the best way she could.

The two behemoths who made up the point of the wedge in front of her towered high above, yet Laura didn't see them clearly. She was focused on the president whom she could now see between the muscular bodies. Where only seconds before the crowd formed an impregnable barrier, it suddenly parted before the wedge and Laura stood before him . . . alone.

The president turned, teeth gleaming white in a huge smile, until he saw her. Their eyes locked and Laura knew for sure it was him. The visions from her dreams of the bloated red face with flaming yellow eyes raced through her brain. He stopped before her, his smile disappearing, and he stared.

He probed, focusing intently to reach deep inside here. Laura didn't flinch. She struggled against the crushing weight of a force she'd never known. A force borne of malevolent power beyond the world Laura had come to rely so heavily upon. She fought it. Don't panic, she thought, because he would win. She would not permit it.

Others within the president's wedge grew anxious. The president had stopped to stare at a woman who, although attractive, was no more so than the hundreds who threw themselves at him wherever he went. At first Bret Cummings thought it was just another of the stops to let a supporter touch or speak to him. Then he saw the president's face, the concentration he had seen only at times of great turmoil within his life. The chief of staff knew what would come next. It would be control or it would be destruction.

"C'mon Aidan," he whispered into the president's ear as he pushed his shoulder and glared at the woman. He was surprised at the woman's own intensity, something he had never seen in anyone addressed by Aidan Sullivan. Almost in passing, he noticed the medallion dangling from a knotted chain in her right hand as the woman stood transfixed in a struggle with the president. Cummings took the president's arm and pushed again.

"Not here, Aidan. Please," he pleaded.

Cummings could feel the president's physical, as well as mental resistance. He turned to Bill Jackson and Frank Thompson, both of whom were now staring at the president. Cummings' eyes opened wide as he struggled to move the man. He called to the two big men.

"Help me! Now!"

Bill Jackson and Frank Thompson had also seen the president this way before. They could feel the anger surging from the man in waves. They had to move immediately. Jackson grabbed the president's left arm and jerked him forward with all his strength. The president stumbled slightly and his concentration was broken. He let them move him the remaining steps to his waiting limousine.

"It's her," he mumbled.

Bill Jackson and Charlie Gilbert, who had run to them from the limo, pushed the president into the car as Frank Thompson and others held the crowd back. Bret Cummings jumped in with the president and the car moved away, cameras following its departure and people lining its route, cheering loudly.

Laura was exhausted. Never in her life had she experienced such a thing. Before the world, the president of the United States was using some invisible power to reach into her . . . to hurt her . . . even to kill her. She breathed deeply as people around her hurried after the departing motorcade. Laura staggered to a bench and slumped onto it. It had come so slowly to her. Now she knew, however, that she really wasn't some inconspicuous journalist who had merely gone out to make a name for herself. The feeling she'd had for days was overwhelming her consciousness. The president wanted her. She didn't know why. Somehow, she had to stop him because her life depended on it.

Zac Morgan sat back in the worn leather chair in his state office in Seattle, Washington. He wore a broad smile as he clapped his hands sharply. His top aides stared at him.

"He did it," he finally declared gleefully. "The son of a bitch just cut his dick off!"

His aides stared blankly at each other. They all thought the president had done a masterful job of getting the crowd back. They couldn't understand the senator's sudden joy.

His long-time aide, Gordon Mason, finally said what everyone else was thinking.

"You're seein' something the rest of us dolts aren't seein', senator. Care to enlighten us?"

Senator Morgan smiled. His clear blue eyes sparkled under his thick white hair and eyebrows. "Don't you see, Gordie?"

Gordie shook his head, bewildered. "It looks to me like he pulled 'em right back in, Zac. The guy got 'em all," responded Mason.

"He thinks he's God, Gordie. The guy just came out and told the world that he is bigger than God."

Slowly, Gordon Mason began to smile. He was followed by the three other aides, all of whom suddenly realized what the president had done.

"He's never said it before," continued the senator. "He's always been so careful. Now he's done it."

Senator Morgan stood up to pace the room.

"He's opened the door for us. We've got to run through now." He turned back to his aides.

"Sheila," he continued, "I want it played up in the papers. Most won't see what he did unless we tell 'em. Others will forget unless we keep it before them. He says he's God, folks. We ain't the smartest people in the world and we haven't been the most God-fearing in recent years, but when a man takes himself out of the 'regular folk' category and says he's God, Americans won't take kindly to it. Take care of the papers, Sheila."

Sheila Blackburn smiled as she nodded and took notes.

"Gordie, you and Sam," he pointed to Sam Phelps sitting next to Mason, "set up a meeting for Thursday morning in D.C. for me and my republican brethren in the Senate." He hesitated before continuing, "Just those opposing the repeal, for now. We'll let the others stew for awhile. Let them think they're out and then see what happens."

The senator turned to the last aide, Seth Jacobs.

"Dig a little, Seth. Get me some other reactions. I want to know who else heard it? Who can we count on to help us here?"

Seth nodded and the senator again smiled broadly, relishing the fact that the enemy had provided the first opening.

"Let's do it! And let's not let that door close on us!"

CHAPTER 19

By the time Laura reached her apartment, she could no longer waste her energies bemoaning her recent losses. She couldn't wait any longer for others to move. She had to understand what was happening in her world, why it was coming apart and why the president of the United States was so interested in her. What was it about her stories that had concerned the White House, particularly when she had been so thoroughly humiliated? Why was she a threat?

Laura sat before a yellow legal pad, writing notes and jotting thoughts that might lead her down the path to the answers she needed so desperately. Her senses grew sharp as she felt the surge of energy that came whenever she started an important investigation. This time was the most important; her very life might depend on the outcome.

Her immediate thought was to talk to Ned McDonough. Bill had taken the boxes of notes and materials she'd gathered for her stories, saying he'd keep them until she returned from her parents' home. Deep down, Laura didn't believe any of this information could hurt the president because it all pointed to something that had already been proven a hoax. Yet Bill had indicated to her mother he'd found something and needed to talk to Laura when she returned. And there were the deaths, two of the three people most responsible for the stories. Was it just a coincidence that Michael Stoner and Bill McDonough were suddenly dead? Was it Laura's turn next? Maybe her box of materials held the answer. She dialed Bill's number. Ned answered.

"Ned, this is Laura Miller."

"Yes, Miss Miller."

"I'm so sorry to bother you right now. But," she wasn't sure how to broach the subject when he was still so obviously distraught, "Bill has some of my notes on a story I wrote. He picked them up for me from the *Herald*. I was wondering if I might get them?"

There was no response. He could care less about her notes. He was probably wondering how she could be so callous. She wondered the same.

"The funeral is on Thursday, Miss Miller. You can come by on Friday if you'd like. My family and I will be here to clean things up for Bill and Nell."

"Yes, of course. Thank you, Ned. I'll come by on Friday.

"Will you be at the funeral, Miss Miller?"

"Yes . . . I'll be there." she stammered, wishing now that she hadn't bothered Ned before the funeral.

"Please say hello to me. I'd like to meet you. Bill thought so highly of you."

"Yes, Ned, I will."

After she hung up, Laura felt worse. She wrestled with her feelings of sympathy and her own need for information. In the past there had never been a conflict. The story was always first, as it should have been now because of the stakes she perceived. Yet she felt badly.

Of course she'd wait for Friday. That's the least she could do. She should never have called in the first place. Yet there was that urgency that wouldn't permit her to wait.

Laura went back to the legal pad. She started several lines of thought and then crossed them out again and again, unable to get a handle on her direction. Every time her pen touched the paper, his name repeated itself in her mind.

Aidan Sullivan . . . Aidan Sullivan . . . Aidan Sullivan.

She wrote it down. Several times. With each stroke of her pen she began to feel that this man was something more than the president of the United States. The speaker across from the Washington

Monument evidently thought so. There was no mistaking the power he had exhibited to her. Laura wasn't hallucinating. She had seen his face. Felt the power. The concentration. The . . . was it possible she had felt fear? Yes, her own for sure. But had she felt the president's as well?

Her mind's eye replayed the scene of the massive crowd and the numerous security men, of the adoration and then her own thoughts at the sight of the security.

Albert Smith . . . Albert Smith . . . Albert Smith.

The name came suddenly, as it had in the park when she first saw the security. In the park, it had merely been her subconscious mind answering her query as to the number of security. Now it was different. After his name she'd written the single word "Why?" and suddenly she knew where she had to go to find her answers.

Two minutes later Laura was on the phone with Jimmy Reese, the keeper of the archives at the *Herald*. She made arrangements to have the note files of the *Herald's* reporters who had covered the assassination attempt seven years earlier available for her to see in the morning. Most of the basic facts were easily accessible in any periodical. Albert Smith had been dubbed by the press a religious fanatic who had gotten a message from God to destroy Aidan Sullivan. This information was gleaned from notes he'd written and from interviews with his wife, who Laura remembered, was a kindly looking middle-aged woman. Laura didn't need the archives to get the basic information; she did need them for the reporter notes and thoughts.

The newspaper articles were purged of editorial comment. It was only on scratch paper and notepads that a true understanding of the story could be obtained. Laura was hoping she'd get a better feel for the man's motives. She hoped they would shed some light on her own predicament.

She sat for several more hours, writing notes and concentrating on her course of action until at six-thirty, her thoughts were interrupted by the ringing of her phone. She picked it up absently and heard the voice of Tom Stafford.

"Laura, you're home. Good."

"Tom?"

"Yeah . . . I'm returning your call." He hesitated. "From this weekend?"

The tension in his voice was obvious. She wondered if she should tear into him for being such a cowardly ass for leaving without talking to her and then coming back to leave the place a mess. There was no time to debase herself for a whim, though.

"Did you come by the apartment while I was gone?" she asked, fully expecting a positive response and intending to simply tell him that she called because she was angry.

"No, Laura, I didn't. I," he hesitated again, "I went out of town a couple days after you did."

"Did you send somebody by to get your stuff?"

"No. I already had it. Why?"

Laura's eyes darted around the room. The knot in her stomach began to rise towards her throat.

"Laura, what happened? Are you okay?" asked Stafford.

"Yeah," she struggled. "I gotta go."

"Laura . . . wait . . . Laura, I'm really sorry about . . ." Stafford sputtered.

"I can't talk now," she blurted. "I'm busy. Call me later."

She hung up and the knot surged upward. She wasn't even safe in her own apartment. They knew where she lived. They had already been there. Searching for something. Of course, they knew. Indeed, if it was the president who pursued her for some reason, he would certainly know where she lived. The government knew what they wanted to know about everyone. It was omniscient. It could snuff a person out without a trace.

Laura had to leave. She had to hide somewhere where no one could find her until she understood what was happening and could come up with some idea of what to do to protect herself. But where could she turn? She couldn't go to her parents' home; she would only put them in danger. Again, she tried to convince herself that it was ridiculous to think that the president of the United States meant her harm. But it had to be true. How else could all this be explained? The inevitability of her situation debilitated her. There was nowhere to go where they couldn't find her. What hope was there?

Laura ran to her bedroom without any idea what she would do. She pulled a duffel bag from her closet and began stuffing clothing into it. She had to go somewhere. Anywhere. Before they came for her.

The knock came seconds later. It was a sharp, firm rap on her apartment door. She jumped, shocked that they had come so soon. She ran to the nightstand next to her bed to get the hand gun that Tom kept there. She had no idea how to use it. As she reached for the drawer, chastising herself for not going to the shooting range with Tom when he'd suggested it, she found the weapon was gone. She stared frantically at the door. Another sharp knock sent Laura running to the kitchen.

The next one was more persistent and demanding.

Hurry!

She grabbed the large butcher knife, dulled beyond normal kitchen use, but sharp and imposing enough to cause significant damage. Whirling at the sound of yet another knock, knife clutched tightly in her hand, she heard a voice through her near hysteria. It was a man's voice. She thought it was familiar, but she couldn't place it. She strained to hear it again, trying to make no sound of her own. One more word was all she needed to recognize it and know if it was friendly.

"Laura, it's Mark Tucker. Are you in there?"

"Mark?" the name registered slowly. "Mark?" she stammered, finally finding her voice.

Running to the door, knife in hand, Laura pulled the door open without even thinking it might not really be him.

"Mark!" Tears filled her eyes as she stood, dazed, in the doorway.

"Laura, are you okay?"

Mark was taken aback by her appearance. The beautiful woman he'd met in Manhattan Beach was haggard and drawn. Her eyes searched the hall behind him as she reached for him and dragged him inside. Mark stared at the huge knife and held back fearfully, not knowing what to expect from the woman he'd known for such a short time.

"Hurry! Come in!" Laura said breathlessly.

She slammed and locked the door behind him, before turning and leaning against it. The knife fell from her hand and lay menacingly next to her.

"Thank God it's you," she mumbled as she slid down the door and held her head in her hands.

He knelt down in front of her. "What's going on?"

"They're after me," she said through her tears.

"Who? Who's after you?"

She looked up slowly, "The president."

Laura waited for Mark's reaction and knew immediately that he wouldn't believe her. No one would believe her.

"What president? What are you talking about?"

She dropped her head again and pushed herself to her feet. This was her problem. Hers alone. How could she hope to convince anyone that the most popular president the country had ever known was out to get her? She stood slowly and staggered past Mark to her bedroom.

"Laura, wait. What's going on?"

"You won't understand, Mark. It's crazy," she laughed and turned slowly. "Maybe I'm crazy. Look, I'm really not up to seeing anyone now. You should go. Call me later, okay?"

Mark was ashamed of his initial reaction. She was deeply troubled. He wondered if he should leave and let her work out her problems. Perhaps he would try again, later.

"It looks to me like you could use some help. What's the matter?"

Laura studied him closely. She needed an ally. There was nowhere else to turn. Yet she barely knew him.

"No, Mark. There's nothing you can do. I'll be okay."

"Look, Laura, I've been trying to get in touch with you for two solid days. Either you're not home or the damn phone's busy. I figure I don't have a chance of reaching you by phone and I'm beginning to think that if I walk out that door without you, that'll be the end of it."

He hesitated as she smiled slightly, wanting desperately to confide in him.

"It took everything I had to call you for lunch. Now that I've broken the ice, I can't stop. I don't know if I'd have the strength to call another woman."

She smiled again.

He held his hands up and continued with a smile, "I'm not so sure I should be doing this, but I'd like to help you. I think you need someone to talk to."

"You'll think I'm nuts," she said warily. "It doesn't make any sense."

"Try me, Laura. If I think you're nuts, I promise you, I'll leave."

She nodded slowly and then turned toward her bedroom.

"We can't talk here," she said. "I've got to leave this place."

"Where are you going?"

"I don't know. But I have to leave this apartment."

Laura finished packing her bag quickly as Mark stood in the bedroom doorway pondering his next step. He was hesitant but finally made the decision.

"I'm staying at the Hyatt Hotel. If you don't have anywhere to go, it has a sleeper sofa. You can stay there tonight," he offered. He was surprised when she accepted.

CHAPTER 20

Bret Cummings thought the American wrist symbol would be a hard sell. That evening, however, at a White House party under the stars on the South lawn, the idea received rave reviews. Everyone seemed to agree that despite the placard carrying protestors outside the White House grounds, it was the only way to protect Americans. After all, with everyone in the world aspiring to American life and with the world becoming so homogenous in appearance, true Americans would only be safe if they were clearly identifiable. The beautiful skin graft patch, which could not be duplicated or counterfeited, was the perfect mark of American loyalty.

Bret heard rumors that Zac Morgan had called a special meeting of the senate's opposition Republicans. His spies were trying to find out what was planned. For some reason Senator Morgan had loved the President's speech. Although receptive to the possibility that the president's remarkable performance had inspired the old goat from Washington to switch sides and convince his colleagues to join the president's followers, Bret knew better than to count on such a hope. It was more probable that Senator Morgan had seen something that no one else had. It was vital Bret find out what it was before it did any damage.

Cummings hadn't told the president about Senator Morgan's meeting. It was clear the President was in no mood for any news, let alone news of potentially strengthened opposition. He decided to wait until he knew more about the senator's intentions. The chief of staff's immediate concern was the president himself. His performance before a world audience from the Washington Monument was stunning. Reports from around the globe, although not effusively positive because of the fear of growing American power and influence, were grudgingly complimentary. President Sullivan had handled a seething crowd with a sure-handed confidence that defied logic. In simple words he had brought them all back from the brink of dangerous chaos. Yet the president brooded.

When he made his appearance at the evening's festivities, Aidan Sullivan smiled and accepted congratulations and assurances of undying support from all the monied guests. He went through all the motions and no one knew his anger. None, that is, except the beautiful Marianne Cornhauer.

The Cornhauers were among the last to leave the party, confident in their position at court with the knowledge that their daughter was again the president's favorite. They spent freely to support the presidential staff's efforts to remove constitutional obstacles from the president's continued hold on the highest office in the land. They also planned, secretly, for the wedding that would forever place them at the head of American families.

Marianne Cornhauer had felt something. During the entire evening, the president was brusque and nasty. It had even gotten to the point that she wanted to leave. She intended to simply go home quietly, without telling anyone. She would let Aidan Sullivan work the anger out of his system. Alone.

She hadn't been able to, however. When the party was over, Marianne Cornhauer still clung to the president's arm. Afterwards she stood alone in the eerie dark of his bedroom. The bedroom had never bothered her before. Its austere decor was unusual, and it seemed out of place in the midst of the ostentatious trappings of the rest of the White House. She'd often wondered how anyone could stand the room's utter darkness, that not even a single moonbeam penetrated. Yet she had never before been afraid. On this night, however, a terrible fear enveloped her. The only light came from the small lamp on the stand next to the bed. Black shadows danced menacingly around the room and her thoughts drifted to pain and evil things. Her mind begged her to run before he returned, but she couldn't.

"I want her found! She will not stop us," she heard him shout.

Suddenly, the door burst open and he entered, taking from her what little hope of escape she still had. Her mind was not hers as she stood transfixed, unprotected before his approach. In the background, Bret Cummings' voice pleaded, "Aidan, don't do this now. We'll find her."

And then the president was in front of her. Breathing quickly. Eyes wild. Angry. Deadly. Aidan Sullivan's hatred was boiling. His mind's eye saw only the enemy that would bring him down. The enemy he thought no longer existed. He reached with both hands for the sides of Marianne Cornhauer's backless dress. In one motion, he tore it from her upper body. She stood before him as an offering, her supple flesh quivering under his control. Her firm breasts bobbed as he pulled again and removed the rest of the gown. He squeezed one breast and with his other hand pulled her to him.

Marianne struggled desperately against the numbness in her brain. She screamed without a sound as he tore her panties off and fell on top of her on the bed. His hands tore at her breasts, twisting and squeezing, and then he was inside her, driving hard and Marianne knew she would die. Her mind fought for freedom. Her only chance. She had to be free of the raging animal that was Aidan Sullivan.

The president felt the power. He was dominant as he drove himself with all his might into the woman beneath him. She was just like the others. The ones who had tried to stop his rise. All of them were in his way and they would all be punished.

He opened his mouth and ran his tongue down her throat to her right breast. He sucked until the nipple stood erect, hard in his mouth. Then he bit down, suddenly, tasting blood. The warm, sweet taste of life trickling from her breast.

The pain was excruciating. Marianne's scream was loud and agonizingly clear. She turned, kicking against his weight. Tears and more screams until suddenly he was gone. She rolled quickly off the bed and grabbed the sheet to cover her nakedness. She ran to a corner of the room and cowered, staring wild-eyed.

"Enough, Aidan! That's enough!"

Bill Jackson held the president in a bear hug from behind. Aidan Sullivan flailed at him and struggled to free himself, but the big man held tight.

"It's finished, Aidan," said Jackson.

Slowly, as a frantic Marianne Cornhauer stared in disbelief, the president calmed. Bill Jackson put him down and Aidan Sullivan slouched onto the corner of the bed.

"It's over, Aidan," the big man said again.

The president looked up at Jackson and then beyond him to Charlie Gilbert who stood with Marianne, trying to soothe her. She flinched at his touch but he continued to speak softly, "It's over, now. Everything will be okay," he purred mechanically.

The president's eyes moved to those of his chief of staff, who stood, shaking with revulsion, in the doorway. The seething hatred continued to surge through the president in ever diminishing waves. Bret could feel the intense power even as the president tried to calm himself. For long seconds the president held his gaze and took control, his anger flooding Bret Cummings's consciousness until the chief of staff felt he would drown.

"I want to go," whimpered Marianne Cornhauer.

Aidan Sullivan turned slowly away from his focus on Bret Cummings, who immediately stumbled away from the doorway, suddenly angry himself. The president stared, unashamed, at the frantic young woman, who finally let the blood stained sheet fall to the floor in exchange for an overcoat. She staggered out of the room under Charlie Gilbert's arm, eyes darting to the president and then quickly away when they caught his gaze.

The president sat quietly, breathing deeply to regain control as he gazed intently through the retreating woman. She wouldn't say a word. Her fear was so palpably intense that she wouldn't dare test the rage and anger she had just barely survived. Their relationship would simply fade away and the tabloids would jump over themselves for the scoop on the president's next gorgeous paramour.

Now the president had to rest his mind. He had much work to do.

★ CHAPTER 20 ★

The phone in Mark Tucker's room rang at four o'clock the next morning. He was startled out of a deep sleep that had started just two hours earlier after a long night of talking with Laura who lay on the sleeper sofa in the corner of the room. Mark was barely conscious as he reached frantically to stop the insistent shrill of the phone. Finally, he found it next to him on the night stand. Laura rolled awake and lifted her head to watch Mark's shadow in the moonlit room.

"Yeah," he mumbled into the phone. "Hello."

He listened intently for several seconds. "I'll be ready," he said finally and hung up the phone.

"Everything all right?" Laura asked as she watched Mark rubbing his face and then throwing off his sheets. He sat on the edge of his bed, yawned, and rubbed his face again.

"There's been another murder. Commander Escobar's coming by right away."

"Is it the same kind?"

"I don't know. Escobar thinks it might be. It's in the same area. I gotta get ready."

Mark stood and stumbled into the bathroom. He pushed the door closed behind himself.

Within a few minutes he emerged wearing jeans, a flannel shirt, and sneakers. He felt energized.

"I don't know when I'll be back. I've got to believe this is going to take most of the morning. If you need anything, charge it to the room."

He threw on a light jacket to protect against the early morning chill and by four-twenty he was walking out the door to meet Commander Escobar.

Laura watched his departure from the bed. She was unable to fall back to sleep again immediately. To her surprise it wasn't because of her fears or the recurring dream. She had experienced neither of them this night. She felt strangely safe in Mark's room, where no one knew where she was.

Over the course of the evening, she had told him everything. Mark listened intently, occasionally asking for clarification, but otherwise letting her finish before discussing it to any great extent.

191

When she reached the mind interplay at the Washington Monument, Mark raised his eyebrows in surprise but again said nothing. Finally, she related someone other than Tom Stafford had been in her apartment searching for something.

"It's probably best you're not there tonight. I don't know what's going on or why, but it's for damn sure you wouldn't figure it out if you're afraid to be in your own apartment."

At first, Laura wasn't sure if he was mocking her. After awhile she realized again that Mark had real character. Maybe he didn't agree with her conclusions, but he agreed something strange was happening.

"What are you going to do?" Mark had finally asked her.

"I don't know. I thought I knew Monday morning when I drove out to the Sunford Home. Until I lost it again when I realized someone else had been in my home. I'm not sure what to do."

"You can't just sit and wait for things to happen. It'll drive you nuts."

"Yeah, if I'm not there already."

Mark laughed uneasily until she finally joined him and a lighter mood of trust prevailed for the rest of the evening.

"You're going to have to find out why the president would want to come after you. If it's true," he emphasized the 'if,' "there's something that you either know or have access to that he believes can hurt him. I think you should do what you originally planned. Go over your notes of your investigation and go to the *Herald* to check the archives. You can't go to the police saying the president wants to kill you unless you have something significant to support your claim."

They spent the rest of the evening talking and planning. Laura asked about the murder investigation, and Mark explained that they were having difficulty finding any pattern to the killings. If indeed they were by the same person, there didn't seem to be a reason for the sudden shifts from Los Angeles to Sacramento, then suddenly and for an extended period of time to Washington, D.C.

Laura dozed again and was soon asleep. It was true that no one would believe her unless she had something significant. Maybe they wouldn't even believe her if she found the facts to support her position.

Commander Escobar screeched to a stop outside a cordon of black-and-white police cars, whose lights flashed a sinister red glow over the macabre scene.

Street people, bedraggled and sopped in the comfort of the brown bags they grasped so tightly, loitered together as if at a meeting of old friends. None seemed surprised by the event that had brought the police careening through their streets to the dark alley between the crumbling hulks of former business establishments.

"It looks like your boy again, Ralph," said Homicide Detective Keneel Fulton, shaking his head and walking away from the gruesome scene. "It's a mess."

The girl's body was literally strewn atop the rubble in the alley. She lay open, from throat to groin, her entrails, cold now from exposure to the evening air, about her. Although Mark Tucker had seen all the photographs and had been able to overcome the nausea he'd experienced the first time he viewed a picture, the horror of the real death was too much for him. He ran out of the alley and vomited against the wall of one of the old buildings.

Ralph Escobar blanched. No matter how many times he viewed such horrific scenes, he could never get used to them. He was able to keep his stomach, but he grew dizzy with the stench of death, and he too turned away.

"Son of a bitch!" Escobar whispered. "This is one sick bastard."

He walked over to Mark Tucker who was leaning on a hand against the building, his head down.

"You okay, Professor?" Escobar asked.

Mark nodded, turning slowly to face the Commander. He could feel the blood rushing back to his face.

"You think it's our guy?" Escobar continued.

Mark nodded slowly.

"Any chance it's a copycat?"

Mark wasn't able to look at the body long enough to make a full investigation. He doubted very much that he could look again. But he knew. He had seen one telltale sign immediately, before he had staggered away to leave his dinner on the ground. The girl's right breast nipple was gone. It was immediately apparent despite all the blood. Mark had no idea if it had been bitten off like all the rest, but it was gone. He had definitely seen that.

"No chance," he finally said.

"Hey, Ralph!" shouted Detective Fulton. "Quick!"

The detective was waving to Escobar as he held his car radio transmitter.

"We'll meet you there," he said into the transmitter as Escobar and Tucker ran up to him.

"We've got someone," Fulton said.

"What are you talking about?"

"Patrol unit picked up a guy about an hour ago. He's at the station. They got him about a half mile from here. They say he was covered in blood."

Escobar turned and again surveyed the scene.

"My boys'll take care of things here. I'll see you at the station," said Fulton.

Escobar and Tucker followed Fulton's unmarked car to the Eighth Street station.

Despite the early hour the old station's lobby was already teeming with life. It was crowded with hookers, pimps, drugged-out street folk, and other denizens of the night. Fulton elbowed his way through the raucous crowd, leading Tucker and Escobar to an interrogation room tucked away at the end of a dark hall behind the main desk.

Next to the interrogation room, behind a two-way mirror and window was the standard viewing room. It was one of the few modern-day conveniences added since the station's initial construction in 1922. It was to this room that Fulton led Tucker and Escobar.

"I'll have him brought in. Hang tight, guys," Fulton said as he stepped back out into the hall.

The interrogation room on the other side of the glass was dark. Neither Escobar nor Tucker knew what they would see when the lights were finally turned on. Visions of numerous faces flashed through Mark Tucker's mind. They were the faces of other serial killers and mass murders from around the world. They were faces he'd studied over the years in his attempts to discern that single telltale feature that would link them all, the one common physical trait that could identify such animals for all the world. He saw Adolf Hitler's pointed dark eyes, which bore no resemblance to the ivy league good looks of Ted Bundy. And the sharp-faced demonic leers of Charles Manson and Richard Ramirez had nothing in common with the round pouty features of Angelo Bono. Like many others who had tried before him, Mark found nothing. He was never able to discern any commonality of appearance. The only commonality was something in their sick, twisted minds. As he waited for what the Washington, D.C., police believed to be the D.C. Ripper, all the faces disappeared to blackness and he had no guess at all.

When the lights finally came on and the young man was led to the hardwood chair in the stark gray interrogation room, Mark stared in shock. The handcuffed and manacled man was huge. A full head taller than the six-foot Keneel Fulton, he must have approached three hundred pounds in weight. His enormous body was spattered with dry blood, most of which was from a source other than himself, but at least a portion of which had to be his own as several cuts, streaks of blood and bruises were visible about his head and face. What most captured Mark's attention, however, was the clear indication of mongolism in the man's face. The large forehead, flat back head, small-featured round face, and upward-sloping eyes spoke clearly of Down's syndrome. Although Mark had never studied the effects of Down's syndrome in any great detail, he had taken several psychology courses in which the condition was reviewed. His recollection was that those suffering from the condition were generally responsive, loving, even-tempered people, definitely not the types that could harbor the deep-seated hatred and ill will that were the cornerstone of the psychological makeup Mark was constructing for the D.C. Ripper. If this man was the monster who had committed such heinous crimes, the study of Down's syndrome sufferers would take a hideous turn for the worse, particularly in a society that had already grown so intolerant of all save the "beautiful American."

As Mark stared at the empty eyes and blank expression, he felt strongly that this was not the man they sought. Nothing he had ever studied would remotely suggest a person of this man's obvious mental makeup. He believed the real killer still walked the streets of D.C. How then did this behemoth get himself covered with blood so close to the scene of the most recent murder? Blood samples, no doubt, would help explain a few things. They would simply have to wait and see.

Jason Sullivan stared straight ahead. He wasn't seeing anything. He didn't hear what his interrogators were saying. All he could see was the dead woman. She lay before him, torn open and silent as he sat moaning and wailing, her blood covering him.

"Monster," he mumbled. "The Monster came again. I couldn't stop it." Tears rolled down Jason's cheeks. He'd been crying off and on since they'd dragged him into the station. He didn't notice the tears. He only thought of the Monster and how he'd failed to stop it. Again.

CHAPTER 21

"*Washington Herald*. May I help you?" answered the receptionist's voice after the third ring.

"May I speak to Jimmy Reese, please?" Laura asked.

"Who's calling?"

Laura hesitated, feeling strangely that the simple question had some other meaning. Her wariness was heightened by the fact that the voice sounded so efficient and formal, an unusual combination in the *Herald's* past receptionists. Maybe the paper had indeed, tried to class up it's act and teach its people how to deal with the public.

"Laura Miller," she finally responded.

The receptionist hesitated.

"Hello," said Laura.

"Yes . . . sorry Miz Miller, Mister Reese is not in."

"Cherie, is that you?" she suddenly recognized the voice and found it hard to believe that the formal tones flowed from the lackadaisical, apathetic receptionist Laura had known for the past two years.

"Yes, Miz Miller, it is."

"Why so formal, Cherie? Are you okay?"

"I'm fine. Mister Reese is not available right now."

Laura was starting to get angry as she began to feel that Cherie was trying to put her off. "You just said he wasn't in, Cherie. Which is it? Not in or not available?"

Again Cherie hesitated, stammered, and then her formality seemed to disappear. "He ain't in so he ain't available."

After another pause, Cherie became formal again.

"May I take a message?"

"No. Thanks."

Laura hung up wondering for the thousandth time what the hell was going on. She'd only called in the first place to tell Jimmy she was going to be a little late. Rather than brood, however, she decided she would just pop in on him. He wouldn't be upset if she was a little late. Laura knew Jimmy.

After a quick shower and a bowl of cold oatmeal crunch, a special breakfast concoction of the hotel's cafe chef, Laura drove to a public parking structure across the street from the *Herald*. She stepped to the sidewalk in front of the building's double-door entry. It looked the same as it had for the past eight years, yet it felt so different. The building had become home, as most of her waking hours had been spent there. Now as she stood staring at those two doors, Laura no longer felt their inviting warmth. Instead, they barred her way and promised nothing except the pain of memories on the other side.

The lobby was crowded, as usual, and Laura hid her face, preferring not to be recognized. At the bank of elevators, she chose one whose direction arrow pointed down. She boarded and rode it down two floors, to the basement level where the paper's archives were kept so well organized by Jimmy Reese and his two assistants.

Laura stepped off the elevator and headed over to the long counter that served as Jimmy's work station. Jimmy was not there. Instead, a young man, whom Laura had never met, sat there, flipping through a card box and placing new cards in alphabetical order.

At either side of the counter were security guards, both of whom watched her suspiciously.

"Excuse me," Laura said to the man behind the counter.

He placed a card into the box before looking up.

"Is Jimmy Reese in?" she asked.

"Who wants to know?"

"I'm Laura Miller."

"No, he ain't in."

"Do you know when he'll be in?"

"No."

"Well, I'll just wait here for him." Laura pointed to two chairs against the wall behind her. The young man stood up.

"Can't do that."

Laura looked surprised and then noticed that the two security guards were moving toward her.

"Why not?"

"Look, Miz Laura Miller, you caused a lot o' problems here at the paper and you ain't welcome," the man said, barely masking his contempt.

"Where's Jimmy Reese?" Laura demanded.

"He ain't available right now and you ain't welcome here."

"Dammit . . . I want to talk to Jimmy. Right now." She'd had enough of not knowing what was happening. She couldn't believe that Jimmy would avoid her.

"You'll have to leave, miss," said one of the security guards as he grabbed her arm and pulled her away from the counter.

Laura jerked her arm out of the man's grasp, trying not to grimace at the pain it caused.

"Keep your hands off me!"

The guard reached for the baton at his side and pushed his way in front of her, unimpressed by her reaction. Laura stared at both guards before she turned suddenly and stormed to the elevator. The three men were nonplussed and simply watched her step aboard.

Back on the sidewalk again, Laura was lost. She couldn't believe Jimmy was dodging her. It sounded that way, though. Oblivious to the pedestrian traffic about her, she stepped away from the building having no thought about her next move, until she heard her name being called.

"Laura. Hey, Laura."

She turned to see Cherie, the receptionist, running awkwardly on red high-heeled shoes.

"Laura . . . damn, girl, don't be moving so fast." She breathed heavily as her eyes darted furtively from face to face around her. "Jimmy told me to come and stop you."

"Where's Jimmy?"

"He's in that ol' basement," Cherie said. "Like he always is." Then, lowering her voice, she continued, "He wants you to meet him out back of the building. Says he has something for you."

Laura looked at Cherie suspiciously.

"What's going on, Cherie?"

"Damned if I know, honey, but since you wrote them stories, all hell's broke loose."

"What do you mean?"

"It's like some damn gestapo state around here. You know . . . phone taps, cameras. They're watching us and listenin' all the time."

"Who's watching and listening?"

"Hell, I don't know. All I know is someone's watchin' and I got to be real careful if I want to keep my job." She paused and watched Laura shaking her head. "I'm real sorry at the way I acted on the phone. I just got to be careful and you're one of the people that ain't real popular around here."

"Why? What are people saying?"

"Your stories spooked a lot o' people and," she paused, "well, it's got pretty ugly around the place. Everyone's real careful all the time." She looked around quickly before continuing. "I gotta get going, now. My break's almost over and I ain't supposed to be talking to you, anyway. Go on back to where Jimmy's waiting."

Cherie walked away quickly. Laura turned down the alley next to the building and followed it to the loading docks in back. Jimmy was standing on the deck of one of the loading bays, a box, about two feet square at its base and about eighteen inches deep, was at his feet.

Jimmy Reese, a short man in his late sixties, was a crusty old guy who was fanatical about history, which explained why he worked in the archives. He loved the feel and smell of history and he knew of no greater chronicle of history than a newspaper that had covered it since the birth of the United States. Had he not found his niche in the newspaper industry some fifty years earlier, he could certainly have become a jockey. Where once his small frame may have sported the wiry musculature of a physically active man, it had now rounded out from long hours of cataloging and indexing. He had a reputation as a harmless old fool who knew his place in the dark stacks of the archives and did little to make waves.

Laura had always liked Jimmy. She'd often taken advantage of his steel-trap memory to collect historical information for stories she wrote. He was not only faster at recalling specific points than were the periodical computer indexes, he was easier to work with. All she had to do was give Jimmy a general idea of what she wanted and he'd get her centered. Laura never had to pick a specific word or phrase and hope she would find what she wanted. Jimmy knew his archives well. Even those from before his time. It was the ancient records that he spent so many hours reading and learning about when he wasn't cataloguing the more recent materials.

Jimmy also liked Laura. She had been the only person who truly valued his knowledge and expertise. She'd always shown him great respect. When he spotted her, Jimmy began waving his arm for her to join him.

"I'm glad Cherie caught you, Laura." Jimmy said in his high-pitched, cracked voice.

"What's happening, Jimmy?"

"They don't want me talkin' to you."

"Who doesn't?"

Jimmy motioned with his eyes to the top of the building, which towered above them. Laura knew he meant John Kursh, owner of the paper, and his board of advisors and editors.

"Why not?"

"They're scared, Laura. They got a terrible fear in 'em. All of 'em do. Even Mister Kursh." Jimmy shook his head. "Never thought Kursh would give in so easy."

"What happened?"

"Your stories. You know, about the president. His people came down real hard on us here at the *Herald* and Mister Kursh got real scared. First time I ever saw a Kursh back down so quickly. His daddy woulda never done it. But this Mister Kursh got real scared.

He's been apologizing ever since and the paper just ain't putting out anything."

Laura shrugged, knowing all of this information well.

"So why can't you talk to me?"

"Cuz I think they figured that I might help you do some more snoopin' around and maybe cause more trouble."

"Who's concerned about that? Not Mister Kursh?"

"You wouldn't think so, would you? But he had a real scare thrown into him. It was almost immediate that your name was off the most-favored nation list."

"Tell me what you know, Jimmy."

He shook his head slowly, "Not much, I'm afraid. But one thing I know is that they sure as hell don't want you having a look at any archives. I suspected before that someone was monitoring our phone calls. Right after we hung up yesterday, these two big ol' security guys come down and told me I'm not to see you or let you into any of the archives.

"Well, that just pissed me off. I mean, the archives are my territory and only Mister Kursh himself can tell me what I can and can't do with 'em. He knows me. Hell, I used to bounce him on my knee. If he was so damned concerned, he could talk to me and we could decide this thing like the men we are. So I decided I wasn't going to listen to two concrete brains. I just put that box together for you and hoped I would catch you before you left."

Jimmy gave Laura a gap-toothed smile and pointed to the box at his feet.

"Is this the information on the assassination?" she asked, smiling, because she already knew the answer.

Jimmy beamed back at her. Laura flipped the top open. The box was full of paper and other materials.

"You go ahead and take it before someone comes out here."

"Do you have any thoughts for me, Jimmy?"

He smiled again, happy that she asked.

"I got to thinking why everybody was so up in arms about things. They acted the same way about poor old Mister McDonough when he got in touch with me. So I started thinking and I came to something which isn't really clear, but it's something."

"Enlighten me," said Laura.

"I don't think all the fuss is really over your stories. There's nothing you don't already have in your own files that we have here in the archives. So I figured it's something more. But it wasn't until I thought a little about what you'd asked for that it struck me that they're afraid of something else.

"I'd always wondered why Albert Smith tried to kill Aidan Sullivan. From what I saw in the records, Albert was just a nice old guy who was real religious and wouldn't go off half-cocked trying to kill a president. I suppose it's possible he just flipped his cork, but I didn't see it that way then and, after looking at some of this stuff last night, I don't see it that way now."

He pointed again at the box, "There's an interesting copy of the AP tape in there. I think you should take a look at it. Mighty strange how the whole thing happened."

Suddenly they heard the sound of slamming doors from the front of the warehouse.

"I better get going," Jimmy said. "You call me at home after you've had a chance to review it all. Maybe the two of us can figure this out."

"Thanks, Jimmy," Laura whispered as she lifted the box and ran awkwardly to the alley.

"Yo, Jimmy," she heard one of the dock men yell. "What you doin' out here?"

"Having a smoke, Billy. Makes me live longer."

Laura was anxious to review the contents of the box. Jimmy had seen something there, but he was either too scared to voice his opinion or he simply didn't understand enough to have an opinion. She wanted to get started on it immediately. Laura made her way through the heavy lunchtime traffic and headed for her apartment, thinking she would watch the Associated Press videotape to learn whatever it was that Jimmy had seen. As she drew closer, however, she felt the anxiety and fear that she'd felt the previous evening. Someone had been in her place. Since her contact with the president, there was a good chance someone would be waiting and watching.

Laura parked at a metered space one block south of her apartment complex and walked to the corner. Stopping just outside the bakery, she peered around the building. The usual cars were parked along the curbs and pedestrian traffic gave no indication that anything was amiss. She saw nothing unusual. She had hoped it would be easy to see the man with his collar pulled up over his chin and the brim of his hat casting a shadow over his face. Realizing that she wasn't in some movie where the bad guys were so easily identifiable, however, she grew more concerned. For all she knew, the watcher could be any of the people walking the cracked and uneven sidewalk in front of her building or any of the sorry-looking people across the street in the park.

Leaning back against the bakery wall, her eyes turned up to the sky. Clouds were gathering above her in formations of white and gray cotton. As one patch of cloud passed across the face of the sun, she felt a chill. Again, Laura peered around the corner of the bakery. This time, however, she concentrated on the park across the street. Her heart sank when she didn't see the homeless family she'd befriended. They weren't in their usual spot under the big oak tree, probably chased away by the police. She searched frantically until the little girl ran into view. She was being chased by her brother and was giggling excitedly.

Laura crossed the street quickly and approached the children.

"Sam," she called.

He turned quickly, stared for a moment, not sure whether to run or respond. When he finally recognized her, he smiled.

"Hi."

"How are things going?" Laura's eyes searched the park for signs that anyone might be taking too keen an interest in her.

"Great! Dad worked yesterday. He was hoping to get something again today, but I guess they didn't need anyone."

Hannah was now standing next to Sam and grinning up at Laura. She wondered at the seeming happiness of these two waifs who couldn't even count on their next meal.

"Is everything okay with you, Miss Laura?" asked the boy. His smile disappeared and he too glanced around the park to see what was having such an impact on Laura.

"Everything's fine, Sam. Are your parents close by?"

"Sure, right over there," he pointed to a park bench where a man and woman sat, resting amidst their meager worldly belongings.

"I'd like to talk to them."

Sam and Hannah led Laura to their parents and Sam introduced everyone. They shook hands. When Mr. and Mrs. Sykes recognized Laura, they thanked her again and again for the good fortune she had brought their way. Laura tried to eschew the gratitude but finally smiled and accepted it.

"Is there anything we can do for you, Miss Miller?" Mr. Sykes finally asked.

The parents couldn't have been much older than thirty. They were obviously without means of any kind, yet Mr. Sykes offered aid with a sincerity that was unequaled in anyone Laura had ever met.

"Actually, there is something you can do for me, Mister Sykes."

He smiled and stepped forward, ecstatic that he might be of some assistance. Mr. Sykes was a thin, wiry man, whose body looked well-muscled despite the difficult life he and his family lived. Laura wondered if she should ask assistance that might put them in jeopardy. "It may be very dangerous, Mister Sykes."

"Please, Miss Miller, my name is Bill and my wife is Molly. We'd both appreciate you calling us by our first names."

Laura smiled in agreement. "And I'm Laura."

"You go ahead and tell us what you need and we'll decide if we can handle it."

"I'm leaving town for awhile and I need someone to stay in my apartment . . . to keep an eye on things for me," Laura dropped her head and hesitated. The Sykes family waited patiently.

"Actually, Bill, I can't go back to my apartment right now. I think someone might be trying to cause me some harm. They might be watching my place."

Bill and Molly Sykes listened intently.

"I'm not sure of this, but I really have to find out," she hesitated. "I was wondering if you could walk over there and see if anyone is waiting." She hesitated again, looking around helplessly. "I don't really know what you'd look for. . . ."

"I could go into your apartment . . . to get something . . . see if I'm stopped by anyone," suggested Bill Sykes immediately. "Do you need anything?"

Laura shrugged and then remembered that she'd started back to her apartment in the first place to watch the AP tape on her VCR. "My VCR. If anyone stops you, you can say you've come to get it, to repair it," Laura offered.

Bill held his hand out for the key, but she held back, still not sure that she should bring these wonderful people into her nightmare.

"It could be dangerous," she repeated.

"I can handle myself. It's the least we can do for you after the generosity you've shown us."

Almost reluctantly, Laura dropped her key into his hand.

"It's unit four eighteen, on the fourth floor."

"If I walk out with the VCR under my arm and don't come across the street, you'll know I'm being followed. There's an electronics repair shop down the street. I'll take the VCR there and meet you out back."

Laura nodded as Bill Sykes turned to cross the street.

"You stay here with Molly and the kids. I'll be back soon," he said before sprinting across between cars.

Laura watched nervously as Molly stepped forward and threw an arm around her, "Bill'll be all right, Laura. Don't you worry. He's a good man."

Bill walked past the wall of mailboxes to the two elevators at the center of the building's lobby. The lobby was clean and well ordered. No one else was visible on the first floor. The elevator responded quickly to his call. The doors opened immediately after he pushed the button for the "up" arrow.

The fourth floor smelled of new paint. Bill could only imagine the cost of the units in the building. Definitely beyond his reach, even when he was working.

★ CHAPTER 21 ★

A placard on the wall across from the elevator indicated that units 401 through 410 were to the right of the elevators and 411 to 420 to the left. Because the rest of the building had been so well maintained and well lit, Bill noticed immediately that two hall lights near the end of the left corridor were out and drapes were drawn across the window at the end. He figured Laura's suspicions were correct.

As he walked slowly down the hall, Bill's breathing came in short bursts. His stomach muscles tightened with the anxiety of a coming confrontation. It reminded him of his experiences in the second Arab War, just six years previously when he was an army private preparing for a night raid against one of the Iranian well heads. The major difference, of course, was that he was now on a tightly closed battlefield instead of the open deserts of Iran, Iraq, or Saudi Arabia. The anxiety was the same, however. Bill slowed and began purposely to breathe deeply, the way he had been taught by one of his buddies. It enabled him to regain control and again sharpen his senses for any eventuality.

To the right of the corridor were the even numbered units beginning with 412. The lack of light from the missing overheads didn't affect anything until he was midway between units 416 and 418.

Bill's eyes played through the darkness to either side of the corridor.

No one.

Finally, at 418, he turned, stepped into the recessed archway, and tried to push the key into the deadbolt lock. Because of the darkness and his intense concentration, he had some difficulty finding the hole. When he finally did get the key into the lock, it turned easily. He immediately moved the key to the knob lock and fiddled with it until it slid home. When the knob turned and the door began to open, Bill wondered if his premonition that something was amiss had been wrong. Then just as suddenly he realized he had been correct.

"Hey," came the voice from behind.

Bill pushed the door open wide for an escape route and then turned sharply with his leg bracing the door open.

207

"What are you doing?" asked the dark figure stepping into the light of the open doorway. Bill tensed, prepared to defend himself. He crouched slightly and waited. The man stopped about two feet away.

"I asked you what you're doing here?"

It was still too dark for Bill to make out features. He could clearly see that the man before him wore a business suit and that there was another man behind him.

"Who wants to know?" asked Bill, standing firm in the doorway.

"Apartment security," the first man responded and reached into his coat. "That's Laura Miller's place. Who are you?"

Fat chance these guys were security, Bill thought. Particularly since they had come from the apartment across the hall. He could see from the dim light behind them that the door across from his was still ajar to the darkened interior of the apartment.

"You're right. It is Laura's apartment. I'm watching the place for her while she's gone." Bill lied. "She asked me to get her VCR repaired while she was out of town."

The second man stepped forward immediately. "We have no record of Miz Miller permitting anyone into her place while she's gone."

"I guess she forgot to notify you guys," Bill shrugged, suddenly unsure of whether they weren't some kind of security. "Anyway, she asked me to take care of it so that's what I'm doing."

Bill turned.

"Hold it!" shouted the first man grabbing Bill's arm.

Bill whirled around out of the man's grasp only to face the barrel of a hand gun aimed at his chest.

"Who are you, asshole?" demanded the first man.

Bill held his hands up in surrender.

"Hey boys, look, I'm just here to help a friend. If it's so damn important that she notify someone, I'll just tell her that when she returns."

Bill slid past the two men as the door closed behind him and the hall was again in total darkness. He stayed close enough to the gun to strike out at it if he had to, knowing full well that he'd never make it down the hall if he had to run with the gun still in the man's hand.

"She'll be happy to know the security's so tight around here. Damn dangerous neighborhood. I'll see you fellas later."

"I think you should come and have a little chat with us," the first man said as he moved the gun towards Bill and motioned quickly with his head to the door of the opposite apartment.

Bill knew he would have to act quickly. His eyes searched the hall behind the two men until he saw the square box holding the exit sign. Although the lights in the exit box were also out, he felt certain that was the only thing the sign could mean. Bill dropped his head and stepped slowly, submissively, toward the gunman.

As the gunman reached for Bill with his empty hand, Bill lashed out pushing the gun hand away. He lowered his shoulder and ran into the gunman's midsection knocking him off balance and into his partner. They fell against the opening door and into the apartment with nothing to stop their fall. Bill darted past the open door toward the darkened end of the corridor where he hoped the overhead box really was the exit direction sign.

The men grunted behind him and banged their way to their feet and back into the hall.

"Shit!" one of them yelled.

Bill's hunch was correct. He slammed into the door's cross-bar release lever and it flew open just as a bullet shattered the glass at the end of the hall. His muscles strained more than they had since the desert war as he vaulted down entire flights of steps, using only the handrail to slow his deadly descent.

Behind him, the heavy feet of his pursuers clanked on the metal steps. He was moving faster than they were, but he couldn't stop to rest or lose the hand/foot concentration he needed to avoid breaking the bones that would bring him to his end.

On the bottom floor, Bill staggered and fell to one knee. He picked himself up quickly, stumbling as he realized he may have sprained his ankle. He stepped on the ankle gingerly, listening. They were still at least two flights above him, but he couldn't wait to see how badly he was hurt. He decided the ankle could hold him. He ran out into the lobby as quickly as he could, through the front doors of the building, and turned up the street toward the corner where he hoped he could lose them. Despite the pain, he ran at full speed, knowing if he didn't get to the corner before his pursuers made it out of the building, they'd ultimately catch him.

Across the street, Laura, Molly, and the kids watched wide-eyed as Bill limped out of the building and then, at the bottom of the entry steps, turned to sprint up the street. When he reached the corner, two business-suited men emerged from the building behind him. The lead man was holding a gun. As soon as they stepped outside, the pursuit stopped and the gunman hid his gun hand in his jacket while the other man looked up and down the street.

"Laura! Get down quickly!" whispered Molly Sykes frantically. She'd been tugging at Laura ever since Bill had started his sprint but Laura had been too stunned to feel the tugs. As the pursuers emerged from the building, Molly pulled harder until Laura understood her own danger and crouched onto the park bench behind a shielding tree.

"Sammy," Molly called to her son, "keep an eye on your father. Follow him at a distance. When it's safe, go to him and see if he needs any help."

Sam joined other pedestrians in crossing the street to the bakery, ever mindful, through his peripheral vision, of the two pursuers who appeared to have given up the chase.

Laura, Molly, and Hannah continued to watch the two men who started one way, stopped, started back the other way, stopped again, and finally gave up in frustration. Pedestrians gave the two angry men a wide berth.

Finally, the two men went back into the building.

Laura turned away slowly. Although she had felt someone might be waiting for her, her intellectual mind had not fully accepted the fact that murder or mayhem could really happen to her. The reality of her situation was again striking home. She was not floating in some dream story from which she would soon wake. Bill's pursuers had actually been holding guns and they were chasing him with the intent to hurt and possibly kill him. This whole thing that she had been conjuring was real and the stakes were the highest they could possibly be.

"I'm so sorry I got you into this," she finally said as she turned to Molly Sykes, who stared anxiously after her son and the figure of her fleeing husband.

"Bill's okay, Laura. I can tell." She shook her head. "I guess you were right, after all. She suddenly turned to Laura. "We should go to the police," she said.

"I can't."

"Why not? They had guns."

"These are big people, Molly. If we go to the police, they'll know where I am, and they'll know who you and Bill are."

"So what? They'll be arrested," Molly rejoined.

Laura shook her head. "No. These people are bigger than the police. I don't think the police will act against them. At least, not yet."

"What are you involved in, Laura?"

"I don't know, yet. But I'm going to find out."

Five minutes later a black and white police car rolled up in front of Laura's building, the lights atop it flashing and siren shrieking. Two officers emerged from the vehicle and met an old woman at the doors of the building. She had heard a gunshot on the fourth floor and called immediately.

The officers entered the building cautiously as two other squad cars rolled to a stop in front. People stopped to stare, while officers backed them away from the area.

When two new officers entered the lobby, the first two pushed the button for an elevator, one of which was already approaching the lobby from the fourth floor. They waited, guns poised as the door opened on two men who held their free hands above their heads and their other hands before them exhibiting badges and identification.

"Federal officers, gentlemen," one of the men said.

"What is this?" asked the first police officer.

"Federal stakeout, guys. We blew it."

"This lady heard a shot," said the officer.

"Accidental discharge," said the federal officer.

The two federal officers walked right past the policemen to the lobby doors.

"Wait a minute," yelled the first officer. "What the hell are you guys doing here? We didn't know anything about a stakeout."

"I told you, officer, we were on a stakeout. We lost our man. That's it!" The federal officer glared at the police officer. "Now back off and let us get outta here."

The police officers let the two men pass.

"Fuckin' feds. They're arrogant sonsabitches," mumbled the officer as he motioned his men to leave the building, while the old woman stared dumbfounded after them.

Laura and Molly watched the two men walk right past the police officers, get into their car, and drive off unchallenged. Molly stared at Laura, realizing that Laura had been right about these men.

CHAPTER 22

At two o'clock that afternoon, Mark Tucker was called to the telephone in Commander Escobar's office.

"Mark Tucker," he answered when Escobar handed him the phone.

"Mark?"

"Laura. Where are you?"

"At a pay phone. Can we meet?"

"Sure. Are you okay?"

"I need help."

"Can you come and get me?" asked Mark.

"Yes."

"Okay, I'm ready now."

"Meet me outside in ten minutes."

On the way back to the hotel, Laura explained the morning's events to Mark. If he had any doubts the previous evening, they were now gone. Laura told how she'd waited for about an hour after the two business suits departed. When Bill Sykes finally returned, he described his meeting with the two men in the hall outside her apartment.

Although Mark was satisfied that someone at the *Herald* wanted to keep something away from Laura, it was difficult for him to believe that someone highly placed might really want to cause her some harm, until he heard that the two men who had accosted Bill Sykes, knew he was entering her apartment.

"Is it possible they really might have been security guards?" asked Mark.

Laura shook her head, "Not a chance. We've never had security guards walking the floors or hiding in vacant apartments. They couldn't have been security."

Mark and Laura stared straight ahead, deep in thought for several minutes. They paid little attention to the shops, traffic, and pedestrians about them. Laura drove mechanically as her mind raced.

"I think you missed our turn," said Mark when he finally realized they had driven well past their destination.

"Damn! I'm sorry. I'm not totally here," Laura said as she entered a left turn lane, made a U-turn, and headed back in the proper direction.

"What are you planning to do?" Mark asked.

Laura gave a short resigned laugh.

"I can't go back to my place, that's for sure. I asked the homeless family to keep an eye on it," she smiled. "I gave them the keys and said they could stay there until the lease expires at the end of May."

"That's kind of dangerous for them isn't it?"

"I guess they figured with those goons gone, they wouldn't have much trouble. I called my landlord and told him I was having people watch my things for me."

Laura glanced quickly at Mark.

"Can I stay with you for a few days . . . until I figure out where to go?"

Mark shook his head slowly, "I'm supposed to be checking out tomorrow morning."

"I thought you were going to be here for a few weeks." Laura was counting on Mark's help. She couldn't rent her own room. No one would know if she stayed with Mark. "Is something wrong at home?"

214

"No . . . it's not that. Nickie's fine and my classes are covered for the semester. I've been taken off the case."

"What happened?"

Mark was shaking his head slowly, trying to figure out for himself what had happened.

"We had a suspect. He was a big kid with . . . looked like . . . Down's syndrome. It didn't make sense that a Down's syndrome person could commit such a crime, because they're normally so passive. But there he was, near the scene with the dead girl's blood all over him."

"What happened?" Laura asked as she parked her car in a self-park stall and turned to Mark.

"They had several sessions with the kid and weren't getting anywhere. It looked like he was in shock. They just got a first name . . . Jason . . . I think . . . and then something about a Monster coming. I went into the office they'd given me, to review some of the files and suddenly, about noon, Escobar comes in and tells me it's all over. He said the feds were picking the suspect up and we were through."

"Did he say why?"

"He didn't know," Mark explained. "He'd gotten orders from his chief to back down. An hour later, the kid was gone, taken away by two huge guys who had Justice Department credentials.

"Obviously, I was stunned and Escobar was pissed. I don't think either one of us necessarily thought that this kid had committed these murders. He was strong enough, but he was just too clumsy to make such precision cuts. Yet the feds stepped in for some reason."

"What are you going to do now?" Laura asked, concerned about what she would do.

Mark smiled. "Until I heard your story, I was planning to head home. Escobar made it clear that the department was pulling the funding for the task force and I'd have to be out by tomorrow morning." He paused for a moment. "I haven't seen much of D.C. on this trip, so I guess I'll stick around for awhile. Besides, I think you could use some help."

Laura returned Mark's smile, relieved that at least one thing in her life was going her way.

★ ★ ★

Mark carried Laura's box up to his room and called room service for delivery of a VCR.

Since he'd missed his normal morning shower and shave, not to mention valuable hours of sleep and any semblance of a nourishing meal, Mark decided to shower, clean up, and get a bite to eat before diving in to help Laura with her box of information.

She couldn't wait to review the AP video, however.

The tape depicted a scene from the Biltmore Hotel in downtown Los Angeles. The cameraman panned the crowd from the entrance and then picked up the arrival of a black limousine out of which stepped the handsome California state congressman, Aidan Sullivan. The angle was perfect to catch the cheering crowd of supporters, straining against the backs of the police and security line.

The first time Laura watched the video, it moved very quickly. Aidan Sullivan was smiling broadly, when suddenly from the right of the screen a middle-aged man was pointing a gun at him. A loud explosion was heard as the candidate was pushed aside and two burley men jumped into the crowd after the attacker. The cameraman was apparently jostled and pushed as the picture lost focus and direction. When the picture again became clear, focused on the back of someone in the crowd, a second explosion was heard. An enormous black man sat atop the assailant straddling him as she heard the third explosion. Witnesses were sprayed with the blood, brain, and head fragments of the assailant.

Again, the cameraman's view was blocked and the camera moved crazily around until it focused on Aidan Sullivan. The congressman held a hand to his bleeding cheek and security forces were pushing him into the safety of the hotel lobby, while shielding him from further assault with their bodies.

The rest of the tape was of chaos and crowd reaction. Laura switched it off and rewound it. Her mind again wandered back seven years. She remembered turning on the news when she heard of the attempt from a coworker, while working late at the *Herald*. She watched with considerable interest and admiration as the wounded candidate refused to call off his speaking engagement. Instead, he gave the first of his nationally televised impassioned speeches calling for a new American order, an order of winning and taking the lead in the world again instead of sitting back and letting foreigners take the place that only America should hold. Laura remembered feeling a certain pride in young Congressman Sullivan's resilience, which, as he shouted, was just a mirror of America's resilience if everyone would only follow him.

From that day until the November election, Laura Miller and the rest of America watched one rousing speech after another with the jagged path that the bullet had cut across Sullivan's face blazing a trail for the next president of the United States. At the Democratic Convention, the vote had gone to the electoral delegates on the third ballot when no clear winner could be found. The delegates defected, en masse, to the rising star of Aidan Sullivan.

From then on it had been easy for the young congressman. He won the presidency by a large margin, garnering fifty-eight percent of the vote. Even Laura had been taken by his rhetoric and voted for him.

★ ★ ★

When Mark emerged from the bathroom, wearing a white terry towel robe, Laura was midway through her third viewing of the tape.

"Anything?" he asked.

She shook her head, "No. Not yet. It's what we all saw a million times on TV."

Mark watched the final frames of Albert Smith's death and Aidan Sullivan's bleeding face before he shook his head and turned away.

"I'm going to take a short nap. I figure you've got a lot of work for me later," he said as he pointed to the box.

"Is the TV going to bother you?" she asked as she rewound the tape again.

"No. I doubt anything could bother me right now."

Within minutes, Mark was snoring softly, obviously exhausted from his early day. Laura continued to rewind and rewatch the videotape. Every time she did, however, it was the same. There was nothing that would make Jimmy feel it was "mighty strange how the whole thing happened." Of course, it was strange a man could get so close to a presidential candidate, but it had happened numerous times throughout history. As long as these politicians walked among the people, they were subjecting themselves to the whims of lunatics. Jimmy must have seen something more.

Laura stood up slowly and stretched. Her watch read four o'clock when she walked to the window of the tenth floor room. From there she could see the D.C. skyline and off in the distance the numerous points of the capital city's historical landmarks including the glistening columns of the White House.

Stuffing her hands into the front pockets of her Levi's she stood staring absently until her right hand touched the chain in her pocket. She looked down and extracted her hand, which held Father John's silver chain and Mary medal. The late afternoon sun glistened off the medal. She stared at the Virgin's imprint and smiled at the thought of her uncle. He was always such a positive, happy man, one of the few people Laura had ever met who was truly spiritual. Not just in the sense that he knew the Bible and theological teachings but also from the heart. He was always so self-effacing and humble, wishing only the best for others.

As she stood wondering about him, she heard his words again.

"This medal is a constant reminder to me that all I need do if I am ever in need is to call on her to intercede for me with Our Lord," he'd said.

"I'll tell you, Mother Mary, I'm in need now." Laura said softly as she stared at the medal. "If you can hear me and your Son can hear me like Father John says, I could use some help. Let me know what to do."

Laura had never really learned to pray. Although she'd been to Catholic schools, she'd only learned the words. She had never prayed "with the heart" as Hilary had called it when she described her experiences in Medjugorje. Even now she didn't know how to do it or even if she really wanted to. She simply stood there and stared at the medal.

"Help me find some answers . . . please," she said.

Laura turned back to the television, which sat ready with the tape still in place. The tape held some secret and she'd have to try it again.

Still absently clutching her uncle's gift, she again pushed the "play" button. The screen went black for a few seconds and then the images of the crowd, leading to the black limousine, appeared. In her previous viewings of the tape, Laura had tried to see everything that was happening. She now concentrated only on Aidan Sullivan.

The candidate emerged from the car, smiling, waving, and marching with a reckless self-assurance through the arms that reached for him. He paid little attention to the guards, whom Laura had previously recognized as the two men who'd formed the point of the wedge that had led the president to her at the Washington Monument. He drew closer, paying no heed to the man on his right who would suddenly point the gun at his face and squeeze the trigger. When he stood in front of Albert Smith, he stopped. He turned slowly, spread his arms out from his sides and stared directly at his assailant. Then came the weapon, the explosion, and the chaos . . . and there! She saw it! Suddenly, she understood what Jimmy meant.

Again, she rewound the tape and scanned the front of the machine for the slow motion button. She adjusted it quickly and pushed "play" again. She watched the president's face closely.

The smile with which he'd left the car had changed. His eyes were no longer floating over the cheering crowd, seeing all yet seeing nothing. They were pointed. Although his smile was still aimed at the camera, his eyes were focused to the right. Then he had turned slowly . . . ever so slowly as he stopped.

The side view showed his smile as the gun rose to his face. His eyes stared directly at the assailant, unflinching. The arms were outstretched, beckoning the bullet that would soon emerge from the barrel of the weapon before him.

He knew!

The thought came suddenly, without any prodding. He knew what was coming. This man who had the power to probe a person's mind knew that Albert Smith was there. Aidan Sullivan knew this man would point the gun and pull the trigger and somehow . . . *somehow* . . . he knew the man would miss.

He didn't flinch, even after the explosion. His first evasive move was when he was suddenly pushed aside by the big black man who pounced on Albert Smith. The move was not prompted by his fear but rather by others who were there to protect him. Even when he held his hand over his wound, blood streaming through his fingers, he wasn't fazed. He simply smiled.

Laura switched the machine off and sat down hard in the chair by the window. Over the balcony ledge she could see the White House in the distance. The realization of what had happened that day, seven years ago, flooded her consciousness.

Aidan Sullivan's lack of fear at any time during the entire ordeal and the knowing smile led her to only one conclusion. Somehow, he'd known what was about to happen and he had welcomed it. He had opened his arms to the assailant as if to say, "take your best shot," with a confidence of prescient knowledge.

Who was this man? This man who had stolen the minds and hearts of an entire country. What kind of man was he? How could he possibly know?

And, who was poor Albert Smith? Was he a modern day Judas Iscariot? The sacrifice for a man who would become king?

"Laura? You okay?" asked Mark as he leaned on an elbow and stared at her through the coming dusk.

Laura turned sharply, jolted out of her thoughts. She stared at him. "I think I found it."

"What?" He sat up and rubbed the sleep from his eyes.

She pushed the reverse button and watched as the machine worked its way back to the moment before Albert Smith raised the weapon.

"I think I found what Jimmy was referring to. Watch this. Watch his face," Laura said excitedly as she pushed "play".

The machine was still moving in slow motion and Laura pointed. "There, watch it."

When the sequence ended she pushed "stop" and turned expectantly to Mark. He shook his head and shrugged.

"I didn't see anything except the assassination attempt. What did you see?"

"He knew it was coming, Mark." She reached for the reverse button again. "He knew it. Somehow he knew this poor guy was going to shoot at him and he welcomed it. It was like he knew it was the one thing that would get him where he needed to go. It was staged, except that the poor son of a bitch who pulled the trigger was snuffed out."

Mark stared at her and she again pushed "play."

"Watch," she said, pointing again. "You see? Look at the way he's turning. Look at his face and his eyes. Watch the smile. There, he doesn't even flinch. It's like he was asking for it. 'Here, take your shot.'" She continued to point at the screen. "Now watch. They've got him completely under control. He's down . . . but they blow him away."

"Hold it, Laura," said Mark. "You're suggesting that this guy planned this attempt on his life and then had his accomplice killed so he wouldn't talk . . . all to win over the American public?"

"I don't know if he planned it. He sure as hell knew it was coming. Didn't you see his face?"

Mark shook his head incredulously.

"Why? How could he know it would work?" he finally asked.

"I don't know, but it looks obvious."

They stared at each other for several seconds. Mark leaned forward at the foot of the bed so he could get a better look at the screen.

"Look," he started, "take it back to the beginning. Let me see the whole tape. It doesn't make sense."

Laura rewound the tape to the beginning. She pushed "play" and it started again in slow motion.

First, Mark saw the slow pan of the crowd and then the limousine. The door opened slowly and Aidan Sullivan stepped out followed by someone else who was only in the frame briefly.

"Let me speed it up until we get to the attempt," Laura leaned forward.

"No! Hold it a minute." Mark was suddenly excited. "Go back. Quick! Leave it in slo-mo."

Again Laura rewound and the scenes rolled by.

"There," Mark pointed.

He jumped up and pushed reverse again.

"Watch Laura. The guy who follows him out of the car. There!"

221

Again he rewound but stayed at the machine until the frames holding the face of the person following Aidan Sullivan appeared. He pushed "pause" and then stared closely at the picture through which lines ran in a horizontal pattern.

"Damn if it isn't him." Mark said.

"Who?"

"That's the guy we picked up today. The Down's syndrome kid. He's much younger here but still huge. I'll be damned if that's not our Jason."

Suddenly the name clicked for Laura.

"Jason?" she said. "Jason Sullivan?"

Mark turned to her.

"That's Jason Sullivan," Laura said. "The president's son. I remember now. Aidan Sullivan has a Down's syndrome son named Jason. I saw his name on the register at the Sunford Home when I went to check on Michael Stoner. The name struck me then because he had a whole wing to himself."

Mark pushed "play" again and the frames flicked by, not catching the youth again but picking up the two huge body guards who stepped forward to lead the young congressman to the Biltmore entry.

"And those are the two sonsabitches who came to get him today," Mark said with an eagerness that showed that things were becoming clear for him.

"I think we're onto something here, kid. And it isn't over," Mark said as he turned and stared at Laura.

CHAPTER 23

Mark and Laura worked late into the evening reviewing the tape several more times and then completing a thorough review of the box's remaining contents. They ate in again, ordering a hardy room service meal as the last expense on the D.C. police force's tab. The prime rib, baked potatoes, and desert made up for the near full day of involuntary fasting and junk food.

The box contained very little that might help Mark gain a greater understanding of the mystery that he had come to D.C. to help solve. Nor did the contents shed any more light on the mystery of Jason Sullivan and the bodyguards. So Mark kept his mind busy by throwing himself into a review of the contents to help Laura in her quest.

There were reams of notes by various writers who had covered different aspects of the story for the *Herald* over the years. Jimmy had not just gathered materials generated at the time of the attempt, he also provided Laura with relevant notes and information from other files created as much as five years later. Laura silently applauded Jimmy's initiative as she wondered how a man of such wonderful insight and intelligence could be satisfied burying himself in the basement archives of the *Herald*.

Most of the papers, notes, and photographs pointed to the same simple conclusions reached by most of the people who had followed the story as it originally unfolded. They described Albert Smith as a committed family man who was a pillar of his Rialto, California, community. He and his wife were devoted members of the local World Christian Church, a small strict Christian sect of which Albert Smith had been one of the founding members.

Interviews with neighbors, friends, and his two grown sons revealed that Al had been an unassuming and self-effacing man who gave of his time willingly to anyone who asked. He never spoke ill of anyone and always espoused peace and love of God. None of the people interviewed believed for one minute that Al even owned a gun, let alone used it to try to kill Aidan Sullivan. When the evidence from the video footage made it clear that Albert Smith was the assailant, Al's friends and neighbors simply stopped talking to reporters. Their shock was too great.

Notes from initial interviews with Al's wife, Martha, didn't shed much more light on the subject. She said that Al had spoken to her about dreams in which he'd seen that Aidan Sullivan was evil. Apparently he'd also said that God was telling him the young congressman should not be president and that he had to be stopped. Martha hadn't listened to her husband. She had been surprised that Al was suddenly so interested in national politics, but she never believed that his interest would lead him to such a terrible act.

By two o'clock, Laura was bushed. Her back ached and her eyes burned.

"I've had enough for the night," she said. "I don't know what it all means, but I can't think anymore. I'm going to bed."

She stood and stretched, working the kinks out of her back and legs while Mark continued to read, unmoved by her suggestion that they pack it in for the night. Instead, he concentrated intently on the sheets of paper in his hand.

"Listen to this," Mark said. "It's a freelance submission by Jake Laford. He sent it to the *Herald* about," Mark glanced at the top of the page and silently calculated, "eighteen months ago. It's entitled 'What Did Al Smith Know?'

"It says here that he found Martha Smith in an Amish community in Lancaster County, Pennsylvania. Did we know she was Amish?" Mark asked.

Laura crouched back down and nodded.

"I read something about it here but I didn't think it meant anything," she said.

"Well, Jake sure thought it did. He interviewed Martha at Al's family's home. Apparently, she went back after Al's death," Mark continued.

"You sound like you know this Jake," Laura pointed to the author's name.

"I did. He was a constitutional law professor at USC."

"Was?"

"Yeah. He's dead."

Laura sat back on her haunches.

"What happened?"

"They called it a drive-by shooting. It happened about two weeks ago, in California. While you were at your parents'."

"You don't think it was a drive-by?"

"That's how it looked. But there were too many things that didn't fit. Wrong part of town and too specific a target. It sounded like a hit of some sort, to me. LAPD wasn't looking at it that way."

"If he was a con-law professor, why was he writing an article about Al Smith?"

"He was shot while working on a weekly throwaway newspaper devoted to one thing." Mark hesitated and stared at Laura. "He was obsessed with stopping Aidan Sullivan's move to a third term."

"Are you saying he was killed because of that?"

"I don't know. But if all this craziness that we've both been seeing is real, it could definitely follow that they were afraid of him and they killed him. He was gaining a pretty strong following in California . . . Aidan Sullivan's home state . . . essential to his bid."

"What did Al have to do with this?"

"It looks like Jake was on his kick even before it became widely known that the president's people would move to abolish the presidential term limits. He always read those boring congressional records and he must have picked something up there."

Mark glanced down at the article again and scanned it quickly.

"Here, in his opening paragraph, he explains it." Mark then read from part of the opening, "'Was Albert Smith a lunatic who ran off to kill a presidential candidate simply to satisfy some psychopathic hunger? Or did he know something about Aidan Sullivan that no one else did? Was he really trying to save us all?'"

"So what did he learn?" Laura asked.

"Unfortunately, it's not really too clear. That's probably why the *Herald* didn't print it." Mark shook his head as he read on. "He seems to be taking the position Al knew Aidan Sullivan was a megalomaniac bent on world domination for his own personal interests." He read further with a frown on his face. "It just isn't clear, Laura. He goes into the constitutional arguments relating to term limits. He hints that Al Smith really did have some kind of spiritual premonition that should not be taken lightly. It's not well written."

Mark put the pages down with a frown.

"Maybe we should go see . . . Missus. . . Schmidt, is it now?" Laura asked.

"Apparently, she changed it back to Al's real German name when she went back to his family," said Mark.

"Can you come with me?" Laura asked hopefully.

Mark wanted to follow up on his own mystery. He had planned to spend the next day in the library, checking on some ideas he'd had.

"I have to do some things tomorrow. We can go Friday, though. I think it's only a couple of hours away."

"Thanks, Mark," Laura said, relieved.

Mark offered the bed to Laura for the night. Laura declined saying she was comfortable on the sleeper.

As Laura drifted off to sleep, she thought about how she was beginning to like Mark Tucker. He had selflessly agreed to help her in what looked like it was becoming a hopelessly dangerous adventure. She wondered what might have happened had they found themselves together under different circumstances.

CHAPTER 24

Zac Morgan sat in his Washington, D.C. office waiting patiently for the arrival of the final two of eighteen senators that he and his aides had called to the special meeting in his conference room.

Sheila Blackburn had done well with the Seattle newspapers and the other major Washington state papers. Although the president hadn't actually said he was God, the headlines read that he had. It raised a tremendous furor in Morgan's home state similar to the time John Lennon had nonchalantly said the "Beatles were bigger than Jesus Christ," in the late 1960s. At that time, the heartland of America erupted in rebellion against the English group whose influence had so swiftly swept across America. People burned records and challenged the band at every stop, until the wayward Beatle was forced to apologize and say he didn't mean it the way it had sounded. But overnight the public's attitude changed toward its former idols. No longer were they the untarnished gods of an entire cultural and societal revolution. They were suddenly just rebellious rock and rollers at the top of a much smaller music hill.

Zac Morgan hoped for a similar response to Aidan Sullivan's faux pas. So far, in Washington state, it was working. The movement was started, but it would take a substantial effort to move it beyond Washington state. As the senator had learned from his other aide, Seth Jacobs, virtually no one else had heard it the way Senator Morgan had. They'd all been mesmerized by the young president's rhetoric and by his masterful handling of the unruly crowd. That's why this morning's meeting was so important. Although he only had fourteen states represented, he would have to get them all fired up to follow his home state's lead.

A knock at the senator's door was followed by the entry of his top aide and good friend Gordon Mason.

"Everyone's here, Zac. They're ready for us," said Mason.

"Thanks, Gordy. I hope *we're* ready." He paused and smiled as he stood up. "I'll be right there."

Mason nodded and closed the door as the senator took several deep breaths. This would be his most important play. He truly believed it was the only way to save his country.

Bret Cummings read all of the Washington state papers. He understood clearly where Senator Morgan was going and the impact the old senator could have on an audience. Although Morgan wasn't the speaker the president was, he did have a certain charisma. Bret also knew which senators had been called to the Zac Morgan meeting. Most of them were from states Bret had not been counting on as part of his nine. One, however, was the junior senator from Nebraska, which was one of the nine. Two others were from Alabama and Pennsylvania, two states Bret had already counted among the original twenty-five in the president's stable on the term limits issue.

Bret ordered his own media people to get to work in every state other than Washington. He had to diffuse the impact of the storm Zac Morgan was brewing.

The chief of staff also had a larger concern. The president's son had been arrested in conjunction with the D.C. Ripper murders. His sources told him that the media had not gotten hold of the story. The murder itself wasn't reported until the afternoon editions of the daily papers, and Jason had been under wraps by the time the stories were released. The Washington police department was ordered to keep a lid on the story and say only that an investigation was still pending and that the feds had stepped in. The White House now had enough influence over both the *Herald* and the

Post to keep them from nosing around. Bret Cummings was still concerned, however. That damn Commander Escobar was up in arms about the transfer of jurisdiction. Then there was that professor from California. Escobar had made it clear that the professor wouldn't quit on this one, no matter what.

Laura and Mark slept in the next morning. When Laura finally did wake at nine-fifteen, she did so with a start. She would have to hurry if she was going to get to the funeral.

Since she hadn't thought clearly when she'd stuffed things into her bag, she had no dark-colored garments. The only thing she had that was even remotely appropriate was a charcoal gray business suit that had somehow found it's way into the duffel bag. She requested an iron from room service to take out as many of the awkward creases as she could. Finally, when she was reasonably satisfied, Laura yelled into the bathroom to Mark that she was leaving.

The drive to Park Lawn Cemetery took about thirty minutes. Traffic was light at mid-morning with most people already ensconced in their offices for the day. The prior day's white clouds had turned gray and were threatening rain. It didn't bother Laura, however. She had become accustomed to D.C.'s spring rains and actually welcomed them. Where early summer by the beach in Southern California always brought a dreary overcast that sometimes didn't lift for weeks in May and June, the east coast's spring storm clouds had character. They would float or roll in, depending on the intensity of the downpour they presaged, drop their allotment and run off leaving blue sky and hot sun glistening off the wet world of earth, shrubs, grass, and concrete.

These clouds foretold a light cleansing rain. She only hoped it wouldn't interrupt the funeral services.

The Chapel of Our Savior was crowded with family and close friends of Bill and Nell McDonough. The services started at eleven o'clock and were presided over by the Protestant minister of the church Nell had frequented. He spoke eloquently but in general terms of death and the journey to God's kingdom, upon which Bill and Nell had embarked.

Bill, Jr. and Anna, the son and daughter of the McDonough's, stood before the assemblage barely able to contain their grief. Despite Bill's devotion to his work, it was clear he was also a well-loved father. When Ned McDonough stood to speak some final words about his brother and sister-in-law, the resemblance to his younger brother was apparent. The two of them could be mistaken for twins.

Although she fought back tears throughout the entire service, Laura was unable to contain herself while Ned spoke. As she watched Bill's look alike speaking about the loving devotion of the two for each other, their families, and their coworkers, Laura's own loss was firmly driven home. Despite his oft-times tough, hard-driving exterior, Bill was one of the least personally ambitious men Laura had ever met. His intensity was not for the benefit of his own pocketbook but rather for the loyalty to his employers, his employees, and most of all to the public, which looked to the *Herald* for a clear and unbiased picture of the world.

Laura had fine-tuned her craft under Bill McDonough's tutelage, but she had never truly understood Bill's advice to write with soul. She presumed that was exactly what she had done because her writing was good. Good enough, in fact, to win many of journalism's top awards. Yet Bill was never completely satisfied. He always praised her work as good reporting, but knew she did it for only one reason . . . the notoriety and praise that would one day bring her a Pulitzer and the financial rewards that would follow.

Even with Laura's fateful stories about Aidan Sullivan, Bill had questioned her motives. When she'd first approached him with news of the meeting at Murphy's Mill, expecting praise for uncovering such a meaty story, Bill eyed her coldly.

"Why do you want this one, Laura?" he'd asked.

"Because it's news, Bill. It's big news," she remembered saying triumphantly.

It was only now that Laura was realizing her real motives. None of them had anything to do with news or information or any altruistic purpose at all. She'd sought the stories with the greatest potential for giving her career advancement and financial independence. As a result, she'd given little thought to the potential impact of her words or, for that matter, to their actual truth. She was such a good writer that she could always use the words necessary to make an untruth sound true without jeopardizing her all-important personal reputation. It wasn't until two and a half weeks ago that it all finally caught up with her.

She cried with the rest of the mourners knowing deep down her misplaced commitment had led to this sad day. Bill tried to teach her. Even her father and her uncle had spoken to her about the need to use her gifts for the good of all people. Yet until this very moment when she listened to Ned McDonough's moving eulogy, it had never been clear. She only hoped, through her tears, that her realization, which came too late for Bill and Nell McDonough, would not be too late for her.

At the gravesite, Laura stood to the rear of the group of black-clad mourners. She was surprised that so few people from the *Herald* had showed up. Those that did acknowledged Laura with a sad smile and nod, and she again felt the guilt of responsibility. Only Jimmy Reese, wearing a threadbare black suit, even bothered to come up and stand with her. They stood together without words, feeling the pain of their loss.

Later, as the crowd of mourners dispersed and walked slowly back to their cars for the trip back to Bill and Nell's home where the family had prepared a farewell party, Ned McDonough stayed at the gravesite. He stood, head bowed, praying. At the end of his prayer, he leaned forward slowly and placed a crucifix atop the casket.

Laura and Jimmy approached him. "Mister McDonough," Laura called respectfully.

Ned turned and stared at her. His eyes were red and the skin around them was puffy. Suddenly, as if he recognized her, he smiled warmly and extended a hand to Laura.

"Miz Miller. Thank you for coming. Bill and Nell would appreciate it."

Laura was surprised at Ned's warmth at a time of such obvious intense personal tragedy.

"I just wanted to thank you, Ned," she stammered, "for such a marvelous eulogy. They were wonderful people." Laura strained to hold back the tears.

Ned nodded.

"I felt badly after our last conversation," he said to Laura. "I shouldn't have cut you off so quickly. I wasn't thinking clearly."

"Please Ned . . . don't apologize. It was callous of me to even call and ask for such nonsense."

"I searched the house for the box of notes and things you wanted. I found nothing. I'm terribly sorry."

Laura nodded slowly, not surprised that her things had disappeared. She was becoming accustomed to this game in which she found herself inadvertently involved.

"Will you come to the house, Miz Miller?" asked Ned.

"Oh, no. I'm sorry, Ned. I can't. I . . ." tears came to her eyes again. "I can't come by."

Ned nodded slowly and he took her hand. "Bill and Nell are safe now. Be at peace, Miz Miller." He walked past her toward a waiting limousine where his own wife sat waiting. Laura stared after him, wondering at his strength as she and Jimmy turned to their respective cars down the hill.

"You okay?" asked Jimmy.

"Sure. How about you?"

"Mister McDonough was a good man. I never knew his wife real well. I only saw her at some Christmas parties, but I'm going to miss him."

"Me too, Jimmy."

They walked in silence for several seconds, each immersed in his or her own thoughts. Finally Jimmy spoke again. "Did you see the tape?"

Laura glanced down at the little man. "I saw it, Jimmy. It took me about a dozen times but I think I saw what you meant." She stopped at her car and turned to Jimmy. "He knew it was coming."

Jimmy smiled. "I knew you'd see it, Laura. I knew it. Somehow ol' Aidan Sullivan knew Albert Smith was there. He knew what was going to happen."

"Do you have any ideas?" asked Laura.

"You're the investigator, Laura," Jimmy said with a smile. "What are you going to do?"

Laura stared at him, unsure whether to tell him, not because she was concerned about Jimmy's loyalty or whether he would consciously tell anyone, but because she feared for Jimmy if someone tried to use force on him. Laura's brain was still having trouble accepting a real world in which she was a potential victim. Yet the events of the past weeks made her wary. As Laura's thoughts wandered, Jimmy began to smile.

"You know what I'm going to do don't you, Jimmy?" she asked.

"I got a hunch."

"That's why you put the Laford article in the package."

"I think it's a good place to start," he said, grinning broadly.

Laura was glad she didn't have to actually utter the words. Jimmy knew that she would go to see Martha Schmidt. Because she didn't have to say it, however, she could content herself with the belief that he didn't actually know. If he was ever questioned, no matter how intensely or painfully, he only had a hunch, no actual knowledge.

She hugged Jimmy and thanked him again for his help before she got into her car and started the slow drive out of the cemetery.

It wasn't until Laura was outside the cemetery grounds and heading back to the hotel that she noticed the nondescript charcoal-colored car behind her.

The rain started, light and intermittent at first, when she turned out of the main exit. She didn't switch on her wipers for several minutes until enough water had built up on the windshield to wash away the overnight parking dust. It was when she looked absently in her rearview mirror, however, to see what impact the rain was having on the convertible top back window that she first noticed the car following her.

She'd seen it exit the cemetery grounds after her, but she'd paid no attention. Since the exit, Laura had already made several turns to avoid the traffic of late lunches. That's why she was surprised that the same charcoal car was behind her. It would be one hell of a coincidence if the driver had been thinking exactly what she thought.

As Laura approached a new corner, she lifted the arm of her turn signal so the green arrow on her dash blinked to the right. Her car moved into the right lane and began to slow for a right turn. The charcoal car moved to the right with her. She suddenly stepped on the gas as she reached the next corner, causing her car to jump out in front of a car to the left. She proceeded straight ahead. The charcoal car sped up, swerved to the left to gain Laura's lane again, swerved back to avoid a collision, then finally merged left three cars behind her.

The driver of the charcoal car wasn't even being coy about following her. Laura thought that was supposed to be part of the game. The follower was supposed to make it look like he wasn't following. It was suddenly obvious that this guy was trying to pull himself back into the spot behind Laura and he didn't care who knew.

As Laura's car pulled out of the cemetery, Jimmy's car, an ancient Volkswagen Vanagon, wouldn't start. He'd been having battery problems for a couple of days. He hadn't had time to get a new battery, so he tried to park on hills. Jimmy loved the van and would never consider a new vehicle despite its 200,000 miles. It was marked in several places with gray primer where Jimmy had mended dings, nicks, rust spots, and dents. He'd painted the rest of the van psychedelic colors and earthy slogans reminiscent of the hippy days of the 1960s and early 1970s.

Jimmy shifted into first, lifted his right foot off the brake while his left rested on the depressed clutch, and the van began to roll. Slowly, at first, it gradually gathered sufficient speed for Jimmy to lift his foot off the clutch. When he did so, the van jerked, coughed, and suddenly sputtered to life. Jimmy quickly stepped on the gas and the van stopped coughing and began rolling smoothly toward the exit.

When Laura's car stopped at the cemetery exit, Jimmy noticed a late-model charcoal-colored Chevrolet pull in behind her. He rolled to a stop as the Chevy cleared the driveway and turned right onto the highway. The license plate clearly indicated it was a government car. Jimmy maneuvered his van behind it and joined the parade.

Traffic was heavy and slow as the rain suddenly came down harder.

By the third red light, there was only one car separating the charcoal car from Laura's. At one point, as the charcoal car swerved around another vehicle by venturing into oncoming traffic, Laura saw its occupants. She didn't have a clear view, but it was enough to know that there were two men in dark suits following her.

In the past, Laura may have succumbed to her initial panic and lost total control, but the events of recent days had taught her how to reach into her mind and direct it away from that panic. She no longer permitted her brain to fight with itself, on the one hand arguing that none of this could possibly be happening to her, while on the other hand screaming to run and hide because it truly was happening. She didn't even question the fact she was being followed. Although she still had no idea why, she accepted it. It was now up to her to lose the tail.

Laura's immediate thought was a ploy similar to the one she'd used on the Hermosa Beach Strand while riding her bike. She searched the lanes ahead for any openings into which she could slide and put some distance between her vehicle and that of her pursuers. Unlike the Strand, however, she found no openings. Nor did she find any pattern of breaks of any kind in the traffic.

The rain fell much harder than Laura had expected when she first noticed the day's clouds. The sun filtered through clouds up ahead promising that the downpour would be short-lived. While it continued to fall, however, drivers were cautious and Laura could do nothing to gain any advantage.

In her rearview mirror, she watched the charcoal car weave back and forth in its lane behind a Jeep that was crawling behind Laura. Up ahead, the traffic light turned yellow and the two vehicles in front of Laura sped through, the second one on red, making him last in line at the next red light.

As cross-traffic began to move, Laura suddenly realized what she had to do. She berated herself for not thinking of it sooner. She hoped she wasn't too late. The cross-traffic was lighter than that heading in Laura's direction. She searched for an opening and even though she wasn't in the right turn lane, took the first one that looked reasonably safe.

Her Shadow darted into the opening behind a Ford pickup and a slower moving Nissan. Her car swerved and slid, causing other drivers to stand on their horns and scream epithets as arms shot out windows and offered Laura their expected advice.

She fought the swerve by backing off her accelerator and then immediately hitting it again as she turned into it. Her car suddenly righted itself and gained too quickly on the Ford. Laura shifted her right foot to the brake pedal and pushed hard, released quickly and pushed again until she slowed almost to a halt behind the Ford.

Laura's heart was pummeling the inside of her chest and her arms were shaking from the tight grip she held on the steering wheel. She glanced back to see the intersection light turn yellow and she realized her pursuers would soon be on her tail again.

The pickup began to roll faster and Laura looked quickly to the left. She squirted into another tiny opening and was again greeted by horns and angry shouts. That maneuver had put her past the pickup. Her car moved faster now and she had a better view of the road ahead, unobstructed by the cab of the pickup. Two car lengths ahead she saw an opening in front of a slow-moving yellow car. She pressed the vehicle in front of her by leaning forward and riding dangerously close. Slowly the strategy began to work and she soon found herself astride the small opening. She moved in quickly and then immediately turned right at the first corner onto a street with virtually no traffic. She could now move freely through the back streets to the safety of the Hyatt Hotel, hopefully leaving her pursuers behind.

★   ★   ★

Jimmy was scared for Laura as he craned his neck to watch her daring maneuver. He held his breath and finally smiled when her car reached equilibrium without hitting the Ford pickup.

"She's got balls," he said approvingly.

The occupants of the charcoal Chevrolet had also witnessed her daring move. The vehicle's passenger was reaching out the window and gesticulating to the driver in the car next to it. The adjacent driver apparently didn't see the gestures, at first, because he too was watching Laura's crazy adventure. Finally, however, he rolled his window down slightly.

The traffic light turned green and the Chevy jerked to the right with the passenger still gesturing wildly. The driver of the adjacent car simply smiled, rolled up his window, and flipped the charcoal car's passenger a gesture of his own. He then stuck close to the bumper of the vehicle in front of him.

The driver of the charcoal car grew impatient and moved further into the right lane, determined to make the lane change. Jimmy stared, frantic for a plan to assist Laura's escape.

In his younger days, Jimmy had used vehicles in various forms of protest. He remembered taking part in a protest against the Vietnam War when he was a graduate student at UC Santa Barbara in the late 1960s. He'd used his hippie van to block a lane of Highway 101.

He now used his van as a battering ram.

Without a second thought, Jimmy Reese stepped on his accelerator and drove his Vanagon into the right back quarter panel of the charcoal car. Although the impact was not great, the slick streets and the front vehicle's awkward position made the backend whip forward so that the front end swung backwards into an oncoming car in the adjacent lane. That collision pushed the front of the charcoal car forward again, and it spun around completely, barely missing several other vehicles that swerved and came to quick stops.

Jimmy sat in his psychedelic van, knowing he'd done right. He smiled as the driver and passenger of the charcoal car jumped out of their vehicle and stared angrily in the direction Laura had escaped.

★ ★ ★

CHAPTER 25

Before leaving the hotel that morning, Mark Tucker had made arrangements for a rental car. He'd also called Commander Escobar to see if there had been any new developments.

"Aren't you gone yet?" Escobar was surly.

"I'm staying over for a few days . . . on my own nickel," Mark was quick to add.

Escobar hesitated before he finally smiled and said, "This wouldn't have anything to do with a certain woman, would it?"

"Nah," dead panned Mark.

"Right, Professor. So what do you need from me?" asked Escobar.

"Do you know who the guy was?"

"What guy?"

"The guy we picked up yesterday."

"No. You know that. The feds picked him and his prints up before we could track his identity down," Escobar's moment of friendliness ended quickly at the mention of the abruptly terminated investigation.

"I know who he is."

"Well spill it, Professor. What are you waiting for?" Escobar's interest was piqued.

"It's delicate. That's why the feds stepped in. He's Jason Sullivan, the son of President Aidan Sullivan."

Commander Escobar was silent. His mind raced. "No shit?" he finally whispered.

"The two gorillas that picked him up are the president's body guards."

"How do you know all this?" asked Escobar.

"It's a long story. I'll tell you later. Just believe me for now."

"You know, I remember he has a son. He always hid him away. Geez, no wonder the feds are involved. They're probably going to bury that kid."

"Look, commander, I may need your help over the next few days."

"For what? We're off the case. It's just lucky they were all hookers. Otherwise the press would be all over it."

"I'm going to be looking into a few more things. Can you help me if I need it?"

"Look, Professor, let it lie. The feds have it and they obviously don't want anyone to know that the president's son is the killer."

"I don't think he's the killer," Mark said slowly.

"What're you talking about?"

"It doesn't work. If he was the killer, he committed the first murder when he was eleven or twelve years old. Although it's possible that one could have such a hatred at that age, it's not likely, especially with Down's children. They're passive people. I don't think we've seen the end of the Ripper killings."

"What're you going to need? We can't officially be involved." Escobar's voice had regained some of its strength. He was excited that Mark would stay with the investigation because he too felt it wasn't over.

"I don't know yet. I need to know that I can call on you."

Escobar hesitated. Mark held his breath knowing both he and Laura would need the commander's assistance if they were to have any hope of putting to the test whatever their investigations unearthed.

"I'll be here," Escobar finally answered. "You'd better be careful, though. If someone up top is trying to hide something, they'll be damn uncompromising about it."

"Thanks." Mark was relieved. "Oh, one thing. Have you heard anything from any other jurisdictions? Any similar murders?"

"Yeah. As a matter of fact, I've got two reports." He paused as he searched his desk. "Here they are. Let's see. This first one talks about one murder in Denver . . . three years ago."

"Just one?" asked Mark.

"That's what it says here."

"What month?"

"Says it happened in . . . April."

"Same time as the D.C. killings."

"The other report describes two more murders." He paused to read. "Well, if these are related, they support your position on the president's son. He would have been about five or six years old. These happened seventeen years ago in a place called Eureka, California."

Mark knew the city to be a small one along the northern coast of California, north of San Francisco.

"Were they hookers?"

"Doesn't say."

"Can you follow up on them for me? Check on other body marks. Oh, and one last thing. Can you get me the police records relating to the death of Aidan Sullivan's wife? I believe it was somewhere in California, about twenty years ago?"

"What do you need that for?" asked Escobar.

"I don't know yet," Mark paused and smiled into the phone. "I think you police guys would call it a hunch."

"I'll check it for you. Stay in touch, Professor."

The Martin Luther King Jr. Memorial Library at the end of "G" Street was a huge edifice with voluminous resources. Mark Tucker loved libraries and had ever since his youth, when he first learned the wonders of fantasy travel through adventures written by Jules Verne, Mark Twain, and J.R.R. Tolkein. In his college and law school days, the marvelous university libraries had become the friend from whose indices he'd learned history and discovered the thrill of reading actual accounts of events at the times they occurred.

Mark spent the day reviewing newspaper accounts of the D.C. Ripper murders. He intended to test a theory he'd finally fallen upon the previous evening. After watching the video with Laura and seeing Jason Sullivan, Mark's mind had again wandered to the original Ripper killings in Whitechapel, London. The similarities between the century and a half old murders and their modern American counterparts seemed to be growing.

The most obvious similarities were the brutal killings of prostitutes in the tawdry slums of the respective big cities. The killers in Whitechapel and D.C.'s redlight district had each picked victims who were part of a world in which murders and other violent crime were so commonplace that in many cases they either went unreported or found themselves relegated to back pages of the newspapers that did report them. Of so little consequence were the victims in both cases, that it took several killings to generate enough political interest to even investigate them beyond the perfunctory review given by the responding homicide detectives.

As for the manner in which the killings were performed, it was as if the current Ripper had followed the old Ripper's lead. The women were all slashed and ripped in the abdomen by a precision craftsman. Some even suspected a crazed surgeon in the Whitechapel killings. It was in the potential suspects, however, that Mark Tucker found the most interesting similarities.

One writer, a Dr. Thomas Stowell, wrote an article entitled "A Solution to the Jack The Ripper Mystery." It had been published in *Criminologist* magazine. In his article, Dr. Stowell posited that the Whitechapel murders were committed by His Royal Highness, Prince Albert Victor ("Eddy") Duke of Clarence. Apparently Eddy was the eldest son of the future King Edward VII of England. Dr. Stowell relied heavily on the notes of Sir William Gull, Physician Extraordinary to Queen Victoria at the time of the Ripper killings. Dr. Stowell gleaned from Gull's notes and other information, that Eddy was a homosexual who had contracted syphilis. The disease had driven Eddy crazy. According to Stowell, it was during this time that Eddy committed the murders, before the Royal Family could lock him away.

242

★ CHAPTER 25 ★

Stowell's theories had caused a mild sensation among Ripper enthusiasts. Mark had read it as part of his own study of the serial mind. The theory had never received wide support, however, as subsequent commentators found numerous holes in Dr. Stowell's reasoning.

Mark thought of Stowell's theories after watching the tape, simply because a member of the current "royal family" was the main suspect in the present-day Ripper killings. It was this simple comparison that led him to consider a possible pattern.

The fifteen murders, now sixteen, as a result of the one for which Jason Sullivan was arrested, had never shown a clear pattern. They occurred in batches separated by years of seeming inactivity on the part of the killer. Mark originally believed that the suddenness with which the murders would occur could only be attributed to some event that set off the anger of the killer. He decided to look at events on a world scale. When he considered world events, however, he dreaded the search because the spectrum was so wide. The killer could be anyone from an Arab terrorist enraged by specific events in his homeland, to any blue- or white-collar worker who reacted to events that somehow carried special meaning for him.

A window had opened when Mark learned who the suspect really was. It was through that opening that he was peering as he read the *Washington Post* and *Herald* dated in January through March, six years earlier. He directed his review to events that would affect Aidan Sullivan and his royal family of advisers, his son, and his hangers-on. Although Mark didn't believe Jason was the killer, he had a hunch he wanted to follow up on.

The lead story on January 10, six years earlier, in both the *Herald* and the *Post* related the decision of the OPEC countries to immediately reduce oil production and raise prices around the world. It was a surprise announcement, effectively ending diplomatic attempts by the still-new President Sullivan and the European community. The first Ripper murder in D.C. occurred two nights later. Yet only the *Herald's* January 13 morning edition mentioned it. The paper ran a clipped report on the last page of its Metro Section.

Over the next two months, during which the other three murders occurred, the war of words with the Arab leaders escalated. Aidan Sullivan fought with Congress over his desire to use force and the Arab leaders scoffed at the barbarian world beyond their borders. Editorial writers in both papers captured the mood of many as they wrote about the president's inability to do anything to prevent the back-breaking impact of the embargo. One caricature even showed the president ducking behind a placard reading "America First," while jewel festooned Sheiks threw syringes filled with oil at him. The caption read "Stand by me and I'll protect you."

The morning of the third murder was the start of the day upon which the president's ultimatum to the Arabs ended. They were to either come around and lower prices by that day or they would feel the wrath of American might. By the end of business that day, the only thing clear was that the president had virtually no support in Congress to back up his threat. No one wanted to argue that force was proper to prevent the Arab action. Force was only proper to protect people in immediate peril or to remove invaders from a strategic country as in the Iraq War of 1991. The president was stuck in his first major test in office.

The next day, President Sullivan unilaterally ordered the pre-emptive military strike that would come to define his presidency. His forces in the gulf region attacked, without congressional approval and the president spent the next two days fighting members of Congress and reporters. At the end of that second day, the fourth murder had occurred.

Although the Arab conflagration was receiving top billing, the murder was front-page news in both papers. They reported there had been three similar murders and an investigation was underway.

The murders suddenly stopped.

On the afternoon after the fourth murder, American smart bombs took out the palace of the Saudi Arabian leader and he was killed. One after another, reports of American successes flowed in and by the end of the day, members of Congress were silently applauding the president's action. The deaths of thousands of innocents for the sole purpose of reducing oil prices didn't seem to phase any of them because they could suddenly see the benefit of Arab oil controlled by the United States. Suddenly the president was a hero. Within two weeks the Arab leaders threw up their hands in supplication.

The scenario was similar three years later with the Japan crisis. After weeks of nail biting and three more gruesome murders, the might of America won out again.

By the time Mark had read the *Los Angeles Times* and *Sacramento Union* accounts of the California murders eight and ten years ago, he was convinced he was on to something. The then California state congressman, Aidan Sullivan, had faced similar crises at the exact times of the murders. These crises had ultimately resulted in dramatic leaps forward for the young politician. In each case, however, he dealt with intense pressure and strain to his political and personal fortunes before coming out, almost miraculously, on top.

It didn't seem possible in the real world, but if Mark's theory was correct, the heinous murders were being committed as a type of tension release by the most powerful man in the world. The crazy thing was that if his position had any merit, it was immediately after each string of killings that the killer experienced wild success and surges in renown. It was as if some other worldly force of evil bestowed such enormous success only after its hunger for death was sated.

Mark had nothing with which to determine if similar circumstances surrounded the Denver murder or the even more distant Eureka murders. He would have to wait for Commander Escobar's additional information. For now, however, he proceeded to the Washington papers of the past two months.

In spite of the fact that there was no clearly defined world event, Mark was able to find what he believed were events of significant importance to the president and his future.

The third term issue to which Jake Laford had devoted, and perhaps lost, his life was vital to the dreams of a president who was beginning to look like a man of unbound ambition. For over two months that story had dominated the headlines followed closely by the president's continued jousting with the Germans. Mark wondered if Germany would be Aidan Sullivan's next Japan.

Although the pressure from Congress and the press was not nearly as great as during the previous events, it was clear that the term limit issue and the Germans could be construed by the president as yet additional defining moments in his career. His opposition, during these two crises, was much more subtle, led by powerful foes.

On the term issue, Washington Senator Zac Morgan was a major thorn in the president's side. This day's *Post* reported Morgan had held a special meeting of republican senators on the issue. The senator was quoted, after the meeting, as saying, "I don't believe folks'll take kindly to a president when he likens himself to God Almighty." The people of Morgan's state had started their own movement to stop the "man who would be God."

With Germany, frictions had smoldered for years, ever since the United States again began to emerge as the dominant world power. It was two months ago, just two days before the first of the recent murders, that the German chancellor made it clear he intended to pull the European community away from America's feet and bring it back to its own power base.

Although both things occupying the president's mind could certainly have created the same concerns that the president may have felt during his other two crises, neither of these seemed far enough advanced nor, for that matter, did there appear to be much concern from the White House. The term limits issue seemed to be moving in the right direction, and it appeared that the German problem was under control.

Mark was confused again. As shocking as it might be to consider the president of the United States a suspect in a string of bloody murders, his research of the past killings could certainly have pointed to a basis for such a conclusion. It all seemed to unravel with his research of events surrounding the most recent murders. Although the issues were vital to the president, the fact that they seemed under control dictated against that conclusion.

The only other thing Mark had found was the attack by Laura Miller in the *Herald* and the furor surrounding it. But even that seemed under control from the White House's perspective. If Laura was to be believed, however, someone apparently didn't think it was under control. The answer had to lay with Laura.

★ ★ ★

That same day Senator Morgan's press corps, made up of his top aides and volunteer supporters from his home state, were working furiously to disseminate press releases and clipped stories to as many newspapers and radio and television stations as they could.

The previous day's meeting with his republican Senate cohorts had gone reasonably well. They voted unanimously though not jubilantly to support the senior senator's proposal for stopping Aidan Sullivan. Although all eighteen senators expressed the standard party desire to have the incumbent's term end in favor of a wide-open presidential election in which the Republicans might have a chance of again attaining the top seat in the land, several harbored silent reservations. They liked the way things were going for them. Their respective states were prospering economically, some for the first time in decades. Their constituents were content to let things lie. Sure, violent crime had risen to all-time highs in most American communities, but police, National Guard, and military units had begun to take tight control of communities to protect the "better" people, who also happened to be the voters. These senators, who balked inside, were really quite happy with the state of the country and their positions. They were all getting rich with a government that actually encouraged the backroom economic politics that made politicians wealthy.

Yet they knew their duty to their party. They voted to support Senator Morgan's plan. They would all continue to vote "no" on every vote relating to the abolition of term limits. They would continue to voice the party line opposing the democratic president's moves. They would even vote to encourage influential people in their communities to help spread the word Zac Morgan felt was so important. Deep down, however, they all felt there was no chance to stop Aidan Sullivan. And that was just fine.

Senator Morgan was happy with the unanimous vote. He had been around long enough, however, to recognize the vibrations of cautious dissent. He knew he didn't have total support. As with most politicians, the republican senators would sit on the fence, nod in agreement, voice support, and then fall whichever way the wind blew. It was, therefore, imperative that Morgan's efforts bore immediate fruit. If they did, the fence sitters would throw aside caution and join him to press harder for the defeat of the proposed constitutional amendment.

As it stood now only five of the eighteen senators were whole-heartedly behind Morgan. These were the oldest five, the ones who could sacrifice their political futures, which were limited anyway. These were also the five who carried the greatest national influence. They, like Senator Morgan, saw clearly the perils of unlimited terms, particularly with a megalomaniac like Aidan Sullivan.

"Forget about her, Aidan. We've got bigger concerns right now with Zac Morgan," cautioned Bret Cummings.

"Fuck Morgan," bellowed the president. "Those spineless bastards aren't going to follow him. I want this bitch."

The president stared hard at his chief of staff and at Charlie Gilbert who sat opposite him in the Oval Office. He couldn't get her off his mind. It was becoming an obsession. He knew with all his soul that she was the one who would bring him down unless he stopped her. He had seen it. He had recognized her in his dream. She didn't fully understand it yet, but he knew. He knew, for sure, the minute he'd probed her mind at the Washington Monument. She would try to destroy him.

"Aidan, please. This woman is nothing. She has no forum. She can't do anything. If we don't concentrate on Zac Morgan, we will be through before the term issue even gets to a vote of the people. He's trying to delay the process."

Bret suddenly stopped short. His head jerked back as if he'd been struck.

"Aidan," he pleaded breathlessly, "not now."

Cummings had no resistance at all. Years of control had torn down all his barriers. Whether of his own choosing or because of the constant probes, the president's chief of staff had long since given himself over to his leader. His mind was always open to be read and directed as the president desired. At most times, Cummings didn't mind. In fact, he welcomed the intrusions because it brought him closer to the man he adored. This time, however, he did not want to succumb. They had to act now to stop Zac Morgan or there would be no third term. He wished the president could see that the woman could not harm him now. But he could no longer speak. His mind was no longer his.

Aidan Sullivan got little pleasure as he focused his awesome powers. He could crush this creature whose mind he held so tightly. It had become so easy. Neither of the men, who sat before him, offered any resistance anymore. Both were unequivocally loyal and neither feared for himself. They were already his.

The president was angry enough to destroy them both now. Yet he needed them. He longed to meet the woman again. In a place where he could test her strength. A strength he hadn't seen in years. She had a power that he knew was growing everyday. He wanted her now before it matched his own.

Charlie Gilbert could feel the probe next to him. He sat quietly knowing, without fear, what the president could do on a whim. He accepted it, as had so many others who worshiped this president. The wrist graft of loyalty, which more of his supporters were wearing, was their public testimony of that commitment.

The chief of staff's body was limp. His mind lay open, brain tissue, tendons, veins, and other matter pealed aside to expose its core. Open for the taking.

Aidan Sullivan's anger filled the room. He was impatient. Slowly, however, he realized Bret Cummings was correct. His grip on the chief of staff's mind loosened and Bret's slack body twitched to life. As the president pulled away completely, Bret opened his eyes and stared dazedly at him.

The president pushed back into his chair and grew pensive. Cummings struggled to clear his mind. His head ached more and more after these episodes.

"Senator Morgan is becoming a problem," said the president calmly. He spoke as if nothing unusual had just occurred. "I want you to stay on top of it, Bret."

Cummings nodded slowly, as he struggled to fight off the last painful effects of the intrusion.

"You don't worry about the woman." He turned to Charlie Gilbert. "I want you to take this on yourself, Charlie. Find her and bring her to me alive."

Charlie Gilbert nodded and the president stared at him.

"Find her now!" he said.

CHAPTER 26

Mark and Laura were on the road by nine-thirty the next morning in Mark's rented car.

After Laura's escape the previous day, she had hidden herself in Mark's hotel room, afraid to venture out on her own. By the time Mark returned to the hotel, she had worked herself up to a fear that paralyzed her mind. She had no idea where to turn. Her life was in danger, yet no police officer would believe her. No person in any position of significance would understand. She could try to hide, of course, but how was that possible from the most invasive and highly structured intelligence force in the world? A force that was at her enemy's disposal.

It took Mark most of the evening to calm Laura's fears. After they finally were able to exchange stories, Mark explained that they had a hope. If either of their theories were supportable, Commander Escobar stood ready to help. In addition, he'd found another possible ally in Senator Zac Morgan, who was the one major voice of opposition to the president. If there was any truth to Mark's theories of presidential involvement in the D.C. Ripper murders, or if there was any provable truth to Laura's fears, Mark was certain they could call on the senator for his protection.

These revelations calmed Laura. She was able to concentrate on the visit to Martha Schmidt. Martha had to be a key.

They again reviewed Jake Laford's article, as well as other materials from the box given to her by Jimmy Reese. From these they determined that Martha was living on a farm with Albert's family, off Route 30 in western Lancaster County, Pennsylvania. It was Laura's suggestion that they take Mark's rented car rather than Laura's sports model, which was known by her enemy.

Traffic was light as they entered U.S. Route 1 heading out of Washington. Mark drove while Laura turned constantly from side to side, back to front to scan the faces of the people in all the vehicles that dared come within a car length of them. By the time they had made the transition to Interstate 95, Laura's neck and head ached, but she was able to relax, somewhat satisfied they had made it out of D.C. without pursuit. She sat back to enjoy the remaining two hours of their drive to Hebenville, Pennsylvania.

As miles of open fields of sunflowers began to roll by, Laura closed her eyes and sucked in the fresh warm air that poured over her through the open window. She began to feel a freedom that made her think maybe there really was a way to just hide . . . to run from her pursuers and find a remote community somewhere in the Appalachian backwoods. A place where no one would ever find her again. Just as suddenly, however, thoughts of family crept into her consciousness. If she ran she would never see the only people who loved her. Besides, she hadn't done anything wrong. She couldn't envision a life of looking over her shoulder and never seeing a friendly face. This was one she would have to carry through to the end.

"You okay?" asked Mark.

"Better," she opened her eyes and glanced at him before shaking her head. "I can't figure what he's so worried about."

"Maybe he's just after you for your looks," Mark said, making an attempt at levity.

"I doubt it." Laura smiled, again glad Mark was accompanying her through this craziness.

"Do you think he's really involved in the murders?" she asked.

"The facts sure support that conclusion. Of course, they could also support a hundred other conclusions including the possibility that his son is the murderer."

Laura nodded and stared out the window. "You know, if he really is after me, it can't be for something I've already done. There's got to be something he fears I'll do in the future."

"He could be out for revenge," Mark suggested.

"Possibly," she nodded. "But I don't see it, Mark. He's got more important things on his mind with the term limits and the German thing." She hesitated for a moment and then brightened, as if struck suddenly. "Unless I know something or learned something that I might reveal that could hurt his plans for a third term."

"Like what?"

"I don't know. Maybe Martha Schmidt knows. Isn't that why we're going to see her?"

"I'm not sure, Laura. At first I thought it was just a hunch of yours. Recently though, I've felt the need to see her, too. I hope we can find her."

Laura stared at Mark and smiled. She reached a hand out and touched his arm softly.

"Thanks Mark."

"For what?"

"Thanks for helping a crazy dame."

They both smiled and watched the Maryland countryside drift by.

Hebenville was a quaint country town of small shops along the Susquehanna River. Upon entering the town, Mark and Laura immediately noticed the contrast between the modern-day motor vehicles parked in front of business establishments and the black horse-drawn carriages of the Amish people of Lancaster County.

Laura's knowledge of the Amish was limited. Although she'd been intrigued by movies in her younger years which depicted the Amish as peace-loving simple folk, she'd never studied their ways or known anything more than what was fed to her through fictionalized accounts. As she now watched the real-life contradictions of the bucolic, old-country lifestyle in the modern world, she felt as if she had stepped into some surreal, paradoxical painting by Dalí.

Lancaster County is located in the southeastern part of Pennsylvania and is bordered to the south by the state of Maryland and to the west by the majestic Susquehanna River. It encompasses an area of pastoral beauty with the greatest concentration of farms in the state. Laura felt if Hebenville were any indication, the towns and cities interspersed between the acres of rich farmland were just as rustic and peaceful. A far cry from the dizzying life style of D.C.

As Mark drove slowly down Hebenville's Main Street, he and Laura watched the small groups of Amish men, women, and children dressed in their simple finery, doing their best to avoid the rude, gawking tourists who tried desperately to snap photographs.

"What a life," Laura thought with a mixture of envy and disgust. She wondered at the simple lives she envisioned, free of the stress and anxieties of the modern world. Yet they lived as exhibits in a freak show under constant surveillance by people who had little regard for human decency and discretion.

"Well, we're here. What do we do now?" Mark asked. "There's a gas station. Let's check the phone book."

Laura turned slowly. "I don't think they have phones. At least the movies I've seen indicate they don't."

Mark nodded slowly and continued scanning the streets for any clue or thought that might assist them. Finally, he stopped the car in front of the U.S. Post Office at the end of Main Street. "Maybe they'll be able to help us find her," he offered.

The building was a single-story brick structure with immaculate grounds and an oak-doored entry. Inside, the decor was simple with a work counter behind two glass doors that stood open and standard metal stamp machines and mail slots in the main mail room.

Laura nodded to a pretty young Amish woman and her young man. They smiled in return, bowed their heads in humble acknowledgment, and walked out of the building. The man wore black pants and coat over a simple white shirt clasped at the throat with hook and eye clasps rather than buttons. His beard was sparse and scraggly and his hair long, over his ears. He carried his black hat until he stepped out of the building. The young woman wore a royal blue dress that covered her from neck to ankles. Over the dress, she wore a slightly darker blue breast cloth, which was a triangular piece of cloth with the apex at the small of her back, the two long ends over her shoulders, crossed in front and attached around the waist to the apex with simple straight pins. From her waist hung an apron of the same material and color, while atop her head she wore a white rounded cap that covered her from the middle of the head and back and had two tails hanging lazily below the simple knot in back. The young woman's dark hair in front framed her plain beauty.

Laura caught herself staring a little too long. She clearly understood the tourist attraction of these simple folk.

At the counter stood a short, overweight man in his early sixties.

"Can I help you folks?" he asked cheerily.

Laura smiled and approached him, while Mark stood behind her and listened. They had previously decided that Laura would do the talking in the hopes that if there was any resistance, she, as an investigative journalist, might be better able to direct the conversation toward a satisfactory response.

"Yes, I hope so," she said. "We're looking for a woman. We were wondering if you or someone here might know where we can find her."

"I'm the only someone here, miss. If I can't help you, there's no one else," he responded with a smile.

"It's an Amish woman we're looking for."

"That explains why you came here. They don't have phones you know," he shook his head with another smile. "Them Amish are unusual folk. The way they don't take to the modern world. They don't like people asking about them much, either." The man eyed Laura and then looked behind her to Mark. The smile never left his face.

"Who you looking for?" he finally asked, seemingly satisfied that he could at least take the next step.

"Martha Schmidt."

The man smiled and shook his head again.

"Shoulda known that one," he said. "Quite a few people have wanted to talk to Martha since ol' Al tried to kill the president. She come back to get away from all the people and for awhile, anyway, they just followed her."

"Who's they?" asked Mark.

"Oh, the police, FBI, you know. And the press of course, like you folks, I reckon. You from the press?"

"I am . . ." started Laura and then she corrected herself, "was a reporter for the *Washington Herald*. We're not here for the paper though. Do you know where we can find her?"

The man nodded, "Sure I do. But I don't think I can tell you. You see, Martha's a good woman. She was hurt real bad when Al did what he did. Bringing it up will only hurt her more. I reckon I'd be doing Martha a favor if I didn't tell you where she lived."

"Mister . . ." Laura hesitated as she began to plead her case.

"Wiley. John Wiley," he answered self-assuredly.

"Mister Wiley, I understand your hesitation, but it's very important to us. We believe Martha's husband knew some things about the president that Martha may know. We need that information desperately."

"That's the same thing this other fella told me about three years ago. Real egghead-looking guy. He comes in and tells me that Al knew things that were important. He said he'd write about them and let the world know that Mister Sullivan wasn't such a great guy."

"Did you tell him where she lived? asked Mark.

"No, sir. Never did. I kinda liked the president then despite what ol' Al might have thought. Don't care for him all that much now because he's getting a little too big for himself, but then I didn't care much to see him brought down. Besides, Martha had asked me not to tell folks where she lived."

"She asked you?"

"Sure. Martha isn't like the rest of the Amish. She's been out among us regular folks and she knows that some of us are good people, too," Wiley finished pointedly.

"Was the man Jake Laford?" asked Mark.

"I don't remember. The name sounds familiar, but I'm not sure. I heard later, from Martha, that he found her after all. I never saw any story, though."

"We'll eventually find her just like Mister Laford did," said Mark trying to make it sound inevitable.

"I suppose. If you want it bad enough and you've got the time, which it appears you don't. Anyway, you won't find it out from me." Mr. Wiley was testy in response to Mark's attempt to force the issue.

Thoughts of reviewing voting records and other public information raced through Laura's mind. She didn't have the time.

"Mister Wiley, this is very important. You may think it strange for me to say this, but I believe it's a matter of life and death."

Wiley eyed her quizzically. He was surprised she appeared sincere.

"Since Martha knows you," Laura continued, "can I impose upon you to take her a note from me? If she will see me, she'll tell you and then you can direct me there."

"I don't get out her way too often," Wiley said half-heartedly.

"We'll make it worth your while Mister Wiley," Mark offered.

Wiley turned sharply on Mark. "Look, mister, that's the second time you've tried to push me. If you're talking about paying me to give up a friend, you're talking to the wrong man."

Mark backed off immediately as Mr. Wiley stared hard at him and then turned slowly back to Laura.

"Please, Mister Wiley," Laura pleaded.

The postman stared for several seconds and then nodded slowly as he again tried to judge the sincerity he saw in Laura's eyes.

"I'll do it for you Miss . . ." he started.

"Miller. Laura Miller."

"I'll go see Martha tonight, Miss Miller. But if I feel that you or your friend here are up to something like following me, I'll come right back and you'll be on your own."

"For what it's worth, you have my word that we will not leave this town, Mister Wiley. We'll stay here tonight and come to see you in the morning."

Wiley again eyed Laura and Mark, then nodded as he pointed to a space at the end of the counter. "You can write your note over there. I'll take it to Martha."

Laura and Mark stepped aside to let another customer approach the counter. Laura pulled a lined pad from her handbag and began writing.

"Mrs. Schmidt," the note started. "My friend and I have come here to discuss your husband's attempt on the life of President Aidan

Sullivan. We believe we are in danger. That it is somehow connected to what your husband may have known or suspected. We don't have any provable evidence to support our belief, but our fear is genuine and we feel strongly that you may be able to help us. We promise you we will not compromise you without your permission." Then as a thought about Amish spirituality struck her, she completed with, "In the name of Our Lord Jesus Christ, we beg you to see us for just a brief time."

Laura signed and printed her name and she had Mark do the same with his. They waited until a second customer left the counter before they handed the folded note to the postmaster.

"We really appreciate this, Mister Wiley. Can we come by in the morning?"

"Yes. Around ten o'clock," he nodded.

Laura and Mark spent the rest of the day walking through the town acting like tourists, gawking at the Amish and their horse-and-buggy mode of transportation. They were taken by the quaint beauty of Hebenville. Spring breezes carried the sun's warmth and the smells of jasmine to them as they tried to stay focused, but found themselves continuously wandering to days past, of the peace and nonresponsibility of springs in their youths.

They rented two rooms for the night at a colonial-style bed and breakfast nestled amidst budding cherry blossoms just off Main Street.

The next morning, Laura was more anxious than Mark had ever seen her. She didn't tell him that she'd had the dream again, but he could tell by the hollow, sunken look in her eyes that she hadn't slept well.

Laura could barely contain herself until ten o'clock when they were to again meet with John Wiley. She was outside at five-thirty when the sun rose in the morning and by the time Mark walked outside searching for her at eight-thirty, she had already circled the huge grounds of the bed and breakfast and the surrounding neighborhood twice. When Mark spotted her, Laura was resting on a park bench under a cherry tree. She stared absently, lost in thought.

"Good morning," Mark greeted her cheerily. "The lady of the manor has a sumptuous breakfast of Canadian bacon and eggs awaiting us." He bowed gallantly and she smiled slightly in spite of her melancholy.

Mark ate heartily, but Laura barely touched her food. She satisfied herself with a small glass of freshly squeezed orange juice and several cups of coffee.

They arrived at the post office at nine fifty-five and waited impatiently for Mr. Wiley's arrival. Although the building was open for mail deposits all day, the business office wasn't open until the postmaster wandered in. He did so punctually at 10:00.

Mr. Wiley noticed them as soon as he unlocked the door separating the business office from the mail room. He motioned them in.

"Were you able to see her, Mister Wiley?" asked Laura, barely able to mask her anxiety.

Wiley nodded slowly. He wasn't wearing the genial, self-assured smile he exhibited at their previous meeting.

"I did, Miss Miller. Damndest thing, though." He stared hard at Laura, as if he wasn't sure he should proceed. "Martha seemed to know you were coming. I expected her to say no. I kind of thought I was doing her a favor in warning her about you folks, so she could go off and hide."

"What did she say?" asked Laura.

"She wants to see you. She said she wants to put all of this behind her once and for all. She'll see you today."

Laura smiled at Mark, her first genuine smile that morning.

Mr. Wiley handed her a folded piece of paper.

"I wrote out directions for you. It's not difficult to find. Should take you about fifteen minutes."

She stared at the instructions and then looked back to Mr. Wiley. "Thank you, Mister Wiley."

"You go on, now. Martha's waiting for you." As Mark and Laura turned, he continued, "Martha's a good woman, Miss Miller. You be careful you don't do anything to hurt her."

They waved as they walked out of the building. Mr. Wiley followed them to the door and watched their car move north along Main Street towards the highway.

They were immediately out in the country again. U.S. Route 30 heading east was devoid of any significant traffic, so the drive was easy. They passed several miles of flat farmland. Because of the early spring, the rich dark soil was already evenly furrowed for the planting of potato, corn, oat seed, and tobacco seed. Few of the farms along Route 30 showed signs of workers in the fields, this Saturday morning. Where Laura and Mark did see field workers, they were not Amish. On the Amish farms, the only activity visible from the highway centered around the farmhouses and barns, far back on the land.

Mr. Wiley's crude map directed them to a Penn Road, off the main highway. It was a narrow two-lane road that worked its way north and south through the farming valley.

They traveled along the road for about a mile before they came upon another of the many roadside fruit and vegetable stands found in the Amish communities. The stand was a wooden stepped structure rising three levels above the ground. Each step offered a few fresh vegetables and fruits but was stacked primarily with jars filled with preserved fruits and vegetables that had not been consumed by the family during the winter. Next to the stand was a wooden mailbox in the shape of a house atop a white post. Hanging from the front of the mailbox was a sign that read "Schmidt."

A hand-printed sign above the fruit and vegetable stand read "Self-Service. Place money in basket. Thank you." An arrow pointed to a basket below the sign.

Mark turned the car onto the dirt roadway leading from Penn Road to the two-story farmhouse, a simple white wooden structure, perfectly kept and immaculate. It was surrounded by a colorful garden of sweet-smelling spring flowers, which formed a buffer zone between the front porch and the play and work yard in front.

To one side of the house sat what appeared to be a second house, much smaller than the first but of the same simple, symmetrical design and construction. On the other side was yet another house, identical in all respects to the smaller house. Across the yard from the houses was a large white barn that dwarfed the houses. Undoubtedly the last structure was the one that provided for the economic welfare of the family.

Two young boys who had been running around playfully chasing each other before Mark turned down the approach, suddenly stopped and ran into the large barn.

As Mark stopped the car, a man in his late fifties strode out of the barn followed by a younger man in his thirties and the two young boys who held the second man's hands. Both older men wore the same black hats as all the other Amish men Laura and Mark had seen. They also wore suspenders over light blue shirts with sleeves rolled up above the elbows. The sweat and grime on the men's faces, arms, and shirts showed that they'd been hard at work for several hours already. Laura smiled as the older man approached, eyeing her suspiciously.

"You are Miss Miller?" he asked, expecting an affirmative response.

Laura nodded and extended a hand. The man took it in a firm, calloused grip.

"I am Daniel Schmidt." He then looked beyond her to Mark. "And who is this gentleman?" His voice inflection made it sound more of a statement then a question with the emphasis on the end of the last word.

"This is Mark Tucker."

Mark and Daniel shook hands and nodded to each other. Daniel then turned to wave the younger man forward.

"This is my son, Amos, and his youngest two boys, Eli and Samuel."

The young boys hid behind their father's legs and peaked out at the outsiders. Laura and Mark smiled at the youngsters and acknowledged their father with another handshake. It was quite obvious beyond the identical dress and beard similarities that all of these males were related.

"Martha is expecting you," said Daniel as he turned and motioned them to follow.

Daniel's manner was abrupt. Although he was not hostile, he certainly was not overly friendly. It was clear that Daniel Schmidt was not happy Martha was having visitors from outside the Amish community.

They followed Daniel to the small house to the right of the main house. A plump woman with simple gray hair tied back behind her head awaited them. For the first time, Laura and Mark also noticed two other women, three younger girls, and an older boy staring at them from the porch of the main house. They were obviously the wives and additional children of Daniel and Amos.

"It is Miss Miller and Mister Tucker, Martha." Daniel called to the gray-haired woman in front of the small house. Martha nodded and smiled to greet the newcomers. She didn't appear overly excited they had come either.

"Amos and I will be in the barn if you need us."

Martha nodded at her brother-in-law. "Thank you, Daniel," she said. "We'll be fine."

As Daniel, Amos, and the two young boys walked back to the barn, the young boys glancing back continuously, Martha invited Laura and Mark to be seated on cushioned wood chairs. She offered them a tray containing a pitcher and three glasses clinking with ice.

"I have lemonade, if you'd like. It's cold, too. I learned to appreciate a refrigerator on the outside. Mine runs on kerosene." She seemed nervous, her speech rapid.

After serving the drinks, Martha sat down and stared out over the yard to the fertile fields beyond. She breathed deeply of the fresh warm air as if she was trying to calm herself and prepare for a long-awaited ordeal.

"We appreciate you seeing us, Missus Schmidt," said Mark.

"Please call me Martha. There is no need for formality here."

"I'm Laura and this is Mark."

Martha nodded and smiled.

"We know how hard it must be for you to again be reminded . . ." continued Laura.

"I know why you've come, Laura," Martha interrupted. "I've been waiting for you for some time."

"You've been waiting?"

"Grandfather told us you would come. He told us we couldn't hide here and hope it would go away. We have a duty, even to the world outside our Amish community."

Laura and Mark looked at each other quizzically. This woman was indeed expecting them.

"I thought perhaps the man who came here before would be the end of it. But Grandfather assured me you were yet to come."

"Was the other man Jake Laford?" asked Mark.

Martha nodded.

"How did Grandfather know?" asked Laura.

"He has a gift. A sometimes terrible gift, I'm afraid."

Laura and Mark sat silently, unsure of whether the remark was directed at them. They wondered if Grandfather had seen that they might bring some harm to this peaceful family.

"You have come to discuss Albert. I have spoken to the police and reporters and many other people since that awful day," Martha said sadly. "What is your interest?"

Laura hesitated in her attempt to respond to that simple question. How could this woman, completely cut off from the outside world in her sheltered community, fathom the fears and suspicions with which Laura was dealing? How could Laura explain that the president of the United States wanted her for some reason? Perhaps he even wanted her dead.

"It's difficult to explain, Martha," Laura stammered. "We feel . . . we believe that your husband may have known something about the president. Maybe he told you."

"He told me much, Laura. Unfortunately, I did not listen closely. Why do you need to know these things?"

Laura felt as if Martha was testing her, looking for a specific answer. Finally, she decided to state the truth as best she could.

"I think this man intends to cause me harm. I have had several experiences recently that convince me of this. They are impossible to understand, yet I know. That's why I must hear what your husband knew. It may help me understand."

"You've had the dream?" Martha asked pointedly.

"Dream?" asked Laura as she turned to Mark, wondering how the woman had known. She then turned back and stared into the now calm blue-gray eyes. "I've had a dream. Several times," she said warily.

"It is the devil's dream," Martha said matter-of-factly. "Albert had it, too. I didn't listen." Martha bowed her head sadly, obviously feeling she could have prevented her husband's desperate act if she'd only responded to him properly.

"Please, Martha. What is this all about?" Laura pleaded.

"I must take you back to the beginning so you will understand completely." She stared hard at Mark and Laura.

"Albert was born here," pointing to the bigger house. "This was his father's house before Daniel, Albert's younger brother, took it for his family. At a very early age, it was clear to his family that Albert would be different. When he and the other Amish children went to school in the public schools outside the Amish community, he would come home with his head full of questions about the outside world. Whereas the other kids questioned and were generally satisfied with the responses of their parents, Al wasn't. He had a fire in him . . . . He wanted to know the world out there. Even when there were strictly Amish schools and Al's parents made him attend these instead of the public schools, Al wanted to escape.

"I grew up on a farm just outside of New Holland in eastern Lancaster County. My family's farm is about thirty-five miles from here. My oldest brother and his family operate it now."

"When I was sixteen, a pretty young thing back then," she smiled and Laura thought that she was still very pretty, "Al came to one of our Sunday services. He had made a practice on off-Sundays in his district to venture out to other districts.

"When I saw Al, I thought he was the most handsome man I'd ever seen. He was eighteen, tall and strong. He was exciting," she smiled with the recollection. "And he wasn't like the other boys. I could see immediately that he was bold and uninhibited, like a wild animal. I was very taken with him. Our district always had Sunday picnics after services. That particular Sunday was no exception. I guess Al must have seen me at services because he found me at the picnic and we talked the whole day. He got home very late that night," Martha smiled again and sipped her lemonade.

"After that, Al made that long trip to our district every other Sunday. Soon he started coming out on Fridays and staying the weekends with some of his friends. His father got angry, because Al left part of Friday's and Saturday's work to his brothers, but we were in love. We were married eight months later, when I was seventeen and Al was two months away from nineteen.

"We didn't tell our parents until after the wedding that our plans were to leave the district and go to live among the English. I was convinced the world held adventures untold for us. We left despite the excommunication from the church.

"We had our first child, a daughter named Rebecca, the following year. We lived in Pennsylvania for a few years so we could see Albert's family. Even though we were shunned by our families' communities, Al's family welcomed us. It was after they were threatened, however, that we decided to leave for good. That's when we moved to California. It was the most difficult thing we had to do. I cried for weeks because we were going so far away, but deep down I knew Al would be able to take care of us and I loved him so."

Martha bowed her head to hold back the tears. After regaining control, she started again.

"We were very happy in California. We raised three children and made a good life. We got involved in organizing a church, much like our own here, and we were involved with the church and community. We missed our families in Pennsylvania, but with each passing year, the hurt lessened." Martha stopped and emptied her glass of lemonade. She looked sadly at Laura and Mark.

"Our lives came crashing down about seventeen years ago," she continued softly, swallowing hard and obviously fighting tears. "When . . . when Rebecca was killed."

Laura's own throat went dry. Despite all the death and suffering she'd been associated with recently, she was shocked to hear of Martha and Al's tragedy.

"Al was . . . we were all devastated," she stammered. Then gaining strength, she said, "Al acted like he'd lost his life. He loved her so."

"What happened, Martha?" Laura asked.

Martha placed a hand over her mouth, breathed deeply and continued.

"She was murdered. She'd gone away to school . . . a place called Eureka." She looked to Laura and Mark to see if they recognized it. Laura nodded and Mark was jolted. He waited for her to continue.

"She was in her last year of school there. Within five days of each other, our Rebecca and another girl were murdered. They were cut open in the abdomen and left to die. The killer was never found."

Mark couldn't believe what he was hearing. Was it possible that these two murders were the ones referred to by Commander Escobar?

Laura stood and stepped over to Martha who was crying into a white handkerchief. She put an arm around her and pulled the woman to her breast.

"We can stop for awhile," she said.

Martha pulled away, shaking her head. "No. I have to finish this."

"The police couldn't track down the killer, so Al left us at home, in Rialto, to seek his own vengeance. I blamed Al for taking us away from the safety of our home and community here in Pennsylvania and throwing us into the decadence of California. I was wrong, though. I hurt him so badly at a time when he was already so distraught.

"For two years, Al searched. He took care of us financially from afar, but he didn't come home until one day he just suddenly reappeared.

"He was a changed man. It seemed that the spark of life had left him. His Rebecca was gone, and he had not gotten his revenge. Slowly, over the next five years, we put our lives together again. We could never forget what had happened, but we were still a family, with our two sons, and we did our best. Al worked hard. We all shared our lives and prayers again.

"Then one morning, Al woke suddenly. He'd been thrashing and churning all night. He was soaking wet when he sat up. I thought he was in a fever. He told me it was just a nightmare.

"The next morning while reading the *L.A. Times*, Al read about a murder in Los Angeles. It was a terrible thing that Al didn't describe to me until much later. Then within two weeks, there were two more murders. The thing that struck Al was that the killings were the same as Rebecca's except that in Los Angeles, the dead were prostitutes. That set Al off again.

"He spent hours going over materials he'd gathered while in Eureka and comparing them to the sketchy information on the Los Angeles killings. It wasn't until two years later, however, that he finally put it together.

"Two more murders were committed in Sacramento. They were identical to Rebecca's and the Los Angeles murders.

"By this time, I had accepted Al's obsession. It seemed he'd never let it die. That it would haunt him for the rest of his life. I decided I would live with it and not chastise him any more.

"That's when he started telling me about the dreams. He described a demon, red faced and bloated, with yellow eyes. He described it coming for him, devouring everything in its path," Martha hesitated as she saw Laura's recognition.

"Al believed he was being given a message of some sort. What I didn't realize was that he was writing Grandfather at the time, for advice. Whenever we received letters from Al's family there was always a personal one enclosed from Grandfather to Al. Apparently Grandfather, too, felt it was a message.

"It was around this time that Aidan Sullivan let it be known that he was running for the democratic nomination for president. I think that's when Al snapped.

"He said he knew who'd been doing all the killings. He said Aidan Sullivan had been there for all of them. He was a city councilman in Eureka when Rebecca and the other girl were killed and a state congressman from Los Angeles during the other five killings. Al had evidence that Sullivan was in Eureka, Los Angeles and Sacramento at the very times that the killings occurred. I couldn't shake him from his belief. I was getting concerned, particularly when he said he'd seen Aidan Sullivan in his dream. I prayed that Al would come to his senses before it was too late."

"And then suddenly it all ended."

Laura and Mark stared at her questioningly. They were both too stunned to speak. Al had been following Mark's theory. He believed that Sullivan was the murderer and had tried to get his revenge. It explained nothing relating to Laura, but it put the older pieces into the overall puzzle.

"For six months prior to the attempt, Al turned back into the man I'd married. He was happy and he didn't speak again of Aidan Sullivan. I was ecstatic and I quickly forgot my fears, thankful for the first time in years that Al was truly back."

Martha grew sullen as she continued, "Even when I was putting his morning paper into the recycler and saw Sullivan's name outlined in red, on the morning of the attempt, it didn't strike me that anything was wrong. Later that day, however, when I was cleaning our dresser drawers, I found Al's gun receipt.

"We are a peaceful people, Laura. Even when Al was so distraught with Rebecca's death, I never believed he would attempt anything like taking a man's life. It was not in him to do so. But he did."

She stopped abruptly and left Laura and Mark pondering all the information she'd given them. Martha stared out across the yard again, conscious for the first time in two hours that children were frolicking joyfully.

"So he did it for revenge?" asked Mark.

"That is what I thought. Until later, when I found a note he'd written that morning. In it, he asked my forgiveness and said he had to perform this terrible act. He wrote that God had come to him and told him that Aidan Sullivan was evil and he had to be stopped."

"That's what the papers picked up," said Laura.

"Yes," nodded Martha "They made Al look like a crazy man. I suppose I believed it too, for awhile, until Grandfather explained something to me for the hundredth time. He said that God had indeed spoken to Al, but Al had misunderstood the message."

"How so?" asked Laura.

Martha shook her head.

"Grandfather couldn't explain it to me clearly, Laura. He did say, however, that there would come another person who would have to understand. He believes you're that person."

"What do you mean?" asked Laura defensively. She'd come here to find out why the president was pursuing her. She'd been a little disappointed during Martha's story when it became apparent that Al's act was one of vengeance, and although it helped Mark, it only moved Laura further away. Now when Martha was telling her she had some significant part to play yet, she grew defensive. Her disappointment turned to fear suddenly and then again to confusion.

"You must speak to Grandfather," said Martha slowly. "I have told you all I can."

"Is Grandfather here?"

"He is at a meeting of the elders. He had hoped to return by now. He asked if you could return tomorrow, after services, if he is not back before you must leave."

Laura felt cheated. It was like one of those "to be continued" television movies that forced the viewer to tune in the next day. But what choice did she have? She had to see it through to the end.

"The preaching service will be here tomorrow," Martha added. "That's why there is so much cleaning and cooking going on today."

Finally, Laura nodded thoughtfully.

"Are you followers of our Lord?" Martha asked.

"We're both Catholic," answered Laura trying to avoid the question.

"If you wish, you could come early and join us."

"Oh no . . . that's okay," said Laura. "We don't want to interfere."

"Grandfather said to invite you. He said it may help you understand."

Laura shrugged. "We'll just come afterwards. What time is it over?"

"The preaching services usually end about noontime. They begin at nine o'clock if you wish to join us."

Laura and Mark nodded their thanks and then stood to leave.

"I'm glad you've come," said Martha.

Laura turned and smiled wanly. She wasn't so sure she was glad.

"I can't join you tomorrow, Laura," said Mark as he pulled his car out of the Schmidt family road onto Penn Road.

"Why not?"

"I've got to follow up on this stuff. If what she said about the Eureka murders is true, we may have the last link. I think we may have the guy. Anyway, she wasn't all that interested in me. You're the one the old man wants to talk to."

"What are you going to do?"

"Find an open library somewhere. You'll be okay won't you?"

"Hell, I don't know."

CHAPTER 27

The Hyatt Hotel's parking supervisor stood behind the red Dodge Shadow trying again to match the license plate against the list of guest names and rooms. He remembered the attractive woman who had driven it a few times earlier in the week. He thought she had left the previous day. In any event, he hadn't seen her since Thursday morning. Yet by Friday afternoon, her car was still parked in its slot. He reported the car to the front desk clerk who passed it on to the manager.

The manager also remembered the pretty woman who'd been with Mr. Tucker. They had definitely checked out the previous day. He wondered if either the little red car had been abandoned or if maybe the quiet Mr. Tucker had committed some heinous act upon the woman. He quickly dismissed the latter idea and made the call to police headquarters to report an abandoned vehicle.

The desk sergeant took the information and fed it into the computer. Almost immediately, the name Laura Miller appeared on the screen next to all of her vital information and a hold notation for the FBI requesting information relating to the whereabouts of Laura Miller.

Within minutes Charlie Gilbert knew the car had been found and that Laura Miller had left with Mark Tucker. By the end of the evening, Charlie also knew what car Mark had rented.

★ ★ ★

Ralph Escobar took Mark's call immediately. He'd been anxious to hear from Mark since their last conversation. He had some additional information about the past murders.

"Nice to hear from you, Professor," Escobar answered sarcastically.

"I'm sorry I didn't call sooner. It's been hectic here," Mark said excitedly. "Listen, commander, do you have any other information on the Eureka murders?"

"Just came in today."

"Was one of the women Rebecca Smith?"

Escobar paused.

"Anne . . . there's an Anne Smith . . . . Wait. Her name was Rebecca Anne Smith."

Mark closed his eyes, knowing now that his hunch had been correct. He didn't understand why, but he knew the president was involved.

"Professor, you still there?" asked Escobar.

"I'm here. I was just thinking."

"Well, what do you got?"

"I still have to check a few things out. I'll get back to you Monday morning or maybe tomorrow night at your home."

"Hey!" interrupted Escobar. "Where are you?"

"I'm in Pennsylvania. With Laura Miller. I'll explain everything next time I talk to you."

Mark hung up quickly. Too quickly for Ralph Escobar to tell him that the feds had put out an all-points bulletin for Laura Miller. What Escobar didn't know was that he and Mark had been on Mark's call together long enough for the feds to home in on his general location.

Mark was anxious to get moving early the next morning. He'd convinced Laura to let him drop her off at the Schmidt farm early, so he could get to the main library in the county seat of Lancaster, some fifteen to twenty miles east of Hebenville.

"Drop me here, Mark," said Laura, indicating the top of the earth approach to the farm from Penn Road. "I'll walk in."

Laura had woken in a melancholy mood. Because of Mark's excitement over his own quest, she wasn't able to discuss her confusion with him. Her logical, investigative mind was unable to organize the facts into anything that made any sense.

It was certainly possible that Mark's theory as to the president's involvement in the Ripper murders had some merit. The facts seemed to fall in a neat little puzzle and, at least arguably, point to him. Putting aside for the moment the fact that the president was the most visible, well known man in the world, whose nighttime meanderings would be easily noticed, it was possible that he could be the killer. Unlikely, as far as Laura was concerned, but certainly possible.

Laura's greater concern was her own dilemma. Although she appreciated the fact that Mark had chosen to help her, he was not able to suggest any theories because he was now so immersed in his own mystery.

She wished she'd never written those damn stories or even become a journalist, for that matter. Yet even as she harbored these thoughts, she knew deep down she could never have done anything else. She had been driven to write. It had been her obsession since her youth when she wrote her first investigative piece in seventh grade. In it, she condemned the failure rate of the school vending machines. She even suggested that it was the result of some sinister plot to steal the dollars of the innocent students.

Once Laura stopped questioning her career choice for the thousandth time, she came back to the confusion of her predicament. Where once she'd had no particular feelings one way or the other for Aidan Sullivan, she suddenly hated him. He was pursuing her for reasons she couldn't fathom. As she stood at the top of the dirt path leading down to the Schmidt farm, she felt that she would soon find her answers. Although she desperately wanted to know, she was afraid of what she'd learn. She needed time alone, even if it was only the time it took to walk slowly down the path to the bustling main house.

★ ★ ★

Mark watched Laura for several seconds through his rearview mirror as he drove slowly away toward Highway 30. She stood staring before starting her descent to the house. "She'll be okay," he said to himself.

Mark's mind immediately moved back to the awesome implications for world politics if his theory was correct. He had much work to do. So much, in fact, that he barely noticed the two dark-colored sedans pulling off to the side of the road about one hundred yards away from the Schmidt farm. Nor did he notice the first of the two vehicles enter the roadway again and make a U-turn after he passed them.

CHAPTER 28

A dozen black buggies were lined up outside the barn. Their horses were nowhere to be seen in the yard. Men stood outside the barn talking, as women were moving about the house completing the service and meal preparations. The children walked quietly together, not yet fidgeting uneasily in the early morning.

Halfway down the path, the clip-clop of yet another approaching horse and buggy became muffled as it moved from the paved road to the hard packed earth. A young driver smiled and tipped his hat to Laura, while his wife and four children stared at her in surprise. The buggy stopped in front of the house where the woman and children disembarked. The husband then directed his horse to the barn where another young man helped him unhitch the steed and escort it inside.

Laura breathed deeply, trying to find the courage necessary to continue her walk into the throng of simple folk. She was suddenly conscious of the pinks and yellows in her spring dress. Eyes turned toward her as the new arrivals directed attention her way.

"I'll come back later," thought Laura. She couldn't walk any further and she began to wonder if all of this wasn't a mistake.

"Laura. I'm so glad you came early." Martha's voice was cheery. The wavering sadness of the previous meeting was gone and she smiled broadly as she approached Laura, her arm extended.

"Come, let me show you the way."

Laura's trepidation upon entering the main house on Martha's arm, disappeared immediately when she was greeted by the peaceful smiles and blessings of the women. No one showed any rude interest in Laura. They all politely introduced themselves and welcomed her to their services.

Shortly after Laura entered the house, the men from in and around the barn began to enter.

"Those first five are our ordained preachers," whispered Martha.

These were followed by three very old men, each of whom struggled in his own way to enter the house unaided. In turn and in descending age came the rest of the men, each of whom greeted the ordained ministers with handshakes as they entered.

"Grandfather is the third of the ordained," said Martha, pointing. Although Grandfather appeared to be in his early eighties, he stood erect. His snow white hair and beard were thick and his blue eyes sparkled from below the black rim of his hat.

The men walked single file into the house's main sitting room, where backless benches were lined up in rows that extended back into the kitchen and dining rooms. All three rooms had their partitions removed, to form a large room capable of holding the 150 or so worshipers and to enable everyone to see the preachers as they spoke.

After the men, came the women and younger girls, also by age. They too greeted the ministers with handshakes before proceeding to their seats. Martha explained that although the unmarried women share the sitting room with the men, they sit separate and apart from them. Martha escorted Laura to one of the benches in the sitting room and sat down with her. The married women and mothers sat nearer and inside the kitchen with the younger children. The older boys sat next to their fathers and the girls sat with their mothers.

When everyone was seated, the five ministers moved to chairs placed in the middle of the congregation. Four of the ministers took their seats and Grandfather stood alone.

"We have a visitor in our midst, from outside," said Grandfather. Laura's immediate inclination was to hide so she wouldn't be noticed. When no one turned to stare at her, she relaxed again.

"We will honor our guest by trying to conduct our service today in English. We hope she will forgive us if we fall back to our native tongue on occasion."

Grandfather looked at Laura, who nodded and smiled.

Grandfather then said, "We will now join together in our first hymn."

As if on cue, each man in the congregation removed his hat and placed it beneath his bench in one uniform motion. The hymns began.

After the first hymn, the ordained ministers left the room and marched upstairs, where, Martha explained, they determined which would speak and in what order. During their entire absence the congregation sang one slow melodic hymn after another, each one being led by a different man in the group.

The preaching service extended beyond three hours, presumably because of the difficulty some of the worshipers and ministers had in dealing with the entire service in English. Yet they all sat patiently, reverently, listening and joining in.

Several times during the services, younger children became antsy. Even some of the older ones fidgeted. Parents didn't seem to get angry or even exasperated, however. At one point several of the women passed trays of cookies and water around for the children to snack on. Some children slept and even adults would occasionally drift off during the long sermons. For all its length, however, Laura was surprised at the level of attentiveness and intense reverence.

As the morning drifted on and she resigned herself to sitting through the entire service, a peace came over her. She'd heard most of the words before in her Catholic past. She'd also heard them recently from her father and uncle. Until now, however, they'd just been words. In the midst of these people whose lives revolved around Jesus Christ and how to best serve the Lord on earth to attain the only goal they all sought—eternal life in heaven—Laura heard something more. The preachers seemed to be talking to her to provide order and purpose to her life, a life geared to the material world outside these simple farms in Lancaster County, Pennsylvania.

The preachers spoke of the evils of materialism, saying that striving for higher standards of living and wealth were nothing more than worship of the golden calf. They read from the New Testament that people cannot serve two masters, money and God. To serve and seek money is to cast aside the Lord. And to love the Lord is to avoid the pursuit of wealth for itself, something many in Laura's world could not bring themselves to do. They all feared life without money and never realized, until they had spent their lives pursuing the golden calf, that it had no life and offered no succor. It was an empty dream.

It wasn't until Grandfather Schmidt stood and preached his sermon, though, that Laura finally began to understand the words she'd heard from her uncle and father. He began with a quote from Matthew's gospel.

"After Jesus rose from the dead, he went to his disciples and said, 'Full authority has been given to me both in heaven and on earth; go therefore and make disciples of *all* the nations. Baptize them in the name of the Father, and of the Son, and of the Holy Spirit. Teach them to carry out everything I have commanded you and know that I am with you always, until the end of the world!'" (Matthew 12:18–20).

Grandfather Schmidt continued without reading: "My brothers and sisters, for over two hundred years, we have lived lives we believed were of God. We have gathered amongst ourselves in prayer. We have taught our children the ways of our Lord and we have condemned the outside world as a place of evil, steeped in decadence and self-righteousness. And we have been happy.

"We have tried, at every turn, to follow our Lord's teachings as brought to us again through Matthew when he wrote, 'If a man wishes to come after me, he must deny his very self, take up his cross, and begin to follow in my footsteps. Whoever,'" Grandfather Schmidt shouted the word and stared pointedly at the faces around him, before continuing more softly, "'Whoever would save his life will lose it, but whoever loses his life for my sake will find it. What profit would a man show if he were to gain the whole world and destroy himself in the process?' (Matthew 15:24–27).

"Finally, my friends and family, our Lord has told us through St. Paul that we must 'Have the same attitude towards all! We must put away ambitious thoughts and associate with those who are lowly.'

(Romans 12:16). Today, these words have special meaning for us in the Amish community.

"We have lived together and helped each other to a better love of Jesus Christ, yet we have removed ourselves from the boiling cauldron of corruption beyond our borders. The word of Jesus is not a word meant only for us. We can no longer sit safely within our own borders and wait for the end, in the self-indulgent hope that at least *we* will be saved. We must hear God's word and we must go forth amongst them, and spread His word. The world beyond our community cries out for help. Only the minions of Satan respond. It can no longer be so."

Grandfather Schmidt paused and turned slowly to look into each person's eyes.

"We have all been given gifts by our Lord. It is up to each one of us to look deeply within to find that gift and ask our Lord's guidance to use it for him. Not for our own individual salvation alone, but for the salvation of all our brothers and sisters. We can no longer cower here in our solitude. Our Lord has given us a mission to help him bring back all his children. It is to that end that we must use these gifts."

Grandfather Schmidt sat again and all in the congregation bowed their heads in silent prayer of thanks for the wisdom imparted by their brother. Laura sat quietly through the final parts of the service. She heard the beautiful chords of the closing hymn and watched mechanically as the congregation filed out of the room in reverse order from youngest to oldest.

The old man's words hung in the air. Laura didn't even notice she was alone in the sitting room. Even Martha had left her side, choosing not to disturb her thoughts until suddenly she felt a light prodding at her shoulder. Grandfather stood before her, his eyes alive and caring.

"Will you join me, Laura?" he asked softly, almost reverently.

Laura stood then and let him lead her out of the main house, down the steps to the small house opposite Martha's abode. She was aware of men moving benches and women and children going about the task of preparing lunch. Snippets of conversation analyzing Grandfather Schmidt's words drifted to her. She even heard words of shock that the old man would suggest venturing out beyond the safety of the Amish community. Such acts had previously been the basis for excommunication from the church. Had times changed so dramatically?

Laura sat at a finely crafted table opposite the old man. Her head began to clear in the moments of silence before he spoke.

"We are all happy you have joined us. We've been waiting for a long time."

She shook her head, a dour look crossing her face. "I don't understand," she stammered. "How could you know I was coming?"

"Our Lord has told us to be ready. We never knew exactly when. But when our friend, John Wiley, told us you sought Martha, we knew you were the one."

"The one? The one for what?"

"I know your dream, Laura. It is the same dream that my son Albert had. Many times. He wrote me about it, and we prayed he would understand the message it brought to him."

"What message?" she asked, unable to bring herself to believe she was even having a conversation about the meaning of a nightmare.

"I did not understand it either for a long time. I did know, however, the action Albert planned in response to the dream was wrong. If indeed the message was from our Lord, he would never ask one of his children to commit an act that violated his own commandments. He would never ask Albert to kill a man. Albert misunderstood."

"Wait. Are you saying that he really believed God told him to kill this guy? For what?"

"He believed that Aidan Sullivan murdered Rebecca. He also believed he had murdered others in the same way and that if he wasn't stopped, he would continue to kill."

Laura nodded, clearly understanding the words that fit into Mark Tucker's easy puzzle.

"I believe our Lord's message was greater than that, however," continued Grandfather. "He was warning Albert of a greater evil to come. An evil that has now manifested itself and is growing stronger each day." The old man stopped because he could see he was losing Laura.

"Grandfather Schmidt," Laura started, "your words today really moved me. I've heard them before from others, but I've never really listened. I think you're right. I believe we've all got an obligation to work for the good of our entire society. We aren't here just for ourselves. That much, I suppose, I've had in me for years. I guess maybe God really does want us to go out and help others." She smiled reflectively. "Things sure aren't working out right the way I've been going.

"But you're talking about something way out there," she continued. "You're suggesting there is some powerful evil force out there that needs to be stopped, but we can't kill it."

"It is no force, Laura. It is Satan himself. As our Lord walks with those who call upon him, so too does the Prince of Darkness walk with those who call upon him. The president of this country walks boldly in the shadow of the evil one."

"What are you saying?" Laura asked incredulously. "You can't really believe we're involved in some great battle between good and evil here. That's fantasy. It's not real life."

"You have felt his power," responded the old man aggressively. "You have felt it very recently. It was only through your own call to our Lord that you've been spared until now."

Laura stared at him, not knowing how to respond. She'd felt it, and she knew she'd held the medal of Christ's holy mother when she'd escaped the president's clutches. But it was only a charm or crutch that distracted her into reaching deeper into her own mind to fight him off. It wasn't God or the devil. It was only a man and a woman using the elusive ninety percent of the brain no one uses.

"Even now he works his will with the people of this country, Laura. You heard his speech. You saw his mark. As we speak, his followers take his mark upon their wrists as a sign of their loyalty to him and his country. But it is truly a sign of loyalty only to one. They accept his call under the mistaken belief that they are truly chosen." He stared at her pointedly. "And they are . . . by the evil one, himself. They are accepting *his* mark upon their hands."

He spoke the truth. She didn't want to accept it because it wasn't real. This was America, where money and greed ruled supreme. Where people lived to grow wealthy and powerful. When they

281

reached those goals they turned to charity and got their names placed on museums and children's homes. That's what it was all about. This talk of evil demons and spirits and God wasn't part of the picture. You live and then you die. That's all. As simple as that.

"He has destroyed the Arab world to take its oil. He has destroyed Japan to take its economic might and he now seeks the rest of the world. Look around at what is happening. He seeks a constitutional amendment for one purpose. Continued dominion over this world's most powerful nation and ultimate dominion over all the peoples themselves. His quest will not stop with a third term. His quest will not stop until he has all the peoples of this world in his hands and those of his master."

"This is crazy," Laura mumbled as she shook her head and avoided the old man's eyes.

"Do you deny that you have felt his power?" he continued softly. "If you do, you are fooling yourself. Do you know why he pursues you, Laura?"

Laura's head jerked up and she glared at him.

"How do you know all this? Where did . . ." she stopped, confused and angry that her mind would not give her the words she needed to refute those of the old man.

"You came here seeking an answer to that very question. He pursues you because he fears you."

"Fears me?" she almost screamed, tears of frustration forming in her eyes. "He has already destroyed me. What does he have to fear from me?"

"Your gift," he said simply.

"Gift? What gift?"

"You have the gift of the written word. A powerful weapon in the hands of one with a following. And you, Laura, have such a following, even amongst the Amish. There are many of us who read the papers outside our community."

"Don't you understand? He has destroyed that." Laura was beside herself, fighting a losing battle and knowing only that none of this could be true.

"You have many loyal readers. There are many throughout this country who seek simple words from one of their own. Words that can show them the proper path. They are all being led by the only voice loud enough to get to them. They need another voice so they can hear the truth. You can stop him, Laura."

"Why me? If you and others are so concerned, why don't you just kill him and be done with it?" She knew immediately that she was wrong, but she needed the old man's words to make it clear.

"That's what Albert thought. He misunderstood, for God will not ask us to break his own commandment. 'Thou shalt not kill,'" the old man quoted and then paused. "It is only through our Lord's hands that life may rightfully be taken."

"Then why doesn't he take this guy out?" Laura pleaded.

"Our Lord will not interfere, directly, in our lives. He has given us the will to choose our own destiny. It is up to each one of us to choose between the false gifts and riches of Satan and true eternal life of God. As man has chosen for Satan, so must man choose for God or forever be cast into the abyss."

Laura was too exhausted to argue with the man. She'd felt the awesome power that had come from Aidan Sullivan. She'd known the fear of being pursued by an insurmountable power for no apparent reason. She had no more resistance and revelation spread through her body. She stopped questioning. Stopped analyzing. Stopped arguing that it was all nonsense. She simply let her consciousness be overwhelmed with the realization of what Aidan Sullivan was really doing.

The man on the microphone in the abandoned building across from the Washington Monument knew. He tried to warn them all. If someone would have had the strength to step forward at that critical time, it would all have come crashing down upon Aidan Sullivan. Yet the only person with the strength to speak and the charisma to manipulate was the president himself. His words brought them all back with greater conviction borne of their shame at having doubted him for even a moment.

It was all becoming clear. The seemingly unconnected facts were suddenly coming together to form one undeniable conclusion. He knew that Albert Smith would try to kill him and that he would fail. He clearly understood the impact such an act would have on a seething electorate grasping for a hero to pull them out of a decade- long socioeconomic slump.

In seven short years he'd risen to become the most powerful man in the entire world. He commanded the mightiest military force and used it with impunity for the "welfare of the United States of America." He spoke the patronizing words of another twentieth century despot to win his people over, telling them that they were indeed the chosen people. They were the best because they were Americans. He espoused the American dream and quickly destroyed any interference with it.

In her mind's eye, Laura saw the exaggerated vision of the suffering of millions in foreign nations subjugated by America. She saw the people of her own country separated by greed, all seeking their own selfish interests and clinging to Aidan Sullivan as the god who would certainly help them all achieve them. In the same light, she saw the millions of dispossessed Americans. Those in the streets without even a piece of the dream. Without hope and without the power to change any of it.

She then saw the demon growing larger and ever more powerful with each passing second. Families disappeared. Mothers and fathers were replaced by the specter of one man. Gone was God and order of any kind except the order of chaos controlled by the power-maddened mind of Aidan Sullivan.

It was all so clear. He had taken the step that would lead to the subjugation of all peoples to the depressive state of worldliness in which no man or woman could be truly happy. Without family, without God, without hope, it was all pointless. Yet that is where he pointed. If it worked as he planned, all people would reach higher for the cold heart of the golden calf and never again attain the warm contented comfort of peace in their own hearts.

Laura realized Aidan Sullivan was a modern-day despot. More subtle perhaps than his predecessors, choosing not to openly alienate any single segment of his society. His pursuit was not borne of hatred of a people but rather of power, the cold, unbridled desire for complete and unchallenged control over all people. He had the tools that could carry him to his goal with barely a voice raised against him.

★ CHAPTER 28 ★

For so many years Laura sought the riches and praise of this world, thinking always that it would lead to that moment of peace when all was right for her. She was just like all the rest, content to let things lie provided she could attain her own personal goals. When suddenly a man of great strength arose to promise fulfillment of all those dreams, Laura began to understand the lies. She understood what her father and uncle had meant when they'd said she would have to write from the heart and for the benefit of others around her. She'd never been satisfied with the treasures of this world. For the first time she could remember, she saw clearly the elusive peace everyone pursued so intensely would never be found so long as people continued to search this world for it. If they lost the only real hope, they were all lost forever.

Aidan Sullivan had to be stopped! He was leading them all, like lemmings, to the precipice. How could it be done? How could anyone convince an entire populace this guy was guided by Satan to make everyone rich and powerful *and that wasn't good*. She stared at a grim-faced Grandfather Schmidt.

"You carry a heavy burden, my dear," said the old man softly.

"But why me?" she asked in a subdued voice. "Why is he pursuing me? I can't possibly hurt him."

"You've been chosen, Laura. Just as Albert was chosen. You are not the only one who has been given the call. There are others who fight his evil. The young people in Medjugorje. The clergy of our nation who struggle to keep the faith, and many others. He resists them as he's always done. But you," he pointed at her, "you, he fears. You have the ability to influence others in the way of our Lord. Your pen is mighty, my dear. You must use it now to stop him."

"I'm an investigative reporter. A 'sleaze journalist'," she spat back at him. Then she bowed her head and spoke softly, "What words can I write that could possibly make people forget my blunder and listen?"

"You must have faith in Him. If He has indeed chosen you, and the enemy believes He has, He will not abandon you."

The old man pointed to Laura's clenched fist. She glanced down and opened it slowly. The Mary medallion and chain lay in her open palm.

"In our faith, we attribute no special blessing to the Holy Mother. I believe, however, that she is amongst us in Medjugorje and other places in this world as a messenger for her Son. Call on her and call on our Lord, for what parent would refuse a child in need? He will give you the words."

Laura fingered the medal and the two sat quietly. Outside, a cool breeze carried the sounds of receding horses' hooves as guests departed at midday. Finally, Laura looked up at the old man.

"I have to go," she said quietly.

"Yes, I know. Shall I have someone take you back to town?"

Laura glanced at her watch. It was four o'clock. She was surprised at the time because Mark was supposed to have returned for her a half hour earlier. She shook her head.

"My ride should be here soon."

Together they walked out to the porch of Grandfather's little house. He directed her to a chair.

"You can wait here if you'd like. I will send some refreshment. I'll be back."

Laura nodded and smiled absently at a little girl who peeked around her mother from the front seat of a departing buggy.

CHAPTER 29

Mark's search had been productive. The Lancaster County Library had access to virtually every periodical in the country through an elaborate computer research center. He was able to piece together a brief history of Aidan Sullivan.

Apparently the young Aidan had been orphaned at the age of six, when his mother died of a drug overdose. Since his father had simply disappeared shortly after the death and no other relatives were ever found, he had no one to care for him and he was placed into the custody of several homes for orphans, the last of which was the California Boy's Home in Salinas, California.

From there the story read like a standard rags-to-riches tale of a lost youth who fought his way through a system which, although overstrained by the awesome demands of a society growing less and less interested in the lives of its children, still gave him the rudiments of the character that would make him president of the United States. Sullivan had gotten a scholastic scholarship to Georgetown University in Washington, D.C. It was there he met his bride June Wilson and became interested in government. He fought tragedy after tragedy, from the birth of a son with Down's syndrome to the death of his wife and to an attempt on his life.

For Mark, however, one event in the president's life was particularly intriguing. He looked back at the periodicals chronicling the death of June Wilson and found that she was killed when her car flew headlong over the cliffs along the coast of Humboldt County in Northern California. The car plunged two hundred feet to jagged rocks and pounding surf. June Wilson's remains were found, thrown free of the exploding wreckage, with her abdomen cut open by jagged rock and the fetus in her womb dead. The accident had occurred in broad daylight on a clear day.

Also strange was that there had been no skid marks near the top of the precipice. It was as if the woman had committed suicide. Was it possible this death started the avalanche? Had Aidan Sullivan been so devastated by the loss of his baby, torn from its mother's dying womb, that he murdered women in a symbolic search for the child?

By the time Mark finally looked at his watch, it was already three-thirty, the time he was to pick Laura up. He spent ten minutes gathering his notes and pulled out of the parking lot, hoping Laura wouldn't be upset. For his part, he was excited with the research. Everything now pointed to the president. It would be a delicate matter, however. You don't just go in and arrest the president of the United States for murder.

On Route 30, Mark found himself pushing his vehicle along at eighty to eighty-five miles per hour. So engrossed was he in his thoughts, he didn't realize how fast he was going until he was almost upon a slow-moving hay truck. He jammed his right foot on the brake pedal. Nothing happened. He pumped his foot and stepped down hard on the brake again. The pedal hit the floor with a sickening thunk, and the car hurtled forward toward the unsuspecting hay truck.

Mark started to pull the steering wheel left into the eastbound lane, but an oncoming car made him swerve back in to his own lane. Only seconds remained before impact. Mark swerved again, this time to the right, toward the soft shoulder. He gripped the wheel hard and turned sharply, clipping the right rear bumper of the hay truck with his left fender. The glancing blow sent his car skidding into the dirt and gravel shoulder. Mark turned into the right angle skid, but the car spun once on the loose gravel and was airborne over the drainage ditch at the side of the road.

★ ★ ★

Jacob Hochstetler saw the whole thing. He'd brought his family home early from the Schmidts' preaching service. After dropping them off at the main house, he'd taken his eldest son and ridden his buggy out to the middle of his fields to smoke his pipe and ponder Grandfather Schmidt's words. He, too, had often felt the Amish had a duty to go out among the English and preach God's word. He wished to discuss this with his son.

He'd seen the hay truck lazily crest the rise at the east end of Route 30 several minutes earlier. When the light silver automobile came along a short time later, he sat forward, sure that it would have to take some evasive action because it was moving too fast to stop in time.

When the silver car skidded left and then right, Jacob began to pray. As it flew over the ditch it spun slowly and when it landed, it rolled crazily several times and then exploded, sending a geyser of flame and black billowing smoke high into the sky.

Jacob stood for a moment, craning to see if there was any movement near the burning hulk of the vehicle. He'd seen this car before. Wasn't it the one that had dropped the visitor at the Schmidt house? A second and third explosion surprised Jacob. He had some knowledge of combustion engines and knew that once the gas tank blew, there should be no more explosions. He wondered what could have caused the other two.

"Go get Simon Lapp, David. His medical knowledge will be needed here. Take him to the accident. Don't get too close," he warned his son.

Jacob then grabbed the reigns of his buggy's steed and whipped the animal to a gallop toward Daniel Schmidt's place. He would have to bring the news to the Schmidts.

The first explosion attracted everyone's attention. They all looked around, unable to distinguish the direction from which the sound had come, until young Eli Schmidt pointed to the curling cloud of black smoke to the East.

"It's from the highway!" shouted Daniel Schmidt. "Amos, hitch up the buggy. We must see if any help is needed."

Laura stood at the porch rail listening to the frantic talk in a language she didn't understand. The explosion had shocked her at first and the smoke was a curiosity. Only after the second and third explosions did the thought cross her mind that Mark might be held up for some time if it was something on the highway. She stared at the rising cloud for several seconds before a sickening thought began to take hold.

For several minutes prior to the explosions, Laura had wondered why Mark was late. She fought the urge to think that something may have happened to him. Surely, he was just held up at the library. When the late afternoon peace was shattered, she knew deep down Mark was in trouble. "Please, please keep him safe," she prayed softly to no one. "I don't know what I'd do without him."

Amos led the black horse and buggy out of the barn. He jumped aboard and went to meet Daniel, who ran out of the main house carrying a leather bag. Before Daniel could take his seat next to his son, another horse and buggy came thundering down the slope. Jacob Hochstetler jumped from his seat before his buggy had fully stopped. He ran to Daniel gesticulating and talking frantically. Grandfather Schmidt, followed by another man, walked up to the two and listened intently. As Jacob stopped talking and Daniel plied him with questions, Grandfather glanced at Laura, concern written on his face. A lump came to Laura's throat as the old man turned away again.

Laura walked hesitantly down the front steps toward the four men.

"What happened, Grandfather?" she asked slowly.

The old man turned and stared sadly at her. Jacob, Daniel, and the other man stopped talking and also looked at her.

"There was an accident on the highway, my dear. A terrible accident. We believe it was your friend's vehicle."

Laura's breath left her. She glanced quickly to the still rising pillar of black smoke and then turned back stunned. She shook her head.

"No," she whispered. "This can't be happening."

Laura knew immediately that it hadn't been an accident. Mark had become the latest casualty in this game in which she was the only real intended victim. He had joined her to help and now was it possible that he too was gone? What would happen to Nickie? Her mind raced with thoughts and fears.

"Is he dead?" she mumbled as tears came to her eyes.

"Jacob didn't know," the old man answered. "He came immediately. Daniel and Jacob will go back to help."

The old man turned and said a word. Daniel and Jacob boarded Jacob's buggy which immediately headed back up the path. Grandfather Schmidt turned back to Laura as the last man stood with Amos.

"You must be strong now, my dear. If your friend is alive, he will be taken care of." The old man was unable to hide his own doubts as to Mark's welfare. He had heard from Jacob's own mouth, the destruction wrought by the explosions.

He stepped forward and took Laura's arm in a firm grip. "You must leave this place now."

Laura stared at him in surprise.

"There is another automobile waiting, Laura. Jacob saw it when he left earlier and he saw it again on his return. He also saw three men holding weapons and standing outside the vehicle. They were looking in the direction of the explosion. I fear they wait for you."

"I have to stay here. I have to see if Mark is all right!" Laura said nervously. She had no safe place, now. Where would she go? It was obvious that they'd been able to track Mark and Laura to Hebenville.

"We have no means of protecting you, my dear. They will come soon. Amos will take you from our farm."

"But where . . .?" Laura stammered.

Grandfather stared at her sadly.

"Joseph Stoltzfus," he pointed to the man standing next to Amos' buggy, "has offered his farm. You may hide there for a while if you wish. But it will not be safe forever."

Grandfather's point was clear. They would do everything they could for her, even at the risk of their own lives. Joseph Stoltzfus wore a brave face, but he couldn't mask the concern for his family's welfare.

Such simple, giving people, totally committed to the welfare of all people. They would gladly give their lives to do God's work. Although they seemed to believe that Laura had some important purpose in the Lord's plan, she could not endanger them any further. She would have to go alone. Too many others had already been killed. She simply couldn't bear the thought of others dying. Eyeing the two men carefully, she said "Is there a way back to town other than the highway?"

Grandfather Schmidt didn't smile, but the relief he felt over Laura's decision to act rather than hide was apparent.

"Amos will take you to Hebenville along back roads. Come, let us prepare you for the journey."

Fifteen minutes later, Martha was hugging Laura, who had changed into the simple garb of an Amish woman, while Grandfather Schmidt instructed Amos in German.

"God be with you, Laura," said Martha.

Amos directed the buggy behind the farmhouse to a path that ran west through symmetrically furrowed fields of rich dark soil. He urged the horse on quickly with sharp flicks of the reins, heeding Grandfather Schmidt's call for haste because the pursuers would soon decide to come onto the Schmidt family grounds.

Laura watched the farm as the buggy trundled away. Even when they left the fields and were on the tree lined dirt road beyond, she kept a wary eye. Finally, when the farm was out of view, she sat back with her thoughts, grateful that Amos was content not to talk.

Despite Grandfather Schmidt's assurance that they would find and care for Mark Tucker, Laura knew he was gone. Her heart was torn with concern for his young daughter and, although she didn't want to admit it, for her own loss. Now she had no safe haven. Nor did she have the quiet comfort of Mark's strong reassuring manner. She was alone against a formidable foe.

How did they know where to find her? If they knew, why did they wait? They could have simply destroyed both of them before they'd even reached the Schmidt farm in the morning. Unless they hadn't known exactly where they were or maybe they wanted Laura alive.

It suddenly struck her that there was only one way they could have known. Commander Ralph Escobar. He had either told them or his phone had been tapped. Either way, he was not someone Laura could trust. Even if she could, what could she say to him? Mark was dead. How could he possibly believe that the president of the United States was pursuing Laura for some reason that even Laura couldn't understand? Laura only had one real weapon at her disposal. She was a writer. She could still do that. All she needed was a forum. Even though she wasn't exactly sure of what she would write, she had to sit down and start. She was drawn to it. She'd have to find a safe place to write and then someone to publish it.

The seven-mile journey to Hebenville took nearly three hours over hard packed dirt roads and asphalt country lanes. It was dark when the bed and breakfast came into view. The inn was well lit and inviting to weary travelers. But to Laura it suddenly looked ominous. She envisioned dark-cloaked villains hiding in the shadows along the walls and instructed Amos to keep right on going.

"Where shall I take you?" asked the Amish man.

"To a telephone," she instructed, confident now of the action she must take.

As the buggy passed the post office, Laura grabbed Amos' arm. "Do you know John Wiley?"

Amos nodded.

"Does he live close by?"

"Yes. His home is at the back of the postal office."

"Take me there, Amos. I'd like to use his phone if he will permit it."

Sheila Blackburn didn't usually work on Sunday. In fact, none of Senator Morgan's staff worked on weekends except when something urgent pressed the senator. This happened to be one of those occasions. Sheila found herself yawning at eight o'clock in the evening as she walked past the reception desk on her way out. She'd been approving copy for press releases all day. Slowly but surely she was making the rounds and getting newspapers from around the country to print Senator Morgan's propaganda.

The phone rang for the third time as she passed the reception desk. She heard a click followed by receptionist Mary O'Donnell's even voice, instructing the caller to leave a message and the call would be returned during normal business hours.

The voice of the caller sounded frantic as Sheila reached for the door.

"Damn," it said. "Senator Morgan, this is Laura Miller. It's urgent that I speak to you, sir."

Sheila recognized the name. Laura was the marvelous writer for the *Herald* who had recently made the mistake of attacking the president without sufficient support. Sheila turned away from the door and back to the telephone.

"I can't talk on this machine senator, but I have something that I think is very important." She paused. "About the president." Then she seemed to turn away from the phone and Sheila could barely hear her say, "Mister Wiley, what is your number, please?"

Sheila had felt badly for Laura. Although they were never friends, Sheila had spoken to Laura on several occasions. She always read her well-crafted pieces. Laura had been a hard person to like because one always got the feeling she was looking for an angle from which to write an exposé. Yet she was a damn good writer.

"I . . . I can't give you the number, senator. I'll call early tomorrow. Please, senator, wait for my call."

Sheila reached for the receiver.

"It's urgent. If anyone else hears this, please tell the senator . . ."

"Hello. Laura, I've got it."

"Hello?"

"Laura? This is Sheila Blackburn. Hold on a minute while I turn this damn machine off."

"Thank God."

"There. Laura, what's so urgent?"

"It's a long story, Sheila. I can't explain now, but I have to talk to the senator. Can you get him?"

Sheila hesitated. Despite Laura's need, she didn't trust her. "It's Sunday night. The senator's at home with his family."

"Listen to me, Sheila. You're working on a Sunday night to find a way to stop the president. I've got the way. I need help. I need the senator's help."

Sheila didn't respond.

"Please, Sheila. No bullshit. I promise you."

"Okay, Laura. I'll try to get him. Can you hold on the line? I'll see if I can patch him in."

"Please."

Sheila pushed the hold button and then another button for a free line. She dialed the senator's D.C. home number.

"H'lo," answered the senator after the third ring.

"Senator Morgan, it's Sheila."

"Hi, Sheila. You still at the office?"

"Yes, sir, I am."

"What is it?" The senator sensed the urgency in Sheila's voice.

"I was just leaving, when a call came in from Laura Miller. Do you know her, sir?"

"If it's that writer from the *Herald*, sure I know her."

"She's scared, sir. I didn't want to bother you at home, but she pleaded with me to call you."

"Does she want to join our team?" the senator asked.

"She says she has some information about the president. I think she wants to help us."

"Then put her through."

"I'm not sure I know how to do this, senator. If I lose you, I'll call back."

"I'll be right here," he answered.

Sheila again pushed the hold button. Then with both lights blinking, she pushed "hold" a third time and immediately pushed both blinking lights simultaneously.

"Senator, are you there?" she asked.

"Here."

"Laura, are you on the line?"

"Yes."

"Miz Miller?" asked the senator.

"I'm sorry to bother you on a Sunday evening, Senator Morgan. I believe I have a story for you that will help you in your campaign to defeat the president's move for a third term."

"We're always interested in help, Miz Miller," he said warily. The senator was well aware of Laura's previous mistake. He was concerned she might suggest a sensational story that, if proven wrong, would only add strength to the president's position. "A writer of your talents could be of some assistance."

"I understand your hesitation, sir. It will do you no harm to hear me out. Will you see me?"

She was right, of course. It would not harm him to speak to her in his office in the morning.

"Can you meet me at my office in the morning?" he asked.

"Well, senator, that's part of the problem. I'm in Pennsylvania. I have no means of getting to you."

"They have car rental agencies, buses, trains, and airplanes in Pennsylvania, Miz Miller." The senator was again wary.

Laura hesitated. How could she explain all that had happened in just a few words? What could she say that would make him understand?

"Look, Senator Morgan, it's impossible to explain to you what's happened over the last two weeks. It all seems so crazy. I can't hope to make you understand in a few seconds over the phone.

"I need a ride. I can't explain why right now." Both the senator and Sheila could hear the resignation in her voice. "Can you send someone to get me? I promise you it will be worth your while. If it isn't, you can do what you want with me."

"Are you in some kind of trouble with the law, Miz Miller?" asked the senator.

"I truly don't know, senator. I can't take a chance on the police right now, though. I've got to tell my story to you. If, after you hear it, you don't believe me, and I won't blame you if you don't, I'll go quietly. You can call the police or whoever else you want."

Senator Morgan nodded slowly, pensively. He could ensure his own safety. He was not concerned with that. And he was curious.

"Okay. I'll have someone come to get you. Where are you?"

Laura closed her eyes in silent thanks.

"It's a small town called Hebenville. Off Highway 30 in Lancaster County, Pennsylvania. It's about a two-hour drive."

"Yes, I know the town, Miz Miller. Where can we meet you?"

"In front of the Post Office. I'll see your driver," she paused. "How will I know him?"

The senator hesitated and Laura spoke again quickly. "Can you send Sheila Blackburn with him? I know Sheila."

"Sheila's put in a long weekend already, Miz Miller," started the senator.

"It's okay, sir. I'll go." interrupted Sheila.

"I'll have Tom come by the office in fifteen minutes, Sheila. Is that okay?"

"I'll be here," she answered.

"Thank you, senator," Laura said and then hung up.

After his call to Tom Gifford, his driver, the senator sat back in thought. This could prove to be interesting.

CHAPTER 30

A few minutes before eleven, a white Lincoln limousine rolled slowly to a stop in front of the Hebenville Post Office. Laura stood behind locked doors in the inside office with John Wiley and Amos Schmidt at her side. They peered through the mini-blinds as the door opened and the smartly dressed thirty-year-old Sheila Blackburn, her black hair pulled back loosely, stepped out of the passenger compartment.

Sheila was surprised to see an Amish woman, accompanied by an Amish man and another man, emerge from the post office. The Amish woman's head was bowed but flicked furtively to the left and right as she walked quickly to the car.

"Thanks for coming, Sheila," said Laura.

"Laura? Is that you?"

"Disguise." Laura smiled sheepishly. "Can we get in?"

Sheila opened the door and followed Laura into the car. Amos and John Wiley stood on the sidewalk, as Laura poked her head out quickly. "Thank you both so much. Amos, please tell your wife I'll return the clothes as soon as I can."

"I will, Laura."

She smiled again. "And tell Grandfather Schmidt that I'll do my best. He'll understand."

Amos nodded. He and John Wiley waved as the door closed and the car moved back onto Main Street and out of town to Highway 30.

★ ★ ★

Laura gazed through the automobile's tinted back window for signs that anyone might be following them. She was satisfied after they'd been on Highway 30 for ten minutes that they had escaped undetected.

Sheila stared at Laura without saying anything until Laura had stopped fidgeting and settled in for the ride. It was almost comical to see the always cool investigative reporter so shaken.

"You okay?" asked Sheila.

Laura smiled and shook her head saying, "I don't know. What do you think? Is the outfit becoming?"

They laughed to break whatever tension still hung in the air.

"How about a drink?" Sheila asked.

"Sure. Do you have VO?"

Sheila nodded.

"VO and seven if you have it," Laura added.

"Coming up."

Sheila poured one for each of them and then sat back herself.

"Do you want to talk about it?" she asked.

"Not now, please. I'm still trying to sort it out myself. I'll explain it all tomorrow, when we meet with the Senator."

Sheila nodded. "Where can we take you?"

Laura frowned. "I'm not sure. I can't go back to my apartment. I suppose a hotel would do. Nothing too expensive, though. I haven't worked in awhile."

"Why don't you just stay at my place, tonight?" Sheila offered.

"No, thanks. I don't want to put you out."

"Look, I'm already put out," she joked. "I can take you in with me in the morning. Besides, you look like you don't have much to wear. I'll probably have something that'll fit you."

Laura nodded her agreement. "Thanks."

She then leaned back and turned to watch the darkened countryside flit by. Thoughts of Mark disturbed her for the rest of the trip. They made her even more committed to the path upon which she'd embarked. It wouldn't bring him back, but it might help to end the coming terror.

The meeting with Senator Morgan took place at eight o'clock the next morning. The senator sat patiently through two and a half hours of one of the most unusual narrations he'd ever heard. He interrupted three times for minor clarifications and when it was over, he sat back pensively staring beyond his guests.

"That's quite a story," he said finally as he cupped his hands at the fingertips in front of his face and continued to stare off into space.

"I don't really expect you to believe all of this, senator," said Laura when the he offered nothing more. "It would be hard for me to believe, too, if I hadn't actually experienced the things I'm relating to you. Even as I sit here, I'm still not sure if it's all real. I do know one thing, though. It's clear to me what Aidan Sullivan is trying to do. I think a lot of people feel it. Deep down they sense something is happening but they can't define it. I see it, senator. What I see puts me on your side."

"What do you propose?" asked the senator, still wary.

"I can write what others are trying to understand. I have a flair with words. I can make difficult concepts seem simple. Understandable anyway."

Morgan stared hard at Laura. Her words were not those of conceit. She was simply stating a fact. She was damn good. He'd read her work for years. Although he hadn't liked the content of some of her most recent pieces, he had to admit that she was talented.

"Go on," he said.

"I don't plan to attack. I just intend to organize facts concisely and present the actual picture in simple form and in some historical perspective. The people will make the right decision, if they know the real facts."

"What specifically do you intend to write?"

Laura bowed her head, shaking it slowly before looking up again and responding, "I'm not sure. I . . . I'm hoping to get some guidance."

The statement was made warily but made nevertheless. Morgan was impressed she had the nerve to come back to hints of the supernatural, when she was already winning on a "real world" level. The woman was committed.

"Why do you come to me?" he finally asked. "There are many editors throughout this country who would welcome a controversial piece from a writer of your caliber."

Laura responded slowly and deliberately. This was delicate.

"I'm not looking for controversy or notoriety, senator. I don't even care if I get a byline. I just know that what I'll say will have to be told."

"My question still stands, then."

"I have two reasons. The first deals with time and practicality. It's possible I could sell the idea to a few editors. They may publish it in some of their papers. But they may also be afraid to get involved with a blackballed journalist. You have the network in place to get the articles immediately published nationwide. You've been fighting this term limits issue primarily from your home state. I bet Sheila's working late for the big push nationwide. My articles can be part of that push. If you like them, that is."

"And the second reason?" he asked noncommittally.

"Basically, sir, I'm afraid. To some, it may be ridiculous to think the president of the United States wants me dead. I believe it, though, with whatever twisted sense I'm dealing, I believe it." She paused and stared at him. "I need protection. A safe place to write and a place to stay until this is over.

"And when will this be over, Miss Miller?"

Laura sat back resignedly shaking her head. "I don't know. Maybe never," she said wistfully.

Everyone sat in silence for several minutes. Sheila Blackburn had sat quietly during the entire exchange. She had never seen such quiet conviction from anyone before. It was clear that Laura had resigned herself to do something she was compelled to do by some force beyond herself. She relished the thought of having a writer of

Laura's caliber side with the senator. She hoped the senator would say yes.

"I'll help you, Miss Miller," the senator finally said as he rocked forward in his chair and leaned his elbows on his desk. "I'll provide you with a place to write. I'll protect you the best I can. I will also do some of my own investigation. If I find you are wanted for any reason, I will not hesitate to turn you over to the proper authorities. Is that clear?"

"Yes," she responded quietly.

"You will write your articles as quickly as possible. If, after I review them, I feel they don't serve our needs, I will go no further with you. You will be on your own. There will be no appeal. Do you understand?"

"Yes, senator. Thank you."

"Sheila, do we still have our place available at the Oakmont?"

"Yes, senator."

"Get Miss Miller over there so she can get to work. What is our current time table?"

"Press releases in all the major newspapers tomorrow. We start a series of editorials on Thursday."

"When can I see your first article, Miss Miller?"

"I'll have it for you on Thursday evening." Laura wasn't sure when she'd have anything. She was used to working under pressure, however, and she knew she could have something for him by then. She just hoped it would be worth his trust in her.

"Good, I'll be expecting it. Thank you, Miss Miller."

The senator stood, signaling an end to the meeting. Laura and Sheila followed his example, and Sheila led the way to the door. Laura paused at the door and turned back to the senator.

"One more thing, sir?" she asked.

The senator stared at her.

"While you're investigating me . . . would you please check on Mark Tucker? He's the man I told you about. Could you see if there's any news about the accident?"

"Yes . . ." he wrote a note on a pad in front of him. "What is the policeman's name? Mister Tucker's friend?"

"Escobar, I believe. Commander Escobar."

"I'll see if there's any news."

Within a half hour Zac Morgan was on the phone with Commander Ralph Escobar.

"Do you know a man named Mark Tucker?" asked the senator.

"Yes, sir. Professor Tucker has been helping our department in the investigation of the Ripper murders."

At least that part of Laura's story checked out.

"I understand there was an automobile accident yesterday in Lancaster County, Pennsylvania, in which Mister Tucker may have been involved. Have you heard anything about that, commander?"

"Yes, sir."

"Do you know what happened to Mister Tucker?"

Escobar hesitated. He wasn't sure what he could tell the Senator. In view of recent events, he wasn't sure who he could trust.

"May I ask your interest, sir?" he finally asked.

"I am calling for a friend, commander."

"Is it a woman?"

It was the Senator's turn to be anxious. Laura had said during her narration of the events leading to her meeting with him Escobar had either informed on them or his line had been tapped.

"Commander, can I impose upon you to come by my office and speak to me?"

"When?"

"Can you come by right away? I'll have lunch brought in."

"I'll be there in forty-five minutes."

"Do you know where my office is?"

"Yes, sir."

"Good, I'll see you in forty-five minutes."

Charlie Gilbert didn't hear the conversation until much later in the day. Although the tap had been running continuously, he believed Mark Tucker was dead and Laura would not call the Commander. He never suspected that Senator Morgan would call.

Charlie had been directing his field operatives on a careful search of every Amish farm in the Hebenville area. He used the pretext that Laura was wanted on federal charges involving interstate drug trafficking. His people had no official arrest or search papers, but their badges and weapons gained them access to most homes. The Amish didn't resist strenuously anyway. As it turned out, none of them had anything to hide. Laura had disappeared.

When Charlie finally did hear the tape, he got two surprises.

One was that Senator Zac Morgan was interested in Mark Tucker on behalf of a woman. Although he didn't say it, his silence was enough for Charlie. Laura had escaped his net and was now being hidden by the senator. The second surprise he expected even less. An earlier phone call to Commander Escobar had established without a doubt Charlie Gilbert had failed the president completely. He would have to start from scratch and do it properly this time. He just hoped he wasn't too late.

"Ham sandwich okay?" asked Senator Morgan.

"Great," responded Commander Escobar.

The young man from the building's restaurant handed the ham sandwich and a carton of milk to the policeman and a tuna on wheat and iced tea to the senator. The senator signed the tab and the carrier left.

"I'd like to cut right to it if I may, Commander," started Senator Morgan as he unwrapped his sandwich. The senator eyed Escobar carefully before continuing. "I know where the woman . . . Laura Miller is." He paused as Escobar looked up, unable to mask his interest through bites of the sandwich. "Is she the woman you referred to on the phone?"

Escobar nodded and swallowed. He took a gulp of milk to help.

"Where is she?" he finally asked.

"She's safe. Now I'd like you to tell me if the same can be said for Mister Tucker."

Escobar still wasn't sure. He took another bite and chewed slowly while he tried to determine how to respond.

"If I'm not mistaken, commander, we're on the same side."

"Well, I don't know about that, senator." Escobar finally spoke. "I don't know much these days, it seems. I can tell you that Tucker is safe. Some of my boys are picking him up right now. He survived the little surprise someone planted for him."

Escobar watched the Senator carefully. If Mark's suspicions were correct, there was federal involvement in the loss of his brakes and in the bombs that caused the second and third explosions.

"As for being on the same side," Escobar continued, "I'm just trying to catch a killer. What are you looking for?"

"From what I understand, Mister Tucker believes that your killer is the very same man that I'm trying to unseat."

"That may be. The professor has a good imagination. Anyway, someone seems to think he's on to something."

"You believe his mishap was no accident?"

"I didn't say that. That was the professor's position. Me, I'm not sure what to believe. I'm just going to bring him back safely and see what he has to say."

"Was he hurt badly?"

"Broken arm and a few cuts and bruises. Seems he wasn't wearing a seat belt. He flew out when the car was rolling. I'm thinking of having him cited," closed Escobar with a smile.

Morgan ignored the comment. "I'd like to know if I can help you, commander."

"Look, I gotta be honest with you. I don't know if we can trust you. It turns out maybe my phone was tapped by some of you federal government people. All we're trying to do is find a killer and all kinds of weird things start happening. First, our suspect is whisked away from us by you feds and then the professor's almost killed."

"I assure you that my office has no involvement. I understand you can't believe that, yet. However, if I am not mistaken, we are both under significant time pressure here. So if we can help each other, we must find common ground."

"Amen to that, senator. I'll just hold off until I've got the professor and I've had a chance to talk to him without someone else listening in. I'll be in touch with you, okay?"

Morgan nodded, "That's fine. You know where you can reach me."

Escobar stood and let the sandwich crumbs fall to the floor at his feet. He put the crumpled wrappings on the tray and carried the half empty carton of milk with him.

"Thanks for the lunch."

Morgan stood and nodded.

"Please call me, commander."

"Will do," he smiled and left.

The senator sat back down to finish his own sandwich. Maybe Laura's story wasn't so farfetched after all.

CHAPTER 31

The single-bedroom apartment at the Oakmont was a finely appointed affair in one of the ritzier security buildings in D.C. The senator rented the unit as housing for traveling dignitaries from his home state as well as for family members outside the D.C. area. Although he had his staff monitor its use, the senator paid for the unit out of his own personal funds.

The apartment was on the eighth floor, overlooking Pennsylvania Avenue just three blocks north of the White House, the grounds of which were within view from the apartment's main window.

Laura stared in the direction of the White House as she leaned against the window sill. She was glad there was no balcony at the living room window. It gave her an even greater sense of security despite the proximity of her enemy's home.

Just to the right of the window sat a desk with a computer pushed off to the right and a yellow legal-sized pad of paper directly in front of the chair in the middle of the desk. She preferred to write longhand and then transfer her product to the word processor. It brought her closer to her work and gave her a better feel for the words. She was able to think more clearly through the movement of her pen across the paper.

Laura had already tried, several times, to start her story. Her efforts were attested to by the balled yellow papers piled in the round wastebasket next to the desk and littering the floor around it.

She'd suffered writer's block many times in her career. There were times when she could sit with her pad for long minutes without writing a single word. She usually had an idea where she wanted to go with her writing, but she would have difficulty getting started or working a transition. On those occasions, she was able to overcome her block reasonably quickly. She would simply start writing anything in a stream-of-consciousness manner and suddenly her opening or transition would come.

This occasion was different, however. Free-flow writing simply wasn't working. She had no clear understanding of ultimate direction despite her assurances to Senator Morgan. Not only did she not know specifically how to approach her subject, she had also lost even the semblance of an idea as to the general direction she should take. Her mind was in chaos. Struggling with emotions of fear, anger, and the need for vengeance, Laura's thoughts drifted to Bill McDonough, Michael Stoner, five hundred innocent victims aboard Flight 384, possibly Jake Laford, several women over the years, and now Mark Tucker. They had all died brutally. Was it at the hand of one man? One power-hungry lunatic whose drive for true world control was a real possibility? And what of Laura herself? Why her? If only he'd leave her alone, she'd go away and forget it all.

Duty? What duty? Her only real duty was for her own preservation. She didn't owe anyone anything. Yet she was called, according to Grandfather Schmidt. She hadn't slept peacefully for weeks because of this supposed call. Maybe she really was the only one who could save it all.

Her thoughts were a jumble of contradictions. A battle raged within her head, stifling her to the point of mental paralysis. Coupled with the pressure of a deadline, her anxiety level continued to rise as she stood breathing deeply in an attempt to control her mixed emotions.

When she turned away from the window, she surveyed the room, searching for anything that might help her clear her mind and get down to business. Her eyes darted frantically back and forth until they landed on the Mary medal laying on the desk next to her. The broken chain lay knotted around the medal. She'd taken it out of her purse and laid it next to her when she'd sat down to write, hoping it would serve as a good luck charm.

"Some charm," she mumbled aloud. She continued to stare at it as a new thought struggled into her consciousness.

"Maybe you're not a charm at all," she spoke to the medal as she lifted it. "Maybe you're just a reminder. Like Father John said."

Her hand closed around the medal and tangled chain as she looked up at the ceiling and walked away from the window musing aloud. "A reminder of what? You're just a piece of metal that my uncle loved to carry. What do I have to do?" She closed her eyes and held both fists up in frustration when suddenly she heard the voice.

It was clear and steady. Almost melodic and definitely soothing. The voice was a woman's perhaps, but that was not clear. Only the words stood out and seemed to hang in the air.

"Why don't you just ask?"

Laura spun around. She saw no one. It couldn't have come from outside . . . eight stories down. It had been so clear. No radio was on. No television. There was no source that she could discern, yet she'd heard the words so clearly. As if someone had been standing before her, speaking to her alone.

She repeated the words in her own mind. A story she'd seen years before on the TV series "Unsolved Mysteries" came back to her. The story was about a woman named Rita Klaus who'd been stricken with the debilitating disease of multiple sclerosis since her late teen years. After leaving her studies as a nun, getting married, and starting a family during a time when the disease had appeared to be in remission, it came back, permanently. By the time she'd reached her mid-forties, her legs had atrophied and were completely useless. She was forced to use braces and crutches or a wheelchair. She pulled away from her faith in God, growing bitter and angry. In the process, she alienated everyone who had grown close to her.

One day, a good-hearted former friend suggested that Rita go to a healing mass at their local Catholic Church. Although she was bitterly opposed to the idea, her husband demanded it as the only hope of saving any semblance of their family relationship. Shielded by her intense anger, she accompanied the friend to the service and stood at the end of a pew shakily bracing herself on her crutches when a priest suddenly walked up behind her and took her in his arms from behind.

He held her tightly against her struggles and said softly, "May the peace of the Lord be with you."

Rita later reported that a sudden calm came over her. A warmth coursed through her body and filled her with a joy that she hadn't felt in years. After that day, Rita proclaimed although she had not been physically healed, her spirit had been healed. Her anger had left her.

A few months later, as she lay in bed one night praying before sleep, she too heard a voice. It had asked a question similar to the one Laura had heard, and somehow Rita had understood. As she lay in bed, she created a prayer asking the Holy Mother to pray for her for whatever other healing Jesus felt she needed. Again, a warmth coursed through her body, and although she woke still needing leg braces, later that next day she felt a tingling in her toes for the first time in years. As the day wore on, the sensation moved up her legs. Suddenly gone were the inward-turned knees. Her legs appeared supple and full and when she removed her leg braces and threw aside her crutches, she was miraculously able to walk, run, and dance as never before. Her doctors were beside themselves with shock at the miraculous recovery. No one could explain it. Yet Rita knew unequivocally that she'd been cured because she'd made the commitment to ask the Lord for help.

Despite Laura's Catholic upbringing, her own belief in God had become more of a conversation piece than anything to which she really gave much intellectual thought. She believed, deep down, that the tenuous balance of the earth's life forces could really only have been created and maintained by a Supreme Being interested in its continuance. The entire structure was just too fragile to have happened and continued by accident or coincidence. Yet she had drifted away from a practicing belief.

The words "God helps those who help themselves" had been imparted to her at an early age. She repeated the words occasionally as she matured and as time passed they had taken on a new meaning. Through her struggles to achieve and gain recognition, she came to believe that if there really was a God out there, he or she had more important things to do than to assist an able bodied self-achiever. From thinking that maybe she had no right to impinge upon God's time, her thoughts had evolved away from God completely. She was on her own and that's how it was supposed to be.

It had all worked well until she was derailed and now found herself in despair, unable to form even the first word of a series that she had to write.

Slowly Laura went to her knees in the middle of the room and clasped her hands together in her lap. "Are you really there? Do you really care what happens to me? Or anyone else in this world?" She asked the questions angrily, still struggling with her own beliefs that she was solely responsible for her own destiny. She couldn't be weak. Yet she was. She could think of no other way.

Laura's right hand moved slowly, so that her fingertips touched her forehead and she made the sign of the cross, whispering, "In the name of the Father, and of the Son," as her fingertips touched her abdomen and then moved to each shoulder with the final words, "and the Holy Spirit."

Head bowed, she spoke softly as if she was still not sure.

"Grandfather Schmidt says you're calling me, Lord. If you're up there. I don't understand. I know this president is wrong, but we've had others who've been bad. Why am I in the middle of this? Why did Mark Tucker have to die? And Bill and Nell? And all the others?"

Laura was building confusion for herself again. Her mind raced with seeming inconsistencies. If God really did care, why would he permit such pointless deaths? Why wouldn't he step forward and stop this evil?

She sat silently brooding until tears of frustration came to her eyes. She held the medal tighter in both hands and brought her hands slowly to her mouth.

"Please, Lord, help me understand. Show me the proper path."

Instantly the confusion disappeared. She had no specific answers to all the "whys," but her mind no longer struggled with the questions. No more self-indulgence. There wasn't time for worrying about her personal concerns and beliefs. As Grandfather Schmidt had tried to relate to her, her burden was great. She suddenly understood if she didn't act now, the burden would only grow to overwhelm her. She knew what she had to do. She'd known it all along. There was nowhere to hide. To run from the task that awaited her. Even when she'd sat down earlier to write, she'd fought with herself. Now she knew. She would write what she'd told Senator Morgan she'd write. A simple, clearly understandable account of events. The path was clear.

Without thinking, Laura was suddenly on her feet and at the desk lifting her pen. The words gushed forth in a torrent and in minutes, the blank yellow pad was filling with a chronicle of Aidan Sullivan's presidency.

CHAPTER 32

The receptionist buzzed Senator Morgan at six o'clock that evening.

"Commander Ralph Escobar is on the phone, senator. Line three."

"Thanks, Mary," he said as he lifted the receiver and pushed the button next to the blinking red light.

"Commander?"

"Can I come by to see you?"

"When can you be here?"

"Half hour?"

"I'll be waiting."

Zac Morgan had been anxious to hear from the Escobar since he'd left the senator's office five hours earlier. The senator and his aides had continued to work at a fevered pace to coordinate press releases throughout the country and to ensure space for editorials in newspapers. But he couldn't take his mind off the events related to him by Laura Miller and at least partially confirmed by Commander Escobar. If the story was true, his struggle was over. The senator's attempt to derail the president's move to a third term would take on a twist that would assure his ultimate victory and the destruction of the most powerful man the world had ever seen. On the other hand, if it was all a hoax, intended—perhaps by the president himself—to diffuse the senator's burgeoning support, it could all backfire on Zac Morgan. The only true voice of opposition would be shut off and the path to the president's ultimate goal would be smooth.

Senator Morgan was anxious to know the truth. Yet he'd have to be careful and control the natural tendency to seek the sensational without knowing, for certain, of its truth.

Commander Escobar arrived at the senator's office with Mark Tucker in tow. At the same time, Charlie Gilbert was listening to the taped conversations from earlier in the day. The auto accident had done a number on Mark. Contrary to Escobar's previous assertion that he'd suffered only a broken arm and some minor cuts and bruises, Mark's torso was tightly wrapped to protect the two cracked ribs, he limped noticeably as the result of a twisted and sprained left knee, and his exposed flesh was mottled with bruises in various stages of discoloration. Bandages and dressings covered numerous cuts and wounds. He was lucky to have survived the accident at all.

"It all fits, senator," said Mark Tucker after finishing his story. "Anytime he's under career-threatening pressure, there's a murder. It's as if he's got to perform a sacrifice or something to some angry god. Then after the murders, something great happens for him."

Morgan sat staring at his two guests.

He was now convinced that Laura and Mark were being truthful. Mark's recitation of the facts leading to this meeting were the same as Laura's, albeit from a different perspective. Even Commander Escobar was no longer simply saying that it was the "professor's belief" the president was involved in the Ripper murders. He had apparently bought into Mark's theory.

"This is a delicate matter, Mister Tucker," rejoined the senator. "Obviously the commander here will need much more than a theory to obtain a warrant for the arrest of the president of the United States."

Mark smiled through the discomfort of his injuries.

"I'm well aware of that, senator. I'm also well aware of the fact that the evidence to support the theory will be almost impossible to find. The president will undoubtedly have unassailable proof of his whereabouts at the time of each murder. The commander himself will tell you that there is absolutely no physical evidence linking him to the crimes."

316

"That seems to defeat your position," said Morgan.

"Yes. It would appear that way," continued Mark. "But there is a possibility. This latest string of murders is the longest to date." Mark leaned forward anxiously and then winced in pain and leaned back again. He smiled. "Sorry, I'm getting too excited." He paused and readjusted himself.

"The problem," he continued "is that I haven't been able to put together a clear picture of the real threat to him. In the past, the threats were easily identifiable."

The senator nodded, acknowledging Mark's previous explanation of those events.

"Germany seems to be quiet right now, and he's moving smoothly on the third term issue. But something's wrong."

"Miss Miller thinks he believes she's a threat to him," interjected Senator Morgan.

Mark looked at the senator warily, not sure if he was mocking Laura. Finally he nodded slowly, saying, "I think she's right. There is no question that someone has been pursuing her. Laura's a smart woman. I don't think she'd go off and make any of this up. Even if you're inclined to think she would, however, I can only refer you to this." He lifted his arms and winced. "This was no accident, senator."

"But it was directed at you, Mister Tucker. Not Miss Miller," said the Senator.

"There was another car waiting for Laura. I didn't recognize it when I drove past. Later, I remembered it. One of the cars followed me and the other stayed put."

"What do you suggest?" asked the senator.

"I don't think this string is played out yet. Whatever has pushed him so far is still out there. If Laura's the threat, he won't rest until she's out of the picture. If he's frustrated in his efforts to get at her, I think he'll act again. We have to be ready."

"How will we know when he'll move?"

"We don't know exactly. So we force his hand."

Morgan looked at Commander Escobar, who shrugged.

"You said earlier that Laura is writing something she thinks will help your cause, senator. If it really can, then it will threaten his chances of gaining a third term. I don't know if that's all it'll take to set him off. However, if he really is after Laura, it may be because he's concerned about what she can do with her pen. She caused a sensation once. Maybe she can do it again."

"You're suggesting he had some previous knowledge Laura would write a series of articles that could actually destroy him?" the Senator asked incredulously.

Mark was treading on thin ice now. It sounded like he was bestowing some supernatural power on the president. He spoke slowly and carefully.

"I don't know what knowledge the president may have had. All I know is that if he is the animal we've been looking for, he's a sick man. A man who relies on whatever twisted perceptions he may have. If he is indeed pursuing Laura, it's because he perceives she'll do him great harm. You said she would have the first article available on Thursday. If it's his true concern, he'll act on it."

Mark paused and looked from the senator to Commander Escobar.

"We can stake out the White House and wait," he finished.

Morgan shook his head and smiled, "Stake out the White House? Do you have any idea the amount of security there? Do you think it's possible to stake out the White House without being seen?"

Mark was angry at the senator's patronizing tone.

"Look, senator, if you've got a better idea, let's hear it. We all want this son of a bitch. I haven't seen anything from anyone else that will get us close."

"I'm sorry, Mister Tucker," said Morgan. "You're right, of course. If there's any merit to any of this, we must catch him in the act. It's just so difficult to comprehend the possibility that the president is a killer."

"No more difficult than any other white-collar criminal in this country, senator."

Morgan nodded at the rebuke and then turned to Escobar.

"What do you think Commander?"

He nodded slowly as he thought of the logistics of such a stake out.

"Let's do it," he finally said.

The meeting ended at ten o'clock that night. Mark longed to see Laura, but Senator Morgan suggested they meet her the next day.

318

On parting, they resolved to meet outside the Oakmont the next morning.

Tuesday dawned bright and warm. By the time Mark Tucker and Ralph Escobar left the commander's modest, single-level colonial in Arlington, Virginia, it was clear that they were in for a hot, humid day.

Mark called Nickie the prior evening upon his arrival at the Escobar homestead. He hadn't spoken to her since Saturday, his and Laura's second night in Hebenville. Prior to that, he had called her every day. Because of the three-hour time difference between the two coasts, Nickie was still wide awake and embroiled in a cut-throat game of *Risk* with her best friend, Julie Stuart, with whose family she was staying.

When Nickie expressed her concern he hadn't called on Sunday, Mark assured her that he was fine and that his meetings had gone on until late in the evening. Nickie missed her father terribly and said so.

Mark missed Nickie, too. They were a team who did everything together. His ache for his daughter grew even more intense in the morning when the commander's six kids, ranging in age from two to sixteen filled the house with their morning chatter in preparation for school and other activities.

"You've got a beautiful family, commander," Mark smiled as they pulled out of the driveway and waved to Escobar's wife Margie.

Escobar nodded and said, "Yeah, thanks. How's your daughter?"

"Good. She misses me." Mark smiled wistfully and looked out the window. "I've got to get back to her."

Mark turned to Escobar who nodded and turned his attention to the road. They had a job to complete.

★ ★ ★

Laura was awakened early by a phone call from Sheila Blackburn. Apparently the senator was coming by the apartment at nine o'clock to speak with her. Laura didn't tell Sheila that she had already completed two parts of the articles and was well on her way with the third. She wanted to save the news for the senator.

Shortly after nine, Laura responded to a knock at the apartment door. She checked the view hole and saw the senator's distorted face smiling at her. She also saw the figures of other people, but she couldn't make out who they were. Upon opening the door to welcome the senator, she was stunned as she glanced behind him to Mark's beaming face.

"Mark?" she whispered. "Mark!" The senator stepped aside and she threw her arms around Mark. "I thought you were dead."

Mark winced in pain as Laura squeezed him tightly.

"Not yet," he said happily. "But I will be soon if you're not careful."

Laura took the hint and escorted him carefully into the apartment.

"God, I'm glad you're alive, Mark," she said softly as Mark sat down in a chair.

"Me too," he answered with a smile. "How 'bout you? You all right?"

"Yeah," she nodded with a sly smile. "I'm ready for the son of a bitch."

Laura handed the senator a stack of paper.

"These are the first two installments," she said. "Two more are coming."

The senator immediately sat and started reading as Laura turned to Mark. They spent the next twenty minutes reciting the events that led them to their present meeting. Mark spoke first, at Laura's urging, but he was more anxious to learn of Grandfather Schmidt's words to her. He told his story quickly and then asked for hers. When Laura was finished, Mark was confused.

"It's difficult to understand," she said. "I know that struck a chord with me, though. I know what I have to do." She pointed to the articles in the senator's hands. "That's it."

Senator Morgan stood at the living room window staring out toward the White House. He held the articles loosely in his right hand, which hung at his side. Laura and Mark watched him expectantly.

"They're beautiful, Miss Miller." He turned slowly and held the articles up for all to see. "It's the best writing I've seen in years. You've made it so clear that anyone who reads these will understand what's happening. When can I have the conclusion?"

"I think I can have it by tonight," Laura said happily.

"We can run them on four consecutive days," he said. "Let's see, if we start on Thursday, Friday, Saturday . . . we can conclude on Sunday. Perfect.

It was far better than he'd hoped. Laura's words were lyrical. They pulled him along on a ride of clarity. So easily was he ensnared, that when he finished, he wanted more. He couldn't wait for the conclusion. The conclusion that, by Monday, would turn the tide on President Aidan Sullivan.

"The senator just left," the voice said into Charlie Gilbert's ear.
"What about the cop and Tucker?"
"Not yet, sir."
"Is she there?"
"We don't know yet."
"Keep me posted."

Charlie hung up knowing that Laura was in the building. After the first call, he'd checked and learned that Senator Zac Morgan kept an apartment on the eighth floor. He would like specific confirmation even though he didn't really need it. The senator had hidden her away, but he hadn't done a very good job.

Phone calls were pouring in to Bret Cummings from Third Term Headquarters all over the country. Senator Morgan's press releases were simple statements hitting hard at the president. There was no question they would do some damage, and the leaders in the various state headquarters were looking for direction.

Bret mollified them all, saying the senator was grasping at straws. He was trying to incite a society with little or no spiritual values to be outraged that the president was likening himself to God. Bret was confident that his own press people could easily counter the attacks by first pointing out their falsity, as the president had not said he was God, and then by again driving home the realities of life before and after Aidan Sullivan. His state coordinators were comfortable things were still in hand after they spoke to Bret. That, after all, was his strength, making things right for the president.

The chief of staff had concerns of his own that no one would be able to make right, however. He was able to deal with the business of marketing the man he'd followed since they first met at Georgetown University nearly twenty years before. There was no one better at it than Bret Cummings. What he was unable to do, however, was fathom his man's obsession.

Cummings had learned over the years to go with the president's hunches. He had an uncanny ability to see things in the future. He anticipated rough spots and attacked them, often physically, before they could hurt him. This time it was different. The object of the president's ire simply didn't make sense. As Cummings saw it, she was nothing. A woman who'd been quickly undone by her own obsession. The obsession for the American Dream, its riches, prestige, and power. What more could she do?

But the president was concerned. He reviled his aides for their ineptitude. And, as he berated them, he paid no attention to the real challenges that mounted. It was left to Bret Cummings to anticipate and respond. He had to be there to make sure the president's train was not derailed. But he could not hold it forever. The obsession had to be dealt with quickly . . . before the momentum was gone completely.

CHAPTER 33

The last of the secret meetings of the heads of the European community took place via video phone at nine-thirty Wednesday morning. Chancellor Heinrich Adler of Germany had been playing his own game for several months. When he met with Secretary of State Henry Trotter, he spoke the right words of supplication. Of course, he'd stand by the Americans after Mr. Trotter's assurances that America really had no imperialistic motivations.

"The Americans have become so arrogant again," he thought then. "They are complacent in the belief they are invincible behind their president."

For three months Chancellor Adler had stepped up his efforts to unite the EC in a common front against American interests. Although European economic fortunes had initially taken a leap forward with that of the Americans during Aidan Sullivan's early days in the White House, American demands for tribute escalated continuously thereafter. The EC's combined economic output stagnated while American fortunes continued to flourish. It had become increasingly apparent that America and its president had one goal sought by so many power-maddened leaders of the past. The major difference was that America had the power to attain the goal of world domination if it was not stopped.

It had taken nearly every waking moment for three months for Adler to move his counterparts in the other EC countries to the momentous decision they had just made, but he had done it. Even the English were behind his plan.

That night the Chancellor made the announcement. His address was carried live, with translations, to every country in the EC during their prime viewing time. Simultaneously, U.S. networks carried the address to millions of Americans.

Bret Cummings sat alone to watch Heinrich Adler strike the blow he and the president thought would never come. They had grown smug in their belief that Henry Trotter's diplomacy was working and the German problem would hold until the world saw that Aidan Sullivan would be cleared by constitutional caveat to run for a third term. They had planned a grandstand play at that time when the world would be watching closely and the American electorate would be most malleable. But they had miscalculated.

Adler's square jaw was firmly set as he announced the EC was cutting diplomatic relations with the United States, effective immediately. Only the president himself, in a meeting with the EC heads, would be able to open diplomatic channels again. In addition, all American goods being dumped on the European populace would be subject to immediate tariffs tripling their costs and making them all but unmarketable. Finally, American military bases in Europe would have all support, utility, and supply lines cut off. They would be required to move from European soil within thirty days.

Adler's expectations were reasonable. He demanded simply that oil be made available to all at competitive rates and that the EC be brought into the global planning that had been totally usurped by the United States. In closing, the chancellor begged the American people to understand what was happening in their country and to step up to force a change that would create a unity of strength rather than the imperialist power structure sought by their president.

Bret Cummings dropped his head as Adler completed his address. In the past, Adler's words would have been countered quickly by the eloquence of Aidan Sullivan. He had done it before when similar pleas were made by the Arabs and the Japanese. The American people would hear Adler's words and wait for a response from their leader. They would then assume his posture as they always had. Only this time, things were different. Aidan Sullivan wasn't seeing straight. Bret wondered if he would even understand what was happening, so steeped was he in his anger that a woman could so easily escape his clutches.

For the rest of the day, Bret attempted to reach the president to plan the next move. They could diffuse the impact of Chancellor Adler's speech only if they responded quickly in Aidan Sullivan's inimitable way. But the president was unavailable. He sat seething with Charlie Gilbert. He demanded an immediate end to his nightmare.

The next morning, Chancellor Adler's address was the lead story in every newspaper and on every news program in the United States. And the first installment of Laura Miller's series appeared in column one of the nation's leading newspapers.

Charlie Gilbert had planned his hit for Wednesday night. He, too, had become complacent in his belief in his own capabilities. He didn't even suspect a guard awaited him outside Laura's eighth floor room. He was sure Zac Morgan had no idea of the workings of the underground world. The senator didn't really believe someone was out to get Laura Miller.

What Charlie hadn't counted on, however, was the mind of Mark Tucker. Mark knew the world of psychotic killers. He knew its unpredictability. And above all, he knew anything was possible.

When the elevator door opened, Charlie Gilbert, dressed in black denims and black work shirt, with a silenced, clean Luger tucked into the back of his pants, stared into the barrel of a police shotgun. The man behind the weapon was alert. Obviously, his first evening on this job. Understanding immediately that it would take a couple of days for the man to let his guard down, Charlie thought quickly.

"Is this the ninth floor?" he asked and looked above the guard to the placard which identified the floor as the eighth.

"Eighth," blurted the guard.

"Sorry," Charlie smiled again as the doors closed and he pushed the button for the ninth floor. From the ninth, Charlie rode the elevator back down to the lobby and exited. He needed a new plan. One guard would not be difficult, but he had to be prepared. He'd be back.

CHAPTER 34

Laura's story had impact. She hadn't gone off like some half-cocked fanatic, preaching fire and brimstone to a skeptical public. She'd played his game . . . appealing to her audiences' own selfish interests and manipulating them. Some were even believing the president himself was one of those fanatic types.

Aidan Sullivan sat bleary-eyed staring at the third installment in the *New York Times*. Neither of the Washington papers would dare print it for fear of White House retribution. Every other major paper in the land had run the story, thanks to the efforts of that son of a bitch Zac Morgan and his staff.

Even the nation's TV news magazines and special news shows had picked up the story and analyzed its contents. Every major network was seeking an interview with Laura Miller, but she was hidden from the public's eye except for the story in which she promised more.

The president had read all three installments and was shocked, initially, at Laura's insight. She started with Albert Smith and accompanied the story with a photograph depicting the president's knowing smirk in the face of Al's .357 Magnum. The caption asked, very simply, "Did he know?" The president answered the question again and again emphatically. "Of course!" But how had she found out?

In their brief encounter at the Washington Monument, she'd known nothing! She was like a baby, naive and scared with not even the slightest conscious hint of his intentions. He could see the seeds planted deep in her brain and he had tried to crush them, but he'd been stopped. For the first time in his memory, he'd been stopped. He'd felt resistance and been unable to overcome it. His first thought was the distance between himself and the woman. Yet when he confronted her again, in the crowd, the resistance still was strong. He could have overcome it then had they left him alone to deal with her. None of this would now be happening if he had.

Things started to move quickly after the first story. Laura's approach was to present the events of his presidency simply. She created a masterpiece, showing the pattern of power and might that had made America so strong that once friendly countries were afraid. They were wary of the president's reach, and they were beginning to turn away into the arms of the powerful Germany. Laura wrote that even now the president made plans to attack his former European allies. Was that what the American people wanted? Did they really want to control a world that hated them?

In the second installment, she wrote a lyrically sensitive piece decrying the greed and arrogance of those who surrounded the president. She hinted at the lessons she'd recently learned about the lack of inner peace when the only goal was wealth, but she touched it softly. Just enough to make readers think, for it was only through revelation, when a seed has had a chance to take hold, that understanding occurs. Aidan Sullivan knew that well, as had many well-loved power mongers of modern times. They planted the seed in the minds of their subjects and nurtured it to reality with smooth rhetoric.

In the third installment, Laura struck the hearts of folks from once-bucolic middle America to the smoldering coastal metropolises. She wrote of family values. They had to remember years—long gone—when families played together and mothers and fathers actually loved their children. Of times when God was at the center of their lives and they could actually sit on a sunny spring afternoon, in a park and be at peace with their lives and families. She wrote of Sundays at church and other days of prayer and a simpler life when it really didn't matter whether one had wealth and power. People were happy simply to be alive and to share moments with family and friends.

After setting the stage, Laura struck the blow of contrast. The sickly present times of street families and constant striving for the unattainable golden calf, the preoccupation with hedonistic pleasures at the expense of the very soul of all Americans. "Where has the kindness gone?" she asked. "Where has the giving gone?" It has gone to the mark, she concluded. The mark of loyalty to the megalomanic who sat atop the throne of the world as the president of the United States.

Bret Cummings' morning briefing was the sign her attacks were working. From across the country, word from Third Term Headquarters was that support was slipping. The president had no doubt that this latest piece would continue the slide. Every effort to prevent the publication of new installments had failed. She'd struck a chord with readers and they were anxious for more. Suddenly, it was no longer clear the president had the support of even the first twenty-five states.

At four-thirty Saturday afternoon, Bret knocked softly and entered the president's office. He could feel the raging tension emanating from the president. No mere massage would appease him now. Still, Bret had to do something to bring him back. It had to be now before time slipped too far away.

"Aidan?" he called softly.

The president was sitting forward in the shadowy gloom of a cloudy afternoon which filtered, dully, through half drawn drapes. His hands, palms down and first knuckles tensed, gripped his desk pad on either side of the *Times'* Section One. He'd been like this since shortly after their morning meeting. For almost seven hours he'd brooded, uninterrupted by the thousands of calls that flooded the White House. Bret drew closer.

"Aidan," he called again.

Slowly the president lifted his eyes. Even in the shadowy light, Bret could see they were bloodshot. Cold. Deadly. And with the eyes came the searing pain of an angry probe. Bret lurched backwards as if struck.

"Aidan, please," he screamed.

Bret fell to the floor and grabbed his head as the president stood slowly and stared at the writhing figure of his chief of staff. Then after causing enough pain, he turned away, released him and walked to the window overlooking the west lawn. He sneered at the clouds churning dark and ominous in the distance.

"You've all let me down," he said in a low raspy voice. A voice Bret had heard only rarely, when his power was truly threatened. When his almost maniacal anger would overtake him and invariably show him the way back. It was different now, however. It had gotten worse each time. It had gotten more difficult to bring him back. Bret feared that this time he might not be able to come back.

The chief of staff pushed himself up on to shaky legs while he continued to clutch his head. The dizziness subsided slowly, but the pain persisted.

"It's not over, Aidan," he pleaded through gritted teeth. "Your address to the nation is in three hours. They're waiting to hear from you. They still want you. They want to hear *you*!" Bret's emphasis was intended to awaken in his leader the subconscious energy that had carried him through every previous trial. "We all need you, Aidan," he finished softly.

Bret wished the president would accept the assistance of speech writers. There was no question that Sullivan's best speeches were when he spoke without aid, but he was concerned that the current situation needed truly delicate handling, a thing for which the president was not suited. Bret stared at his back before turning slowly to leave.

"I'll be back for you at six-thirty, Aidan."

Aidan Sullivan continued to stare at the churning mass of bulbous black clouds.

When his father didn't send him back to the Sunford Home, Jason was happy. He was glad when Big Bill and Frank had taken him away from that cold room with the bright lights at the police station. He didn't know why they'd taken him there in the first place. He was just trying to stop the Monster.

Jason had cried several times since he'd been brought home to the White House. He liked being at the White House because that's where his father was. Even though his father didn't come to see him much, and when he did he was usually mad or something. Jason still liked to be close. He was happier here. Still, he cried because of the Monster. For longer than he could remember, he'd had dreams of the Monster. In the beginning, he'd simply thrashed about in bed and begged it to leave him alone. After a while, however, he knew that he had the dreams because he was supposed to try to stop it. Maybe if he'd been a little smarter, he'd have been able to do so. That's why he cried. It was for all those ladies. The ones the Monster had taken. And he had done nothing.

Jason occupied a group of rooms in the east wing of the president's home. The area was off limits to visitors and well shielded from public view. Even the yard area outside the rooms was hidden. He liked the surroundings because there were no bars. Although Frank Thompson slept in the same room with him, Jason really didn't look at him as a guard. He wasn't even concerned about the huge gun that Frank carried with him everywhere they went.

Jason liked Frank. He'd always liked him more than the others who helped his father. Other people joked around about the fact that it was probably because Frank was almost as dumb as Jason. At those times, Jason didn't like Frank as much because Frank would get mad and act mean to show the others that he was smarter than Jason. When he wasn't being mean, Frank was a lot of fun. He'd wrestle with Jason and play the kind of running and hiding games Jason liked. Frank would even watch cartoons with him. He was a good guy.

In the last few days Jason had started to get nervous. He hoped Frank hadn't noticed because he didn't want Frank to interfere with what he might have to do.

The Monster was coming again. It wasn't ready to act yet, but it would be soon. He'd tried to tell Frank about it once, but Frank wouldn't listen. He'd gotten mad and a little mean. He'd even pointed the gun at Jason and told him never to mention it again. So Jason didn't.

The feeling was getting stronger. Something was going to happen soon because the Monster was coming. He didn't know when or where it would strike. But he would know soon. He always did, just before.

At seven forty-five, Senator Morgan, Gordy Mason, and several other of the Senator's aides crowded his office in anticipation of the president's speech, just fifteen minutes away.

A network newscaster was summarizing the week's events, covering the European Community Summit first, then moving quickly to the stories that had sparked such intense interest. No one had yet spoken to Laura Miller about the sensation she'd caused. Some commentators mentioned the previous story that had almost destroyed her career but most stuck to the current series. Although the White House wouldn't admit it, the commentators boldly speculated it was the waning support for the constitutional amendment that prompted the coming speech and press conference before a live audience outside the White House. Despite the president's supporters' recommendations that he not answer questions after the speech, the press corps felt he would anyway. They anticipated the pointed questions raised in Laura's articles.

"This is it, ladies and gentlemen," said the senator softly to his cadre.

Laura stared through the gloom of night at the coming storm. It promised to be a big one. Unusual for spring in Washington. But then everything that had been happening recently was unusual. She stood next to her desk where a copy of the final installment of her series of four stories sat. She had already submitted the original. It would be appearing in newspapers across the country in the morning. Barring anything unforeseen, it would vie with the president's speech for the lead story of most newspapers.

★ CHAPTER 34 ★

By the last article was the start of a new one, which she'd entitled, "The Rise and Fall of Aidan Sullivan." It had simply come to her as the others had. She'd asked for help and always kept the Mary medal close by, as a reminder. Laura didn't yet know the ending of her new endeavor, but it would come. Unlike Mark, who was convinced it would end with the president's arrest just seconds before his attempt at another murder, Laura felt deeply that she would yet have to face him. She dreaded it.

"Here he comes," shouted Mark from the adjacent room.

Mark had talked Commander Escobar into letting him work stakeout with him for the past three nights outside the White House. He was convinced that all the conditions were ripe for another nighttime attack by the Ripper. If he hadn't missed his guess, Laura's articles and the surprise action by the European Community were just the things that would create the tension that begged for its murderous release. Although they'd followed limousines from the capital garage on two occasions in the previous three nights, neither one proved to be what they awaited. Commander Escobar was growing leery, despite the evidence supporting Mark's theory. He wouldn't last much longer. It was all too crazy.

Laura walked into her apartment's living room and sat down next to Mark. She smiled, again grateful he was with her. He grasped her hand as they prepared to watch the president.

Fingering the medal with her other hand, she listened as the president began to speak.

His voice was calm. Mechanically slow. He spoke softly at first as if he was trying to find the proper path.

"Americans. I've stood before you many times over the past fifteen years. First as a representative in my home state of California and then as your president. We have come a long way together. We have accomplished much."

He spoke directly now, starting to build his energy and firmly driving a message that was coming clear to him with every word he uttered. Bret Cummings stood to the side, tense at first but slowly calming himself with the realization once again that the president was in his element.

"I have done everything within my meager capabilities to strengthen this great country of ours. To make it the mightiest nation in the world for you. At every turn we have faced formidable foes from Arabia, Japan, Central and South America, Africa, and other parts of Asia and Europe. We have vanquished them all. For what?"

He stared at the camera, his blue eyes piercing the heart of each of his viewers.

"For you, my friends. You are the only people in the world worthy of all the gifts of this earth.

"Before our presidency, we were all adrift. Led by weaklings who put the welfare of foreign peoples ahead of our own. They opened this country to every kind of trash from abroad and we were sinking. The weight of our burden was killing us all. We were unemployed and scared. It was only with the tremendous effort of the past seven years that you have a prosperity never before seen in this world.

"As I have told you before we still have enemies. You have read about them. In Europe, as we speak, our so-called friends stab us in the back. And at home, we have those amongst us who turn our words and acts to their own evil purposes."

He moved smoothly to Laura's series of articles, comparing them to her previous attempts to discredit him and his work. Although he continued to speak well, many of his listeners had seen the difference in Laura's pieces. Where the first was clearly directed to selling newspapers and gaining notoriety, the most recent series simply recited known facts in a form conducive to concise analysis. His chief of staff didn't smile as broadly because the president hadn't quite hit it squarely. But he was satisfied, nevertheless, that the president had presented himself well. With sufficient politicking and time, they might yet win the day.

As Aidan Sullivan completed his speech to mild applause, Senator Morgan sat back disappointed.

"He's good," he mumbled to anyone within earshot. He and everyone sitting with him were overcome with a certain melancholy. They had expected either a rousing speech that would blow them completely out of the water or a major mistake that would further strengthen their resistance and give them more ammunition. Instead, they got nothing. It wasn't great. Yet it wasn't bad.

As they all looked around, no one really knowing what to say, Morgan suddenly sat forward again and pointed.

"Wait a minute," he said expectantly.

Aidan Sullivan had just stopped and pulled away from his body guards to turn and walk back to the podium. For a moment it seemed as if he would not respond to questions as had originally been planned. Apparently, however, one question caught his ear.

"What is that question again?" asked the president as he took the microphone.

"How do you respond Sir, to comparisons between yourself and Adolf Hitler?" asked BBC reporter John Marshall.

"To the extent that we have both brought our countries back from socioeconomic ruin, I applaud the comparison. Beyond that, however, there is none. He was an evil man, bent on destroying the world."

"And you, sir? What is your goal for the world? Do you wish to have it all under your control?"

The president smiled and shook his head slowly. "My wish, Mister Marshall, is to make the whole world a place in which Americans can walk free from fear. It's that simple. If it means using our might to protect our interests, we will."

"Does it also mean subjugating the rest of the world?"

Bret Cummings stepped forward. "We'll take another question. You've had your turn Mister Marshall."

The president pushed Cummings aside. "I'll answer that!" He was growing angry. "I will do, for my people, what is needed to make them safe. If it means controlling the world, then it will be so."

"There go the allies," muttered Senator Morgan with a smile.

The president glared at John Marshall who bowed his head and wrote feverishly. Several other hands went up and Bret Cummings pointed quickly in the direction opposite John Marshall.

ABC correspondent Wendy Kroven waited for the mobile microphone.

"Mister President, do you believe this country is in need of the spiritual revival alluded to in Laura Miller's stories?"

Sullivan turned sharply, a scowl covering his face "Our spirit has never been stronger," he spat. "The American spirit is power and strength. It makes us great."

"At what expense, sir?"

"What do you mean?" he challenged.

"Our country is first in the world in suicides. We have more homeless families than any civilized nation in the world. While the powerful bask in the wealth and strength of their positions, our cities are patrolled by heavily armed military."

"Are you complaining, Miz Kroven?" asked the president with a sneer. "You are safe in your Washington bungalow. You don't have to fear the streets at night. Why is that, Miz Kroven? Because we are protecting you."

"But would it—" she was cut off as Bret Cummings directed the microphone to the middle of the crowd of reporters.

"I'm Jarad Paulson, Mister President. The new Washington, D.C. correspondent for the *Seattle Sun*."

The president nodded absently as Bret Cummings' eyes bulged at the name of the newspaper most vocally opposed to the move to amend the constitution. Zac Morgan held his breath, excited his man was getting a shot.

"Many people are saying, sir, you are nothing more than a power-hungry man looking out for your own interests."

The president's jaw tightened.

"That is the American way, Mister Paulson. We all seek power and wealth. That is what makes us great. It is that ethic that will make all who follow me great and powerful as well."

"Some say you think you're God," continued Paulson.

The president flared. His eyes pierced Jarad Paulson and Jarad flinched backwards suddenly. When he again leaned forward, fear was etched on his face. Aidan Sullivan smiled smugly.

"Maybe I am, Mister Paulson," he said slowly, deliberately. "For what is god, Mister Paulson, but a crutch for man to lean on? For seven years this country has been leaning on me. And," he turned from Paulson to the main camera, "if it wishes to continue its prosperity, it will continue to do so."

A stunned silence fell over the crowd. The reporters stood awkwardly, eyes flitting back and forth between a shell-shocked Jarad Paulson and the intimidating President Aidan Sullivan. The small crowd of people behind the press grew silent, also. Bret pushed at the president's arm but he stood firm, staring over the crowd. Suddenly, from far back, an orange came flying and struck the lectern in front of the president.

"Satan!" came the shout from one person.

As security guards wrestled the young man to the ground, others began to boo. Other objects began to fly toward the president's podium.

"Look at him," pointed Mark Tucker, surprised at the evil countenance that leered menacingly into the camera lens.

Bret Cummings and Bill Jackson pushed and pulled the president from the podium to the safety of the White House as security forces struggled with the small crowd which was growing rowdier than it's size would suggest possible.

"It's going to happen tonight, Laura," Mark said softly but emphatically.

He picked up the phone and dialed Ralph Escobar.

"Did you see it?" he asked.

"Yes," Escobar said slowly as if he too were shocked by the words he'd heard.

"It's going to happen, tonight. We've got to get over there."

"It'll be like an armed camp, professor. Those security guys are already calling for help."

"I'm telling you, it's tonight, Commander Escobar. Did you see him? We've got to be there."

"I'll pick you up in half an hour."

"I think we'll need another guard here. If he really believes Laura's the cause of all this, he may come after her."

"I'll send another guy over."

Charlie Gilbert and Bret Cummings approached the door to the Oval Office warily. It had been three hours since the fateful speech and the White House grounds were finally clear and secure. The president wanted to see them both.

Charlie knocked firmly and opened the door. Aidan Sullivan stood in front of his desk. The drapes were drawn shut and three lamps lit the room. The two approached the president. He stared at their approach without emotion as black rings beneath his eyes joined the shadow of resignation that covered his face.

"It's over, gentlemen," he rasped.

"No, Aidan," pleaded Bret Cummings. "We can still—" He was stopped short by Sullivan's quick glance. The president didn't even move his head. He simply flicked his eyes toward Cummings, and the chief of staff knew his entreaties fell on deaf ears.

"You fucked up, Charlie. You were supposed to bring her to me and you failed."

For the first time in many years Charlie Gilbert feared for his life. He'd done everything he could to find the woman and bring her in before the first installment was printed. He could not. But it would do him no good to attempt to defend himself. He had long since given himself to Aidan Sullivan. He knew when he had, that he would live or die at his leader's whim. He had hoped that his death would be in victory.

Slowly, almost caressingly, Aidan Sullivan entered his mind. With the care and skill of a highly trained technician, he ensnared Charlie's brain and slowly began to squeeze. Sullivan knew his strength well. He also knew there would be no resistance. So he worked slowly, reveling in the pain that was now gripping his once valuable soldier.

"It's over, Charlie," he sneered and then suddenly glared.

He squeezed with all his might and surprisingly felt some resistance. The resistance of a dying man struggling reflexively to hold onto the last vestiges of life. Charlie was on the floor, writhing without sound. His feet kicked at the desk and chairs and his hands clawed at his head, opening wounds around the ears and eyes as he struggled to rid himself of the terrible pain, until, suddenly, it was over. A final spasm and then blood from the mouth, ears, eyes, and nose. A brain hemorrhage had taken Charlie Gilbert.

★ CHAPTER 34 ★

Bret Cummings stared at Charlie's struggle, aghast. He grew dizzy and weak with the knowledge he was next. He stared pleadingly at the president who turned to him and entered his mind.

"Aidan, please . . . it's not over, Aidan," he shouted as the first stab of pain sent him reeling backwards.

Sullivan toyed with Cummings, squeezing for the screams and then releasing to grant false hope of continued life. With Bret, however, it was only a game for the time being. He still needed Bret Cummings.

CHAPTER 35

Jason had been unable to sleep from the moment he was put to bed at ten o'clock. Even when Frank finally came to bed an hour later, Jason wasn't asleep. The Monster was coming.

When he glanced at the clock on the table between his and Frank's bed, it read twelve-thirty. If he stepped out of bed he'd wake Frank just like he always did. He had no choice, though.

Quietly Jason threw his huge legs to the floor and stood.

Immediately the sensor in Jason's bed triggered a beeper under Frank's pillow that warned that Jason had risen. Half asleep still, Frank told himself the kid was just going to the bathroom again as he'd done every night since they'd brought him here. He silently wished that Bill Jackson or someone else had the job of watching over Jason. As Frank lay between the worlds of sleep and wakefulness, however, he sensed Jason standing over him and he suddenly sprang up to a sitting position.

"Dammit, Jason," he said. "What are you doing?"

Jason's huge bulk formed a silhouette at the side of Frank's bed.

"I'm sorry, Frank. The Monster is coming. I have to stop it."

Frank stared after the silhouette as it moved away.

"Wait a minute! Jason! Where are you going?"

"To stop the Monster."

"No Jason," Frank fumbled at the table next to him until his hand rested on the hilt of his gun. He couldn't find the lamp switch quickly enough, so he leveled the gun at Jason's departing shadow. The click of the hammer as he drew it back, stopped the big man.

"Stop Jason!" he shouted. "You know what I have to do if you try to leave."

Frank stared at the silhouette. He couldn't tell exactly whether Jason was facing him or had his back to him. All he could see was that the big man was at least one full bed-length away. With the gun still trained on Jason's silhouette, Frank again searched the table for the damn light switch.

"I have to go, Frank."

The shadow moved. Frank squeezed the trigger and vaulted out of bed as he heard the silenced explosion followed by the thud of a hit and Jason's scream. Turning, he struggled again with the lamp, this time finding the switch. The room was awash in the eerie yellow glow as Frank turned and faced Jason, who stood before him bleeding from a wound in the upper chest.

Jason grabbed the gun hand in a vice grip that kept the barrel pointed downward. In his other hand he held Frank by the throat. Even though they were of comparable size and weight, Frank had never felt the crushing strength now exhibited by Jason. He was in a death grip. While he kicked and struggled, the room turned black again as if the lights had been turned off. He slumped in front of Jason and fell to the floor.

Jason bent down to hear the big man's unconscious gasps for air.

"I'm sorry, Frank. I have to stop the Monster."

Jason winced in pain as he turned and moved quickly to the door.

They'd been waiting for over three hours at the corner of Jackson and Pennsylvania Avenues. Mark and Commander Escobar had seen the capital's grounds cleared and were sitting patiently. They'd talked for a while, but Escobar was tired after three consecutive nights, so he began to doze off. By twelve-thirty Mark was also starting to drift away when suddenly headlight beams preceded a black limousine out of the garage of the White House.

"We're up, commander," said Mark as he shook Escobar and pointed.

Escobar watched for several seconds as the limo pulled out onto Pennsylvania heading east toward New York Avenue. He lifted his radio transmitter and spoke to another police vehicle along the path taken by the limo.

"Wake up, kids. Our boy's on the move. He's coming your way, Sam. Up New York. Should be passing your position soon."

"Got 'im, commander," came the response.

"Keep me posted, Sam. Out."

"Roger. Out."

Escobar took streets paralleling those taken by the limo. He kept in contact with other squad cars whose drivers formed a grid around their prey and kept Escobar within a block of the vehicle at all times. Within minutes the sleek black car was cruising the streets of D.C.'s red-light district. Mark and Escobar each silently anticipated what was to come. They believed they had their killer.

Escobar's unmarked car was stopped at a corner as the limousine passed slowly, its occupant seemingly oblivious to the police vehicle's presence.

"I'm behind him," he reported to the others as he turned right to follow.

A few blocks further down, well into the city's seedy red light district, Escobar turned right again.

"I'm right on 'L' Street," he said. "You got 'im, Jake?"

"Right boss," came the reply. "He's slowing down, commander."

"Keep an eye on him."

"Looks like he doesn't like the crowd. He's turning north on Thirteenth."

"I'll pick him up," said Escobar as he moved the car East on "M" Street and saw the limo pass his position at Thirteenth. Escobar stopped at the corner. He switched off his headlights and moved slowly into the unlit intersection.

"He's stopped!" Mark exclaimed. "Someone's getting in."

"He's got one. Stay loose boys. I'm north on Thirteenth." He switched his lights back on.

"Let's go, commander. Before it's too late," said Mark anxiously.

"Relax, professor. We've got him," Escobar responded calmly as he peered forward. He then picked up the transmitter and spoke again, "I've got to cut out at 'N' Street guys. I'm west. Who's got him"

"Watson, sir."

"What are you doing?" asked Mark anxiously.

"Let me do my job, will you, Professor? He can't suspect we're onto him or he'll abort."

Two blocks further north on Thirteenth Street, their paths crossed again. This time Escobar kept his car in the unlit intersection and watched carefully as the brake lights of the limo came on. The black car veered slowly to the right and stopped. No lights except the tail lights of the limo marred the night black. Even the moon was hidden behind the clouds that continued to threaten but didn't unload.

They looked south on Thirteenth to determine whether any back lights might expose their approach. As in the rest of the area, however, most of the street lamps had been blown out.

"Move in slowly. No noise, guys. Keep your heads down," Escobar ordered before turning off his machine and moving north on Thirteenth again. He hugged the right curb and the shadows along it.

"There," Mark pointed. "Someone's getting out."

A slim figure stood outside the vehicle. Escobar stopped. A second figure emerged, black against the night.

"Stay in the car, Professor."

Escobar slid out of his car, revolver poised in his right hand and flashlight in his left.

The two figures moved slowly over the rubble of gutted buildings. There didn't seem to be any struggle from the woman. Yet from a distance she didn't seem to be overly willing either. She moved mechanically.

Escobar clung to the battered walls of buildings and moved as quickly as possible while trying to avoid a misplaced step on a brick or piece of wood in his path. When he kicked a stone he stopped short, knowing the sound would carry. When nothing happened, however, he moved again until he stood behind the limousine.

Crouching, so as not to be seen by the driver, he stared into the darkness between two buildings.

A tearing sound directed his eyes to the two shadowy figures. One standing erect as the other reached forward and tore again at a garment. The second figure moved toward the first and seemed to pin it against the building. Escobar strained for any sound that might alert him to move. Finally, a whimper broke the silence.

The flashlight blazed to life. "Police!" he shouted.

The light caught the shine of a blade held low in the second figure's hand.

As the door to the limousine opened, the headlights of three police cars came on and shouts of "Police!" broke the silence again.

Escobar didn't move his eyes from the figures in the alley. He crouched low and yelled, "Drop the knife."

The figure didn't respond. It didn't even look. It simply turned the blade toward the woman.

"Drop it!" he shouted again before he fired.

The explosion was deafening as the figure fell back out of the light's glare. Escobar ran forward crouching over the rubble. The first figure did not move. Suddenly, however, the second one lurched back into the light seemingly oblivious to the oncoming Commander Escobar.

"Stop!" he shouted.

Again the figure paid no heed. It lunged at the girl and a second explosion caught it in flight, sending it sprawling backwards over the garbage in the alleyway.

Then the girl crumbled to the ground.

"I need help," yelled Escobar.

Mark, upon hearing his call, started the car and raced the last hundred yards to the scene. The limo driver was already handcuffed, lying face down on the pavement. Two other officers had run in to help their commander. Mark followed them to the alley.

"Take care of her," said Escobar to the first of the two officers.

The girl lay unconscious, in the arms of the policeman who removed his jacket to cover her. The front of her skintight top had been torn away and she was bleeding from a wound to her right breast.

Mark approached Commander Escobar and the body laying face up in the glow of the flashlights.

"It's not the president, Professor," he said shakily. It had come too close. He'd almost been too late.

Mark peered at the lifeless face of Bret Cummings. He recognized the chief of staff from his many appearances at Aidan Sullivan's side. Mark struggled with the realization. It didn't fit his profile. Or maybe it did, but he hadn't considered Cummings. Had he been there with the president for all those years?

Within twenty minutes the alley was swarming with detectives and paramedics. The young black woman was stabilized and taken by ambulance to the city hospital. Commander Escobar leaned against the hood of his car, sucking on a cigarette and slowly calming his shaking.

"You did good, Mark," he said with a smile. It was the first time he'd used his first name.

"Wrong guy," Mark smiled.

"No. We got the right guy. Thanks to you."

"Thanks . . . Ralph."

Escobar smiled and offered him a cigarette. Mark declined and leaned against the car next to him.

"It's kind of weird, though," said Escobar.

"What's that?"

"He didn't hear me."

Mark looked at him quizzically.

"I warned him three times," Escobar continued. "He just kept on going. It was like he was in a daze or something. The girl too."

"What did they do?" asked Mark.

Escobar shook his head, bewildered.

"They just kept doing what they were doing. Like they didn't even know I was there. It was like they were hypnotized."

The word hit Mark like a brick. Of course. Hypnotized. That's why they didn't cry out. That's why they didn't react. There was some kind of mind control. That face he'd seen on TV from the president was not an innocent face. It was a face of rage. Laura had seen it too. She'd felt the power. The power to control a mind.

"We've gotta go, Ralph," Mark jumped forward.

"What—"

"It's not over. Laura!" he shouted as he ran to the driver's side. "Get in!"

Ten minutes after Mark Tucker and Ralph Escobar began their pursuit of the presidential limousine in which Bret Cummings rode, a second vehicle emerged from the shadows of the White House garage. This second vehicle was unlike the first. It was a compact American made vehicle that bore no American flag or other sign of a government purpose. It was a regular passenger vehicle like any other driven by the millions of Americans who owned cars.

The vehicle rolled slowly out of the garage, headlights off, and clung to the shadows of the trees overhanging the driveway. The guard at the security gate paid little heed to the late night departure because he'd seen so many before. Even without the markings, he knew the vehicle was on some presidential mission, perhaps to return yet another of the president's paramours to her home or any number of other reasons he didn't even bother to consider.

When it rolled into the street, the vehicle merged quickly with the few cars out at this late hour and no observer would have guessed the vehicles' occupants. Nor would anyone have guessed the intent of those occupants.

Laura found it difficult to sleep, even more difficult than she had on the previous three nights that Mark had been out with Commander Escobar. It gave her little comfort to know she had guards at her door. They would not be there forever.

Laura had taken the step she felt so deeply. She'd written the series of articles that had come from deep within her. She'd written them with the sincere conviction that the people of the United States had to open their eyes and understand what was really happening around them. She had girded for an immediate response from the enemy that she believed stalked her. When none came the first night or on any of the subsequent nights, she began to wonder. Was it all some trick of the mind? Was her own subconscious playing with her simply to get her to use the pen for the vengeance that brewed deep down inside her? The president wouldn't really be interested in her.

When she had these thoughts and her brain became muddled again, she turned to the comfort of the prayer she'd used while writing the articles. Each time, her thoughts were cleared. Memories of her encounter with the man at the Washington Monument reminded her again it was no trick. There was definitely contact of a kind she'd never known. It came from him. It was real and painful and suffused with a malice that was palpable. Whenever doubts crept into her mind she banished them with the knowledge of her own personal contact with the evil she knew awaited her.

On this night her sense of foreboding was heightened. She'd seen the anger in his face. He'd tried to control it on camera, but the rage boiled up and Laura could see the ending of her dreams. The face turning red and the cold blue eyes, ringed in the yellow of deadly strain. She saw that face again and again every time she closed her eyes and tried to sleep. Even when she asked for help, when she prayed, it came to her as if she wasn't supposed to sleep. She had to be ready.

By twelve forty-five Laura's head ached. She was exhausted, but sleep wouldn't come. Maybe she just wouldn't let it. Too many thoughts raced haphazardly through her brain. Finally, she gave up the fight and stepped out of her bed.

As she had done several times before, she walked to the door of the apartment and peered through the magnifying glass of the viewhole. The guards continued to sit far enough from the door for her to see them clearly. They played gin with no sign of concern. Only boredom at having to babysit some neurotic broad.

Laura went to the kitchen to pour herself a glass of ice water. She thought she might turn on the television and watch a late night talk show. Or maybe an old movie would put her to sleep. As she picked up the remote control, however, she heard the first thud. The second thud was preceded by a yelp . . . a high-pitched, strangled cry, so brief as to be almost undetectable.

★ CHAPTER 35 ★

Slowly, Laura replaced the remote. Her breath came in tight gasps as her stomach knotted and constricted the lungs' expansion area. She inched her way to the door and peered cautiously through the hole, now holding her breath to avoid making any sound.

At first she saw only black, as if someone had covered the glass. Then came the eye. Suddenly, the head on the other side pulled away and the yellow ringed ice blue eye stared at her.

Laura gasped and stumbled backwards, a strangled scream coming from her throat. She stared in horror at the door that shook on its hinges under pressure of some great force from without.

She continued to lurch backwards to the wall at the end of the room where she stopped, her mind paralyzed.

With a horrific crash the door burst open, and he stood before her, at the threshold. He did not smile even in the knowledge that his prey was cornered. His face was a mask of terror and hatred, brows, eyes, and nose pointed in a grimace of rage.

Laura grew dizzy as oxygen ceased traveling to her brain. She swooned and then caught herself, forcing herself to breathe as he stepped forward.

"Laura Miller," he rasped in a deep guttural voice that was not the voice of the Aidan Sullivan she had heard before.

She looked beyond him into the hall where a large black man stood over the bodies of her two guards.

"You have haunted my dreams," rasped the president matter-of-factly. "There is no escape, now."

She turned to run to the kitchen. The knife was there. But before she took her second step, he entered her mind.

"Where will you run?"

He reached in. Laura struggled as she turned back, involuntarily, to face him. She couldn't flee, she couldn't even move. She could only struggle, with her mind.

"You resist?" he smiled for the first time content in the knowledge that she would try to fight, perhaps more than any before her had done, but one-on-one she was no match. He had the power of all generations and she had only her own mind.

"I overestimated you, Laura Miller," he sneered as he drew closer.

Laura was transfixed. Panic coursed through her body as images of slow painful death raced through her mind.

"Do you like what you see?"

Slowly, tenderly he prodded her mind. As he had from afar he peeled back its layers, as if it were a fruit hiding some golden treasure at it's core. At the middle he saw the seed, now grown large. It was the seed of the understanding she now had. An understanding that no one else even suspected. Only she knew. And he would crush it.

Laura felt his grip tightening. Her brain was being pulled away from the nerves that controlled her bodily functions and it was being enveloped in his grip. Soon she would resist no more. He was winning so easily.

He stood before her. Only two feet away. From his waist band beneath his coat he withdrew a blade that glinted sharply in the room's dim light.

"From the womb, my heir to the kingdom of this earth was taken. To the devil shall go your womb."

He reached for the top of her nightgown and with one motion tore it downward, but the tear was not clean, so he grabbed it again, holding tightly to her mind.

Laura screamed, not with her voice, but with her mind. She screamed with rage at her helplessness and then she understood.

"Lord Jesus, send this beast from me!"

Aidan Sullivan was suddenly rocked backwards on his heels. His grip on her mind was broken, as he reached for his own head and screamed in pain at the piercing blow dealt him. He stumbled backwards and fell onto the couch, then to the floor. The huge blade flew from his hand, across the room and landed at the far wall.

Laura slumped to the floor at the base of her wall. She lifted her head slowly and stared as he stood again. No more sneers of victory. It would not be easy.

"You have learned some things, Laura Miller."

Sullivan walked, cautiously, around the couch to retrieve his blade, speaking slowly to allow his mind to clear. He gained strength for the next attack.

Laura found her own strength in his apparent weakness and began crawling to the kitchen for her own blade.

He attacked again. This time without prelude. It was no game now as this woman had a power of her own. A power he'd never seen before.

His thrust into her brain was deep. Tearing and squeezing with every ounce of his black strength, but her walls were high.

Laura turned and glared at him. Her pain was great, but she would not give him the satisfaction.

"Lord Jesus, protect my mind from your enemy."

Again he lurched backwards. He was cast out yet again by a power beyond any he'd ever seen. He stumbled and tried again, screaming in anger for his own strength.

"I have served your purpose well! Don't abandon me!"

But there was no entry. He could find no opening as he stumbled to the side, near the window.

Fear now contorted his features. His awesome power was like nothing in the face of the strength within this woman. Yet she was a novice. She didn't know it well. He could see that she knew it only for defense. She had no offensive capability. And she was no match for him physically.

Aidan Sullivan stood erect. The sneer returned.

"You are weak, Laura Miller. You will be mine!"

He stepped toward her blade poised, when suddenly Bill Jackson hurled through the open door backwards and struck his head on the coffee table. He slumped to the ground unconscious.

"Daddy!" bellowed Jason Sullivan as he ducked through the door. "No more Monster, Daddy," he wailed as tears streamed down his face.

"Stay back!" shouted the president.

Jason stumbled as the mind probe caught him.

"Leave me!" said the president with a deadly glare.

Jason rocked back and forth on the heels of his feet struggling as his father tried to control his mind.

"Lord Jesus, help this boy," Laura whispered as she clutched the Mary medal at her throat.

Jason closed his eyes and mumbled through gritted teeth, "No more Monster, Daddy."

Like an animal out of control, the boy burst forward and charged his father. Aidan Sullivan swung his blade and caught his son in the stomach, but the force of the charge and the weight of the son carried him forward into his father. They both crashed through the glass window to the street, eight stories below.

The president of the United States of America lay dead with a broken neck and crushed skull atop the street pavement. A boulevard sprinkler had pierced his back and torn through his heart. Next to him lay his son bleeding from the nose and mouth gurgling his last words.

"The Monster is gone, Daddy."

EPILOGUE

Zac Morgan's task was much simpler after that. The movement to repeal the 22nd Amendment of the Constitution of the United States went down to one defeat after another. For the time being, anyway, there would be no more concern of uncontrolled despotic rule in the United States.

Mark Tucker asked Laura to return to California with him. She declined temporarily because she had to clear up some things in D.C. She promised him she'd be back soon. California was her home. And Mark Tucker figured prominently in her plans for the future.

In the ensuing months, investigators pouring over Aidan Sullivan's papers found materials that would fill the minds of psychotherapists for years to come. There were the letters from the man at the orphanage. They spoke of a morally bereft relationship of animal sacrifice and Satanism. Even more telling, however, was the suicide note of June Wilson, hidden away among his own notes.

"You are evil!" she had written. "May God forgive me for leaving Jason in your care. I can no longer live with the pain of your uncontrolled ambition. Nor will I permit a healthy child to come under your control. The fetus within my womb will die with me and never have to suffer the indignities of a life with you."

For months after Laura returned to California, she was inundated with offers for the rights to her story. Every major studio offered her incomparable wealth. Talk show hosts begged for her appearance. She declined them all. Someday, she said, she'd write about it. Besides, they'd all gotten stories from Bill Jackson, Frank Thompson, and others who had surrounded the president for years. These people spoke of the mind control and the unique power of the president. They described the manner of destruction of Delta Flight 384 and the numerous other deaths.

The investigators had also read the letters. The people of the country shuddered at the thought that he had manipulated them all. Yet they wanted more. They wanted to know what Laura knew about Aidan Sullivan. She told only the facts surrounding the evening of his death, however. For now there was a lot of healing that had to occur. There were a lot of fences that had to be mended by the country's new leaders. And there were a lot of people at home who had to be healed. To dwell on the evils of the former president would only delay the healing. Laura chose to write about something else.

She wrote of a faith that could save lives. A faith that could bring peace. A faith that could bring all people together in a giving world. From that day forward, Laura Miller wrote from the heart.

★ THE END ★